HAVOC

By
Rick Tegeler

PublishAmerica

Baltimore

First printing

ISBN: 1-4137-0625-8
PUBLISHED BY PUBLISHAMERICA, LLLP
www.publishamerica.com
Baltimore

Printed in the United States of America

You taught me strength of character.
You instilled in me the will to succeed.
But most important you allowed me the freedom to dream.
In memory of my Father

"The weather is always doing something... always attending strictly to business; always getting up new designs and trying them on people to see how they will go."
— MARK TWAIN

"Everybody talks about the weather, but nobody does anything about it."
— Editorial, HARTFORD COURANT
(August 24, 1897)

"And, like almost every other piece of technology, anywhere and anytime, it came into existence by accident."
— JAMES BURKE
(The Pinball Effect, 1996)

PROLOGUE

5 JUNE 1944... D-Day minus 1

Jagged bolts of lightning seared across the morning sky as the storm's full fury lashed the Normandy coast. As if in a swarming frenzy, serpents of electrical discharge writhed along the length of heavy cable stretched between a straining generator and two crescent-shaped transmitter dishes. The test area, crowded with concerned technicians and engineers, was cloaked in motionless air. Yet, laced with static energy, the atmosphere around the project seemed somehow alive. The equipment was untried. No one knew if it could withstand fifty thousand watts and forty three hundred volts for a prolonged period, let alone actually function as intended. Indeed, after only a few short hours of operation, the mechanism teetered on the brink of self-annihilation.

In the rush to complete the *VERHEERUNG PROJECT*, and for reasons of economic expediency, most override circuits were simply omitted. While the end result was far from the concept of a deadly high-energy radio beam envisioned by its original creators, the latest version of the thing could prove to be a far more potent and deadly weapon. Everyone involved was skeptical about the slightest potential for even minimal success, let alone production of a fully operational apparatus that might alter or even control the weather. As with the jet engine, the V-2 rocket, underwater tanks, and the atomic bomb, Adolph Hitler liked the concept, ordered its development, and demanded immediate success. Not in their wildest dreams did they imagine it would ever work.

Major General Alfred Gause, Field Marshal Erwin Rommel's chief of staff, gave the order to shut the damn thing down after a banshee wind tore the rock chimney from the chalet being used as his command and control center.

They called him Salt. For as long as he could remember, private Silas T. Marsh had been addressed as such. Much earlier this day, in the gloom and cold of pre-dawn, their sergeant briefed them on the predicted weather for the crossing. It would be calm, making the first part of their journey easy. Yet, here they all were, his platoon and one hundred seventy thousand other young souls, their troop transports breaching the precarious ten-foot seas, pummeled by forty-five knot winds. Hardly a cakewalk so far, and they were still thirty miles away from Omaha beach on the Normandy shore.

At the same moment, in a wind-torn glen on the coast of England, General Dwight David Eisenhower was about to make the first of the two most momentous decisions of his life. The man who commanded nearly three million troops found it necessary to recall the largest naval fleet in history, or risk losing half of his invasion force to the elements. Strike proposals indicated the morning conditions for 5, 6, and 7 June would provide the proposed landing with an early low tide, exposing most of Rommel's submerged defenses. A late-rising moon on these dates would offer a relative cover of darkness for the thousands of landing troops. Meteorologists predicted the weather patterns on these days might yield mild seas for the channel crossing by over 5,000 vessels. Further, on-shore winds on the French coast would clear the beaches of any residual smoke from the naval 'softening up' bombardment prior to the landing. Operation *OVERLORD* began with such promise, and then the cursed weather blew in from nowhere.

"Two years of meticulous planning, not to mention the logistics of assembling the largest fighting force in history, down the chute. How could the best forecasting men and equipment in the world be so wrong? Where *did* this freak of a storm come from?" the man affectionately known as Ike fumed. He glanced at the driving rain one last time before slowly pulling the curtain. Deliberately he turned and faced his very concerned staff. "One gone, two chances left," he muttered to no one in particular. "Let's call 'em back." The assembled officers were silent.

Twenty years of life growing up in Chicago suburbs hardly prepared Salt for the enormity of his current situation. Midway through the war and less than a year before, he felt it his patriotic duty to enlist in the Army infantry. "Infantry," he cursed. "What the hell are we doing on a frigging boat if we're infantry?" he stumbled to a wildly heaving rail of their troop transport to join most of his buddies already retching over the side. "Where in hell did they find this weather?" He hung on for dear life, and tried to catch his breath. "We haven't been off this floating rust bucket for over a week, and now I'll probably drown when we sink. This is calm and easy? Infantry, my ass!"

The encoded recall message began to repeat every fifteen minutes in each radio room up and down the miles of ships comprising the invasion fleet. After personally reviewing the original order to withdraw, Lt. Commander Robert R. Hollis, commanding officer of the destroyer U.S.S. EVANS, cursed to himself, ordered his helm about, and mentally ran through a checklist of new problems he and his many peers faced. *Now the damn Krauts are the least of it. Do I have enough fuel to return, re-group, and ferry out again in the event we get the EXECUTE command for tomorrow? Shit! Can we safely turn a fleet convoy stretching sixty miles long and return to England in the dark without collisions, or some other catastrophe... in this weather? What about crew morale... to say nothing of those poor infantry bastards, all of whom have been locked aboard since 26 May? We've been planning this damn thing for over two years! Have the Germans spotted us? Or worse yet, have they been on to us all along? What a fucking fire drill!"*

The English Channel is notorious for capricious weather, but the speed and fury of this unscheduled tempest surprised them all. Captain Hollis put down his empty coffee mug, braced his feet against the onslaught of the next mountainous wave, leaned into the ship's turn, and swore again under his breath. "Just where *did* this bloody storm come from?"

Despite the wind howling through a gaping orifice in the roof that moments before had been part of the chimney, the raucous celebrating of the Germans and their Japanese counterparts surged in pace with their consumption of schnapps and sake. Theirs was an unlikely alliance, given Germany's notion of Aryan supremacy. However, Japan provided the technical know-how, and did the actual construction of *VERHEERUNG*. Germany contributed (or had plundered) the necessary resources required. For this endeavor, the Germans made racial tolerance an exception.

Since Rommel's departure the day before, Major General Gause luxuriated in the power of absolute command. Now, all the armies of Rommel's *"ATLANTIC WALL"* answered to him. This initial success of the

VERHEERUNG project furthered his delusions of dominance, making him more arrogant than his deserved reputation. After quieting the celebrating staff and technicians, he addressed them, "Gentlemen... we have achieved yet another stunning victory for the Fatherland." As a quick afterthought he included, "...and for Imperial Japan." Cheering resounded anew, this time at decibel levels rivaling those of the screaming wind. "Ours was deemed an impossible task. Our victory made even sweeter, for the whims of nature have never been previously defeated, let alone controlled to advantage. We gather here this morning, the masthead of a now impregnable *FORTRESS EUROPE*. It is said the Allies will invade soon. I say, *LET... THEM... TRY*!! Before this day, down through history, weather defeated the Spanish Armada and the Chinese fleet. So shall the might of the German army, together with our ability to control the weather, defeat any attempted Allied invasion. This time, thanks to you and *VERHEERUNG*, history will record that the weather is ours to command... *WHEN... WE... DEEM... FIT*!" The room erupted in whistles and applause. Gause raised his glass in toast, "Gentlemen... to *VERHEERUNG*!!" The officers in the room had absolutely no idea that the successful test of their new weapon, together with a great deal of metrological coincidence, had in fact combined to repel the Allies' first attempt at the invasion of France. Ignorance is certainly one offspring of arrogance.

By noon on 5 June, the storm in the Channel blew at gale force. All the battered segments of *OVERLORD* hunkered down in the restricted areas of coastal Britain and blessed their luck that mistakes, screw-ups, injuries, and losses received from the recall effort were minimal. They waited, hoped, and prayed.

At Southwick House, S.H.A.E.F. (Supreme Headquarters Allied Expeditionary Force), the American Commander received updates on the recall status and the weather every thirty minutes throughout the afternoon. The logistics of assembling more men and equipment for a military endeavor greater than ever before in the history of the world was a staggering burden. To postpone *OVERLORD* a second time would risk its almost certain exposure to the Germans. To date supreme secrecy and clever deceptions had successfully obscured the magnitude and objectives of the operation from the wary enemy. Yet the decision to go again, given the seemingly identical weather patterns predicted for the coming day, might invite the consequences of another fiasco similar to the one they had just survived. Everyone on the Allied staff knew that a second failure would be certain disaster.

Too soon it became evening. Eisenhower and his staff reviewed the latest weather briefings and finished conferences with the various operational field commanders. For all concerned another postponement seemed a grim reality. If the weather would hold as predicted for just a brief window of time the following morning, the clearing skies would allow essential air cover over the landing beaches. Despite the forecasted conditions being below the minimum hoped for standards, this just might be their final opportunity for success. Indeed, the outcome of the entire war and the future of the world would depend on Ike's next decision. Silence again settled over the room and all eyes turned to the tall, thin Midwesterner.

"That's enough for me... I don't like it, but I authorize you to institute *OPERATION OVERLORD* effective Tuesday, 6 June, 1944. D-Day. I do not see as how we have any other choice. Let's go!"

5 June 1944. Before retiring, Major General Gause left instructions for the on-line technicians to re-activate *VERHEERUNG* at 0000 hours on the morning of 6 June. Further operational testing was required. He had no idea how successful the day's test truly was, or what havoc the weather had caused the Allied fleet now struggling back to England at that very moment. For the Germans, it was merely a positive test result of a highly questionable new weapon. The secret of the invasion date was still safe.

While the German High Command fully anticipated an Allied invasion somewhere along the coast of France, they didn't expect it at Normandy, nor did they suspect it commencing any time before the last weeks in June of 1944 at the earliest. They, *VERHEERUNG*, and the traditional massive weaponry of the German army, were dug into the French bluffs of Calais, directly east of Dover. This strategic location overlooked one of the narrowest points of the English Channel, and was thought by the German brain trust to be one of the likeliest spots for any prospective Allied invasion. In actuality, Calais was well north of the eventual landing zone. At that time, on that date, the German's *Atlantic Wall* force alert readiness might best have been described as 'confidently relaxed'.

Rommel left his coastal headquarters for Berlin on the morning of 4 June, to visit with and celebrate the birthday of his wife on the 6th. He was entirely certain that the Allies were not ready or able to marshal an invasion so soon. The *VERHEERUNG* project, if indeed successful, would be just one more layer of impenetrable armor in his *Atlantic Wall*. None of the German command staff expected *VERHEERUNG* to be productive. But the Fuhrer had to be mollified. In the unlikely event it did work, so much the better.

The switch was thrown at the appointed hour, and the huge generator laboriously spooled up to maximum RPM. The machinery whirred to life for a brief moment, began an ominous hissing, and then shuddered twice as if mortally wounded. It thudded and popped occasionally as the vacuum tubes in its guts finally parted with existence... and mercifully for the Allies, became still. The head technician, still bleary-eyed from the previous day's celebration, noted the time, logged in gauge readings and added his impressions to the primary journal, then headed back to his quarters to sleep off a worsening hangover. Besides, what difference did it make? The Allies weren't expected for at least another three weeks... if at all. This failure was just one more of many.

6 June 1944. D-Day. Gause was awakened at 0315 with the news that the first Allied bombs of operation *OVERLORD* had fallen. At 0500 he was in his staff car en route to Caen, directly inland from the Normandy beaches, when a Japanese officer waved for him to wait. Lt. Takahashi of the Imperial Engineers and in charge of the Japanese involvement in *VERHEERUNG*, sought orders from the fill-in German commander regarding the disposition of the disabled device. Theatrically, Gause stuck his gloved hand out the car window palm up and said with exaggerated disgust, "I don't notice any rain Takahashi, so I presume either you neglected my start-up orders, or the machine has failed yet again. After four years and countless thousands of man-hours, Germany expected much more. I'll give you the benefit of the doubt this time, Lieutenant. I haven't time to fool with fanciful devices and incompetent foreign engineers just now. If you can't repair it in the next hour, ship it back to Japan and correct *your* mistakes. Your country built it in Japan. Fix it in Japan! I'll take a Panzer division any day over the likes of your ridiculous device. Take one of my staff with you and be certain that someone is always with the damn thing. If you ever get it working again, contact me, Field Marshal Rommel, or the office of the Fuhrer in Berlin. Heil, Hitler!"

He prodded the driver's shoulder with his crop using more force than necessary, and in a shower of mud they were gone. Watching the speeding car disappear, Lt. Takahashi ruefully laughed, "*Our* mistake. Ha! The test success yesterday was a mindless fluke. Mere coincidence. The storm would have occurred regardless. We should never have offered these arrogant morons the opportunity to experiment with the machine in the first place. Anyway, I'll be more than happy to get home and have some real food for a change, despite dragging some German lunatic with me. Fate," he muttered, spitefully. "Heil, Hitler!"

0630 hours in the misty gloom of dawn, 6 June 1944 ... D-Day. Private Silas T. Marsh bid good luck and farewell to his buddies, lumbered off the ramp of their landing assault craft, and into the freezing surf pounding Omaha beach. With that first unprotected step he and thousands of other frightened young men waded directly into murderous machine gun fire from the German guns positioned on the Normandy bluffs directly above. His last remembered thought on that fateful day was recalling that he always did want to visit France.

That historic moment was the beginning of the end of World War II in Europe.

Under the direction of Lt. Takahashi and Major Franz Speidel, the *VERHEERUNG* machinery was quickly disassembled, packed in Cosmoline, and crated in eight huge containers. Each was sealed with Field Marshal Rommel's official wax stamp. '*STAATSGHEIM*' was stenciled on each side of every container in bold, one meter high, blood red letters... '*STATE SECRET*'.

Late that afternoon the crates were carefully placed in the bomb bays of four German *Heinkel* HE-111 twin engine, long-range bombers. In Rabaul, New Britain Island, New Guinea, fifty-four hours later, after numerous, often harrowing refueling stops, and nearly half way around the war-torn world, they were unloaded under the watchful glare of the German Major and the inscrutable gaze of the Japanese Lieutenant. From the airport the cartons were trucked three miles to the only remaining operable pier in Simpson Harbor. Earlier in the war, this once beautiful, geographically protected bay was the most active base for the Imperial Japanese Navy outside Tokyo Bay. At this later date, the Allies controlled the air in the Pacific theater. Necessarily then, the last leg of *VERHEERUNG*'s journey to Japan required a well-planned, perfectly timed, clandestine, watery dash. The crates were hoisted aboard the waiting transport freighter, *Italia Maru*. Shortly after *VERHEERUNG* was stowed and sealed in hold number 2, the ship was under full steam, with orders to make Japan under all possible speed. Takahashi and Speidel agreed that Speidel would take the first eight-hour watch in the hold. Takahashi had just retired to his stateroom in possession of the sealed, waterproof pouch containing the *VERHEERUNG* schematics and logs, when the first bomb shattered the calm water 100 meters off their port bow.

While Rabaul was simply by-passed by General MacArthur in his inexorable Pacific land campaign, nevertheless it was reduced to impotency by a continuous barrage of American bombs. Eventually, the entire city was flattened, driving the population to a mole-like existence in over three hundred and fifty miles of hand-dug tunnels. Early evening orders this day were no different for the US airmen, their directive being to engage and sink any and all shipping to, from, or in Rabaul. The only deviance for the American aviators was in the time of day they visited potential death on those below. A relatively slow moving freighter still in the confines of Simpson Harbor would be easy prey for their 500-pound bombs.

The young American pilot watched as his wingman put one directly amidships on the *Italia* with no visible results. "Another God damn dud!" He pounded the yoke of his Mitchell B-25D attack bomber in frustration. "I risk my butt flying around out here in the middle of nowhere, and they give us fuckin' duds. We might as well throw rocks at 'em!" He keyed his mike, and radioed his wingman. "Nice shot. At least you hit it, Mickey."

"Thanks, Bob. Better luck with yours."

"Hey Bobby. Give me a 360 and come out heading two seven five degrees at two thousand feet. And do your pilot stuff good so they don't shoot the shit outta us. I'll lay the damn thing right on their deck. If this one doesn't go off, at least it'll knock some of 'em overboard!" The navigator on the lead flight glued his eyes to the Norden bombsight.

"Roger that, *Mr.* Bombardier, sir," responded the pilot. The lead Mitchell rolled out exactly at the requested altitude.

Cursing the pilot good-naturedly with instructions that would fine-tune trajectory, the bombardier put his own missile right down the huge stack of the inviting target. This time, the results were unmistakable. The eight hundred foot long transport literally blew apart. The stern section, lifted from the water by a secondary explosion in her boilers, settled back into the lagoon, prop still dutifully spinning, and sank in under three minutes. Lt. Takahashi was instantly scalded to death by escaping steam. Along with most everything in the stern compartments not fastened to the superstructure, his sealed pouch and its secrets were blown clear of the sinking hulk.

Deep in the bowels of the condemned ship, Major Speidel was crushed between a collapsing internal bulkhead and the two-ton crate housing the *VERHEERUNG* generator. Had not both arms and his right leg been broken, he may have been able to claw his way free. As it happened, he could only just glimpse the beckoning sky through some twisted hull plates as the crippled wreckage listed bow down. He heard tortured sounds of wrenching metal, punctuated by the doomed screams of the crew trapped in the holds and compartments directly beneath him.

Quickly the calm waters of Simpson Harbor enveloped the shattered remains. The *VERHEERUNG* crates shifted one final time. The forward half of the dying *Italia Maru* slowly wallowed from side to side and teetered bow up, then ponderously sank. Painfully, as he sucked in his final breath, Major Speidel observed what nice weather it was.

PART ONE

Discovery

> "In completing one discovery we never fail to get an imperfect knowledge of others of which we could have no idea before, so that we cannot solve one doubt without creating several new ones."
> — JOSEPH PRIESTLY

1

5 JUNE 1991

"Ten pounds overweight and three months under-trained," Cody Steele muttered to himself. He took another quick swig from the water bottle strapped to his hand and searched for the next striped ribbon marking the trail.

Positioning for a ride home from Riyadh, Saudi Arabia, he promised himself he would celebrate the coming of his fortieth year by entering and hopefully finishing a one hundred mile endurance run. "This was another bright idea. I wonder what I'm trying to prove this time, and to whom?"

The deed was far easier to accomplish in his imagination than in actuality, a reality he was painfully experiencing. Long distance running to keep in shape all his adult life, and entering several 'ultra-marathons' (events in excess of the Olympic marathon distance) in his early thirties taught him what to expect... he thought. "I don't know what made me think a few two hour runs in the desert last month would prepare me for this insanity," he mumbled through labored breathing. "Here I am 8,000 feet up in the Sierra, fifteen hours on the trail, with over thirty some odd miles still to go... and it's getting dark!"

2

Immediately prior to and during the Gulf war, Iraq was desperate for a precise guidance control component, which would increase the accuracy of its Russian-made *SCUD* missile arsenal. The *Partidario* drug cartel, operating out of Sao Paulo, Brazil, offered Saddam Hussein the compatible Soviet systems, while the terrorist, better known as *Wolverine*, represented the more accurate elements developed by the French. Clandestine US government operatives provided irrefutable evidence that *Wolverine* was awarded the contract, tangible proof of which was the direct hit by the new improved *SCUD* on the American barracks in Riyadh.

Certain that *Wolverine* would be in the general vicinity of his many shipments— historically, it was his style—Steele's team of hand-picked specialists surrounded the warehouse believed to contain the second consignment of components at Shannon airport in Ireland. Steele turned down numerous, if not most, proffered CIA, NSA, and other related agencies assignments. However, when *Wolverine* was thought to be involved, Cody couldn't resist the challenge of involvement. Their paths had crossed many times before, seemingly always with unpredictable results. The men comprising his elite teams were Americans, all multi-specialized, and usually Special Forces trained. All normally worked as 'independent contractors', except in unusual circumstances such as this. Israeli operatives of *MOSSAD* working with the Americans assured the team that *Wolverine* was inside. They claimed to have observed him supervising the unloading. An unusual assertion however, as most of the intelligence agencies around the world weren't even sure what he looked like. Seconds before the trap was to be sprung, the building erupted in a series of multiple explosions, literally blowing the lid off the operation. After sifting through the still smoldering wreckage, local forensic experts found what was left of the guidance systems, but no conclusive evidence of *Wolverine*. In fact, what human remains they did uncover were minimal. The burnt-out building was secured and guarded round-the-clock until the stateside lab boys arrived. The temperature at the height of the conflagration was estimated to have exceeded 3,000 degrees Fahrenheit, thanks to large quantities of avgas also stored within the warehouse. The experts concluded that any traces of human existence would quickly have been incinerated. The operation's dragnet following the fire was thought to have been 100% secure. It was believed that no one could possibly have escaped the containment, let alone survived the explosions and resultant catastrophic fire. The action virtually ended there, although for the subsequent two weeks following the war's cease-fire, Steele's team followed elusive residue of *Wolverine*'s operation all over Europe and the mid-east, with no tangible results.

3

Cody chose the East Slope Endurance 100 partly because he knew and loved the locale so well, and partly because of the mental and physical challenge the varied topography would offer. He needed to get his mind focused on something other than his recent incomplete operation. It was truly hard to face the reality that the years of his fixation on eliminating *Wolverine* evidently were behind him, strewn somewhere in the cold ashes of an Irish warehouse. He lifted weights and practiced Akido for muscle tone and flexibility. However, running had always been his panacea, his escape and addiction of choice.

He was a good athlete, or at least had thought of himself as one all his life. The sports, like the professions and avocations he chose, were all individually oriented. He was a swimmer in high school and college, an F-4 Phantom driver in Vietnam, and now basically a mercenary for esoteric government agencies under 'black-op' contract. He was possessed of a multitude of talents, skills, and aptitudes that all who knew him recognized and usually appreciated. The only one who didn't … was he. For most of his youth he was driven to constantly strive for perfection in many and varied pursuits. It wasn't until one day, after catching the biggest fish while on a trip with some friends, he realized that despite all his achievements and accomplishments, he was still tremendously alone and unfulfilled.

Everything I have done has been by myself on my own, and usually for the wrong reasons, he thought.

Raised the only son of a hard working, depression-hardened father, Cody spent much of his existence seeking approval. First and foremost, approval from his father. Failing that, approval from anybody, anywhere, doing anything in order that he might somehow feel worthy. He tried desperately to validate himself... and failed. It was a rare failure amidst a sea of recognition, the latter symbolized by meaningless awards and accolades. He kept raising his sights. His father taught him never to show emotion. "It is a sign of vulnerability," he said. "In order to be the best, to succeed in life, you cannot afford to be vulnerable. Never let anyone know how you really feel. Allowing anyone to know your emotions gives them the key to control. Commit to no one." His father raised the bar yet another notch.

Cody learned these lessons all too well. The result was a life focused on solitary and individual oriented pursuits... from precocious child to calculating adult, in a never-ending search for self-respect. The more he struggled to excel for recognition, the lonelier his world became.

Following a near death experience in the merciless jungles of Cambodia, Steele began to re-evaluate his emotional priorities and values. He explored the boundaries of the known world with a new understanding, in the process testing his own limits and resourcefulness. A market for his skills with the US government was developed. He selectively worked clandestine operations— 'blackops' —with the idealistic hope of making the world a bit better and safer. He discovered a satisfying sense of reward in so doing, particularly with any successful mission. For the first times in his life, on assignment he found a real sense of meaning and respect for self, and in the process, began his escape from a lifetime of programming and manipulation by others. Philosophically, he developed the somewhat plagiarized, but certainly relevant, motto for his life's direction: "Don't be trapped on someone else's trail. Go where no one has been, and leave a path so others might follow."

Struggling with this new awareness after barely surviving the Cambodian nightmare, he still tended to be withdrawn when it came to expressing his feeling to anyone, including himself. OK with working alone, he was having trouble being alone. However, he did begin to examine his motives more frequently, and in the course of this self-exploration, discovered that his life-long insomnia suddenly began to disappear. Albeit grudgingly, he was beginning to seek approval from the most important person in his life... himself. He was learning that the price of maturity is age. Often, as he did now during the run, he debated the issues in his head.

"No for-the-team sports, for-the-outfit war, or for-the-company efforts. The one chance I had to do something that required compromise went south because of the damn Gulf War, or maybe this is just another in a long list of excuses for my inability to make a lasting commitment. I wonder what she's doing now?

Not necessarily handsome or chiseled in a movie-idol sense, his rugged countenance did draw second looks in a crowd on occasion, usually because of his penetrating eye contact. Those eyes smoldered between gray and deep blue depending on his mood. With a tall, athletic build and the effortless way he comported himself, he seldom wanted for female partners or companionship when he so chose. Despite his many talents and social skills developed over the years as a buffer for his lack of self-esteem, he thought himself quite shy. He never sought out relationships. Affairs seemed to just happen, usually at the insistence or prodding of a willing partner. They seemed to *un*happen frequently as well. None lasted much longer than a few years at the very most. Until he met Devoney.

He had dated, gone out with, been with... maybe even loved, Dr. Devoney Marsh for over four years. Every time it seemed as if they were ready to make a lasting commitment, Center from the CIA headquarters at Langley would call and off he would go offering little or no explanation. Throughout their relationship he would occasionally talk to Devoney about a previous operation, or relate some concern over an ongoing one. In the course of these generic discussions, she became aware of *Wolverine*, and the obvious obsession Cody bore for the man. When the call came this last time, Devoney was incensed. They were in her house in Mill Valley, California when Conley phoned. Their lovemaking finished for the time being, they had been warming themselves by the open fireplace, planning their SCUBA diving getaway to the South Pacific. She answered the phone, despite his protests. Sometimes he could *feel* when that call was coming. She had long since ceased quizzing him about these unscheduled departures and prolonged silent absences, which were the usual results of these calls. Instead, she merely acquiesced to his over-worked excuses... "To defend freedom, and duty for the sake of national security."

"This is the last time! I've had it!" she stormed. He replayed the scene in his mind over and over again during the six months of the war. On the few occasions he was able to reach her by phone her demeanor was distinctly frigid. When he rang her from Shannon and again from Riyadh to tell of his unlikely success with his mission he got her message service, which informed one and all that she was gone on vacation and couldn't be reached.

"Bothered," he silently corrected into the telephone mouthpiece.

Fate once again intervened to protect him from, or by his way of thinking, conspire against, making a commitment.

4

Of the many fascinating and often bizarre things that sometimes happen to participants in an extremely physical activity, one of the most interesting is the diversity and clarity of the scenarios — vignettes or daydreaming really — that play across the stage of the mind. Conscious awareness reorients inward in an attempt to avoid confronting the fatigue and pain experienced by the physical body. The first of these extended mental productions occurred for Cody between the thirty and forty-two mile checkpoints. He reviewed his mental files on *Wolverine*.

Wolverine. By definition a small, vicious, solitary member of the weasel family. The boys in Ops always had to have a cogent label. In this case he had to admit the name fit the man. *Wolverine*, the terrorist; the drug smuggler; the arms dealer; the market manipulator... the cold-blooded killer. Steele pursued him for years in all these capacities and many more... and until two weeks previous, with marginal success. *Wolverine* seemed somehow to be involved in the world's most egregious events, his influence with crime and terrorism like a cancer. *Wolverine*, alias Hans Seidelmann, alias Franz Toscana, alias Brook Coleman... names favored most recently by his adversary. Just as had happened in Colombo, Sri Lanka three years before, when it seemed Cody had him finally cornered with no possibility of escape, *Wolverine* always somehow managed to slip through his fingers.

Has he done it again? he wondered. *Teflon Chameleon would have been a better name and description.* He struggled over Deadman's summit, forty-four miles into the torturous race. *This guy's smart and cunning. More like a jackal than a wolverine. A wolverine will at least stand and fight when cornered. A jackal is sneaky and ruthless, and runs when confronted. Damn! We're not even sure what he looked like. At least we minimized his effectiveness in Iraq. I always knew the inevitability of it. One time we would meet where there was no possibility of escape. It would finally be over... at least for one of us.* He let those thoughts drift away, and shuffled on down the trail. Obsessions, like dreams, die hard.

His second mental exercise wasn't a new one. He experienced it many times before during events such as this. Its recollection was like a nice, warm, but very exciting place for his mind to wander. It concerned the legend of the *Lost Conquistador Mine*. He first heard the tale from a grizzled old prospector while sitting at a bar in Bridgeport, California in 1973. He had been exploring the famous old ghost town of Bodie on his dirt bike. Late that evening, he stopped at the *Sportsman's Tavern* to wash the fine, high desert sand and grit from his mouth with an icy beer. Striking up a conversation with the establishment's only other patron soon resulted in the old character spinning him a yarn he was to hear often over the subsequent years from a variety of sources, reliable and otherwise.

Driven by their insatiable quest for gold, precious stones and anything else of perceived value, legend suggested that the Spaniards who conquered Mexico in the sixteenth century, sent far-ranging exploratory patrols into what now is Nevada, Arizona, New Mexico, and California. One of these expeditions followed what today is known as Owen's River Valley, as far north into California as Mono Lake. Their journey then, as the same route most certainly is today, was visually spectacular. It paralleled the junction of the east slope of the rugged Sierra Nevada mountain range of eastern California, and the high Sonoran desert that is now western Nevada. As they continued north at 8000 feet above sea level, many of the peaks forming the ridge to the west of their route towered nearly 4,000 feet above them... a select few even 6,000 feet higher. Except for the interruption of the majestic White Mountains, most of the topography to their right was rolling high desert and flat plains. This transitional zone in the topography of the western United States can be summarized by a plethora of geographical superlatives, and is unabashed in its diversity.

The native Indians they met along their way were very friendly, a welcome change from the violent encounters the marauding Spaniards recently experienced, courtesy of the indigenous inhabitants of Mexico. So friendly were these peoples, in fact, that they openly showed the armor encased 'Gods' where some of the richest gold mines of the area were located in exchange for a few trinkets, beads, and an occasional metal knife or spear point. In those times, Native Americans had little purposeful use or relative sense of value for gold, and used it solely for ornamental decoration and in select ceremonies.

Late in the fall one year, so the story went, the avaricious Spaniards were in a hurry to depart the high country mines. Unprepared, they endured an unexpected early snowstorm. It caused great alarm because of its intensity and the quantities of snow dumped in its wake. They hadn't anticipated, nor were they provisioned for, winter in the area. They had specific orders to report back to Mexico with their loot in time for it to be shipped back to Spain via treasure galleons in December. Their captain, motivated by a desire to save time, decided to take a short cut, which in a previous understanding with the natives they had promised never to use. Often they were warned by their friendly hosts to stay out of the area of this route, for it traversed the hallowed burial ground of their ancestors. "Spirits and bad medicine," they were cautioned.

Giving no heed to those warnings, the Spanish treasure patrol of twelve, heavily laden with gold, purposely marched south across the ancient burial ground... and were never heard from again.

Now and then through subsequent years, someone would find a piece of old armor or some other accoutrement dating to the Conquistadors of the sixteenth century. The legend was born. When the area began to become populated, mostly as a direct result of the California gold rush during the mid-1800s, the occasional prospector would show up in Carson City, Nevada, sporting an extremely high-grade chunk of gold ore. In turn, each told a similar story. For some kindness or favor proffered to an Indian, they were rewarded with gold, and often told a sketchy story of a cave-like mine filled with untold riches, but protected by the bones and spirits of dead ancestors and the ghosts of mysterious invaders. All the storytellers claimed the natives described the walls of the mine to be smooth, dark, and strangely reflective, '...like water that runs slow and deep.'

In the depression era of the late 1920's and early 1930's, the district was overrun with treasure hunters certain they possessed the right map, had done all the proper research, and/or had received previously unreported information that would certainly lead each to the mysterious hidden fortunes of the *Lost Conquistador Mine*. While much dirt and rock were rearranged during this treasure hunt, little of value was ever found. These many failures did nothing but perpetuate the legend. The region most often mentioned in these tales was that traversed by the East Slope Endurance 100.

The area between Bridgeport and Bishop, California the start and finish of the race had some of the richest gold mines in California. The Mammoth Lakes and Mono Craters portion of the territory is geologically young, currently is, and has been, one of the most active earthquake zones in the western US. This area also boasts some of the wildest diversity of weather in the entire hemisphere. More than anything else however, it is incredibly remote and scenic. Cody Steele was drawn to this area for all these reasons, and more.

5

He enjoyed the legends and tales, and had on occasion prospected the high valleys, less in pursuit of legendary riches than for the personal enjoyment of the effort, the realignment of his perspectives and priorities, and most of all for the peace and contentment he experienced just being in this wild country. He speculated, "If there *were* a lost mine, the sheer magnitude of the land would almost ensure its secret unless stumbled upon strictly by accident. But hey, everyone should dream."

The trail used in the East Slope Endurance Run wound through this alpine splendor, and was marked with red and white striped lengths of ribbon. The race organizers attempted to strategically place the markers at eye level, and at different intervals all along the 100-mile course. To this end these ribbons could be found dangling from tree limbs, embracing boulders, fence posts and tree trunks, in addition to decorating all variety of trailside shrubbery.

At the Deadman's summit checkpoint, the course crossed US highway 395 from the west side, at which point there was a supply drop and check point for the runners. The race had a thirty-hour time limit, and began at first light. Comfortable with being a back-of-the-pack participant, Steele planned on finishing in darkness, and had provisioned his drop bag at Deadman's with a flashlight and windbreaker. Hardly a serious competitor, satisfaction in this sort of event for Cody was in the training. If he arrived at the start healthy, participation in the actual event was gravy. He recalled the recurring line from the TV series *Kung Fu*, 'It's the journey Grasshopper, not the destination.' Winning for Steele was merely in completing the race, even if he finished dead last. From this checkpoint on to the finish line, the trail meandered gradually downhill.

"Looking good," called the checkpoint race official.

Steele rummaged around in the piles of runner's gear bags searching for his. "Thanks." As he put on his windbreaker, he noticed what looked like a large ball of orange fur amongst the debris in the drainage ditch to the side of the freeway. "What's that?"

"Looks like what's left of the old stray cat that hangs around the highway maintenance shed up the highway," replied the monitor. "Saw it earlier making a dash across the road in front of a pickup. Guess he didn't make it."

Steele went over for a closer look. The tabby's chest moved irregularly. Sitting on the side of the concrete culvert, he picked the cat up, noticing it was nothing but skin and bones, however still barely alive. He examined it quickly, and found no obvious injuries. Wrapping it as best he could in his windbreaker, he cuddled it protectively in his lap. "Little short on luck this time, eh big guy?" His thoughts ran back to the exploding ball of fire off his right wing so many years ago over Cambodia. His wingman and best friend were gone in an instant. "There wasn't even the same chance to bail as I had." The cat stirred, each successive breath further apart. It mewed softly, as he gently petted its head. Suddenly, its eyelids flew open. Clear, golden eyes stared directly into Steele's for just a fleeting second, then the eyelids fluttered closed. "Dying alone would be hell." He tenderly hugged the cat to his chest.

He buried it in a small rock cairn off to the side of the highway amongst some dense sage. "Didn't want the critters to get it," he said to the race official. The man just shook his head. Zipping up his windbreaker, Steele wiped the corners of his eyes, and jogged into the night down the long trail. "Living alone is even tougher."

Running downhill was never Steele's favorite. It killed his knees. The nagging pain was the result of numerous overuse injuries suffered earlier in his athletic career. At just over six feet, and a sturdy one hundred ninety-five pounds, he knew his physique was not conducive to this kind of prolonged abuse. One of his buddies, a physician, cautioned him time and again to retire his running shoes in exchange for a swimsuit or a bicycle so that he might walk without a cane in his old age. Stubbornly, he kept on running. Several hours earlier in the race, his knees had signaled his brain that they were not in total accord with the pounding punishment they were being asked to endure. He regularly swallowed *Motrin* to quiet the insistent pain. He decided that he had best enjoy this race to the fullest, as it just might be his last long distance event. As he plodded along, the sun slipped behind a distant high peak.

Darkness comes quickly at this altitude. There is no long, low-light dusk, particularly when a ridge of high mountains averaging 11,500 feet above sea level interrupts the light from the setting sun. Too quickly for Cody and most of the other runners, it was pitch dark.

Following the narrow beam of his light, he delicately picked his way down an ancient arroyo on the far south side of Mono Craters, while simultaneously attempting to locate trail-marking ribbons and watch his footing. The loose, round rocks of the streambed provided treacherous footing. In mid-stride he lost his balance as he tried to avoid what looked to be an unusually sharp, pointed stone. Dodging, he was forced to overcompensate his next stride, causing a loss of balance on the uneven terrain. The sudden awkward movement, combined with his momentum, sprawled him headlong onto the riverbed gravel. "Goddamn it!" he bellowed. Stiffly sitting, he ran a hand through his sandy blond hair, and then took inventory of his body parts. Finding no major problems he gingerly stood and retraced his flight path, muttering to himself. "Dumb ass pilot error! Let's see what caused such a nice trip."

He retrieved his light and directed it at the pointed rock, which precipitated his fall. He was surprised to notice it gave off a dull reflection unlike any of the surrounding rocks and gravel. Positioning the light on a nearby stone ledge so he could use both hands, he scraped away accumulated detritus from the object. Accomplishing this, he put all his weight against the exposed point and heaved for all he was worth. Reluctantly, it finally came free. It appeared to be a tarnished, rusty, bent turtle shell. Cody's startled realization was almost instantaneous. The armored breastplate must have been at least four hundred years old.

6

The descent into Rabaul is one of the 'E ticket' rides in air travel. Rabaul is the capital of New Britain, the largest and most diverse of Papua New Guinea's many offshore islands. Cautiously resting on the rim of an enormous, flooded volcanic caldera, the town's setting is unquestionably one of the scenic wonders of the South Pacific. The approach was through, not around, a family of brooding volcanoes which continually threaten the idyllic setting. Violent eruptions have occurred in this area, known as the Gazelle Peninsula, with devastating regularity throughout the last 150 years. These sleeping giants steamed and bubbled to life for a brief few days in 1984 causing serious concerns, and had the inhabitants poised for a fast exodus. In early 1942, Japan successfully invaded Rabaul, intending for the city and its geographically protected harbor to be a major supply base, and a deciding influence for its World War II strategy. Shortly after the takeover, Rabaul became a primary target in the Allies' air campaign in the Pacific. In addition to the devastation caused on shore by incessant American bombing, between fifty and sixty Japanese vessels were sunk in the harbor. To dive to their ghostly remains was why Dr. Devoney Louise Marsh was aboard an Air Niugini flight, gently touching down in paradise.

On the faculty of the University of California in Berkeley, a Ph.D. in environmental science, Dr. Marsh was an enthusiastic SCUBA diver. The sport not only provided her with some much needed time to herself away from her academic pursuits, but the beautiful and seemingly perfect order in the world beneath the surface gave her insights into her own values and priorities, personally and professionally. Diving allowed her to be an observer rather than the observed, the student rather than the teacher. Her friends and colleagues often accused her of being far too intense, to the point of being

30

almost obsessive. It was the reason she never married, they proclaimed. The youngest of three sisters, she was also the prettiest, a reality that estranged her from her siblings. Her father Salt, a decorated WWII veteran, had hoped for at least one son. Devoney was a tomboy from an early age thanks to her father's influence. She learned to excel in a man's environment. She was also very intelligent. As her awareness grew through puberty, she was torn between taking advantage of her burgeoning femininity, or her discerning intelligence. This dilemma plagued her constantly. At university, she chose to pursue academics. It was really an easy choice, given the traumas and uncertainties of relationships in the capricious 1970s. Early in her career, she discovered that the only way for a female to compete in an academic world driven and dominated by men was either to sexually acquiesce, or be better than everyone else. Her beauty brought her many invitations for upward advancement by physical submission, nearly all of which she ignored. The intensity she brought to her endeavors, both in professional and emotional arenas, insulated her from most potentially close relationships. The result was an outward veneer of aloofness, but on the inside she was a very lonely individual. Diving offered an escape from both extremes.

She had been diving for the last ten of her thirty-six years, and visited many 'world class' dive locations around the world, including the famous Japanese wrecks of Truk Lagoon in Micronesia. She was extremely anxious to begin this current adventure, having heard so much about this area of the world from Salt and his war buddies. Further, through her studies, she knew that in this part of the Tropics, specifically in Malaysia, Irian Jaya and Papua New Guinea, there existed some of the last truly pristine areas in the world left to explore, both physically and culturally. She was excited with the opportunity to be one of the first to do so.

She splurged and chartered a boat for ten days, in order to have more flexibility than a shore-based operation would permit. She was met at the airport by one of the crew of her charter, the *Taleo Tambu.* He spotted her immediately, as she was the only unaccompanied passenger coming through customs. Like all divers, she carried what seemed to be every conceivable piece of SCUBA gadgetry known to man.

"Welcome to paradise, ma'am. Have a nice trip?" The youngster wore not much more than a striped T-shirt, which appeared two sizes too large, emblazoned with the boat's name and logo. She thought him to be the skinniest kid she had ever laid eyes on, but soon forgot this thanks to his enormous smile accentuated by ivory-white teeth.

He tossed her dive bag and clothes duffel into what appeared to have been a jeep in an earlier life. "My name is Gratvin, and I'll be your guide." He helped her grab the roll bar and pull herself into the well-used vehicle.

"Thank you, yes Gratvin. It was very long, but worth it." She inhaled the sweet thickness of tropical air while holding her hair up off her neck as they bumped along the airport frontage road. "Will we have time for a dive before dark?" She had lost all track of California time transiting the International Dateline, changing planes in Los Angeles and Australia, spending 36 hours en route.

"You're the boss, ma'am. Whatever you want, we can arrange. There are good wrecks only five minutes from our mooring, and the *Tambu* is five minutes from shore by Zodiac." The formidable smile never left his face.

Ten minutes later she sipped a frosty glass of iced tea in the small but very comfortable, cockpit area located on the aft section of the *Taleo Tambu*. Having arranged the charter from half way around the world sight unseen, she knew nothing more than that the vessel was supposed to be a sailboat equipped for diving. She was awed with the end result, given her previous poor experiences with 'exotic' boat charters. The *Tambu* was a brand new, state-of-the-art, fifty-foot, blue-water catamaran.

In each of the outboard pontoons the craft sported three intimate staterooms. Each side had its own bathroom with vanity, sink, head, and shower. As the only guest, she had free run of the entire starboard quarters. The main salon separated the two sides of the boat, and abounded with luxury. On one wall was a bank of entertainment electronics, including a TV, VCR, CD player and stero tapedeck. Built into the opposite wall was the inboard pilot's station, which looked as if it were right out of an airplane cockpit. Stacks of consoles crammed with switches and dials were arranged throughout the compartment and complemented by radios and other apparatus strewn over a well-lit chart table. There were three built-in, wrap around sofas in the comfortably intimate living area, placed to the sides and rear of the full length, full width, tempered windshields. Additionally, the port pontoon was equipped with a gourmet galley outfitted with all the modern conveniences. It also housed the crew, with whom she was currently becoming acquainted.

In addition to Gratvin, there was Molly the cook, and Xavier, or Exxy, as he preferred, who would do the deck work and handle the topside diving duties. All three were 'Nationals' native to Papua New Guinea. The native PNG population is a mix of Asian, Melanesian and Polynesian. Their skin color varies from almost black to a light caramel, depending on ancestral distillation. Twentyish, plain-looking but extremely buxom, Molly was from the capital city of Port Moresby; Exxy came from a small off-shore island group known as the Trobriands; and Gratvin from a clan in the New Hanover Islands northeast of New Ireland. They all awaited the arrival of the skipper.

"What does *Taleo Tambu* mean?" Devoney asked, her question directed to all of them.

"It comes from the dialect of a small, mainland clan and roughly translates to mean 'sacred north wind'," Molly replied.

"Great name for a sail boat," she acknowledged.

To her questions about the underwater topography, and to what she might expect on the wrecks in the harbor, Gratvin was enthusiastic. "Most of the wrecks in the Rabaul area lie on the flooded interior crater of this ancient volcano, on whose surface we now float. The geography is typical of most volcanic cones found throughout the world. That is, steep, often sheer interior side walls, gradually sloping to a common depth near the center. Here in Blanch Bay and Simpson Harbor, it is not unusual to find over thirty meter depths within ten meters of shore."

Devoney was amazed with the diction and formal presentation of his dialogue, thinking to herself that he obviously must have done this before. "Where did you learn all this, and to speak English so well, Gratvin?"

"I went to the Australian high school in Port Moresby, ma'am. English is our official national language, if you don't count Pidgin."

"Please, don't call me ma'am. I won't know to whom you are speaking," she instructed. "Dev, Devoney, or even 'hey you' will do just fine."

She continued working on her drink, while he eagerly continued, anxious to show off his knowledge. "Yes, ma'am. Oops. Sorry about the ma'am … ma'am. All the wrecks we'll explore in the bay are over thirty meters deep so we will have to watch our dive tables and no-decompression limit computers carefully. We understand from the dive profile you forwarded that you are experienced. It's entirely your decision whether to try this dive or not, however. The waters in the bay are quite clear and calm, so we thought you should be able to handle a relatively deep first dive with no problem. Due to particularly effective post-war salvage effort, much of the best stuff has already been taken off the wrecks, though. But, I'm certain we will see and find things that will interest you. With the skipper's OK, we'll motor across to the Beehives and make our first dive."

Still doing the mental conversion of meters to feet, she glanced in the direction he indicated. Protruding near the center of the deep lagoon, she saw two rock pinnacles about one and a half miles away. "I'm game. I didn't come here to just sit around. Let's do it!"

Just then a second rubber Zodiac approached, its arrival heralded by a bellowed, "Ahoy, mates!" Dominic nosed his boat in beside the one Gratvin had used to ferry Devoney out from shore, threw Exxy a line, jumped aboard, and gave her hand a theatrical kiss in greeting all before she could even set her glass down. "Dr. Marsh, I presume. Welcome aboard. Please call me Dominic, skipper, captain, or anything that pleases you. I answer to anything loud. I hope my crew made you comfortable and showed you around my shiny new toy." Like the rest of the crew, Dominic wore a striped *Taleo* T-shirt. He looked to be in his young forty's, had short sun-bleached hair, and was a bit on the stocky side, but 'muscular', she noted with admiration. He went about the details of readying his craft for departure, his movements fluid with familiarity. Despite a rich tropical tan and contrasting white blond shock of hair, it was his face that immediately drew her attention. It was dark and chiseled into the kind of brooding good looks, which might as quickly explode into a flash of meanness or anger, as melt into a smile. A curious razor-thin white scar blemished an otherwise perfect left jaw. She noticed his strong sure hands went about their tasks with skill and care, an attribute she and many women admired in a man. His movements, while definitely masculine, had a certain feline grace about them. Her appraising gaze took a bit longer to finish its inventory than she intended, and the sudden physical attraction to this stranger startled her. His dark brown eyes seemed to take in *everything,* and they flashed enticingly when he fired up the engine and called out over his shoulder... "Let's get wet!"

On the run across to the Beehives, Devoney became absorbed in the irony of the tranquil beauty that pervaded the Rabaul of today, and the violent episodes, natural and otherwise, that punctuated its past. The afternoon air was laced with the exotic scent of frangipani, the water... vitreous, the weather and temperature... humid, but otherwise ideal. All in all it was a typical day in the Tropics of the South Pacific. Yet in a short while she would be face to face with reminders of the man-made violence wrought on this seemingly peaceful paradise. She couldn't contain a shudder of foreboding. She rationalized, thinking it was probably due to her sense of anticipation and excitement before making her first dive. "And a particularly deep one," she cautioned herself.

As they prepared their tanks and regulators, Gratvin laid out the dive plan.

"The *Hakkai Maru* was sunk in late 1944, and rests upright in about forty five meters. Its holds were filled with spare parts for the famous Zero fighter plane, and we might still find some recognizable pieces for you to photograph. It lies almost on top of the bow section of the *Italia Maru,* sunk earlier in '44. Not much is known about the *Italia.* Because it was almost totally destroyed by the bombing and its orientation on the bottom, there aren't many distinguishable areas on the hulk. Because of this, few divers have bothered exploring her. The majority of the forward section lies about twenty five meters off the center port section of the *Hakkai,* and it came to rest in an unusual bow up position. We call it 'Tojo's nose' because it looks just like a giant nose when you see it from the *Hakkai.*"

Dominic throttled back *Tambu's* engine, and searched the blue-black waters. Gratvin continued, "Skipper will tie off on a submerged buoy ... *if* he can find it." Over his shoulder, Dominic shot him a 'give me a break' look. "The buoy is anchored to one of the mid-section winches on the top deck of the *Hakkai,* at a depth of around 35 meters or about 110 feet. Once on board, we'll do a quick swimming tour of the entire wreck, and possibly visit one of the forward holds. If we have enough bottom time left and you feel up to it, we can swim over to 'Tojo's nose', and go under and into it at a depth of about 45 to 50 meters. It apparently broke in two between the number two and number three holds, and rests upright on that point. At any time you want to stop or feel uncomfortable, I'll be right there. There will be a safety tank with an octopus rig hanging off at ten meters, where we'll make our first decompression stop. If we dive to our plan, there won't be a need for any stops, but we make a habit of doing them anyway for safety's sake. Two minutes at ten meters, five at six meters and ten at three. Got it?"

She flashed him the universal hand signal for OK.

Pulling her diveskin on over her bikini, she noticed the skipper watching her, obviously admiring. *Not too bad for an old lady,* she thought. *I still have bumps in the right places and curves where they're supposed to be.* Instantly, her brain wrestled with years of repressed femininity and practiced conservatism, ignited by the allure Dominic fired in her sexuality. It was a conundrum she had faced many times in her life. Usually her conservatism won. On holiday, in the comfort of the warm tropics, half a world away from the reality of her professional life ... and Cody. This time, there was no contest. Purposefully, she turned to face Dominic so that he might get a better view as she stretched and wiggled into the Lycra bodysuit. *Why the hell not?* she smiled to herself.

In actuality, she looked years younger than her age. At a nicely proportioned five feet one inch and just a tad over one hundred pounds, topped with a tangle of golden hair, she turned men's, and often women's, heads wherever she went. She did her best to keep her shape by mountain biking in the hills of Marin County when she had the chance, and did an hour of aerobics in a class at her local fitness club every few days when she couldn't ride. The tone of her skin suggested as much exposure to sun as to florescent lights of the classroom, and the wrinkles of age seemed to have avoided marking her much, except for tiny 'smile tracks' at the corners of her pale blue eyes. Since her argument with Cody when he left her house that evening seven months ago, she had immersed herself in work. This was the first time since that she acknowledged, let alone noticed or even cared about, the effect her appearance had on a man.

By the time they were suited and geared up, Dominic and Exxy had the *Tambu* tied off and were busily preparing the safety tank and decompression ladder. She followed Gratvin off the rear access platform with a giant stride entry that was a bit on the rusty side. The water was a soothing 84 degrees Fahrenheit. "I may never leave," she sighed. She cleared and adjusted her mask, while admiring streamers of sunlight dancing magically through the clear blue water all around.

They snorkeled to the bow of the *Tambu* and the descent line. Gratvin instructed her to take the lead, and reciprocating a thumbs-up farewell to the topside crew watching from the cat's trampoline above, she positioned the regulator in her mouth, purged her buoyancy compensator, and slid into inner-space.

It took her senses a few seconds to adjust to the underwater environment. By the time they descended to forty-five feet she felt at ease, and her body coursed with the thrill of anticipation for the adventure waiting below. At about this depth in clear water, a diver can no longer see the reflection of light on the surface. While there still is ample ambient light, warm colors begin fading to blues and grays and the surface is no longer a visible dimension. In conditions like these, the diving experience is like free falling in an infinite liquid world, with no sides, top, or bottom. The only thing to spatially orient the two descending divers was a rough manila anchor line disappearing into the velvet indigo below.

As she equalized the pressure in her ears, she recollected Gratvin's report that they might not see many fishes. The harbor in Rabaul is totally enclosed by the surrounding landmass, and the only water funneling in and out of the bay is tidal. Through her studies, and from past diving experiences, she understood that fish life required sustaining marine growth such as kelp or coral, which in turn require the sustenance of nutrient-rich currents. None of these life-supporting systems are present in the ecology of Simpson Harbor. Abruptly, she felt a gentle tug on her left fin and turned to see Gratvin pointing to their right. A small black-tip reef shark effortlessly glided up, took a cursory glance at these strange intruders in his domain, and as if dismissing them, was gone with an imperceptible flick of his tail.

At seventy-five feet she began to make out disjointed, ghostly shapes converging directly beneath them. After descending another ten feet, they could recognize nearly the entire deck and bridge areas of the *Hakkai Maru*. The silent stillness radiated an eerie aura of melancholy. She felt a sudden wave of isolation. A little faraway voice in the back of her brain warned her that part of this emotion was caused by the narcosis of 'Rapture of the Deep'. Analytically she understood that nitrogen narcosis is a physiological state usually affecting all divers to varying degrees at depths below fifty feet. She knew it was brought about by the higher partial pressures of nitrogen in their systems, as a direct result of higher volumes of air being consumed to compensate for increasing water pressure as depth increases. But most stunning to her was the harsh reality of finality engulfing the eerie remains of the old Japanese warship. She felt as if she were walking through a graveyard at midnight.

Her contemplation was interrupted by the tingling sensation caused by a burst of ascending bubbles coming up from inside the hull directly beneath her. Following their undulating silvery trail, she swam around the winch and dropped through a hole in the rusted decking to join Gratvin. He seemed to be buried upside down in a loose pile of debris over in the far corner of what she imagined must have once served as the galley pantry. All she could see were his erratically flailing fins. A moment later, he righted himself and from a cloud of disturbed silt proudly displayed a hand-blown Japanese soda bottle. Inside, the marble that acted as a stopper when the bottle wasn't tilted for drinking could be easily seen. He handed it to her and she bowed deeply accepting this unique, handsome treasure.

They hand signaled mutual OKs, checked each other's air pressure gauges and decompression computers, and then started off on their exploratory circuit of the wreck. Every now and then Gratvin would stop and point out interesting nautical paraphernalia or pieces of machinery, some of which she would dutifully photograph. She thought him a splendid model as he would always hold a photogenic position and exhale just the right amount of bubbles. After about ten minutes he settled back on the top of the forward port deck, and with one hand to his forehead, struck the age old pose of a person looking off into the distance.

Focusing her attention in the direction of his gaze, to her amazement, she became aware of the huge bow section of another vessel looming up from the silty sand and gloom of the dark bottom. It appeared almost as if it were trying to steam vertically for the surface. She giggled out loud, slightly flooding her mask, when she observed that, indeed, from their viewing angle, it did look quite like a giant nose.

Gratvin signaled a question as to which way she wished to continue. Using the quick inflator, she squeezed a short burst of air into her buoyancy compensator vest and without hesitation gently pushed off from the deck of the *Hakkai* and swam across to the shattered section that was the bow of the *Italia Maru*.

He quickly led her to the coarse sand bottom, then under a piece of twisted hull plate and into the remains of the second ship. In the beam of his dive light she could clearly make out the huge bulkheads and twisted beams that comprised the innards of this silent obelisk. About half way into the wreck at the point that once was amidships, Gratvin trained the light through a neat, one-meter diameter hole in the interior decking. The jagged metal at the circumference was all bent inward, indicating the deadly passage of what she imagined correctly was a bomb. The relatively neat hole was the only indication of damage they could see, as the rest of the compartment where they were seemed completely intact. She queried him with raised eyebrows about this incongruity. He responded with a shrug of his skinny shoulders.

With practiced expertise he maneuvered them through the remainder of the ruined hulk. When again she was at his side, he motioned with his thumb toward the surface. She nodded and they ascended at a slow, calculated rate. Passing the huge anchors near the very top of the dead vessel, she could just make out the requiem nameplate... *Italia Maru*.

After swimming up to the shallowest point of the silent bow, they angled upward back toward their buoy line on the *Hakkai*, rising into the clearer, lighter surface water. They were soon dangling at the ten-meter bar on the decompression ladder, where they bobbed gently in rhythm with the slight surface movement presently caressing the *Tambu* directly above them.

Following their scheduled five minute wait at the six meter rung, Devoney was languidly passing her final ten minutes at the shallowest stop, playing with a school of tiny fishes living in a growth beneath the anchor buoy. Suddenly, a muffled explosion jarred them. They felt more then heard the tremendous underwater report. She realized that whatever it was must have come from well beneath them for the surrounding water remained, for the moment, calm and still. She saw Gratvin searching the water all around them when the latent, fast moving shock wave from the concussion swept them uncontrollably toward the surface. The nearly half century old '... Goddamn dud', five hundred pounder, resurrected from dormancy by the agitation of their passage nearby, finally exploded in the guts of the *Italia Maru*. Tojo's nose stood no more.

Through veils of mental gossamer, she wallowed through the abyss of unconsciousness. Abruptly, to a blaze of brilliant white light, she hit awareness, her head and body feeling instantly ravaged and abused, with a feeling of being drugged. Her eyelids fluttered, trying to remain open, and finally she focused on a trio of very concerned faces. "Are you all right, Dr. Marsh?" It was Exxy.

"Devoney," she croaked in response. Her tongue felt two sizes too big for her mouth. "I think so. Is Gratvin OK? What the hell happened?" Stiffly, she creaked to sitting position, and found herself on one of the couches in the main salon. Dominic nodded his head toward the port hatch, through which she was just able to glimpse the youngster cautiously checking their dive gear. He immediately joined them inboard when he heard her voice. While responding to Gratvin's questions of concern, she noticed a thin trickle of blood oozing from his right ear. "I'm better than you look," she said. On reluctant legs, she stood to examine his ear, her voice still sounding somewhat hollow. Dismayed, she noted that his irrepressible smile was missing, and fear still shone in his dark eyes. "My God. What *did* happen down there?" she shuddered.

7

As he strode up University Drive, an unusual package under his arm, he couldn't put aside the growing excitement he felt. Maybe he really was on to something.

The Berkeley campus of the University of California is a compendium of different buildings, seemingly laid out with no rhyme or reason. More than once on his way to meet her he had become lost within its boundaries, after parking in some new lot Devoney recommended. It wasn't until she patiently explained the logistics of orienting oneself to the campanile or the Greek Theater that Cody was truly comfortable finding his way. He was amused with himself, thinking how easy it was to get lost in a city, and how he seldom if ever got lost in the mountains or the jungle. *Cities are no place for sane people*, he thought.

Locating Laura Demming in her laboratory on the third floor of the Life Sciences building was easy. An identifying shock of red hair erupted from a hastily tied scarf she wore on her head. Encircling her from behind with his free arm, he spun her around and deftly kissed her astonished mouth. "And how is my second favorite Doctor?"

"Cody! I didn't expect you so soon. What manner of rocket did you fly to make it back over the Sierra so quickly?" she stammered. She attempted to hide her surprise and pleasure on seeing him. Her emerald green eyes danced with excitement.

"Ah, my dear. Driven on by the mere thought of seeing you again was all the magic I needed."

Dr. Laura Demming had been Devoney Marsh's ace graduate student during Devoney's first year as a fledgling professor. Since then, the three had become best of friends and confidants. The two women even roomed together for a period before Devoney purchased the home in Mill Valley. Steele often kidded them both, claiming that if it hadn't have been for meeting Devoney first, he most certainly would have lustily campaigned for a relationship with Laura. At 33, she was a classic redhead in every attribute; her subtle charm and quick wit were legend on campus. On occasion, Laura would house sit for them when either was away. Laura's forte was anthropology, with strong interests in archeology, and she was his first phone call after he literally stumbled on the armor.

After the fall, Cody excavated the armored piece, hiked cross-country back to highway 395 and thumbed a ride to the nearest run checkpoint. There he informed the race organizers that his run was over, and they accommodated a ride back to Bridgeport. He immediately called Laura. "This trinket better be worth waking me up in the middle of the night," she warned. "I thought you were supposed to be on some sort of death run."

"I was. That's where I found this thing. C'mon, Red. I know you weren't asleep. What was his name?" He carefully unwrapped his find, as they continued their good-natured banter.

"Geez, Cody. Whatever it is, it's really dirty, horribly bent, lousy with rust, but very, very old." Her manner and speech became more academic, as she began to inspect the find. She studiously cleaned away decades of caked dirt with a small, horsehair field brush. "Definitely armor," she said. "Possibly Gothic. So-called Gothic armor was produced through nearly the end of the 16th century, until gunpowder quickly hastened its obsolescence. Notice how it isn't uniformly thick. Pieces like this were made by hand, hammering outward from a central point to the edges, creating thickness where protection was most required, and tapering thin where connections to other pieces had to be made. If authentic, this must have belonged to someone of importance or of rank, as it is exceptionally well crafted. The greater the quality or decoration, the higher the rank or stature of the wearer. Look here, Cody," she prompted.

"Sometimes your expertise amazes me, Red."

Both traced their hands around the edges of the plate, she becoming more intrigued with its manufacture, he with the history it represented. Not to mention the potential provenance of a long lost treasure. "A back plate was attached here," she indicated six holes, two on either side and two at the top. "The connections were usually made by riveting leather strips to the main piece, or by interlocking studs with slots and turnable wooden pegs." She held the piece to her chest in demonstration.

"I think I'd prefer you in something a bit more flimsy."

Often, they kidded each other, to the extent that the practice had become almost an expected game between them. She ignored him, and rifled through some nearby reference material. Showing him an illustration of a man outfitted in a suit of armor, she pointed to the figure's familiar looking breastplate. "Based on the construction, utilitarian style, quality, workmanship and type of metal, I make it most likely Spanish, possibly Italian, early to mid-1500s."

"You mean its *real*?"

"Authentic as hell," she concluded.

Steele wrapped both arms around her waist, hoisted her off her feet and spun her crazily around the cluttered room, all the while shouting "YES!"

When finally they crashed headlong over a chair and were picking themselves up from the floor, she elbowed him in the ribs and commanded, "OK, Fred Astaire. Where'd you find it? Let's hear the whole story."

8

Molly cleared the remains of the dinner feast. Devoney did yet another body parts inventory on herself, the latest of many since the afternoon incident, concluding with relief that she had survived mostly intact; though tired, she was otherwise OK. Maybe it was the fresh-caught tuna, perfectly prepared. Certainly the exceptional wine helped. "Perfect for medicinal purposes," she smiled to herself as Exxy poured the last of the second bottle into her glass.

Repeatedly, she turned down the crew's suggestions that she go to the local hospital just to be sure, and now even the ringing in her ears and the headache had subsided. Dominic rolled the chart he had been studying, discreetly put the afternoon's batch of faxes in the drawer, and turned to Devoney. "The Southern Cross is exceptionally clear at this time of night. Let me introduce you to it." He held out his hand to help her from the table.

As she stood up, her intuition warned her that he had more in mind than simply giving her a visual tour of the heavens. *What the hell*, she thought. *I haven't had a fling since I started seriously dating Cody. I'm on vacation in a tropical paradise. Who knows where he is? I'm a big girl, and this guy is a definite hunk. What's wrong with a little harmless romance?* She let her last question go, lowered all the red warning flags in her cautious brain, and let him lead her out into the warm night.

They arranged themselves comfortably, leaning against two oversize cushions on the foredeck overlooking the mainmast and trampoline. Once outside of the cabin, it was soothingly dark. The reflected lights of Rabaul seemed to dance just for them as the waters of the harbor gently moved, stimulated by some imperceptible breeze.

"I heard a muffled thump that seemed to lift the whole boat," Dominic recounted. "The next thing we knew, Gratvin was yelling bloody murder from just astern. I ran out of the cabin, and saw you floating face down to starboard. We were able to get you on *Tambu*'s dive step within seconds after your unscheduled surfacing."

"You mean... you came in after me?" she interrupted.

"I've never lost a guest... at least not on the first dive of the first day. After we got you on board and checked your vitals, which seemed strong enough, we brought you into the cabin and you came around in a matter of minutes. The rest, as they say, is history."

"What do you think it was?"

"Unexploded ordnance of some sort, most likely. Probably jarred in some way by you two crashing around inside that old hulk. Although Gratvin did admit to me that you handled yourself quite well in the water."

"I'm not so sure about that. I had to be dragged unconscious out of it. I know I'll be more careful if and when I ever go into another wreck."

"How about first thing tomorrow? Let's find out what caused all the commotion."

"You'll be diving with us?" she asked.

"Just you and me. I'm afraid Gratvin won't be doing any diving for a while. I'm no Doctor, Doctor, But I'm certain he ruptured an eardrum. I sent him ashore to have the medics check it out."

Accenting Dominic's last comment was the engine of one of the Zodiacs popping to life at the stern. As the little inflatable sprinted toward shore, they watched its florescent wake tear a white swathe through the black water.

"Dominic..." she slowly rolled the name off her tongue. "And what might be your full name?"

"My mother was French. Married a German SS Major during the war. I took her name after my father vanished right after D-Day. He was working on some sort of secret weapon at the time. My real name is Franz Toscona, but my close friends call me Dominic, as my mother did."

"Exactly what vitals did you check, and what did you check them with, Dominic?"

"Maybe I should do a more thorough examination." He took her hand, and circled her bare shoulders with his other arm.

The warm night air was luxuriant, filled with a heady assortment of sweet, exotic smells. The tropical jungle fringing the harbor had come alive with the magical resonance of night animals and insects, while the catamaran rocked hypnotically back and forth, dark waters gently lapping at its sleek hull. Devoney felt a spark ignite from a dormant ember deep within her. She gazed skyward to the Southern Cross shepherding the peaceful scene, and returned the purposeful pressure of Dominic's hand.

9

At about the same time, on a small island in the St. Matthias Group, approximately 350 miles due north of Rabaul, a young native just beached his dugout canoe. Walking toward the inviting cook fire in front of his modest palm frond home, he thought, *I surely must be the luckiest man alive. I live in paradise. The weather is good all year. Our islands are protected from the typhoons by the fringing reef. The sea, reef, and land provide me with all I could ever hope to eat. I have the most beautiful wife a man could want. She is a wonderful mother to our children, is the best cook in the village, and even after ten years, I can barely keep up with her desire.*

As Tomast strode across the soft white sand, the day's catch of fish and lobster in his palm basket, he could see the silhouette of Majanii in his doorway. She was naked to the waist, her breasts still firm and up-thrust. A lump of pride and passion rose in his throat. Just then his two children burst through the doorway and attached themselves to him, one on each leg. They loved to hold onto his muscular thighs, and ride his feet as far as he would permit. Their laughter echoed back at him from the cliffs of the hill behind their cozy home.

A night breeze murmured fresh off the lagoon, the precursor of yet another perfect day for fishing tomorrow. He gave his wife a robust kiss full on her upturned mouth, and handed her the fish, all the while attempting to disengage the children from his legs. As he walked to the nearby waterfall for his evening rinse, again he acknowledged his good fortune, and thanked whatever gods there were for providing him such a good life.

46

10

Following a leisurely breakfast of fresh tropical fruits, Devoney's attention turned to the serene harbor waters awaiting exploration. She took in the peaceful bay from her position on the foredeck, as they cruised back to the Beehives. The morning air was calm and almost cool, the oppressive noonday tropical heat and humidity still almost four hours away. Once the *Tambu* was again moored to the *Hakkai* buoy, Devoney quickly suited up and readied herself for the dive, with Gratvin's doting assistance. The young man was obviously disappointed with not being able to dive. The doctors ashore confirmed Dominic's diagnosis of a ruptured eardrum. They cautioned Gratvin against any water-oriented activities for several weeks. Nevertheless, he couldn't disguise the excitement he felt about their attempt to find an explanation for their near disaster the day before. Devoney's apprehension vanished as they descended through thirty feet. Columns of refracted sunlight cascaded all around. The whole experience seemed somehow less foreboding than on her previous dive. *Perhaps due to a good night's sleep after a comfortably mellow evening*, she thought. She equalized pressure on her ears, then continued on down.

The events of the previous night on deck with Dominic had been wildly romantic, and certainly an unexpected addition to her vacation. They explored each other like wanton teenagers until she demurely retired to her cabin before all control could be abandoned to their fiery passion. She was certain there would be ample opportunity in the next few days to fulfill her resurrected physical desires. She sensed an animal quality in Dominic, which fascinated yet frightened her. Quickly she rationalized it as anticipation of the unknown. *A forbidden fruit that I really need to taste*, she mused. Still, there was that tiny nagging voice of guilt buried deep within her psyche. Was it simply intuition, or maybe she was moving a little too fast for comfort? What about Cody? *Why not, damn it? I deserve it.* She looked beneath her as Dominic settled toward the bottom, and again felt a warm, stirring feeling as she imagined the potential pleasures their budding romance might provide.

Dominic touched down on the bridge of the *Hakkai,* creating a small explosion of disturbed silt. She already noted how at ease he appeared underwater, but further observed the telltale signs of a novice, albeit seemingly bold, diver. He swam with his arms extended in front, rather than streamlined against his sides, and continually adjusted his buoyancy using the automatic power inflator. All signs of a rookie. Like most sailors the world over, Dominic was not a diver... at least not until it had become necessary for him to quickly learn. "In order to recover a customer's dropped camera," he told her.

"Oh well," she sighed into her regulator. "What he lacks in skill and experience are more than made up for by his enthusiasm." Cody being the rare exception in her experience, she usually found her own athletic and sporting skills to equal, or exceed, those of her male friends and previous lovers.

Devoney settled down gently beside him, and they both took in the panorama of the huge, inhospitable foredeck and king posts stretched out below and in front of their watery perch. Everything was just as she remembered. She triggered a quick burst of air into her vest, and easily kicked up and to port about ten feet. She was astonished when all she could make out of the neighboring hulk *Italia* was an enormous pile of undefined rubble where yesterday the intact, monolithic hull had stood.

By mutual assent, after monitoring each other's air pressure gauges, they moved across the bottom wasteland to the wreckage of the mystery ship. Devoney arrived at the remains first, and easily bounced her way along the sand bottom on the tips of her fins, her performance resembling astronauts enjoying the moon's minimal gravity environment for the first time. She was examining the hull plates as she moved along the keel, searching for a safe entry point, when she heard Dominic's resonating signal. He had continued up the supine port side hull to the remnants of the deck area, where he was banging his dive knife on an exposed steel beam to attract her attention. She joined him and 'thumbs upped' his discovery of an access point through an unobstructed, now horizontal passageway.

The explosion the day before had exerted just enough force to release the *Italia*'s bow section from the vice-like bottom suction, while also dislodging the sand supporting it. The combined effect of sand and suction had held it in an upright position for over forty-five years. Once free, the violence of the sudden motion caused corroded and rusting rivets and bolts throughout the interior of the ravaged vessel to give way under new torques and stresses. The redistribution of weight was just enough to topple the remains of the bow to starboard. The *Italia Maru* finally found its ultimate angle of repose. The corpse of the ship crashed over sideways, then finally and ignobly, collapsed in on itself. The resulting chaos of rubble now confronted Devoney and Dominic as they prepared to breach what was left of her flattened and smashed interior.

Dive lights blazing, they cautiously entered the small companionway, Dominic in the lead. Just prior to leaving the *Tambu,* they had agreed on several basic rules for their proposed dive plan. They wouldn't venture into any space or compartment if either decided it looked too unstable or dangerous. They would immediately exit the wreckage if either's dive light failed, or when the first one's remaining air pressure fell below 1,000 psi (pounds per square inch) as measured and displayed on their pressure gauges. This would give them just about one third of a tank, and ample remaining air to safely exit and swim to the surface. As before, a safety tank and regulator would be hung at the decompression ladder. They calculated their safe bottom time at twenty minutes, and knew they had to get in and out quickly to avoid any required decompression stops. They planned entry through some part of the severed mid-ship section, just as Devoney and Gratvin had done the day before. They were forced into using this entry point, never having considered the new positioning of the vessel, or the extent of debris and wreckage now confronting them.

It took them both several minutes to orient their senses, and recognize reference points within the dark horizontal passage, which had been constructed and used in the vertical. Devoney had a flashback to her childhood visits to the Winchester Mystery House in San Jose, California, where some of the hallways in that bizarre home were constructed sideways rather than upright.

After traversing about twenty yards into the passageway, Devoney caught a sudden rush of movement beneath them at the periphery of her light's powerful beam. Dominic noticed it also, and both redirected their lights down into the adjoining compartment, which opened up to their position in the companionway. Everything outside the circumference of their searching shafts of light seemed a sepulchral, fathomless black. Dominic spotted and illuminated it first, unconsciously back-pedalling into Devoney. Recoiling, she instantly recognized the equally startled animal. The eight-foot long Gray Reef Shark had become trapped in the hold when the collapsing *Italia* fell sideways the day before. Sensing the motion created by the intrusion of the divers with its highly developed lateral line sensors—two highly sensitive, mucus filled membranes running the length of either side of most species of shark—the trapped fish quickly swam toward the diver's erratic flailings.

Once the shark got up and inside the companionway with them, the situation became a momentary standoff. The big fish, which to Devoney seemed to be constructed mostly of very large teeth, did not have enough room to turn and retreat. Likewise, Dominic and Devoney could not hope to out swim it backwards to their point of entry. The shark made the first move. As it came toward them in a burst of speed, all they could manage was to scrunch up against the wall of the passage, which was now their ceiling, hoping to create as much room under them as possible. The shark charged beneath them in a frenzy and was gone in an instant, a gray flash in a roil of agitated silt and water. Devoney felt as though her thighs had been sandpapered. The creature's coarse skin grazed her in passing, shredding her Lycra diveskin, but causing no serious physical damage.

After seconds, which seemed hours, she expelled a frightened breath and looked at Dominic. His dark eyes, wide with raw excitement rather than fear, seemed to completely fill his dive mask. "Is this guy afraid of anything?" she wondered.

Simultaneously they burst out laughing with relief. Dominic noticed the tatters of her ruined diveskin, and took off his glove to examine the tear. The warmth of his hand on her bare skin, even there in 140 feet of water, caused her to shudder and tingle with anticipation. She told him with hand signals, gestures with eyes and nods of her head, that she was fine. Tentatively at first, they resumed their exploration, dropping slowly into the shark's vacated compartment.

Carefully adjusting their buoyancy so not to needlessly disturb any accumulated silt, they hovered just above tangles of cable, containers, and debris, which had settled to the bottom of the dead *Italia*. Discovering that they were almost in the center of the compartment where the rubble apparently was deepest, Dominic motioned her to move to one end of the flooded hold, while he explored in the opposite direction. They could hardly lose one another as the solitary brightness of their lights dominated the cramped, gloomy compartment.

Devoney flippered slowly over and down the heaps of equipment: probing here and there with the beam of her light. She kept on the alert for anything recognizable, which would hopefully offer them a clue to the contents of the hold. There was a variety of cartons and cases which all looked somewhat intact, and others that were completely smashed and broken. Through the splinters in the breached containers oozed a slimy-looking, brownish-black substance she couldn't identify, and was loath to examine by touch. Now and then, within the broken containers, she noticed layers of thin boards plugged to which were what appeared to be vacuum tubes. Most were shattered, but a few appeared undamaged. She wondered what electrical functions such a device might have had nearly fifty years previous. The layout of the wiring and the arrays of tubes she could see reminded her of similar things she had discovered in her childhood explorations through her parent's old *Philco* radio. At the far end of her side of the compartment, near the bottom of the hold, she came upon a large container that looked still fully intact. It was canted at an odd angle, forcing her to squeeze against a bulkhead to get a better reference for observation. She screamed long but silently when she recognized the object beneath the crate, the sound of her cry totally absorbed by the indifferent, black water.

Up until the moment of Devoney's find, Dominic fared similarly in his end of the hold. He was examining what appeared to be an old TV satellite dish when he looked over and noticed Devoney's erratically waving light. Quickly he swam to her and on seeing the object of her fright, tried to comfort and calm her as best he could, given their location and situation.

Devoney had seen a few cadavers in her college days, and certainly a number of skeletons. But none frightened her as this one did. An icy chill shot up her spine the instant she recognized what it was. Never expecting to find such a ghastly thing, and understanding the horror of its owner's last few moments of life put her over the line between curiosity and dread. She momentarily lost it.

All they were able to see was a skeletal hand thrusting up toward them from a mound of brownish silt and debris. The pale bones of the stark fingers appeared to desperately claw at the black water. Dominic gently moved Devoney to one side and began to fan the silt from the macabre hand. His efforts scattered the tiny finger bones, but still he continued. Eventually, he uncovered the broken arm bones clear to the shoulder, where they disappeared under the large container at the point it was jammed against the forward bulkhead. He didn't begin to try and budge the massive crate. Even if he could, he was certain they would find the remainder of the skeleton horribly crushed.

Devoney regained her composure enough to assist in this process by holding both their lights on the area where Dominic worked. Returning his, she signaled her OK, quickly squeezed his gloved hand, and motioned that she was going to explore the other side of the intact container. Dominic followed, admiring her pluck, given the circumstances. Here and there, they were able to break an occasional board from the banded carton, once exposing several gauges fastened to some sort of huge machinery within. Otherwise they weren't able to find any further definitive clues to the contents. On their final pass around, just above the skeletal arm, they were just able to make out what looked to be the first part of a very faded word stenciled on the old, decaying wood, the final letters of which disappeared beneath the dead man.

After checking the bottom time on their decompression computers, it was with a mixed sense of relief and reluctance that they took one quick, final circuit of the compartment, then began working their way up toward the passageway. Once free of the wreck, the blue, almost translucent water near the surface was a welcome sight, and both Devoney and Dominic's spirits lifted as they waited out their safety-stop decompression time dangling on the ladder beneath the *Tambu.* Unbeknownst to either, both their thoughts concentrated on what might be in the mysterious crates aboard the *Italia,* and both speculated about the stenciled word and its meaning.

Serendipity is a capricious benefactor. Though he would never know it, Dominic had also discovered the remains of his 'vanished' father.

Once back on board, as Gratvin and Exxy helped them off with their gear, they jabbered simultaneously and non-stop at each other.

"Did you see the teeth on that thing?"

"Damn, he was a big sonofabitch. I thought he was going to hit us for sure."

"Nice, quick moves for an old guy, eh? You guys blew the whole bloody thing right over yesterday!"

"What the hell was in that hold?"

"That poor bastard."

"Hold it. Wait a second. One at a time. What happened down there?" Gratvin implored, trying to sort through all the excited chatter.

Devoney recounted her version of the events, and Dominic filled in with his interpretation. After they both ran down and were finally silent, all agreed it was quite an eventful and exciting dive. Molly set out some munchies in the main salon and they were all gathered there when Dominic, for the third time since surfacing, posed the question, "So what did it mean?"

"Do you have a pencil or pen?" She glanced around. Exxy quickly produced a pencil and notebook from the chart table. Both agreed the letters Devoney reproduced on the paper were the same they saw on the crate... S-T-A-A-T-S-G-E-H. "So... what do you think?" Devoney asked again. "I wonder what the rest of the letters are, and what it means?"

Gratvin rejoined them, and saw the word. He took the pencil out of Devoney's hand, and filled in the missing letters... E-I-M.

"*STAATSGHEIM*. My German's rusty, but that's what it looks like to me." Dominic stared at Gratvin. "That hold was sealed. We had to have been the first ones to see that crate since 1944. So, how the hell did you know what the rest of the letters were, anyway?"

"Simple," Gratvin turned his palms up. "When you were away last month, a buddy of mine and I were diving the *Hakkai* from the Zodiac looking for bottles like the one I found for Dr. Marsh. There wasn't much on deck, but we spotted a pouch almost completely buried in the sand down beyond the stern. It was pretty much intact when we found it, but began to come apart on the way up.

"What did you do with it?"

"Took it to my friend's house."

"I don't see the connection with the word."

"Inside the pouch there were a bunch of papers, drawings, and books all sealed in some sort of plastic stuff." Gratvin smiled. "On the top of each drawing and book was the word... *STAATSGHEIM*."

11

The cabin of the *Tambu* looked like the copy room of a daily newspaper moments before press time. Sheets of paper and schematics were draped over every available flat surface and clothes-pinned to lines hastily strung throughout the cabin after every other available space was taken. Molly was barely able to contain her verbal disgust with the trashing of her always-tidy domain.

Gratvin and Dominic had gone ashore and retrieved the old pouch and what remained of its contents following Gratvin's story. By early afternoon, they had systematically separated the legible paperwork from that totally ruined by years of water intrusion, and were in the process of sorting everything legible as quickly as their space and patience would permit. Once they began this process and cursorily reviewed the documents, there was no doubt in any of their minds that the language of inscription was German. Unfortunately, none of the crew, including Dominic and Devoney, could translate any of it.

"I learned some as a kid, but my mother wouldn't permit it spoken in her presence. She *really* hated the Germans. I can still understand and speak it a little, but this... I haven't a clue," Dominic shrugged apologetically in the direction of the documents. "A shame it isn't in French."

"No problema, mis Amigos," Devoney said, revealing her second language. "There must be someone around here who can read and translate soggy German"

Dominic thought for a minute. His opportunistic mind was already working on the possibility that the paperwork held information of more than merely historic value. After all, it was a mysterious Japanese ship carrying secret equipment, marked in German, at the height of a World War, destined for who knew where. "I know a couple of local guys who might be able to help, if they're still in town and sober. I haven't been around for a few months, so I'm not certain exactly where to find them. Maybe Gratvin will know."

"Why do we need two?" Devoney wondered aloud.

"We'll have an answer twice as fast, " he lied, his mind racing. *If the translating chore was split, and there was valuable information to be had, it would be less likely for one of the translators to steal the bulk of any secrets if, in fact, there were any*, Dominic reasoned to himself. "If we get anything at all from this, most likely the damn thing will end up being a better pretzel maker," he offered to his rapt audience.

Following a visit to the only local bank to make copies of their collection of materials on one of Rabaul's only two copiers, they started their search for translators. They located the first in the patio bar of the *Kaivuna Hotel,* at the north end of town, two blocks from the harbor. Willie Kaltenbach was German, and the Asia-Pacific marketing representative for *Air Niugini.* His great-grandfather had been the master of a ship, bringing early white settlers to the then pristine area. A robust, bull of a man, with a too quick smile and a penchant for languages, Kaltenbach was arranging group accommodations for upcoming tours at the *Kaivuna.* Over the last few years Willie had become somewhat of a fixture in the cities and towns served by the government subsidized *Air Niugini.* The Germans always seemed to be among the first to explore and visit new tropical destinations around the world, and Willie had his hands full with the current demand for visits to Papua New Guinea by his countrymen.

A century before, Germans were the first foreign entrepreneurs to capitalize on the bounty of resources and opportunities New Guinea had to offer the world economy. In 1884, two years after Captain Simpson sailed into and named the harbor around which the town of Rabaul would soon develop, a large population of Germans moved to the area to escape the ravages of malaria on the mainland north coast and directed their efforts toward the production of large quantities of copra for export. By 1910 the settlement and growth of Rabaul—translated as 'mangrove swamp' from a local dialect— were well underway. Shortly thereafter, World War I ruined what had quickly become a prosperous, very beautiful and peaceful community. The German heritage remained mostly intact through and after W.W.I however, as the area proved to be of little strategic importance to the invading Australians on the Allied side. Other than seizing control of the local politics and perfunctorily managing the affairs of the community, Australian occupiers in particular, and the war in general, had little effect on most of the German population. Following the 'war to end all wars', the more modern, enterprising Australian influence gradually usurped that of the old country Germans, and Rabaul slowly developed into a frontier town on the edge of paradise for expatriates from a variety of countries. This all came to a bloody halt when Japan suddenly invaded at the outset of World War II, taking absolute control of the entire area. Most of the Australians were killed. All agricultural production for profit ceased. Australia was given the job of care-taking the country following W.W. II, up until PNG independence in 1975. Presently, the German presence is mostly in the form of visiting tourists.

12

"So Dominic, G'day mate," Kaltenbach tossed off in flawless imitation of an Australian accent. "And where did you find this rare Bird of Paradise?" An undisguised ogle directed at Devoney, as he stood to shake their hands.

While sharing a round of *Fosters* and routine pleasantries, Dominic produced a partial batch of the copied schematics and drawings. "This is German?" he questioned, hopefully.

Willie took a quick glance while taking another long pull at his beer, and thumbed through the remainder of the drawings. "Sure thing, mate."

"Would you have a chance to go over these and help translate some of it for us? We're not interested in every word: just some of the highlights. I'll throw in a coupla days diving on the *Tambu* with my star attraction here for your services," Dominic offered, smiling at Devoney. He knew Willie had recently become certified to dive, and had taken to it like a proverbial fish.

"No worries, mate. Shouldn't be any problem. Looks like the layout for an electrical generator of some sort. I recognize the gist of it from similar drawings I worked with in my days as a mechanic at the airline. Those were the good ol' days, before they moved me up to this white-collar bullshit. Pardon my American, ma'am," he parodied. "Reluctantly... have to take a pass on the diving 'til next time I'm through, though. I have to run up to Kimbe and Walindi Plantation tomorrow AM to set up a tour for next month's batch of Krauts. I could have these for you in two days when the return flight stops back. Where'd you get 'em anyway? They look *really* old."

Dominic quickly thought through the risks of entrusting the drawings to Willie for a few days, and chose not to answer the last question. Having learned to always follow his gut hunches, he acquiesced, handing over the documents. "Great," Dominic stood, and again shook Willie's hand. "When we see you the day after tomorrow, we'll set up the diving, and I'll fill you in."

Their next stop was the Rabaul Yacht Club, a broken down remnant from the days between world wars when Rabaul was the capital of Australian New Guinea. Like similar waterfront establishments the world over, the premises acted as a magnet for the area's most colorful and eccentric characters. The only pretense of exclusivity was the fading 'MEMBERS ONLY' sign loosely attached to the massive, mahogany entrance door. Most everyone in town, tourists included; ignored the sign. Dominating the interior was a long, oversize, well-stocked bar over which three slow moving fans noisily failed in their attempts to cool. The dining room opened to a tacky, colored concrete deck bordered on the far side by Simpson Harbor. Scattered all over the place was an amazing variety of gratuitous and decaying boating paraphernalia. Devoney thought the place looked right out of Somerset Maugham. And, of course, adjacent to the outside deck and lawn areas, was a covered, but open on the sides, bar. Here, perched precariously on the end stool, they found Felix Hendel.

Hendel was a third generation resident of New Britain. His grandfather settled and developed one of the most successful plantations in the area. His father took the business an additional step and was establishing a reputation in the export of palm oil, when his life was tragically extinguished in one of the area's all too common car collisions in the late '60s. The Nationals of PNG love cars, but don't spend much time or effort learning to drive. It took Felix only five years to squander his inherited fortune and to lose most of the plantation. In 1975, following PNG's independence, Felix developed an affinity for acquiring quantities of native artifacts, trading booze for art. With the advent of tourism to the area, and with almost no forethought of his own, he stumbled into the lucrative and burgeoning market for 'native art'. He added an appropriate line of cheap T-shirts to his inventory, and for a short time became 'the man to see' for the ubiquitous tourist. Unfortunately, Felix was also a serious drunk. The minute he would get a little money he would head for the Rabaul Yacht Club. Without doubt, he was a regular. Sixtyish, thin, fragile-looking, and generally unkempt, but always with a good story, he was the personification of a Hemmingwayesque character in Rabaul. When they found him, he was in the process of drinking his way through his morning's receipts from sales made dockside of a Russian cruise ship.

"Hendel, old boy. How'd you like to make two hundred Kina for a day's work?"

He slowly turned toward them, his bleary eyes struggling to focus. "Illegal, immoral, or both?" he slurred.

"None of the above. Here take a look at these. You *can* still read German?"

Hendel inhaled the dregs of his scotch and water, spread open the proffered logbook, steadied himself by placing both feet on the floor and both forearms on the bar, loudly cleared his throat, and began a verbatim translation of the first three pages of the *VERHEERUNG* project logs. Devoney returned Dominic's knowing grin. They had found their man.

They left Hendel with the copies and instructions to meet them at the downtown pier at 5:00 PM the following afternoon with his translation notes. Dominic ripped ten, 20 Kina notes in half giving Felix ten useless halves. One Kina, the PNG unit of currency, had the same approximate value as one US dollar, and the largest denomination is K20.

"We'll give you the working ends of those tomorrow, old boy," Dominic promised, slipping him a whole 10 Kina note for emphasis. "Depending on the legibility of your efforts, there might be a substantial bonus in it for you. No cruisers are due in for the balance of the week, so this shouldn't interfere with your curio business. Paul... cut him off if he stays longer than another hour," Dominic instructed the young barman.

"Yes sir, Mr. Dominic," the young man winked.

"Well, its four hours 'til dinner. We've got two full air tanks and two full bottles of wine in the jeep. How about the grand tour of the town; then a beach dive?" Dominic proposed to Devoney.

Devoney noted the swift change in his demeanor... from the shrewd negotiator to the mellow, laid-back charter captain in paradise. "Business or pleasure?" she murmured, taking his arm.

"Man cannot live by German translations alone." He hoisted her effortlessly into the jeep. "Let's see where this road takes us."

13

Half way around the world, Cody Steele sat slouched in an uncomfortable chair in a sterile debriefing room, deep within a featureless building known as the '*mall*', at Langley Air Force Base, Virginia. This is the headquarters of the Central Intelligence Agency. Cody's boss, Chuck Conley, *Deputy Director of Operations* and head of the agency's covert, field team operations, was beginning his second hour of analysis and wrap pursuant to the recently concluded *Wolverine* affair.

The 'who's who' of spying, Cody thought to himself, glancing around the room.

The DDO sat at the center of the crescent shaped, polished walnut conference table, flanked by the President's Assistant Chief of Staff, and next to him was a representative of the United Nations Security Council. The Iraq situation still had everyone's attention, as Hussein's remaining arsenal and his brazen subterfuge and obnoxious posturing clearly indicated that he still posed a serious threat to the stability of the Middle East and the world, despite the crushing defeat of his forces in Kuwait. The one and only thing that all Middle-East experts agreed on was that as long as Saddam Hussein remained in power he would be unpredictable. Earlier, Steele provided the assembled brain trust with his usual laconic report, and now all eyes were on the projection of images and corresponding analysis screened upon the far wall.

"We believe they accidentally activated one of their own internal security booby traps while rigging it. The tech boys found minute traces of the highly volatile new C4-S *Plastique* explosive in several critical locations," Conley advised. "While an unlikely scenario considering *Wolverine*'s known involvement, it becomes a much more plausible hypothesis, given the fact that he was working with a bunch of camel drivers." Conley was not at all shy about expressing his personal prejudices.

The transparencies chronicled the Shannon warehouse from a time well before the incident. Then they detailed the occurrence of the explosions and subsequent fire. The projections offered what appeared to be irrefutable visual evidence of the Agency's assertion that *Wolverine,* and many of his operatives, were 'neutralized'.

Barbecued, Cody shuddered ruefully to himself.

The screen silently disappeared back into the ceiling when the lights came back up. Conley theatrically unwrapped a cloth bundle, which had been strategically displayed in front of him throughout the meeting. He held up two, amorphous, charred lumps of metal. "Gentlemen, the last remains of *Wolverine.*"

Cody unconsciously slid forward on his chair.

"Here we have one seriously melted Glock .357 Sig., and one charred, but quite serviceable, Italian throwing knife. As most of you recall, over the years we have established that *Wolverine* consistently, and expertly I might add, employed them both. They were recovered by the lab team in nearly the exact spot inside the warehouse. The knife was still fastened to what was left of a human tibia. Our informants tell us that *Wolverine* always wore such a blade strapped to his inner left calf, and 'never left home without it'." A subdued round of chuckles circled the room.

"That proves absolutely nothing!" blurted Cody.

"Steele, I understand how much you need and want conclusive evidence. You know better than I that *Wolverine* was placed in that building at the time of the fire. You said so yourself in your briefing earlier this morning. While admittedly he seemed a master of disguise, your own handpicked men claim they saw a man matching one of our descriptions of him entering the warehouse just prior to the blow. The Israelis corroborated all this last week. You and your own operatives staged the raid, and coordinated the onsite teams."

Cody tried hard, for the hundredth time, to be convinced by the evidence and his own perceived realities of the events... one way or the other.

"The final and conclusive evidence found... was this." Conley held up a very expensive, heavy gold chain attached to which was a solitary bullet. "Your slug, Cody. Ballistics matched it to one of your company weapons. Apparently, you must have hit him in Sri Lanka three years ago just as you claimed all along. We speculate that a section of the asbestos roofing material must have fallen on it after it was torn from his body by the explosion. It was there we found it and would explain why it's almost intact, and why it wasn't recovered in the area of the weapons. From the few vague photographs and descriptions we do have of *Wolverine* since the Colombo incident, we knew he always wore a gold chain regardless of his disguise," Conley continued as he passed around three 8 x 10 inch glossies highlighting the chain. "Now we know what was on that chain."

Cody was stunned. In his own mind he was certain that no one escaped the burning building. He had been reasonably confident that *Wolverine* was inside. Given this evidence, it would be difficult to further doubt the obvious conclusions. But still…

When finally they filed from the room, Conley tried to induce Cody to become involved in yet another ongoing operation. "You need this work to get your mind off this obsession you have with *Wolverine*."

"It's done!" Cody snapped. "Over! Right now. I want no more!" Steele interrupted the less-than-subtle campaigning, to remind his chief that he was a volunteer. "You need me more than I need you, and after all this I'm not sure I need anyone."

Much of Cody's past success with the agency was in large part due to his ability to involve himself only in operations he knew best suited his singular talents. His clandestine successes post-Vietnam and pre-Agency had been as a mercenary, a hired gun, working alone on his own terms, using his own means. He, much like *Wolverine*, seemed to be drawn to the same actions and conflicts... those requiring self-sufficient performance and single-minded motivation for success. Yet, they were always on opposing sides in every operation. Could it be an issue of conscience? If so, which of them had it and which didn't? Or was it merely fate... the luck of the draw? Their means were often the same, but the ends... always juxtaposed. Maybe these striking similarities were reasons for his fixation with the man... or could the cause of this obsession be rooted in avoidance of something else?

"I was recruited by you guys, Chuck, remember? The terms were case-by-case as a volunteer, solely my choice."

He wondered to himself about the very real possibility that *Wolverine* was the carrot forever held out to him by the Agency to enlist his participation in all those other unrelated projects over the years... with Conley manipulating the stick.

While the Deputy Director prattled on about duty and obligation, Steele's thoughts returned to Devoney... then to a Spanish treasure patrol 450 years overdue.

14

The pure white sand ten feet below appeared to stretch away endlessly in every direction. They leisurely snorkeled the gin-clear water out toward the drop-off. As she swam, Devoney retraced their afternoon. True to his word, Dominic had indeed taken her on a grand, though fast, tour of Rabaul.

They started at the local market, or 'Bung'. It was the most colorful she had ever experienced. Although Dominic informed her that Saturday was the day it really came to life, it was chaotic and feverishly bustling the short while they were there. Scattered throughout the impressive array of fruit and vegetable stands was a variety of booths and stalls staffed by insistent vendors, offering all sorts of shell jewelry, live birds, hand made native furniture, baskets, clothing, and endless samplings of native art. There was even a man with his 'pet' full-grown crocodile. Dominic had to drag Devoney back to the jeep once he discovered that she was an inveterate collector of trinkets. "Tchotchkes," she called them, using the descriptive Yiddish word. "And you thought I was fluent only in Spanish."

Next, they toured the tiny war museum situated in the middle of town, which actually is nothing more than an underground, confined old bunker silently guarded by a small, rusting, Japanese tank. Inside, they examined some fascinating photos and maps from the period of the Japanese occupation, displayed together with some dusty old war relics. But by far the most interesting thing about the place turned out to be intangible. Admiral Yamamoto, architect of the infamous raid on Pearl Harbor, had spent his last night sequestered inside before being shot down the next day on his way to inspect his troops in Bougainville.

On their way to view an old German residence dating from the turn of the century, they visited the Rabaul Orchid Park. Here, they hand-fed the tame, indigenous parrots and cockatoos, and marveled at the incredible beauty and variety of native flowers. From the ruins of the old residence further up the southwest slope of North Daughter, they were able to see all of Blanche Bay in one direction, and the open waters of the Bismarck Sea in the other. Years before, Captain Simpson had named the harbor after himself and the bay after his ship. Looking down the slope of the sleeping volcano at the tranquil bay and recalling all the sights, smells and sounds she had just experienced, made it easy for Devoney to imagine a storybook South Pacific now long gone.

While sharing a fresh pineapple purchased at a little roadside stand, Dominic kissed her. First in jest as he attempted to wipe some of the sweet juice from her lips; then deep, long, hard and meaningfully as they stood arm in arm at the viewpoint. The second time, she found herself lustily returning his passion, probing his mouth with her searching tongue.

As they headed for the beach and the dive site on the ocean side of the peninsula via Tunnel Road, her emotions were conflicted just for a moment when she thought of Cody. But only just for a moment. She was jarred back to the present when Dominic swerved hard to avoid hitting a squealing pig that darted across the road. They both laughed, enjoying the excitement of the moment, the scenery, and each other's company. Her anxieties and guilt about Steele vanished faster than the pig in the jungle.

When they reached the drop-off she turned to shore in order to gauge how far they had come. The view was like a postcard, only better... and real. In the late afternoon photographer's light, the water was turquoise, the fringing sand beach a blazing white, offset to the lush greens of the encroaching overhang of the jungle... the entire scene capped by the peak of North Daughter, crowned with her afternoon mantle of mist and steam. Devoney turned to include Dominic only to find his bubbles noiselessly dappling the surface, marking the spot where he had submerged.

The wreck they were going to dive was not 'high profile' according to her travel/dive literature, which referred to it only as 'George's Wreck'.

The scenery and dramatic drive to access it will certainly make up for any shortfall in the dive, she thought. She descended to join Dominic on the point of the drop-off.

The unnamed vessel was sunk in an upright position while at anchor. Rumor has it that the Japanese skipper, knowing his ship was doomed, drove her straight into the shallows in the hope that she might be re-floated and quickly repaired. Little did he realize that the drop-off was so radical and so close to the shore. She hit the shallows with her bow and the anchor was tossed. Unfortunately, most of the length of the ship was still over very deep water. The bow area came to rest at the top of the drop-off wall in a mere ten meters of water, while the stern section was a dangerous seventy meters below. The ship virtually hung by its bow and anchor on an underwater cliff.

Devoney and Dominic casually explored the upper portions from the mid-section bridge forward to the bow. The water clarity was not as good as it was within Simpson Harbor, due to the constant scouring by the open-ocean current, which nourishes this area of the coastline. It was an informal, easy dive with no real destination or plan. They took turns leading one another through the intricacies and mazes of the decaying forward holds, all the while trying to outdo each other with 'finds' of outrageously colored crinoids, or feather starfish. Reasonably close to shore, and for the most part, relatively shallow, the bow section of the wreck had been picked clean of relics, but did offer the first assortment and quantity of fishes Devoney had seen to date in PNG.

The end of the dive found them walking ashore in shoulder deep water pushing their floating dive equipment before them. They shed their heavy gear as soon as they were able to stand on the bottom, and by inflating both their buoyancy compensators, each created his and her own little raft to which all the remainder of their gear was attached. This unencumbered arrangement made the wade to shore much easier, and they were able to chat on the way, regaling each other with their own versions of this latest adventure.

By the time they reached the beach it began to rain, usual weather, which happened almost daily at about this time according to Dominic. They sought shelter from the warm shower in a convenient three-sided, palm-frond lean-to just off the beach and under some trees.

Dominic sprinted for the jeep, shouting back at Devoney to wait in the shelter. At the vehicle he quickly changed from his Speedo into a traditional sarong, or 'lap-lap'. He returned with two towels, two blankets, and the last half of their pineapple, and the cooler containing the wine. They dried off and stretched out on their blankets to enjoy the wine and shower.

At first, she lay on her right comfortably snuggled in the hollow of his left shoulder and arm. She distractedly played with the hair on his chest, which was bleached nearly white from the sun. Tracing lazy figure eights with her fingers, she abruptly stopped on a bare spot just beneath the large muscle of his right shoulder. A slightly red, circular scar the size of a quarter. "And what's this?" she asked.

"Just a small souvenir, courtesy of an overly persistent and quite annoying competitor. I picked it up a few years back while on business in Sri Lanka."

"Hmm," she murmured, her fingers on the move again.

He, languishing on his back and savoring her caress, methodically toyed with the tie of her bikini top as they enjoyed the sights and smells of the tropical downpour.

As the intensity of the rain increased, it became distinctly cooler. She flipped over to her left side and snuggled against him spoon-fashion... not just for warmth. Firmly but gently he ran his open hand up and down the length of her right side, from her hip to just below her armpit. He could feel her muscles tense and relax as his fingers traveled close by and over her sensitive areas. At the lower end of its exploration his hand began to linger at the provocative curve of her hip, not so subtly massaging it to the full reach of his fingers. She moved against him in rhythm with the motion of his hand. As his arousal began in earnest, he started tracing the underside of her right breast through her bikini top. She softly moaned approval. Not wanting to wait any longer, she seized his hand placing it fully over her breast... and held it there. It was soft yet firm and fit his hand as if made for it. Beneath the pressure of her tiny palm, his index finger escaped and began tracing meaningful circles around her hardening nipple. When she couldn't stand the pressure of it now fully erect and straining against her suit, she quickly spun back to her right side facing him.

Slowly, she raised her head from his chest and locked his gaze, mesmerizing him with the penetrating paleness of her eyes. With a swift, cat-like movement, she rolled on top of him, straddling his hips. She gradually leaned close enough to lick his lips with her darting tongue, while at the same time removing her suit in two, deft motions. She pulled away from his face, her hands tight on his shoulders, never moving her hips from his. "Now... right now!" she demanded.

She felt him grow instantly rock-hard beneath her. Inseparable now, he purposefully rolled her onto her back. Ripping his lap-lap away, he entered her completely. "Now... right now!" she urged again.

The rain pounded down, drowning their passionate cries.

15

"...And now they're off somewhere trying to get them translated," the voice on the phone finished.

"Shit! God damn it! I didn't buy that Shannon story for one second. It sounded too simple. Get that little prick Melissio in here!" Ramon Guillermo Vasquez barked back into the receiver, "All right, all right. They shouldn't be able to interfere with this one. Its too secret, he's too far away, and his organization's been hurt badly. We've a direct line to Hussein and he's really pissed now. We'll have this shipment to him within the next thirty days. That'll calm him down and put him back in business. Keep us informed as soon as there is any movement there, *comprende*?"

"Si, mi *jefe*." Ramon's order was acknowledged immediately following a two second pause, caused by the extreme distance the message signal had to travel via relay from the communications satellite.

He slammed down the receiver. "I thought you told me you took care of the fucking meddler Toscana," Vasquez raged at the cowering Melissio.

"But *jefe*... we did. How was I to know that?"

His last words were brutally interrupted by the spit of the silenced .357 Smith & Wesson. Vasquez emptied the weapon into the still twitching corpse, emphasizing his displeasure and rage, while offering yet another lesson to those witnessing the swift execution. "There is no place for incompetent fools in *Partidario*! I'll deliver this shipment. Personally, if I have to!"

16

"So... what do you do when your not ravaging wanton female guests or skippering your yacht?" Devoney asked.

The rain ceased and the late afternoon sun chased what remained of the storm's drained white clouds. They lazed on the deserted sand beach; she demurely wrapped in a towel ... Dominic, still naked.

"I'm not sure who was the ravagee and who was the ravager," he chided.

"Seriously."

"You did say you were away for a few months. Business or pleasure?"

"Excellent recall, Doctor. Business," he replied, contemplating how best to deflect her questions.

"When did you leave France and what became of your mother?" Her attention was momentarily captured by a colorful crab scurrying by her toes.

"Sally Lightfoot," he said, pointing to the crab. He took a deep breath, releasing it slowly in a long, audible sigh.

"My mother wasn't really married. Those bastards raped her. I just tell everyone she was married. It seems easier for most people. She was a member of the French Resistance during the war, and it was either put out or be shot, once they caught her. They ended up killing her anyway shortly after I was born. Why they spared me..." His voice trailed away. *That's when I really stopped caring about anything"* he thought. *The world owes me lifetimes of revenge, and sometimes it comes in very tasty packages,* he considered, eyeing Devoney.

"I'm terribly sorry, Dominic."

"Not to worry. I heard all this years later from my aunt and uncle who raised me. In truth, they were the ones who barred me from learning German. I never knew which one was my father. I don't think she did either. They all ran like the cowards they were when the Allies came. I swore I'd get revenge the day they told me she was dead."

"So how did you happen to end up in this part of the world?"

"A very long and boring story, I assure you."

"The high points then."

"Well, they tell me I was a bright but problematic student. It seemed I was always a troublemaker. To me, my classmates were slow... quite dumb, actually. Anyway, after countless fights and being kicked out of every school I attended, believe it or not, I lied about my age and joined the French Foreign Legion."

"You're joking."

"No, really. They were made up of recalcitrants just like me. Tough as hell, but a true, caring family to me. My first posting was to Vietnam in the early '60's. What an experience. It was there after three years that I realized how corrupt the world's politicians truly are. Yours, ours here, the French... all of them. Vietnam made me want to kill, and the Legion taught me how," he voiced a recurring thought aloud.

"While in Nam, I stopped trying to make a difference, or to be righteous all the time and started to notice all the incredible opportunities... not only financial, but for a meaningful life. I stopped fighting the river and went with the current, so to speak. After my tour there, I resigned my commission, which is not an easy thing to do with the Legion. They expect you to be in for life. I bumped around Southeast Asia for a while, and learned English in order to survive during this period. Your language is one of the few threads of commonality shared by the countries of Asia and the Pacific Rim... at least for business purposes. That region of the world at that time, as I'm sure you are aware, was in the throes of being thrust into the twentieth century kicking and screaming..." he paused reflecting. "...And was filled with incredible opportunities for those smart and bold enough to take advantage. Plus there was the revenge motivation as well. Actually, quite a similar situation exists right now here in PNG. The Pacific Rim continues to be a growing force in the world economy and those who have the foresight, talent, skills, and knowledge, often benefit by being there for the emergence of a new country," he said. *It also doesn't hurt to be a bit ruthless and to understand whose side to be on*, he smiled at his own silent admission. "Anyway, that's what I did," he continued aloud. "Took advantage of the opportunities in an area of new economic growth. For instance, when PNG became independent in '75, there was no TV in the country, if you can imagine. What a chance to start a broadcast company for someone with the abilities and skills. The newly independent eastern block countries offer incredible possibilities as we speak. There aren't any modern communications systems or supporting infrastructure there. We're talking dark ages. Someone with a truck load of fax machines to sell in East Europe today could retire tomorrow."

Devoney was fascinated. "So what is it that you do?"

"I suppose you might call me a facilitator. When someone or some country wants or needs goods or a service, either I provide it for them, or for a fee or some other benefit, I find someone who can. Over the years, I have developed an excellent network of contact people just like me. They are spread over the entire Asian continent and the Pacific Rim. That network can supply all sorts of things."

"Like what, for instance?"

"Like PNG TV. I still maintain part ownership. The proceeds from the sale of some of my ownership financed the boat I had before the *Tambu*. I keep having to buy bigger and bigger boats as the demands of friends and tourism increase. The diving is new for the crew and me. When I got here in '75, this country was an un-tapped gold mine. I saw an opportunity and took it. As a matter of fact, I've even applied for citizenship. I had no clue I'd end up running a dive operation until three crazies from California chartered the boat earlier this year, and opened my eyes to dive charter opportunities."

They stood and Dominic followed Devoney into the shallows. The water was magnificently refreshing. She thought over his story, concurring with his observations and conclusions and admiring his pioneer spirit. He rationalized to himself that he hadn't really lied to her... just hadn't told the whole truth. A trait that often served him well.

Quickly, they found themselves at a depth over Devoney's head and she gently treaded next to him as he continued to walk into deeper water. He held her around the waist supporting her easily. She wrapped her legs around his torso, her towel discarded at the water's edge.

"So when did you learn to sail?" she asked, playfully licking his ear.

"How can I talk when you're so deliciously wrapped around me?" He threatened to dunk her by releasing his grasp on her tiny waist. She responded by taking his free hand and placing it between her thighs. Her fiery core came instantly alive again. She arched her back pushing her pelvis against his probing hand. His mouth went easily to her nipple, conveniently at mouth level, just above the surface. His fingers slipped automatically inside her. He couldn't believe how wet she felt... even underwater.

17

It was noon, hot and humid. They spent most of the morning provisioning. The plan was for the *Tambu* to sail for the town of Kavieng on the island of New Ireland the next day, where Devoney would rejoin it after her visit to Walindi on the north side of New Britain. It was an easy two-day sail, but Devoney's travel agent suggested the three-day shore interlude, in order to avoid any discomfort that might arise in moving the boat through the open ocean. Given her blossoming romance, she wished she hadn't agreed to those arrangements. Dominic assured her that her stay at Walindi Plantation, a picturesque, working, palm-oil development that was also establishing itself as a world-class dive resort, would be well worth it. "Besides," he kidded, "... it will give my sore, old body a day or two to heal from the workout you gave it." He claimed to have some pressing paperwork to attend to, and instructed Gratvin and Exxy to complete Devoney's tour of Rabaul. They all arranged to rendezvous at the town pier at 5:00pm where they hoped Felix would be waiting.

As the unlikely trio raced around Rabaul in the jeep, Devoney learned more than just the history of the area. Dominic had sponsored Gratvin to the Australian school in Port Moresby because the young man's Trobriand clan was too poor and too small to provide good schooling. Apparently, Dominic had run aground in a storm years before on one of the many uncharted reefs close to Gratvin's home island. During the long process of salvaging his boat, he took a liking to and an interest in the young native boy who assisted him every day. Gratvin now seemed to revere Dominic almost like a father. Furthermore, being one of the first white men ever to visit Gratvin's island, Dominic was also one of the few expats to always treat him as an equal. As the afternoon tour and accompanying stories progressed, Devoney thought

71

she noticed some resentment being directed toward Gratvin from the younger Exxy. She put this aside, deciding it was nothing more than juvenile envy.

They visited most of the tourist spots, from the barge tunnel on one side of the bay, to the wreckage of W.W.II Japanese aircraft strewn throughout the jungle around the airport on the other. Despite the heavy tropical growth and mountainous topography, the road system traversing Rabaul and the Gazelle Peninsula is excellent. Yet another legacy from the days of the prolific German plantations. However, driving was an adventure unto itself, as the Nationals piloting opposing vehicles always seemed to take their half of the road out of the middle. This, coupled with the British/Australian custom of driving on the left side, made the whole adventure seem like a wild ride at the local amusement park. At the airport she reluctantly reconfirmed her reservations for the next morning. Her departing flight was the turn-around on which Willie Kaltenbach would be arriving.

They were parked at the pier at 5:00pm sharp, and watched Dominic's Zodiac on its way in from the *Tambu*. Just as the nose of the inflatable was bouncing off the pier, Felix Hendel turned a corner of the adjacent warehouse and shuffled toward them. Dominic joined them on the pier, giving Devoney a rousing hug of greeting. Felix looked awful. Then again, this seemed to be his normal appearance.

"How'd it go, old boy?" Dominic asked, steadying the older man by an elbow.

"Bloody hard work. Goddamn Germans never did have good handwriting, and I lost my glasses two weeks ago."

"Well, were you able to make anything at all from those?" Dominic persisted. He tried to pry the logs from Hendel's shaky grasp without success.

"Mein Gott! Those crazy Japs built a bloody heat concentrator. Can't understand why Herr Rommel didn't stay with the bloody thing." Felix dropped half of the documents attempting to flip through some schematics. "Look at this. The Axis powers were so close to success they could've drowned the whole pack of Eisenhower's invasion force. Diese bloden! The Fools. It's right here. Look!"

Felix launched off into yet another burst of confusing explanation punctuated with German expletives, and only halted when Dominic handed him an envelope with the other halves of the torn Kina notes.

"Why don't you come out to the *Tambu* and have dinner with us? We can go over your notes and the logs there and be much more comfortable. Besides, you look as if you could use a good meal and Molly always cooks too much."

Emphasizing the invitation, Dominic removed a new bottle of Cutty Sark from the bag under his arm, displaying the label to Felix. In response, Hendel quickly had one foot in the Zodiac. It immediately bobbed away, stretching him between the pier and boat. If Exxy hadn't quickly hauled in the slack, the old German would have taken an unscheduled and embarrassing swim. They giggled to themselves at Hendel's expense, and soon were all squeezed aboard the Zodiac and motoring across the calm harbor, any further conversation effectively extinguished by the whine of its powerful little engine.

"You mean to say," Dominic managed to ask as Felix broke verbal stride for another belt, "...that the Germans and the Japs seriously thought they could build a weather-making device?"

If nothing more, they all would have agreed Felix could tell one hell of a good story. During dinner, and after the first half of the scotch, he took them through two of the three *VERHEERUNG* logbooks. At first, he referred often to the books and his notes. As his narrative and alcohol consumption progressed, he became more and more animated. His translation became less analytical and more theatrical. His words helped them all form a wonderful mental picture of a far-out, but talented group of German scientists running around in the rain, dressed in immaculate, ankle-length, white lab coats, conjuring up the forces of nature. They silently wondered how much of his story was actually derived from the material he had been provided, and how much was fabricated in the pickled brain of the storyteller. By the time Molly removed the dinner plates, he was using his notes less frequently and began to punctuate his narrative with more and more German words and phrases. Devoney looked over at Dominic at one point, not knowing whether to laugh out loud at the presentation or the content. She noticed Dominic also had a bemused look, stifling his amusement in his napkin. Continuously, Hendel kept using that mysterious word... *VERHEERUNG.*

"Well, from these it looks to me like it started out to be some sort of attempt at rudimentary radar, or possibly an experimental development for transmitting a very powerful radio beam. That would explain the huge dish-like apparatus, and all the transmitting gear. But, somewhere along the way they either dropped the radar concept or in the process came up with this other thing. Can't really tell for certain from the logs if the change was an accident or planned. And it wasn't just the Germans and not just a weather making machine," said Felix, quickly swallowing. "The Japs were involved. They built the bloody thing in Japan. They were trying to *make,* not just *control* weather. Unglaublich! Unbelievable. Can you imagine? In the logs after 1942 there is a series of entries in Japanese, and from then on it appears that all the data and observations were transcribed in both languages. Here." He flipped through the book and pointed out a page written in what surely appeared to them all to be Japanese. "That must have been about the time the thing found its way to Germany from Japan."

"That fits," commented Devoney. "Often, my dad would tell me of the war and the collaboration between the two countries. He contended that if the Germans had listened to some of the ideas the Japanese had but couldn't develop for lack of materials, the war might either have gone on longer or ended differently."

"Still... " Dominic pursued, " ...you must be mistaken about the purpose of this thing. They had some wild out-there ideas, but... c'mon Felix."

At this, Hendel stood and erupted in what all took to be a fit of German swearing. Dominic gently but forcefully sat him back down and poured another drink from the bottle of scotch, which was fast approaching empty. Fortunately, just then Molly appeared from the galley with a papaya and ice cream desert, whose delicious appearance alone was more than enough to change the tenor and subject of the conversation.

"Now what exactly is this *VERHEERUNG?*" Dominic asked, easing everyone back into the topic.

"It doesn't really translate all that well into English," Felix muttered.

"In German, the word is used to describe a state or a condition. They kept using *VERHEERUNG* when referring to the project because *VERHEERUNG* is the condition they hoped to achieve if this mechanism ever worked. It means upset or chaos... even 'havoc' would be a reasonable English translation. If they could control the elements and forces of the weather, they could create chaos or havoc for their enemies. So, basically, it translates as the *HAVOC PROJECT*, or simply... *HAVOC.*"

"*HAVOC,*" pondered Dominic. He remembered the chaos poor weather actually had caused in some of the crucial battles and strategies of the Second World War, including the D-Day invasion. "Look what happened to Napoleon and Hitler in Russia." Quickly he segued to the present and pictured the havoc poor weather had done to modern technology, and its important effect on current world events, "The Challenger disaster, and the floods in China. Wouldn't it be something if they actually did it?" he silently asked himself, daydreaming. "Imagine what you could do with something like this, and how much you could make. And better still, if I were able to…"

"So Felix, did they ever get it to work?" Devoney asked.

Hendel was well into his cups by now, and it took him a while to put his thoughts and words together in understandable English. "They really didn't have great successes according to these. But apparently they got some interesting changes in weather patterns in enough trials that they kept experimenting with it until early summer, 1944 when the entries cease. I sure wish we had some drawings or pictures of this thing to look at." Hendel's speech was noticeably slurred, and his head was beginning to droop.

"This is great, old boy. Why don't you stay aboard tonight? It's too dark and too far for you to drive back home from the pier. I'll take you in early in the morning when we go ashore. Devoney's flight out is at 9:00am, and we could kill two birds with one jeep ride," said Dominic, prophetically. In response, Felix Hendel began to snore.

After Gratvin and Exxy carried the sleeping Felix outside to the foredeck, Devoney and Dominic poured over the *HAVOC* materials, all the while verbally speculating as to their veracity.

"Well consider this," argued Dominic. "We know as historical fact that the Allied Invasion was recalled and postponed a day because of unusually bad weather. Weather that was totally unexpected. Fact. That was June 5, 1944. The last date of any consequence in these logs is June 6, 1944. June 6, 1944 *was* D-Day. Fact. The logs for June fifth indicate that the device worked, a successful test. Unfortunately, we don't know what 'successful' meant. *HAVOC* worked, but we don't know for sure what it actually did. Could it have altered the weather? Possibly. History tells us that that storm on June 5, 1944 came out of nowhere."

"Maybe the bad weather and the successful test of HAVOC were just a serendipitous coincidence," said Devoney.

"Well apparently, when they started it on June sixth, it failed," continued Dominic. "Did they know the bad weather the day before delayed the invasion? No. They didn't have a clue about the invasion. Fact. If they knew the thing worked and *did* do something to the weather, do you think Hitler would have let it return to Japan? No way. So where does this leave us?"

They reached no conclusions, but agreed that the Japanese and Germans had certainly spent an enormous amount of time and effort on what was now a pile of worthless junk at the bottom of the bay. "Boy," Devoney exclaimed. "If it could work, just think of what good it might do the world. Deserts converted to gardens for food; floods eliminated; the reduction of natural disasters; fresh water where there is only contamination. The possibilities are endless. Wouldn't it be something if we could rebuild it from these notes using the modern technology of today and have it actually work?"

Dominic didn't respond. He contemplated a far different spectrum of uses and evaluated the potential problems caused by the number of people already aware of the device. *There are always solutions, however,* he thought.

As the evening wore on, Devoney became aware that Dominic seemed unusually distant. He continually ignored her attempts at humor, and even her touch. Obviously he was more interested in the old paperwork and the secrets it might hold. Eventually, she stood and stretched provocatively right in front of him hoping that he would acknowledge and act on her not too subtle sexual signals.

"I think I'd better turn in now," she said. "I still haven't packed for the flight tomorrow. Want to join me and the Southern Cross for a nightcap?"

"You go ahead. I want to go over Hendel's notes one more time," he answered, not even looking up.

Dr. Devoney Marsh tossed restlessly in her bunk, her thoughts confused and divergent. She tried to envision the science of a mechanism that could control the weather. "Just think about the lives it might save, and the extraordinary things that might be accomplished with such a tool."

She experienced a hot, physical rush when next she thought about the adventures and passion recently enjoyed with Dominic. Yet there seemed to exist a form of rejection manifesting itself in her new lover. "Maybe I'm overly tired and overwhelmed by it all, or maybe I went too fast for him. Am I too easy? God, did I want him. And I want him now!"

Then there was Cody. He flitted and lurked just on the periphery of her awareness. "Damn you, Steele! Tomorrow I have to leave this beautiful place to go to who knows where and be with who knows who and nobody cares."

The heedless water lapped at the outside hull just two feet from her bunk. Once again, just when she thought she was through with it, she felt very alone.

18

Devoney, Dominic, and Felix arrived at the airport just as the compact Air Niugini F28-1000 jet was dropping between the resident family of Rabaul's volcanoes. Felix, still a bit drunk and nearly asleep on his feet, waited with the car outside the terminal. Dominic was back to his attentive, passionate self and nurtured Devoney all morning. So much so that she almost believed she might have imagined his somber mood of the night before. He gave her the last half of Felix's translation notes for her to study over the next three days.

"Who knows?" he asked. "Maybe we can put this *HAVOC* thing back together. There's probably a Nobel Prize in it for you if we do, Dr. Marsh."

She wasn't sure if he was kidding or serious. His farewell kiss was indeed serious, and she blushed all the way up the boarding ramp. Dominic and Felix literally ran into Willie as he bounded down the flimsy stair cart.

"I'll see you Thursday. Don't sink on the way over, and tell Gratvin goodbye for me." She waved to them all on the ground as the plane's door was closed.

"Felix, you look like shit!" bellowed Willie. He pounded the older man on the shoulder and nearly knocked him over. "Quite the bird you've got there, Dominic. What's your secret?"

Dominic didn't respond and piled Willie's luggage in the back of the jeep. Felix plopped back into the passenger's seat, and began snoring contentedly.

"Hell of a contraption, this *VERHEERUNG*," Kaltenbach yelled from the back. They jolted along the road headed for the *Kaivuna*.

"How did you know about *VERHEERUNG*?" Dominic shouted.

"Stamped all over the bloody paperwork. Rather a huge waste of effort if you ask me. Hitler was fanatical about new technology though. Just some sort of monster electrical generator."

Dominic listened carefully to all of Willie's comments without saying much in return. They skidded to a stop in front of the *Kaivuna*, waking Felix.

"Got any plans for this afternoon? I've got the Zodiac down at the town pier. I can drop the old man here back at his place and be back around noon to pick you up for a dive. We can explore that new wreck they discovered a few months ago just around the point."

"Sounds good to me," said Willie. "No one knows I'm back in town, so my services aren't yet in demand. Thanks for the lift in. We can go over these drawings at the upstairs bar afterwards. Shouldn't take but a beer or two as long as you're buying. I made plenty of notes. Just honk twice when you get back. Have a cocktail on me at the Club, Felix."

Kaltenbach effortlessly hoisted his duffel as if it were filled with feathers, spun on his heel, and disappeared in the side entrance.

"Good bloke," mumbled Felix. "Mind giving me a lift home? I'd better change before I start spending your money."

"No problem, old man. I've been planning on it."

They headed for Felix's shack on the backside of North Daughter, accessed via Tunnel Road. Soon after turning north off the main track, the pavement becomes a dirt path into lush jungle. The residences are isolated, few, and far between. Once again Hendel fell asleep still suffering from a serious hangover. He woke only when the jeep screeched to a dusty stop. "Where the hell are we, Dominic? You must have missed my turnoff."

"You were asleep again, so I thought I'd take a look at the water conditions from here. We're at the sub base. Willie and I are going diving this afternoon, and I thought this would be a good spot. Won't take a second. Want to come have a look?" Dominic was out of the vehicle and headed toward a high point along an overgrown path.

The Japanese submarine base is at the northern tip of East New Britain, where the island distills into the Bismarck Sea. The base was a major provision depot during the war, and is protected by sheer cliffs easily 100 meters high on the shore side. Perfect for submarines, the boats had over 300 meters of water beneath their keels less than five meters from shore. The path negotiated by Dominic and Felix ends at a dramatic but dangerous overlook. When Hendel finally caught up, Dominic stood at the precipice casually looking down at the water far below.

"Jesus, Dominic. Don't you think you're a bit close to the edge?"

Dominic turned and lunged. Felix Hendel's face registered shocked astonishment, then pain and terror. He looked down at Dominic's fist twisting in his gut. As if seeing it all from a great distance, his mind noted the hilt of a blade. Dominic pulled straight up with all his strength. The razor-sharp Italian steel responded, cutting a deadly, vertical trough through flesh and bone.

"This will be the final time you'll ever spill your guts, German," Dominic spat, and then laughed in the dying man's face.

He quickly yanked the knife out, as Felix's body crumpled to the ground in a bloody, writhing heap. Then after a casual kick of his foot, watched as Felix went over the cliff. Leaning down, he wiped the blade clean on some wet grass, and replaced it in the flat sheath attached to his inner left calf. As he walked to the jeep to retrieve his binoculars, Dominic sadistically hoped the old man would survive the fall. "Ah... sweet revenge. Fuckin' Germans."

By the time he returned to the overlook, they had begun to circle. He adjusted the glasses and scanned the surface of the water. The sharks, dozens of them attracted by the blood, were tearing at the body. For a moment, at the center of the feeding frenzy, Dominic thought he saw Hendel's arm frantically wave.

19

"Thanks for taking care of her, Harry."

"No problem, Mr. Steele. It's my pleasure, I assure you. Great to see you again."

Steele took a final fond look at the old Pullman, and headed for the nearest freeway entrance in the rented jeep.

Three years earlier, following the completion of the Sri Lanka assignment, he arranged to take ownership of the stately old railroad car in lieu of his usual cash fee. At first Conley balked at the idea, but was easily persuaded when confronted with the figures showing the realized savings to the Agency and the taxpayers. Steele didn't work cheap, and Conley recognized the bargain once he had all the facts.

Throughout the 1920s, the quantity of private railroad cars in America burgeoned. They were extravagant emblems of an opulent era, and were visible proof to all that their owner had 'made it' or had it made. Usually built by the Pullman Company, the distinctive exterior of these rolling palaces quickly came to be recognized the world over. Their interiors, on the other hand, could be, and often were, as unique as their owners. They were completely self-contained, luxuriously comfortable, and easily mobile. The great stock market crash of 1929 signaled the beginning of the end for these moving showplaces, their use and production declining drastically over the course of the ensuing depression. The Pullman's indelible ties with the history of an age Steele intensely admired were major factors in his decision to acquire the old car.

He found it forlornly deteriorating on a dead end spur, off the mainline right-of-way in Portola, a once thriving, but now dying railroad community in the high Sierra. He immediately envisioned the uniqueness of owning such a vehicle, and hoped that living and traveling in it from time to time might assuage some of the pressures of his urban existence. When not on a 'project', as Conley called them, and when staying with Devoney, he often wrestled with the concept of finally making a commitment and settling down. But invariably he would feel trapped by the proximity of neighbors, and crowded by the expanding encroachment of rapid development quickly disfiguring the once rural and bucolic San Francisco Bay Area. His Pullman was the answer.

Arranging to have it delivered to a private collector's service barn in Sonoma, California, he worked on it there when he could, bringing it up to current Department of Transportation standards. He and Devoney vacationed aboard her across Canada the previous year. Devoney conceded to the fun of riding it. Steele loved its uniqueness and privacy. And the proud old Pullman was reborn.

The forward section of the old rail car was refurbished into three small, private, but well-appointed staterooms, each with a queen size bed and adjoining bath facilities. Each bedroom had a small sitting area situated strategically around oversized windows. The middle third of the car consisted of a bar, storage area, half bath, utility compartment and a compact, but fully outfitted and stocked gourmet kitchen. Cody had spent considerable money and effort redecorating the coach, and his masculine tastes were evident throughout. The parlor boasted two oversized sofas on each side, both complemented by matching padded, high back swivel rockers. Between them was an eight by three foot polished marble coffee table. To the right center of the coach, perpendicular to its length and facing aft, was an oversized TV screen wired to a small satellite receiving dish set in the roof. Additionally, the monitor was connected to a VCR inset next to the stereo and state-of-the-art communications systems. The decor was all done in very thick and expensive piled velvet. In respect for its era of origin, deep burgundy and plush greens were the understated hues of choice throughout, from the thick carpeting to the brocade drapes. Dark highly polished mahogany shelves and cabinets offset walnut walkways and ceiling panels. Original railroad signal lanterns wired for lighting were positioned in strategic nooks and crannies. Gimbaled tiffany lamps adorned all of the ornately carved end tables, and three overhead Raffles fans circulated temperature-controlled air throughout the parlor area when needed. Unique carvings gathered from countries Steele had visited graced walls, tables and select floor areas. An antique, expandable, English Country table with muted brocade chairs situated just to the side of the rear entryway, served as the centerpiece for meals not taken on the coffee table.

Steele's work area was a refinished postal desk removed from a mail car of the same generation as the old Pullman. The aft outside steps and boarding platform were guarded by a three-foot polished brass railing, the soapbox for many a politician in campaigns waged during an earlier time. The entire ambiance was one of understated elegance, yet styled and designed for everyday comfort.

Cody had 'trained' her to Reno. For a fee, depending on the type of car and distance, many of the country's railroads will place a private car on an existing train, 'training' it to wherever the owner wished. Steele left it in the Southern Pacific yard with Harry, the yardmaster. He ran her often between Sonoma and Reno when testing her track-worthiness, and discovered Harry on his very first excursion. Harry Miller, 64, was a year from retirement and loved the old showpiece, almost as much as Cody.

It was 6:00pm when the train with Steele's Pullman made the Reno station. Using a small yard engine, it took another hour for them to switch the car onto a safe siding. He figured it would take another three hours of strong driving to reach Bridgeport. "I guess I'll have to wait until tomorrow to get rich." It would be dark by the time he reached his proposed search area, so he decided to stop and spend the night in the little town. His plan was to systematically explore the areas contiguous to the mid-point of the East Slope Endurance Run trail, starting where he discovered the armored breastplate. It was his hope to find either more clues to the mine, or the lost treasure cache itself... if there really was one.

"Lost Conquistador or bust!" he yelled, speeding past an eighteen-wheeler.

He loved this country, and he immediately felt less stressed and rejuvenated the minute he merged onto highway 395 heading south from Reno. "Home," was the concept filling his mind when he tried to put a word to the feeling.

Legends and images of the gold country occupied his thoughts as the drive progressed. He felt a special kinship with, and an affinity for, the men who mucked for gold in the high mountain streams and rivers of this area over one hundred years ago. They were a bolder and freer breed of men who dared explore the boundaries of the known world, constantly testing their curiosity, courage, resourcefulness, and always, in so doing, their limits. It had been a special time and place for special people. Their self-sufficiency and rugged individualism had long since been brushed aside by the technology and over population of a modern world. He found by visiting and exploring these areas his own inner spirit was somehow renewed, and he relished the adventure that awaited.

As was his custom, he armed himself with all the latest information about the area he was about to explore. In addition, he brought along the latest in high-tech metal detectors. *The modern world does offer a few advantages,* he thought. A Collins Engineering model GSC-3000 was in the back seat of the jeep, along with a variety of reference books put out by the State of California Department of Natural Resources. He hoped an understanding of the geology of the territory might help in his search.

He arrived in Bridgeport just before 10:00pm, and after checking into the Walker River Lodge, ran over to the Sportsman Tavern for a quick dinner. Striding back to his motel afterwards, he thought it appropriate that his treasure hunt would begin back in the same town where his love for the Sierra was first kindled. He inhaled deeply of the incredibly fresh mountain air. Returning reluctantly to his room, he was soon fast asleep, his dreams vibrantly alive with visions of lost gold mines, Devoney and... *Wolverine.*

After breakfast the next morning, he drove the final fifty miles to the point where he would leave the highway. He reflected about the reasons why *Wolverine* still haunted him. *Too much a part of my life for too long, yet somehow easier to deal with than things that should be more important,* he concluded. He put those thoughts away for later.

Pulling off the road he parked the jeep at Deadman's Summit. He loaded his daypack with water, assorted fresh fruit, a 15-minute section topographical map, and a flashlight. Within half an hour he found the dry wash where he had unearthed the armor. He referred to his map and surveyed the surrounding terrain for landmarks, wondering where a mine might be. The entire area was desolate and uninhabited. The type of landscape one goes through on the way to somewhere else, never a destination.

From information a geologist friend of Laura's provided, he knew he stood in the approximate center of one of the largest dormant volcanic zones in western North America. At some time in the past 100,000 years the entire region existed beneath a prehistoric lake or inland sea, and once was the peak of a huge, underwater volcano. When the submerged volcano ultimately erupted, massive amounts of lava belched out. As the molten rock cooled, it hardened and cracked leaving the area laced with fissures of varying shapes and sizes. After those primordial waters receded, the land probably looked much as it does today. In one of those crevices, Cody reasoned, he might find the Lost Conquistador. *What better place to hide a cache of treasure or secrete a mine than in an endless maze of deep crevices. Hard to find and easy to defend,* he reflected, trying to think like a Conquistador.

Currently, the whole geographic zone experienced strong 'families' of earth tremors, signals to one and all that the dormant volcanic cauldron beneath the land was still very much alive and potentially dangerous. As a native Californian, and somewhat experienced in earthly rumblings, earthquakes never bothered Steele, and he paid little attention to the media coverage when they did occur. Cody fired up the Collins GSC-3000, adjusted the ground tone and volume, and then headed up the arroyo in a northeasterly direction, whistling softly to himself.

After an arduous hour of trudging through ancient cinders, ash and boulders, he came to the base of a non-descript bluff, which according to his topo was three miles in diameter and 1,000 feet higher than the surrounding plain. It was unnamed, and didn't appear to have any access roads or trails. Not unusual or unique in any way. The terrain between Mono Lake and Mammoth Lakes boasts dozens of similar bluffs and outcroppings. Jeffrey and Ponderosa pine flourished on its flanks, but it appeared barren at the crest. "Well, you haven't gotten any significant hits with the ol' GSC-3000, and you haven't anything better to do, so let's see what's up there. Have you seen any hidden treasure?" he asked a kangaroo rat. The tiny creature cautiously observed him from the entrance to its burrow ten yards away. When he broke through the tree line and into open expanse, he had a strange feeling. Years spent in black-ops encounters had honed his 'sixth sense' into a trusted ally, visceral hunches saving his life on numerous occasions. It felt as if some thing or some one was watching him, or at least knew he was there.

250 feet below the summit of the bluff, Cody found a huge outcropping of basalt, and the GSC-3000 started an erratic tweeting in his earphones. He climbed diagonally upward. Just as he reached the edge of the outcropping, he was astounded to see a yawning fissure right at his feet. If he hadn't been paying close attention to his footing at the time, he would have stepped right into it. It was about four feet wide, and ran off to his right in a jagged slice through the otherwise solid rock. Cautiously bending over, he peered in. Nothing. Using a softball size stone for a sounding measure, he tossed it over the lip and slowly counted to eight before he heard it clatter against what he imagined must be the bottom. "Holy shit!" he exclaimed. "By golly what a gully! This baby is one deep sonovabitch!"

It was approaching noon and getting uncomfortably hot on the exposed rock. Steele sat, took a drink from his water bottle, and studied the map. There was no indication of fissures or canyons on it. He checked the publication date. 1975. "Could these have happened since then?" he wondered aloud.

He followed the meandering crack as it traversed across the top and to the edge of the bluff. Standing there, he realized it couldn't be seen from only ten feet away on either side. In a prone position, he inched up to the edge until he could see into the interior with the aid of his flashlight. Using the light, he located a spot where he might be able to climb in and down. He'd have to use a rock climbing technique called 'chimneying' at the top until he could find footholds on some protruding boulders he noticed well down one of the sidewalls. Hanging onto the edge with one hand, he swung the GSC-3000 over and into the void with his free hand. It responded with a steady, insistent chirping. Icy cold prickles of excitement and fear raced across the back of his neck.

20

Despite government literature to the contrary, PNG is a very clan oriented country. Especially in the outer islands like New Britain. Clan members are very much involved with the goings on within their own communities. However, very little concern or awareness is given anyone, or the things they do outside the environs of the clan. This particularly applies to non-clan expatriates or tourists. The presence one day, and the absence the next of most foreigners is given little notice or thought by most Nationals. If anyone even observed the little inflatable and its two occupants speeding across the bay, they paid them little heed. It is usually more expeditious to travel across the harbor by outboard than around it by vehicle. The calm, protected waters of Blanche Bay experience many dozens of similar passages each day. This midday voyage undertaken by Dominic and Willie Kaltenbach was just another everyday occurrence in Rabaul. No one witnessed Dominic's return to the *Tambu* alone, two hours later. The crew wasn't even aware their skipper had been anywhere but ashore with Hendel and Devoney.

Dominic anchored just east of Praed Point at the entrance to the bay, and he and his guest were soon descending through the indigo waters entombing the Japanese destroyer *Suzanami*. Fast and deadly, the compact 370 foot long war ship almost made good her escape to open ocean on the afternoon of November 11, 1943 when she was caught and sunk by torpedo bombers from the US carriers *Bunker Hill*, *Essex* and *Independence*. Discovered by divers late in 1990, she rests upright, though listing to port, her keel plowed into the bottom sands 240 feet beneath the surface. Extreme depth and open water currents conspire to make the dive treacherous, even for the most experienced, so very few divers visit her grave. Certainly it wasn't a destination that a novice diver should attempt, a fact Dominic purposefully neglected to include in his dive plan description to Willie before they hit the water.

The *Suzanami* took the first hit in her stern section. An air-launched torpedo penetrated her hull plates just forward of the rudder. The torpedo's delayed fusing mechanism detonated its murderous warhead seconds after breaching the plates, the resultant explosion crippling the ship's steering mechanism. In addition, the internal blast ruptured many of the ship's watertight bulkheads. With all directional capability lost, the *Suzanami* steamed in a tight circle until the onslaught from the bombers above finally proved too great. Throwing up deadly anti-aircraft fire at her tormentors from her two remaining functional batteries, she defiantly disappeared beneath the surface guns still blazing.

21

Willie Kaltenbach lived his life with reckless abandon, often plunging headlong into situations before fully understanding them or their inherent risks, relying on his instincts and adaptability to see him through. In a really tough spot, his ace-in-the-hole was his tremendous brute strength. To this day, those traits served him well... too well. Cocky in the extreme, he believed in his own invincibility. He took up diving the way he did everything else, all caution to the wind.

Willie received SCUBA training and certification through an abbreviated 'resort course'. These courses are designed to be quick rather than thorough. More often than not, basic training in physiology, and normal precaution are passed over or simply neglected in order that more paying divers can be plopped into the ocean by ambitious instructors and/or tour operators.

While the physics of diving is basic, and the precautions mostly those of common sense, the experience of surviving underwater is still an adventure into a foreign and unforgiving environment. A diver unaware of or disregarding these facts is an accident waiting to happen, and the odds of trouble increase the deeper the dive. A miscue or a wrong move at the surface is usually just an annoyance, but at depths it can be fatal.

Dominic counted on all this and more when he suggested the *Suzanami* as a dive site to Willie earlier that morning. He knew somewhere on or in the deep wreck might be the ideal place to have an accident, and Willie Kaltenbach underwater brought with him all the ingredients for just such a convenient calamity. Dominic was certain the specific details of the opportunity would manifest quickly when they got on the wreck.

Once underwater, all Dominic had to do was point down. Seeing the signal, Kaltenbach purged air from his buoyancy vest and sank toward the bottom like a brick. The correct way to descend is to regulate buoyancy, always keeping just to the negative side of neutral. This provides a gentle, controlled descent with little or no physical effort. Dominic needed to fin hard just to keep up with Willie dropping rapidly below him. Hardly textbook, but the first signal for Dominic that he had read his man correctly.

Willie hadn't noticed the absence of a safety tank. The reality was Kaltenbach had never been deeper than 100 feet, and was oblivious to the need for potential decompression stops, let alone any other effects of depth. Safety never crossed his mind. Diving was just another experience for him to conquer. You jumped in, took your chances, then took over. Simple. What could be easier? Any problems that might arise could easily be dealt with, and after all, didn't he have Dominic, an 'expert' dive buddy to assist just in case?

Going hell-bent in free-fall, they plummeted by the *Suzanami*'s bridge at 100 feet, heading for a hard landing on the deck to the port side of the forward, ten-inch gun mount at 160. Dominic's ears screamed in protest because he wasn't able to equalize fast enough during their brisk descent. He kicked up about ten feet to reduce the pressure a bit, and laughed into his regulator at the sight of Kaltenbach crashing butt first onto the deck. The big German quickly righted himself, and expelling an umbrella of bubbles, proceeded to brush himself off, as if his out-of-control drop was merely how it was supposed to be done and let's get on with it.

Dominic and Kaltenbach swam around the destroyed gun turret, and soon were positioned at the entrance to a dark companionway on the main deck where a hatch had once been. The eerie passageway before them appeared to lead completely through the bridge area. Kneeling at the open entry, they could just make out a faint, bluish-gray light beckoning from the far end of the long, black interior, possibly indicating an exit to open water at the other end. In the heat of battle forty-eight years earlier, all hatches and openings on the *Suzanami* had been closed and dogged. Multiple explosions from within the ship bent a four-inch thick, steel companionway door outward from the bottom. However, the top two thirds of this small hatch was forever jammed shut. This mangled opening to the stern of the bridge was what they saw now.

'Rapture of the Deep', or nitrogen narcosis, is a condition that will begin to affect most divers, novice and experienced, below 50 feet. As the partial pressure of nitrogen in the blood and tissue fluids increases relative to the increased pressures of depth, a sense of well-being is often experienced. Divers the world over compare the feeling to the euphoria or dizziness which follows consumption of alcohol, to the extent that a rule of thumb commonly known as 'Martini's Law' has evolved. For every fifty feet of depth the experience is surprisingly similar to that which results from drinking a martini on an empty stomach. One hundred feet... two martinis, one hundred fifty feet... three martinis, and so on. At this depth, Dominic and Willie were working on their fourth. And four martinis merely added to Kaltenbach's cavalier sense of invincibility.

Dominic had to restrain Willie from charging headlong into the dark opening. Handing Kaltenbach a dive light, he demonstrated with hand signals how they would swim down the corridor and out the apparent opening at the far end. He patiently cautioned Willie to proceed slowly, and to stay off the deck and not stir up four plus decades of accumulated silt and debris. Willie flashed a hurried OK and barged in. Dominic noted with satisfaction that his 'buddy' seemed a bit too sure of himself, and that his eyes appeared unfocused and wild with excitement. Four plus martinis. Dominic knew that the means for his 'accident' were to be found somewhere in this dark hole. All he had to do was wait and seize the opportunity when it presented itself. Without looking, he felt for his dive knife sheathed to the inside of his left calf. "If all else fails…" He cautioned himself not to be overconfident, and carefully followed Willie through the orifice into the innards of the dead ship.

The corridor was narrow and cramped, a claustrophobic's worst nightmare. In addition to being pitch black, it was askew with the list of the wreck. Because the keel was on a slope, the further in they went, the deeper their depth. Dominic was aware that, coupled with their narcosis, these ingredients must surely add to the disorientation of the unwary and inexperienced Kaltenbach.

Venturing down the passageway, they noted that every twenty feet or so there would be black openings to their left off the main corridor. Having explored similar companionways on other wrecks, Dominic correctly realized these were hatches into several of the ship's compartments. Shining their lights inside, they could only speculate on the cabin's functions or purpose. Their probing beams were but pitiful pencils of light shedding little understanding on the uses of the past. Every time they would pause at a compartment opening, Dominic would again have to restrain the wildly thrashing Kaltenbach. He would point at the distant exit, then to his dive watch, and finally to his air pressure gauge, silently instructing Willie that they hadn't the time or the air reserves to broaden their exploration. The reality was that Dominic wouldn't be absolutely certain of his desired result if he let Kaltenbach go in alone.

Their rising exhaust bubbles burst against the ruined overhead, creating a brownish-red cascade of agitated silt and debris above and behind them. Dangling from this corroded and rusting ceiling was a maze of wires. It ran the entire length of the passage, and Dominic had to brush individual strands aside to avoid entanglement where they floated loose in several places along the way. Despite the earlier warnings, Willie was not at all concerned with his buoyancy, erratically bouncing off walls, ceiling and deck, his antics contributing to the quickly deteriorating visibility. Once, while Willie was scanning the interior of an adjacent compartment, Dominic turned around to see how far they had come and became somewhat alarmed when he realized any retreat would probably be a blind one. He couldn't see the entry point through the powder-fine silt they had stirred up. *Man, in this silt-out, at this depth without a light, you could get lost in here forever*, he thought. *Settle down. Four martinis. You're just narc'd.* He carefully moved through a web of wires hanging all the way down to the deck, and as he gingerly waved them aside, the answer came to him.

When they finally reached the far end of the passageway, Dominic knew he must make his move, and soon. His gauges showed their depth was a dangerously deep 180 feet, and that his remaining air would last scarcely another ten minutes at this depth. He was pushing his no decompression limits as it was. The blown exit hatch dictated his decision. Willie knelt at its bottom, evaluating his chances of successfully squeezing out the open section. Dominic could see that if they were able to make it out at all it would only be by removing their gear and either pushing it or pulling it through, a tricky and dangerous maneuver at best. Certainly it would require teamwork on both their parts. Willie turned and excitedly motioned his intent to go for it with his gear *on*. For the first and last time, Dominic did not caution or stop him. He simply gave the big man the 'OK' signal. When Kaltenbach stooped to try and squeeze through, he dropped his light. Dominic quickly retrieved it and while shining it on the hatch with one hand, with his other he began wrapping a handful of loose, but still attached ceiling wires around the first stage of Willie's regulator where it attached to his tank at the back of his neck. Kaltenbach was too engrossed to notice. Accomplishing this, Dominic began to deliberately fan the ceiling and walls adding to the clouds of stirred up silt and debris already swirling around them. When Willie turned and extended his hand for the return of his light, Dominic gently kicked back and disappeared into the passageway now completely obscured by the disturbed silt and the blackness of depth. He immediately extinguished both dive lights and began his retreat the way they had come. Willie tried to follow but the wire noose around his tank held him fast.

The brute power of the huge German's struggle to get free served only to ensnare him tighter. Futilely he kicked at the solid bulkhead door and pounded the walls in mounting fear and desperation. The more frightened he became, the faster he sucked his dwindling air supply. Logic was gone in an instant. It never occurred to him to remove his tank in order to extricate it from the wire trap. Not once did he think of Dominic. His narcotized, terror-filled mind focused solely on his own escape. Frantically, he tore at the efficient snare behind and above him, panic forcing every exhalation into a water-muted scream... screams only he could hear. He felt a forceful, heavy blackness rushing in from all sides.

Keeping both his hands in constant contact with the corridor walls for orientation and direction, Dominic blindly worked his way back up the corridor. He jammed his eyes closed and forced his lids to remain shut to avoid the possibility of vertigo, surely a deadly result should he attempt the impossible and try to see through the clouds of enveloping silt. Instead, he concentrated solely on keeping hand contact with the cold steel plating to his right and left. If he dared to turn on the beam until well back in the passageway, Willie might see its glow. Twice his right hand lost contact with the crusted metal of the interior wall. In the total darkness, he surmised that these voids must be compartment openings, and by their separation he could judge how far he had come. Once well up the corridor, he turned on the light.

Kaltenbach had several chances, none good. One was if he was able to take his tank completely off and untangle himself. A good trick even for an experienced diver given the darkness and the immediacy, not to mention the physiological problems associated with the great depth. Dominic was almost certain that Willie was too large to escape through the blown hatch in any event. Even if by some miracle he did manage to squeeze out, he would have an extremely difficult 180-foot free ascent to the surface. Dominic was also nearly certain that Willie didn't even know what a free ascent was, let alone possess the skills and experience to execute it. If not done correctly from this depth there could only be one result... death, either from a massive air embolism or by drowning. If he were successful at the free ascent, he would probably have to contend with the bends. After all, there was no safety tank for decompressing, and in the elapsed time it would take him to escape he would certainly have stayed too deep for too long. Assuming he were able to free himself from the wires and be unable to squeeze free through the hatch, then the odds were excellent that he would become disoriented and lost in the passageway and bumble into one of the side compartments. There, he would most likely run out of air, blindly trying to find his way out. Not a pleasant way to die, but certainly an almost perfect solution. When and if anyone ever found the body they would write the death off to the over confidence of inexperience.

Once, Dominic thought he heard a distant, muffled scream. He definitely could feel the vibrations of the death struggle in progress behind him transmitted through the metal plates of the corridor all around. *Deep diving alone,* Dominic smiled at the beauty of it.

After regaining the entrance, he casually began his own ascent, never taking his eyes from the stream of bubbles cascading up from beneath the stern section of the bridge. At eighty feet he lost sight of the top most part of the *Suzanami*. He swam over to the rising fountain of bubbles, and holding at 10 feet among their upward expanding, silvery cloud, breathed off his remaining air. When his tank was exhausted, he floated alone at the surface breathing through his snorkel and watching until there was no trace of any bubbles from below. The odds won. Willie wouldn't be back. Dominic leisurely kicked over to the Zodiac, which bobbed on the surface chop one hundred feet away. He wondered what to do about Dr. Devoney Marsh.

22

"There. Right over there!" she shouted, pointing off to her right. They were two days sail out of Kavieng where Devoney had rejoined the *Taleo Tambu,* after enjoying a wonderful stay ashore. Walindi Plantation, as advertised, had been exceptional. They were following a giant school of yellowfin tuna first spotted an hour earlier. "Why do they keep disappearing?" she asked Dominic. He brought the helm two points to starboard following her direction.

"I think its the vibration and noise of our engine that spooks them," he responded. His eyes focused on the area of agitated water about four hundred yards away. "They're schooling on some surface dwelling bait fish. They dive when we get too close. Their urge to feed doesn't keep them down for long though. Damn! Look how large that school is."

The *Tambu* was under power rather than sail, for the wind was non-existent, and the seas were dead calm. They watched a slowly moving, disturbed area of the surface about the size of a football field. Roughly within those boundaries, it appeared as if someone were continuously throwing great handfuls of rocks in the water. The splashing resulted when the small fish tried to escape becoming a meal by bolting out of the water in thrashing, desperate leaps. It was their third effort to close on the school. Each time previous, just when their sleek craft would get within about thirty yards of the surface commotion, the school would sound and the water would become still. They would wait and drift, engine off, for about fifteen minutes. Then, all of a sudden, someone would spot birds massing over some new, distant spot where the tuna renewed feeding on the millions of smaller, slower bait fish. Occasionally, a charging tuna could be seen streaking over the surface tracing a graceful, tail-lashing arc through the air in hot pursuit of its meal.

The scene was a perfect visual representation of the oceanic food chain in action. The tuna forced the smaller fish to the surface by rapidly schooling in circles around and beneath their panicked prey. The hunters forced the hunted into a confined, churning mass near the surface, eliminating a dimension of escape. In this way, the larger fish could feed easily, charging directly across and through the ball of frenzied bait. Beneath them were dolphins feeding on smaller tuna and bait. Lurking around them all were the sharks. Above, all manner of sea birds fed on anything leftover, plunging pell-mell into the fracas when a morsel was spotted, raucously screaming with the frenzy of feeding on such bounty.

Exxy and Gratvin stood on either side of the stern cockpit area facing aft, each with a spool holding 150 yards of fifty-pound test monofilament. On the end of each line a large, brightly colored jig was attached to a four-inch fishhook. This time, as the *Tambu* closed on the moving feast, Dominic cut her engine and she drifted right into it.

The excitement and frenzy beneath them was contagious. It was impossible not to be swept up by the noise and visual spectacle of so many fish boiling the water around the boat. Everyone was yelling; not at each other; mainly just hollering with the sheer awe of it all.

"Holy Christ!"

"Look at that one right there!"

"Sharks under the boat!"

"Geezus!"

"Watch your line, Exxy!"

"I got a monster on!"

"Grab the gaff!"

"Man did you see that one? What a beaut!"

Loud cries and screeches of hundreds of diving birds directly overhead and all around only heightened the chaos.

"Throw out those lines again!" Dominic's voice finally boomed over the din.

"Fish on!" sounded simultaneously from both the crew.

Adrenaline jolted through them all.

Before the jigs could troll out five yards, each of the boys had hooked in. When tuna feed like this they strike at anything that moves in the seething mass of baitfish, even a bare hook. The cockpit instantly became a storm of confusion filled with shouting and laughter, as Dominic and Exxy wrestled a powerful sixty-pounder on the port side, while Gratvin and Devoney were quickly losing fifty yards of line to a running fifty-pounder to starboard. Molly stood in the cabin hatchway excitedly directing them all, punctuating her instructions with animation, and slashing the air with a seven-inch long filet knife for emphasis. The only definitive thought Devoney could recall having afterward was how thankful she was for the leather gloves Gratvin made her put on right before the first fish struck their lure. The monofilament would have deeply sliced into the flesh of her unprotected hands without them.

Ten minutes later, both teams had their respective fish at the boat. Dominic quickly tied his line off on the mainsheet port winch, grabbed the gaffe, and was on the dive platform attempting to bring the reluctant fish aboard. Gratvin and Devoney did it the easy way. When their fish ended its first run, Gratvin deftly spun three turns of line around the starboard winch and easily cranked the struggling creature into the boat, grinding the winch handle as if it were a giant peppermill. Both fish were soon desperately flapping around the deck inside the cockpit. Gratvin quickly ended their hopeless struggle dispatching each with a well-placed blow to the head using the heavy winch handle as his club.

The small cockpit was a shambles. Tangles of line were all over. Spools, jigs, equipment, coolers and happy, laughing crew littered the deck now slippery with salt water and fish blood. There were high fives all around. Molly gave each a congratulatory pound on the back. Dominic disappeared into the salon for a quick moment, only to reappear with two bottles of champagne and five glasses.

"Best damn fishermen... oops, sorry ladies... fisherpeople on the ocean," he toasted, topping off each glass. "Sashimi anyone?"

23

It felt cold. This was the first sensation Steele noticed when he finally dropped to the floor of the fissure. He estimated he was 75 to 100 feet beneath his entrance point at the rim overhead. The narrowness and depth of the chasm kept the lower recesses in perpetual shade, except during those fleeting moments when the sun passed directly overhead.

Climbing down was easier than he anticipated. He put his daypack on backwards wearing it over his chest, and attached the metal detector to it with a length of rope he always carried on such expeditions. Years earlier, when he began exploring the high country solo, he made it a point to travel with a customized survival kit. In addition to the rope and flashlight, it contained a butane cigarette lighter, an extremely lightweight space blanket for warmth, a whistle, some bandages, water, a Power Bar for quick energy, and a Smith & Wesson .38 caliber Chief Special. By bracing his back, arms, and hands against one wall, and muscling both feet against the opposite, he was able to carefully slither down the upper portion of the fissure. About half way in, he found hand and footholds on a tumble of dislodged boulders, and quickly worked his way to the bottom.

Repositioning his daypack, he realized that the almost vertical walls to either side of the area he could see were no more than three feet apart. There wasn't room enough to fully extend both arms out straight at the same time. It took several contortions to organize the metal detector, and he laughed at himself with the effort. "Like trying to get dressed in a broom closet," he thought.

Once his eyes adjusted to the subdued light, he saw that the floor pathway disappeared around a protruding wall some fifty feet away. Cautiously, he started toward it, the Collins GSC-3000 chirping steadily in his earpiece. The footing consisted entirely of coarse, gray volcanic sand, which crunched with each step. It sounded like he was walking on wall-to-wall corn flakes. The only impressions on its surface were tiny, scurrying footprints, mute evidence of some small desert animal's previous passage. At the first corner he stopped and again quickly examined both walls. They were basically smooth, except where an occasional boulder or clump of stones protruded here and there. He correctly surmised that these irregularities must have congealed in the otherwise smooth walls sometime during the volcanic cooling process thousands of years before. He edged around the corner and was confronted by the next section of fissure, which appeared identical to the one he had just exited; only it looked twice as long. The Collins insistently chirped on.

After an hour of steady trudging, he stopped and sat with his back at the base of yet another vertical wall, in this seemingly continuous labyrinth of canyons. Mentally, he checked off what he had learned. He peeled and ate an orange as he contemplated. "About three miles of connecting vertical fissures so far," he calculated. From his years of running he knew that his pace was an easy eighteen to twenty minutes per mile. "Joined on a tangent of at least 45 degrees, and getting deeper as I progress," he thought, gauging his depth with a casually concerned glance upward. The sky, apparent at the crest of the fissure about 150 feet above, appeared to be no more than a very thin blue sliver. "I'm still going generally east." Steele had always enjoyed an excellent sense of direction and he had noted the orientation of the fissure when he first entered.

"If anything, the composition of the walls is changing slightly." He brushed his fingers over the smooth surface, cool and glasslike. "No evidence of any human intrusion since at least the last rain." The path was undisturbed by manmade footprints. With the exception of an occasional tumbleweed or small rockslide, it continued to be monotonous in its uniformity and makeup.

"No variance in the detector readings." He tapped its gauge and fiddled with the volume adjustment knob and then stood, glanced self-consciously over his shoulder, and started off once again, not quite shaking the disturbing feeling that somehow he was not alone. When he wasn't moving, the silence was ominous.

He came upon the first significant geographical change half an hour later. It appeared to be a small inset cave at the base of the right hand wall, approximately in the middle of the section he was exploring. The mouth of the cavelet was a dark arc about four feet in diameter. He was at a depth where ambient light could not penetrate horizontally. On his knees with his flashlight in hand he could see that the cave had a smooth black finish, and extended in about twenty feet. "I'll be damned. Solid obsidian." The light danced across the black, reflective interior.

Ten thousand years previous, miles beneath where Steele knelt, raging volcanic forces released a series of massive, primordial, gaseous upsurges. The resulting bubbles slowly rose through the surrounding molten lava, some eventually boiling to the surface, others trapped in perpetuity within the cooling magma. The entire area of Cody's search was punctuated with these age-old, trapped cavities.

Standing once again after satisfying himself that there was nothing in the cave, he became alarmed when he noticed several small streams of sand and pebbles cascading down the vertical walls to either side of him. He quickly stepped back. The sound of the falling sand was similar to that of air escaping a punctured tire. He stood transfixed, watching the sandfall form small, neat, cone-shaped piles at the base of the fissure walls. After a long minute, they subsided and soon stopped altogether. Oppressive silence engulfed him. He waited. When nothing happened, he bellowed, "HELLOo-o-o! Anybody up there?" When there was no answer or further disturbances from above, again he started off down the fissure. *Maybe a small animal, or probably just the wind*, he thought.

The further he went the more caves he found. In addition to those at the base of the walls, he observed cavities as far up as he could see. At this point in his exploration, the ones he could access from the floor were much deeper and wider than the first one he encountered. All were formed of pure obsidian. He was peering in one at shoulder level with the light when he first heard it.

Felt it actually. At first there was no sound, just a sensation like trying to stand in one spot without support on a moving subway. Icy tentacles of fear and panic shot down his back and involuntarily he flinched in response, dropping his flashlight and the Collins. A quick explosion of vertigo washed over him as the walls started to dance sideways and undulate. Suddenly... the sound! It was a rumbling roar similar to that of distant thunder, only continuous and getting louder by the second. Violently he was thrown to the ground as the noise enveloped him, pounding at his consciousness. Everything was in motion. There was no fixed horizon or stationary point on which to focus. Boulders and debris rained down all around. Somehow he managed to regain his feet for just an instant and lunge for the lip of the cave he had been examining. He gained the entrance on his second try, hauling himself up and in just as a Buick-sized piece of the wall crashed down on the very spot he had just vacated. Now, undulations were coming in time to deafening waves of ground resonance. He was mercilessly tumbled about in the small cavity. The air became filled with fine particles of sand, torturing his lungs and stinging his eyes. The last thing he saw was the opposite wall of the fissure closing in, slowly sealing the opening to the cave. *A perfect tomb*, he thought as a black, senseless tide of unconsciousness swept him away.

24

Kavieng. The name sounds more African than tropical South Pacific. But there it is, and there they were. Almost dead on the equator, juxtaposed between the two bands of tropics, surrounded by a rash of tiny islands. A town calling itself a city, right out of Somerset Maugham. The travel guides refer to it as 'laid back'. Hell, even in the center of the busiest part of town, if you can really find a center, all the men still wear lap-laps. Crowning the northern point of land on needle-thin New Ireland, Kavieng's somnolence defines the peace and tranquility found throughout the entire island. They sat on the grassy area fringing the stunningly beautiful town harbor just north of the local market.

"So... what do you think? Is it possible?"

Devoney slurped on her margarita through a tiny straw wondering the same thing. "Is what possible?" she responded.

They had casually but persistently discussed the *HAVOC* device off and on, over the course of the last few days. Almost automatically they referred to it now as *HAVOC*, ever since the evening of Hendel's translation in Rabaul. They agreed it sure beat the dickens out of having to wrap your tongue around *VERHEERUNG* at every mention.

Separately, each pondered the potential: fertile, creative, intelligent minds evaluating the same topic, but each working in entirely different directions, with different purposes, different ends after different rewards.

For the last three days, they had leisurely cruised New Ireland's offshore islands, diving and exploring. Most of the islets were but tiny dots of palm atop pristine, vanilla-white sand beaches, encircled by that incredible sapphire sea. All but the largest were uninhabited, and rarely, if ever, visited. This privacy afforded Dominic and Devoney the opportunity to further fan the flames of their carnal passion, first ignited that night in Rabaul. They snorkeled naked in the protected shallow lagoons searching for shells and lobster. They walked hand in hand for hours along the deserted beaches by day and by moonlight. They made love at every opportunity. Once, even on the sandy floor of an underwater cavern, their private chamber sculpted from the solid reef by eons of tidal flows, and the relentless action of the waves. They were evenly matched. Each seemed insatiable. The crew of the *Tambu*, in deference to the lovers, purposefully left them alone at every chance.

Devoney slipped into this hedonistic lifestyle faster than she ever could have imagined. As if cast in a spell, the tropical beauty and her infatuation with Dominic combined to lull her into a feeling of well being and trust. And paradise conspired. Thermal currents, born in equatorial heat and nourished by dense jungle, blessed the lovers with an endless cycle of brilliant blue sky, wondrously changing clouds, occasional afternoon rain showers, and incredible sunsets.

On their walks, or during quiet times they quizzed each other and themselves on *HAVOC*. "You know," she said. "After taking another really close look at the schematics, and I'm no engineer mind you, I'm certain the thing can be rebuilt. All the components, at least the ones they listed, are rather common. You know, generator, transmitters, relays, and the like. Whether we can get it to work is another matter. I'd love to have the UC techies take a look at all the drawings. Those guy would love to get their hands on this thing."

"Not necessary, my dear," Dominic quickly responded. He wanted to distract her from that line of thought. "I think I can put together a team of engineers and technicians from my sources here that could give it a go, if that's what we're talking about actually doing."

"Well, either way. But still, it might be worth the effort. Just imagine what it could do. The question is, whether modern technology can streamline and refine it enough to give it some chance of working. It might be that the Japanese and Germans just lucked out with the right combination of machinery at the right time."

"Yeah. And in the right place. At least for one day. Too bad for them, they didn't have a clue what they actually did. The war might have gone a little differently," Dominic grinned. He wasn't yet convinced that he could put the entire project together without Devoney's help. She brought a unique, cost-free expertise to the table, and besides, she was one helluva lay. He would try to keep her around until he was certain he could complete the project, or until she found out too much about his true motivations and intentions.

The most developed of all Dominic's many skills was his uncanny ability to manipulate people: usually without their knowledge, and always for the benefit of his own needs and ends. In this manner he was easily able to compensate for his own shortcomings or lack of skills by using someone else's. He certainly was no fool. The educational and technical know-how required to reproduce *HAVOC* was far greater than that which he or any of his current crew of close associates possessed. Given this, he quickly came to the conclusion that, if he were to proceed with his plan, he must find, hire, coerce, or force someone with the necessary abilities to help complete the fabrications and shakedown. That someone might just as well be Dr. Devoney Marsh. "Love the one you're with," he quietly concluded.

"Say again," she said. Her own thoughts had distracted her attention.

"Nothing. I was just thinking out loud to myself. So exactly how does the damn thing work?" he prompted again.

Devoney took another pull at her drink, and then turned to face him. "You're a sailor. You certainly must know about the Doldrums."

"Parts or regions of ocean, usually at or near the equator, known for squalls and light shifting winds. But they're most infamous for long periods of stifling calm. What's that got to do with *HAVOC*?"

"Hold your lap-lap on, and I'll explain it to you in somewhat simplistic terms. Better yet, take it off." She playfully tugged at a loose corner of his sarong. "Let's suppose you are becalmed in just such an area, and for whatever reason, don't or can't motor out."

"Happened to me once about ten years back. I sailed into the damn thing and was stuck there for four or five days before a Taiwanese fishing trawler came along and towed me out. I'd probably still be there if they hadn't spotted me." He vividly recalled the experience in his mind's eye. "Hotter'n hell, and muggy like you wouldn't believe."

"Okay then. You've got the picture. Dead, flat calm, hot and still with absolutely no air movement."

"Bingo."

"Now I want you to picture the air mass, the bowl of air if you will, encompassing the becalmed area. Completely motionless. Dead still. Got it?"

"Yep."

"What must happen to get that air moving?"

"Some sort of weather change, obviously."

"And what do you suppose causes the doldrums in the first place?"

"Well, as you said, I'm a sailor, and all sailors have to know meteorology to survive, and I've been sailing for over twenty years. So, the Doldrums are caused by uniformity of temperature in the water and in the air mass to a very high altitude with little or no tidal or other currents. No water or air movement of any kind."

"Precisely. Very good so far. What happens when you build a fire?" she asked.

"What the hell do you mean?"

"To the air... when you build a fire, anywhere?"

"Well…" he paused, thinking. "The hot air... rises," he said slowly.

"Exactly! Let's just suppose you were able to build a big enough, sustainable fire on your becalmed sailboat. I know. Unrealistic. But just suppose you could. What would begin to happen to that mass of stagnant air if the fire were big and hot? Think of what happens to the air over a pot of boiling water."

Dominic lay back on the grass and gazed for a long moment at the billowing clouds overhead, while conceptualizing Devoney's analogy. "If I could build a hot enough, sustainable fire, the heat source would cause a column of air to rise above it."

"And then?"

"And then..." he continued slowly, measuring each word to his developing thoughts. "...As the air rose over the fire the surrounding, relatively cooler air would flow in to fill the potential void left by the rising, hotter air. If the heat source were sufficiently strong and concentrated enough to reach sufficient altitudes, you might create…."

"Wind," she completed his sentence. "In theory, with a big enough fire, sustained for a long enough period of time, you just might be able to create movement in the air mass, and effectively induce a change in the weather."

"*HAVOC!*" he blurted.

"Elementary, my dear Dominic."

They gazed at each other in excited amazement.

25

Gently, he depressed the shutter release for the fourth time in the last minute. The venerable old Nikon F responded with a mechanical 'cu-u-lick'. Field agent Kevin Meade had been on-station in Papua New Guinea for three years and found that the heavy workhorse of a camera with its non-electrical innards was far more dependable for tropical duty than any of its more modern, sophisticated counterparts. He thought of it as a "she".

"What I give up in weight and noise is more than compensated for in reliability," he often lectured his doubting field associates. "Those electronic marvels always crap out in the moisture and heat, and always just when you need them most." Meade had been assigned to New Britain and New Ireland three years previous. His routine job was to watch for anything out of the ordinary. This meant people unusual to the area doing things out of the ordinary. His job was like that of hundreds of other field agents around the world. Usually routine. But every once in a while… He had taken notice of the slick catamaran and the sporadic appearances it made in the local ports over the last two and a half months. He was almost convinced that the captain was legit. "I'm just a well-paid, over-educated spook in paradise disguised as a photographer. I hope somebody even looks at this stuff. Let them figure out who he is."

After he fired off another three shots of the couple lounging on the grass, he walked briskly back to his room at the Kavieng Club two blocks away. Standard procedure was never to be in any area of any country long enough to raise suspicions. Meade's cover was that of a travel writer and photojournalist. He looked the part. Two battered old suitcases, worn shorts and faded Hawaiian shirts, an old Olympia portable typewriter in a travel case, and an assorted array of hand-carried apparatus and camera equipment made up his travel kit. The typewriter was actually a well disguised, state-of-the-art portable computer and fax machine.

Once returned to his room, he developed the film in the basin and tub. While it was drying, he arranged to borrow the one private overseas-capable telephone line at the Kavieng Hotel next door. The 'Club', as his small lodging was known locally, did not yet have such modern conveniences. "I need to get some material to a publisher," he explained to the uninterested desk clerk. "Damn deadlines, you know."

He examined each photograph before placing them in a manila folder. With the exception of one, the subject's face was in excellent focus. In the one it wasn't, the man had moved at just the instant he triggered the shutter. All he recorded of the subject was a slight blur in the foreground, and a perfectly exposed photo of the woman who was with him. "Damn. What a babe," he said, wolf whistling to himself. "I'll send it along anyway. Give those lab guys an eyeful."

He flushed out the tub and basin, reopened all his windows, and scattered penciled travel notes over the bed and desk before leaving for the hotel. "Never can be too careful, you know," he said to the uncomprehending native maid as he passed her in the hall on his way out to the street.

Four hours later, in Washington DC, Charles Conley, *Deputy Director of Operations*, CIA was rudely awakened by the phone. His private line.

"This better be damn good," he muttered, rubbing his eyes awake.

"Chief, you'd better get down here right away and take a look at these."

"These, what?"

"Batch of images just faxed in from our guy in PNG."

"There's somebody in 'em we all know well."

"Jeezuz!" Conley slammed down the phone.

"What now?"

26

"It appears they modified some early laser technology in order to create the heat source. The entire basis of the whole apparatus resulted from the Japanese genius in incorporating the principle of *coherence* into their heat transference. "

"I didn't think anyone knew anything about lasers until just lately, at least not until the '60s anyway, and what the hell is *coherence?*" Dominic asked.

"Once they were able to generate heat in abundance, and I mean *abundance* with a capital 'A', they were able to contain and therefore focus it over distance without spreading or significant loss, and you're partially correct about laser technology," continued Devoney.

"Gee, thanks."

"Actually, the scientific community conceptually knew a great deal about lasers as early as the 1920's. It just took them another 40 some years to put all the ingredients together correctly. You know Hitler. He was always encouraging his science community to come up with the latest gizmo that would give him the ultimate weapon. I'm certain the Germans and Japanese were fiddling with this sort of technology throughout the war. I read somewhere that von Braun even thought about it for guidance on the V-2 rocket. The concept and designs are really quite simple, scientifically speaking."

"Do you think we can build the damn thing?"

"Who is we?" asked Devoney.

"Us. You and me. I have the resources and the use of a lab. I'm certainly no expert. But from the schematics we've seen, I think we could do it. And as you said, it's somewhat simple. Maybe we could get lucky."

Devoney laughed. "All we really need is time, probably a few million dollars and most of all, that wonderful ingredient you just mentioned… luck.

All any great scientist ever needs. I thought you said you were just a simple sailor. What're you doing with a lab?"

"Seriously, Dr. Marsh. Wouldn't you like to give it a shot?"

Devoney already decided that she would. She was somewhat surprised that Dominic was showing such apparently genuine interest.

"Think of the good we might do for the world," he added.

"First, I haven't the time. Second, I have no idea what the ultimate cost might be. And third, I'm not sure I have the know-how to do it. Further, I never imagined you to be such a blatant philanthropist." She wondered, *He can't be serious?*

"For a ballsy chick, I'm surprised at you. After what I've seen you do, not to mention what you've done to me these last few days, I'm amazed at your reticence."

"Excuuuuuze meee. Such language. I guess the honeymoon is over," she said. She gave him a playful poke in the ribs.

During their conversation they had wandered down the waterfront and found themselves at the town pier, where one of the *Tambu*'s zodiacs was tied.

"Want to go for a snorkel on Edmago?" asked Dominic, pointing to a tiny island just outside the harbor.

She responded by jumping aboard the Zodiac and untying the lines.

Their snorkel was a trip through a magic kingdom. Protected by the fringing reef, the shallow waters of Edmago teemed with life. They swam through rainbows of reef fish living in and around lush coral gardens. Carpets of anemones festooned the reef top. Having been visited by very few divers, the fishes were still curious rather than frightened. For nearly five minutes, a school of trevally cruised beneath them as they kicked along one canyon. Colorful crinoids were everywhere, even stationed on a number of the huge sea fans they frequently passed. They experienced a moment of near fantasy when they cautiously approached a school of patrolling barracuda. It immediately funneled around, surrounding them completely in silvery brilliance.

"That's why I came to PNG," she said, afterward on the beach.

"Oh? You found nothing else?" he chided.

"I hate to have to leave so soon."

"So why go? Let's sail back to my island, and like all the king's men, let's try and put *HAVOC* back together again."

"I really wish I could. But I just can't, Dominic. I have my classes, my research, my house...and..." she didn't complete her sentence, as the thought of Cody rushed through her awareness yet again.

Neither questioned the other about other relationships. They were content to enjoy each other and what they had for the moment. Instinctively, both knew this would change if Devoney were to stay.

"C'mon, Dev. How many opportunities or offers like this are you likely to receive in a lifetime? Take some time off. Give it a month or so. It's hands on work, right up your alley. It's what you teach, what you do. If it doesn't work, at least we can say we tried and then you can go back to the rat race and get back on the treadmill none the worse off, if that's what you want.

"I suppose I could take a leave of absence," she said, slowly thinking through the proposal.

"So how did this laser make it work?" he asked, quickly changing the subject. He knew a fertile seed had been planted with his asking. Now to set the hook.

"Hmm… Oh, uhhh," she stammered, attempting to change gears in her thought process. "It really isn't a true laser by technical definition. But it does use laser technology. It wasn't until 1958 that all the pieces of the first laser were fitted together into a working prototype. It took them until then to come up with just the right light source, commonly referred to as the lasing medium. One wrong element and it won't work."

"So?"

"So… basically *HAVOC* almost had it, but somewhere along the way one of the engineers must have noticed that while being unable to concentrate a light source, he was quickly able to super-heat an immense column of air. Within the column, which funnels from a point on the ground and expands outward and upward through the atmosphere, the Germans were able to excite the electrons surrounding the atoms of oxygen in the air to an incredibly high state by the use of light pulses. The friction of this excitation causes heat, and we know what happens after that from our sailing analogy."

"Excitation, eh. Sounds awfully sexual," Dominic said, playfully.

She temporarily ignored his hand insistently caressing her thigh. "The electrons in the air column absorb the energy from the electrons of the pulsed light source. They excite the electrons of an adjacent atom, and so on and so on. Theoretically, a large air mass can be quickly affected in this manner. If the electrons in the controlled column can be continuously stimulated for some period of time, the resulting friction will cause them to become super-heated ultimately formulating an enormous, self-sustaining, rising, hot air mass. I think that either the Japanese or Germans lucked onto the right combination of ingredients for this device while probably attempting to create something entirely different. Such are the vagaries of science and invention."

"Tell me more about the rising column," his eyes sparkled with that look she had come to know well.

"You're incorrigible. Pay attention! You started this discussion," she continued. "In laser technology, when the excited electrons within the lasing medium are allowed to return to a lower energy state, they emit built up energy in the form of light. With *HAVOC*, the interaction of these agitated electrons can apparently affect normal weather patterns by reversing the flow of ionization."

"Sounds seriously complicated."

"Not really. I thought you said you knew meteorology. In fair weather, heavy, positive ions drift earthward counteracting the Earth's normal negative charge. It is generally agreed by meteorologists that a change in ionization is usually present in unsettled weather patterns. The technicians presumably were able to use *HAVOC* to reverse ionization and move air masses. If it works, fired off at the right time at the right place for a reasonable duration, in theory at least, you could pretty well be sure you could induce some sort of change in the weather."

"I'm impressed, professor."

"So am I, skipper." An admiring glance at the bulge in his sarong.

"Are you sure you don't want to give it a try?"

Her response was quick and positive. She jerked his lap-lap aside and took him completely in her mouth.

27

After thirty-three years in the service of his country, very little surprised Charles R. Conley anymore. In his tenure with the CIA, and as a career navy man, he thought he had seen, heard, been through it all; double agents, double dealing, double crosses. You name it. His staff thought him to be the personification of cool under pressure. That's why they stood, mouths agape in astonishment, as he raved at the grainy, fax photo reproductions clenched between his two fists. They had never before seen him this agitated. "I'll be goddamned! What the fuck is she doing there...with him? Did the ID boys check these against...?"

"Yes, sir. It's a positive match," interrupted the night duty officer who first placed the call to Conley.

"Dr. Devoney Marsh... and... *Wolverine*. Unbelievable!" Conley sighed, dropping the copies as if they might burn his hands. "This might explain a lot. Where's Steele? Anybody contacted Steele about this yet?"

"Yes, sir. Well, yes and no sir."

"What the hell does that mean?"

"We've got a positive fix on the Pullman, but haven't been able to raise him in person. We left a CIU on his recording scrambler, and you know how he hates to carry a mobile or a pager."

"You know damn good and well Steele has a history of ignoring Call In Urgents. What else have you tried?"

"We were able to raise the yard master in Reno where he left that rolling time piece. We sent the local field agent out to talk to him. The old guy told our man that Steele went out in the desert you aren't going to believe this searching for treasure. Didn't know when he might be back."

"Reno? As in Nevada? Treasure?" Conley roared. "What in bloody hell is going on around here? I'm dealing with a bunch of lunatics right out of the daytime soaps. First we convince everybody, including the Director, that this guy *Wolverine* is off'd in Ireland. Next thing we know he shows up alive and well in Jungleland with Steele's squeeze. And now you're telling me that Mr. Adventure is lost in the desert on a search for treasure? I must be dreaming. I'm going back to bed. I don't care how you guys do it, but get Steele on the horn and get him informed... NOW!"

28

Cody Steele came to with a start. He rapidly blinked his eyes, and then vigorously rubbed them hard. Neither technique worked. Blackness. He shook his head in an attempt to chase the cobwebs of unconsciousness from his brain. Still nothing. *I'm blind"* he thought. Panic in a very cold wave swept up his spine. *Get a grip.*

He lay on his back. With cautious sweeps of his hands, he explored the area immediately around him. The grainy texture of volcanic sand on the cavern floor was the only tangible link to his surroundings. Coughing dust from his throat and lungs, he extended one arm up over his face. When he couldn't touch anything above, he slowly sat upright, his outstretched hand still probing the enveloping darkness. Bringing his hand closer and closer to his face he searched for the sight of it in vain. Using his index finger, he touched his nose. "Can't see it." He opened his eyes to their widest extreme, leaving his open palm on his nose. Still, there was nothing but absolute black.

After determining that the rest of his body seemed more or less in working order, he rolled to a kneeling position and crawled tentatively forward. It took but three 'steps' on hands and knees before he hit his head on a solid, down sloping wall. "Shit!"

With his right hand on the wall for orientation, he began inching along, still crawling, not sure what he was searching for, but was thankful for some activity to divert his mind from his blindness. "Had to have been a quake," he muttered. "Must happen all the time around here. Probably wouldn't take much shifting to open or close those fissures. I should've known better than to get into this hopeless situation. No wonder I didn't see any footprints. Nobody else would be stupid enough to go in."

He scrabbled along the wall for about ten feet before his left hand brushed across rough nylon. "My daypack," he uttered out loud. His voice sounded strangely muffled. With his back to the wall, he felt for the top, and then opened the pack. It was only then, as his adrenaline rush subsided, that he began to feel numerous cuts and abrasions all over his body. "Must have happened when I was bounced around this tomb during the quake," he said. "I wonder how long I was out?"

At first, he thought he would remove and arrange the contents of the pack on the ground around him. Remembering his blindness, he belayed that plan. "Don't want to lose anything in this volcanic sand." By touch, he was able to identify each item of the pack's contents. "Where's the flashlight?" Then he remembered dropping it and the GSC-3000, right before hoisting himself up to the pocket cave. Ultimately, his searching fingers closed around the butane lighter. "Let's find out for sure," he said, hoping for the best but fearing the worst.

Carefully, he brought the lighter directly in front of his face, his fingers positioned on it for striking. He took a deep, slow breath and deliberately held it, then opened his eyes wide and flicked the circular lighting mechanism with his thumb. The spark caught and ignited the wick on the first try.

29

"That ought to give us a good start," said Dominic. He fed the last page of the list into the fax machine.

"What's the world coming to? A sailboat with a fax. Where is that going?" asked Devoney.

"To my crew on *Pavao*. It's that island I mentioned where I have a house. A very rich friend of mine owns it actually, but he rarely uses it. It's really a large atoll, not an island, with one long, habitable stretch. You'll love it. It's quite beautiful, and has all the conveniences. My staff there will take care of running all this stuff down. Most of it will be coming from Asia and Japan."

"Staff?" she wondered to herself. "The charter biz must be *really* good."

They spent Devoney's last, official vacation day canceling her reservations home, calling the university to arrange for a substitute for her classes and making sure through Laura that the rest of her affairs would be handled. It really was much less trouble than Devoney first imagined, once she finally made the decision to stay. Dr. Thomson, the head of her department, was more than accommodating. "Take all the time you need, Marsh," he said. "You've been working too hard and taking yourself too seriously for years. Happy we could oblige. Have fun." Thomson was happy to be rid of the brilliant Dr. Marsh for even longer than he hoped. In keeping with the times and changing attitudes, UC was actively seeking qualified females for department head positions when possible, so Thomson perceived Devoney's intelligence and gender as a threat to his position. "This vacation of hers will give me a chance to entrench my position with the faculty."

Laura, of course, was far more inquisitive. "So who is this guy? And you're going to build a what?" Devoney dodged both questions, assuring her good friend that it was strictly research, and she would be filled in as it progressed.

With Dominic's urging, Devoney agreed to take six more weeks off. He was certain he would know in that time whether or not they could build the thing, let alone get any results. If they did, then he would decide what to do with Dr. Marsh.

That night they pored over the *HAVOC* schematic and log translations yet again. From them they developed a long list of tools and parts they would need. Devoney was amazed when Dominic suggested that he could have them all flown in, and that they would probably be on *Pavao* within a day of their own arrival.

Boy, this facilitator business must be lucrative, she thought. *Amazing what he can conjure up at a moment's notice. There's way more to this guy than meets the eye.*

"I'm not much on electronics," she warned.

"That's why they call me Sparky," he kidded. "Not to worry. One of my crew on the island is a whiz. He takes care of the entire system at the compound, and even wired the *Tambu* for me."

"Where is this place *Pavao*? I've never heard of it."

"Not surprising. Not many people have. It's a really small islet, and that's the local name. There are over 2,000 islands around here and all have at least two names, if not more. It's about a twenty-four hour sail from here due northwest. North of the Admiralty Islands, and northwest of the St. Matthais Group. Out in the middle of nowhere. As I mentioned, the owner is filthy rich and the place is self-contained. Even has its own crushed coral airstrip. We could easily fly there from here, but I thought it'd be fun to have the *Tambu* there with us. We wouldn't want to work around the clock now, would we?" he asked. "Besides, this stuff will take at least forty-eight hours or so to round up, and we can't start work until it gets there anyway."

"Whatever will we do?" she laughed.

Gratvin hoisted in the *Tambu*'s anchor just as the sun set.

30

The tiny flame was brilliant. "Geez. If I wasn't blind before, I am now," Steele said. Holding the lighter at arm's length, he squinted his eyes to help them get accustomed. "Man, this place must really be shut tight for it to have been that black." He recalled his helpless feeling of blindness, and shuddered at the thought. A glance at the fluid level in the lighter, two thirds full. "Evaporation. I've got to remember to replace these in my kit more often ... if I ever get out of here."

Estimating he had about twenty minutes of fuel in the lighter, he was determined to make the best use of it. Quickly he stood, and walked the circumference of his buried chamber. A sheer, solid barrier that once was the far wall of the fissure now sealed the opening where he hauled himself in. "Slammed shut."

He found half of the GSC-3000 sticking up from a crease between the sidewall and the floor directly across from the area where he first lit his lighter. The metal shaft was sheared cleanly in half. "Good thing I made it in here when I did." He imagined what such powerful, earthly forces might have done to his body had it been he instead of the detector.

Moving to the center of the chamber after his quick tour, he turned off the lighter, and listened for a long moment. The silence was spectral. He ran down a mental checklist of his situation. *At least one hundred feet below the surface. Closed in on all sides by solid rock. Chamber is about thirty feet across, and just over six feet high at the center. Twenty minutes of light. Food and water for maybe three days, if I'm careful. And no one has a clue where I am. Not good. They won't find the rental jeep until way too late for me. At least there seems to be plenty of air. Plenty of air...*

Re-igniting the lighter, he held it at chest level and out of the direct line of his breathing. At first he thought it was his eyes playing tricks. Then, there it was again. The flame bent and flickered just a bit. And again. It definitely was wavering and angling to his right. He hurried to the wall exactly opposite from the direction the flame flickered, and had to crouch down as the ceiling curved radically where it joined the floor. His whole being concentrated on the small flame. Now, it showed a pronounced deflection, even though he was motionless. He moved it slowly back and forth to find the point where it was most agitated. "A definite draft."

Finding a vertical ledge at the point where the flame spread the most, he searched the smooth rock with his fingers. The ledge extended out and up. The low light drastically reduced depth perception, so he hadn't seen it at first. At the widest point between the ceiling and wall was a gap. An opening in the rock of about twenty inches. The breeze blew out the flame after he reached the lighter into the opening. Pressing up against the wall, the left side of his face jammed hard against it, he snaked his arm around the jutting ledge, then back around a right angle in the opposite direction. *Definitely a shaft, and definitely fresh air*, Cody thought, hopefully. *Not just a chance, it's my only chance.*

In his mind's eye, he envisioned his way through the unseen opening, planning each move carefully. He would have to bend his back around the first ledge in order to negotiate the second with a bend from the waist. "After that, who knows?"

Safely tucking the lighter in his pocket, he tied his pack tightly closed at the top, and then wrapped the shoulder straps securely around his right hand. "I'll try and lead the way with the pack in my hand. That way, if I drop it, at least it'll be in front of me," he reasoned.

Feeling the vertical ledge again with his hands he bent up and around it, not quite minding the blackness quite so much, now that his mind was working on potential escape. It was a tight squeeze, but the smooth, volcanic walls simplified the task. As near as he could tell, the opening for his next forward contortion was much the same size as the first. He bent around the next corner and scrunched forward by leveraging his toes and worming with his shoulders against the walls of the narrow shaft. Once around the second corner he could stretch out full length. *A claustrophobic's worst nightmare. God, I sure hope that was the end of any earth movement for a while. Just a few inches smaller in here and I'm a dead worm*, he thought.

The passage continued on beyond the reach of his searching hands. Pausing for a moment to catch his breath, he considered the situation. Having no other options, he started working his way forward, knowing there was no retreat. After about twenty feet, the passage quickly narrowed, as did Steele's hope. He blindly traced the small opening with his hand. It seemed impossibly little. Sucking in his diaphragm, he shrugged his shoulders toward his ears, and with a desperate, muscular effort, wedged his way into the funneled section. Once through, any relief he felt was immediately gone. The next section was wider, but sloped down.

Pausing again, he searched the shaft with his hands. The darkness was oppressive. Then, he felt a small opening about the size of his head, up and to the right of the main tunnel. He carefully inched forward and up to it, all the while considering the advisability of retrieving his lighter for a look. "Can't afford to lose my light source now." Curiosity won. Squirming his hand into his pocket, after a good deal of effort in such confined quarters, he worked the lighter free. By angling his left shoulder and head partially through the hole, with his left arm full extended, he was able to take a look. "Holy Christ! I'm not the first to get caught. Or even the second."

The cavern wall fell away directly beneath his viewpoint. Even in the insignificant light, he was able to see human skeletons strewn throughout the volcanic chamber. I'm roughly ten feet above the floor and that tomb looks about the same size as the one where I started." His viewing hole was far too small for him to squeeze through any further. In the far corner of the cavern, his light was reflected by something, but he couldn't quite make out just what it was. "Damn!"

He withdrew his arm and extinguished the lighter. Just as he did, he gradually began to slip. At first, he was able to control his slide by expanding his chest and dragging his toes. Too soon however, he found himself shooting down through the slick, obsidian tube, spinning crazily out of control as the downward angle increased. Concluding that his fall was unstoppable, he concentrated on relaxing his muscles, trying to prepare for the inevitable crash, which he was certain, must await him at the bottom of this primeval slide.

31

Dominic set the compass on the autopilot to 315 degrees, moved the control switch on the autopilot to the 'capture/hold' position, and then poured them each another margarita. The last they saw of New Ireland and Kavieng before complete darkness closed in was a sliver of dark land just on the horizon off their stern. Almost comically, a small puff of a cloud threw bolts of lightning at the ground just at that point. It must have been too far away, for they heard no thunder. With that exception the night sky was beautifully clear, and the stars twinkled like cosmic diamonds all around them. When they got underway at sunset, the sea was calm, and according to the latest satellite report, there was no unsettled weather anywhere along their intended route.

Devoney and Dominic sat on deck chairs in the aft well of the *Tambu*, enjoying the silky smooth ride, the balmy ocean breeze, and the warm night air. They spoke sparingly, choosing rather to enjoy the ambiance of the moment in relative silence. An hour or so later, by the time Devoney was ready to turn in, they had picked up a following sea.

"Nothing to be concerned about. This is quite normal. It'll be an easy crossing." Dominic checked the magnetic compass. "We're just getting out from the lee of the island and into open ocean. This is blue water sailing."

The cat slowed perceptibly as she climbed the back of the big rollers passing under her twin hulls. Then, as if embarrassed by the sluggish upward climb, she surged agilely down the front of the next wave. Devoney said her 'good nights' to the crew, pecked Dominic on the cheek, and went below to her cabin. The steady forward to aft rolling motion of the craft quickly lulled her to sleep.

The first time she awoke, she thought she must have been dreaming. The rolling sensation had increased dramatically. Or so it seemed. She imagined she could hear water angrily hissing just outside the hull from her bunk. The forward part of the roll felt much more pronounced, longer and faster than it seemed when she retired. Listening intently, she heard no sound from the crew, the sheets weren't clanging, but she could feel the boat's steady momentum from the winds insistent force on the sails. Everything seemed normal. "I've been on small boats in the open ocean many times. Nothing to be alarmed about. Back to sleep."

She wasn't sure if it was the noise or the motion that woke her the second time. Instantly awake, she was slammed down in her bunk as the *Tambu* hit the bottom of a trough between two waves. Her bunk was oriented such that her feet pointed forward. As the vessel agonizingly climbed the back of the next wave, Devoney felt the blood flow to her head. *This one must be really big*, she thought, anticipating the fall.

She lay on her back looking up at her feet. There was a calm moment when the boat seemed perfectly level, then it shuddered as it teetered forward and over. Finally, free fall. Again, she was smashed into her bunk as the boat plunged down the face of the next huge wave into yet another bottom trough. As if each of her senses turned on independently, she became aware of a mournful moaning on deck, and realized it was the wind howling through the rigging. The *Tambu* groaned in protest at the rough treatment she was enduring. Next, Devoney heard muffled shouts and crashing throughout the boat. "What in God's name…?" She threw on her shorts and poked her head through the hatch into the main salon.

Even in the eerie glow of the red night-lights, she could make out the mess. Molly thrashed about, trying to tie everything down and maintain her balance at the same time. She didn't succeed at either endeavor, and crashed into the dining table as the *Tambu* was rocked backward by the next wave. Devoney could hear Dominic bellowing something from out on the aft deck. Rain lashed the windscreens obliterating any forward vision from within. The sheets angrily tattooed the mast high overhead. "Christ. What have I gotten myself into this time? An easy crossing. Sure."

Timing her move with the next break between waves, she hoisted herself through the hatch up into the salon. She grabbed Molly, and they tumbled awkwardly sideways onto a couch. The cook was wild-eyed, and obviously terrified. "Hang on, Molly. I'll help you tie this stuff down." Together, between onslaughts, the two women got everything moveable stowed or tied down. Devoney comforted Molly as best she could, not completely believing her own words. "Just a quick tropical storm. We'll be out of it in no time."

Through it all Dominic continued to holler unintelligible commands just outside. She wasn't sure opening the hatch to the weather would be such a good idea, but her curiosity got the best of her. What she saw when she did, scared the hell out of her. Dominic, Gratvin, and Exxy, all three dressed in yellow slickers, were trying to hold the wildly gyrating helm. Dominic was on one side, the two boys on the other. From the looks of it, they weren't being too successful. Right after she opened the hatch, Dominic was thrown violently to the side, just barely hanging onto the wheel with one hand. Both boys were lifted off their feet as it jerked around the opposite direction. All three yelled at the top of their lungs. Devoney looked aft and saw a black mountain of a wave racing at them from dead astern. For a moment it totally filled her field of vision, blotting out everything else. It hissed ominously as it slid under them, tossing the *Tambu* back over its flank, flinging the little craft around like insignificant flotsam. "Anything I can do?" Devoney yelled at the top of her lungs without conviction, and knowing the answer.

The crew didn't even seem to notice or hear her; so intent were they on just hanging on. She watched in morbid fascination as yet another monster walled up behind them. Wind driven spray stung her face. The *Tambu* pitched sickeningly to port as it careened precariously down the face of the huge mass of water. The vision and the motion overwhelmed her senses. Too much out of her control was happening all around. She slammed the hatch closed, staggered back down to her cabin, and struggled into her berth. "I'm going to die," she thought, as the next wave bounced and rattled her off the cabin wall.

The sheer emotion and intensity of the drama quickly exhausted her. She was resigned to the fact that she could do nothing but trust fate. Mercifully, she fell into a frightened sleep, her last cognizant thought of Cody Steele. Somewhere, deep in her sleeping brain, there came a tiny voice she would recall much later. "Just let it be." It was a warning.

32

He ricocheted around a thirty-degree corner still picking up speed. The sweat from his earlier efforts served to lessen the friction, but sped his roller coaster descent. Just when it seemed the chute would drop vertically away, it bottomed out and became level. He pressed out hard against the rock with toes and shoulders, and thankfully came to an abrupt stop. A cool blast of night air washed over his face. An incongruous light after all the darkness he had just endured drew his eyes to the left. Not fifty feet away, he was astounded to see the figure of a man, nonchalantly sitting at the edge of a small campfire. "What took you so long? Care for a beer?"

"What the…? Who in hell are you?" asked Cody, extricating himself from the tube. He tumbled out into the desert night, stood, brushed himself off, and approached the fire. A glance back at the opening in the bluff where he exited. "I'll be damned. Came out the opposite side of the mesa."

"Name's Jeremiah. Jeremiah Wilkins. My friends call me JW. Pleased to meet ya', I'm sure. How about that beer?"

"How'd you know I was in there?" asked Steele. Gratefully, he accepted the cold bottle from the unusual looking stranger.

"Didn't. At least not until about fifteen minutes ago when I heard all that thrashing around. Sound travels well out here. Saw a vehicle over on the other side. Guess it's yours."

"What in God's name are you doing out here, JW?" Cody asked. He tilted the bottle to his dry lips and took a long pull, then let out a relieved breath.

"Come out here now and again just to see what changes there are since my last visit. Strange place, this. Burial ground of my ancestors, you know. You might say I'm here visiting them as well."

"How's that?"

"Kuzedika Paiute. I'm nearly full-blooded."

"You're joking. What kind of a name is Jeremiah Wilkins for a pure blood Pauite?"

"That's my Christian or white name. You couldn't begin to pronounce my tribal name. Besides, I kinda like Jeremiah."

Steele took a close look at the man. Indeed, he had the appearance of a Native American. He looked to be about forty-five years old, jet-black hair tied in a ponytail, high, distinctive cheekbones, and wrinkled olive skin around coal black eyes. But something was wrong, out of place. It was the clothes. He didn't know what he expected a Paiute to wear, but it certainly wasn't a San Francisco Giants baseball cap, a Hawaiian shirt, Levis and Nike running shoes. Steele laughed out loud. More with the relief at his escape than at Jeremiah. Jeremiah joined in. "What're you laughing at?" Steele choked out.

"You sure as hell looked ridiculous," Wilkins roared. "I heard all this commotion coming from that obsidian tube. Thought at first it must be a coyote. They're generally the only ones stupid enough to go in those things. Next thing I know, there's just your head stickin' out that hole, and you with that silly look on your face. Hoo boy, what a sight," he gasped, slapping his thigh. Cody introduced himself, then related his side of the events leading to their unlikely meeting. He felt an unusual but instant liking for Jeremiah.

"Yeah, rumor has it that someone occasionally buys it in there. No proof though. No one ever finds the bodies. I've been comin' out here for forty years. I live in Hawthorne. Every so often the whole maze of fissures will change. Usually after a quake. One closes and a new one opens in another spot, in a different direction. Must have been a little shaker that caused all your troubles. This entire bluff is laced with volcanic tubes and cracks. The guys over at the Ranger station in Lee Vining tell me its common in the geology of active volcanic areas."

"Did you ever find anything unusual in there?" Steele innocently asked. He shrugged a shoulder in the direction of the tube.

"What do you mean *unusual*?"

"You know. Old stuff. Miner's, Spanish, your ancestor's, anything."

"Once, I found a cave with two skeletons. One was suited in old armor. The other was the remains of an Indian. I could tell by her kit. Legend has it that the Spanish visited and traded with us hundreds of years ago. Some even 'married' our women, they say. Such arrangements went against tribal religion, and the couples were banished. I'm sure I found the burial tomb of one such couple that must have been murdered. I left them untouched. When

I came back with an archeologist, I couldn't find them again. The land swallowed them up, much like it just tried to do to you."

"What about the *Lost Conquistador*? Surely you must have heard the stories."

"So that's it," laughed Wilkins. "I knew there had to be a good reason for you to be rootin' around in there. Yeah, I believe the stories are basically true. Somewhere out here, maybe even in there," he gestured toward the mesa.

"One day, someone will be lucky enough to be in there at the right time, and they'll find it. However, our people warn that this place is bad. Sacred ground, you know. Me? I just love the solitude. Another beer?"

33

At first, she thought the sound was just part of another dream. A monotonous drone emanating from some faraway, shadowy realm. She propped herself up and shook her head, not knowing how long she had been awake. The noise was persistent, and definitely real. She felt strange, unsure of herself, as if still in a nightmare. "I haven't drowned after all," she mused. She glanced around her disheveled cabin. The contents looked like the inside of a washing machine just after the spin cycle. Clothes and bedding were strewn everywhere, everything damp. When she opened her cabin door the persistent noise increased dramatically. It dawned on her that it was the sound of *Tambu*'s inboard Volkswagen engine reverberating throughout the twin hulls. "At least the engine still works. I doubt there's a shred of sail left after last night."

She poked her head through the hatch leading into the main salon. Everything seemed normal, with the exception of three sleeping bodies draped over all the available cushioned lounges. Quietly, she climbed up into the living area.

By the looks of it, the crew had as tough a night as I did, she thought. Exxy and Gratvin were collapsed asleep, still in their foul weather gear. Molly had wedged herself between two large sofa pillows and snored softly. Given the state of her cabin, Devoney was surprised to see everything in the salon appeared as it always had, neat and stowed. *Somebody's been tidying up.* She glanced out the forward windshields, and noted that all the sails were furled. To her amazement, nothing appeared out of the ordinary. *Extraordinary,* she thought.

It was then she smelled it. The rich aroma of fresh brewed coffee, subtly laced with the unmistakable smell of tropical jungle. "Land. Thank God." She opened the hatch separating the salon and the aft helm area, the same hatch through which she had witnessed the storm the night before. "I thought I might never have the chance to open this again," she said to Dominic. He stood at the helm, and calmly sipped from a steaming mug, all the while checking the gauges on the cockpit in front of him.

"Ye of little faith. Top of the morning to you too, good lookin'. Sleep well? How about some hot coffee?"

At first glance, Dominic seemed none the worse for his night's efforts. Then she noticed the dark hollows beneath his eyes, and he stood stooped, as if suddenly twenty years older. She joined him, and looked around. The sea was absolutely flat calm. Not a roll, not a ripple or swell. A lone frigate bird soared silently overhead. The enveloping still after the chaos of the recent hours felt surreal. To port, she could see nothing but water and sky. Both were gunmetal gray. In the flat light of early morning she couldn't be certain where water ended and sky began. To starboard was one of the most wonderful sights she had ever seen, even more so because she didn't expect it. "I've died and gone to heaven."

"*Pavao*. Passed through the outer fringing reef about half an hour ago," said Dominic. He nodded at the landfall.

They motored about two hundred yards offshore. And what a shore it was. There appeared to be no beach at all. Just a solid vertical wall of lush jungle, thrusting straight up out of the sea to about five hundred feet. They were close enough to the island that Devoney literally had to lean back to see the palms at the very top. Bursts of different colored flowers interrupted the predominately green wall demanding her attention, their exotic fragrance wafting across the water and permeating the air. The precipice was punctuated here and there by plunging ribbons of vaporous white water. "Purging itself of the rain from our little squall," explained Dominic.

"Little squall, my ass. If that was little, count me out when you hear there's to be a real storm. Where's the pot?" Devoney asked. She ducked back through the hatch and headed for the galley.

And a very nice one at that. Such a shame it won't be with us a whole lot longer, Dominic thought. He admired her backside, as she bent forward under the low hatch sill and disappeared inside.

"It's truly beautiful, Dominic. But I thought you said this was a tiny island." She returned to the cockpit with the pot, and refilled his mug. "Just this section must be about three miles long." She looked over at the jungled cliff. "Where's your house?"

"Up there. Just on the point. Look closely. It's right at the very top. The roof is thatched so it blends in with the jungle."

She looked again at the ridge high above them. At first she didn't see it. Then she saw a flash of light reflecting off something at the very top, directly over their position.

"They must have the glasses on us. Give 'em a big wave." Dominic throttled the engine back a few hundred RPM. "The actual land mass is about five miles long by one mile wide."

"The house at the highest point is about 150 meters above sea level. The outer edge of the atoll surrounding us is about 30 miles in circumference and has only one pass deep and wide enough to be navigable. I'm so tired I almost missed it." He rubbed his red eyes with a fist. "A good dash on the reef would have awakened you a bit sooner, I'll bet. The opposite side of this hill slopes gradually down to a beach and pier area. We should be tied up there in about ten minutes. How'd you like the entertainment last night, anyway?" he asked.

"What the hell happened? I thought you said it was supposed to be clear with smooth sailing."

"Yeah. That was a really good one," said Dominic, ruefully. "Happens now and then out here. Even the best weather instruments and up-to-the-minute data aren't infallible when it comes to the weather. Particularly in the tropics."

"Chaos theory," Devoney said, offhandedly. She put her mug to her nose, and inhaled deeply.

"Chaos theory. What the hell is that?"

"Much too complicated to try and explain now. Especially since you're asleep on your feet. I promise I'll tell you in great detail later. Basically though, it suggests that the weather, among other things, can and will be unpredictable, regardless of any patterns. How did you ever manage to keep us on course and in one piece?"

"I really didn't have much to do with either," he shrugged. "About two hours after you gave up and turned in, the wind really picked up, and with it the seas went even wilder than they were when you were on deck."

"That's hard to imagine," she said.

"Believe it. In a matter of minutes, it was all we could do to hold the helm, let alone worry about a course. The three of us managed to keep her running with the seas. The *Tambu*'s a tough bird, but she'd have been kindling if we ever got sideways to one of those mountains of water. We lost one of the motors for the Zodiacs. It sheared through a half-inch tie line when we bounced off the bottom of one of those rollers. All things considered, we were pretty lucky. I clocked us at seventeen knots surfing down the front of one of those babies."

"How'd you know where we were?"

"Didn't have a clue. At least until the action slowed enough for the boys to leave me solo on the helm, clean up the mess, and take a nap. Just as suddenly as it started, we were out of it. About 4am this morning. Couldn't believe it when I took a SATNAV reading. We cut about ten hours off the usual transit time. Nothing like a little weather to speed things up and make life interesting."

"Interesting! You're delirious. You *must* be exhausted."

Dominic didn't reply. They rounded the point and were headed toward a white, crescent shaped beach. His mind flashed on *HAVOC*, and then quickly he turned his attention to the four figures standing on the distant pier.

34

Cody camped at the base of the bluff with his new friend the Paiute, Jeremiah Wilkins. By the light of the late rising moon, they worked their way around the north side of the bluff and back to Steele's jeep. There they retrieved his sleeping bag, the rest of his camping gear, some food, and a bottle of Chivas Regal. They retraced the same route back to Jeremiah's small campfire. As the contents of the bottle and their fire dwindled they swapped stories. To his amazement Cody learned that in addition to supervising the government's weapons disposal program in the high desert of Nevada, Wilkins was an elder to his people in Hawthorne.

"Doesn't that mean you're a chief?" he asked.

"Sort of," replied Wilkins. He shielded his amusement behind a long pull from the ornate glass bottle.

Wilkins told Steele about several similar volcanic outcroppings located throughout the region. "This one here that nearly ate you…" explained Wilkins, shrugging in the direction of the black wall at their backs, "...covers by far the largest area and probably contains the most fissures."

"Someone really ought to warn people of the potential danger," said Cody.

"Too far off the beaten track, and not a lot of reason for folks to be wanderin' around way out here. Besides, who'd be dumb enough to go in one of the damn things alone, anyway?"

"Just pass the bottle, wiseass."

The more they talked and drank, the more Cody liked Wilkins. A very unusual personal concession for Steele. His line of work demanded that he be a loner, wary and evasive when it came to relationships of any kind, always on guard and uncommunicative. The solitary hunter, always alert and alone. This posture rarely permitted friendships, particularly so quickly. Yet he was at once very much at ease with the big Native American. In the course of their conversation, they discovered both had served in Vietnam, Wilkins on the ground and Steele in the air.

"Figures. Us minorities slogging around in the muck, while you white boys are takin' in the view from above." Both men laughed with respect for their involvement in that conflict, each well aware of the dangers and personal losses experienced and suffered in both arenas.

Wilkins invited Cody to spend a few days exploring the area, and doing some fishing. "I know some of the best golden trout lakes in California. All within two hours of where we sit."

Cody readily accepted, with the concession that they spend the next morning reconnoitering the top of the bluff. "I want to walk those fissures from the top. I have a funny feeling about this place."

"I'll bet you do. It nearly killed you."

"Maybe we'll find something interesting."

"Like the other half of your metal detector?" Steele shivered with the thought. Wilkins chuckled.

The following morning, early, they packed up their camp and hiked to the top of the bluff. "Where's your ride, anyway?" panted Steele. He dropped his pack as they reached the flat of the summit.

"Dirt bike. Suzuki Enduro 250," responded Wilkins. "It'll go just about anywhere. I'm an Indian; remember? Always supposed to be stealthy and sneaking up on folks. Kidding aside, I try to hide the bike as best I can. You never know out here. Two kids in a pickup could leave me with a long walk. It's hidden back down in the scrub brush about twenty yards from your vehicle."

"I'll be damned," exclaimed Cody. "I didn't see a thing and I'm generally good at spotting something out of the ordinary. Let's take a look at these fractures."

They spent the better part of the morning following the clefts across the top of the mesa. Most originated from the sides. A few shallower ones opened from the top. Some meandered the length of the bluff, while others terminated abruptly toward the middle. The monolithic volcanic leftover was about three quarters of a mile square at its top. The two men traced the wanderings of at least a dozen different fissures. At some point, the bottom of each was so deep that it was out of their sight. Cody found his point of entry of the day before. Carefully, he followed the crevice along its top for about 400 yards to a point where it suddenly closed. From there on, all that remained of it was a sliver-thin crack that finally petered out altogether after another hundred yards.

"Like it wasn't even there," he said to Wilkins.

"Maybe it was all in your mind."

"Then how do you explain my dropping in on you?" countered Steele.

"Good spirits. I was almost out of beer when you showed up," he laughed. "If you're about through with this wild goose chase of a treasure hunt, let's go fishing."

They left Wilkins' bike camouflaged in the bushes after retrieving his fishing gear. They stopped in the small town of Lee Vining for supplies. Perched just above the west shore of Mono Lake, the town is the eastern terminus of the only road bisecting Yosemite National Park. By the time they reached town, Cody had already decided to take a few days off and spend some time with his new friend. On the drive in they agreed to fish a basin of lakes they both knew about, just at the east entrance to Yosemite, eight miles west and five thousand vertical feet above Lee Vining.

While Wilkins went to the market to buy supplies, Steele phoned in and retrieved his messages from the coded and scrambled answering device aboard the Pullman in Reno. He hoped there might be something from Devoney. He picked up the CIU on the third of five messages, and cued in the appropriate code to reset the machine. Nothing from Devoney. "What'd you expect, fool?" he cursed himself. He decided to ignore the CIU for the time being, figuring that it was most certainly Conley, wanting to get him involved in some new fiasco. "I thought I made myself clear when I was back there. Hard headed sonovabitch. They can defend freedom without me for a few more days, but the trout can't wait," he grinned and hung up.

Over nine thousand feet high and five miles west on highway 120 the Tioga Pass road from Lee Vining leading into Yosemite, Ellory Lake pools glacial runoff, then spills it over a thousand foot waterfall to the valley far below. A concrete dam at the east end of this high alpine lake controls the falls, preventing a washout of the precarious mountain highway during the annual spring snow melt. Wilkins and Steele pulled the jeep off the road at a spot just below and to the side of the spillway. The stop gave the laboring rental vehicle a breather, and the men a chance to admire the awesome view. Jeremiah stood hands on hips, looking down into the canyon they had just ascended, while Steele pondered the rushing water escaping the lake just above them.

"That's it!" Cody shouted over the roar of the cascading falls.

"That's what?'

"Run enough water at high velocity through those fissures, and I'll bet

you'll flush out the treasure, at least some evidence of it… if it's in there.
   "Now how the fuck are you going to do that?"
   "Details, details."
   "You're crazy, white man!"

35

She was fifty years old, 441 feet long and moved with the grace and subtlety of a bulldozer. Originally christened the *John Nash* after an obscure Revolutionary War captain, currently she sailed under the name, *Star of Persia*. Registered in Panama by a shadowy Brazilian agricultural compendium, the venerable old liberty ship was actually owned by the government of Iraq and operated by *Partidario*. However, the true owner and operators would be nearly impossible to establish, even in the unlikely event anyone were to attempt excavating through the paper trail of ownership. Multiple name changes, walls of phantom companies and constantly changing registries provided more than adequate buttressing.

In the fading light of evening, two Port Santos (Santos, Brazil, just east of Sao Paulo) tugs laboriously maneuvered the *Star* into the narrow confines between two adjacent piers. Empty except for bunker oil, she rode 25 feet higher than she would when fully loaded. Thus, the tugs had an easier time with her and were able to complete their task before dark.

After the tugs departed, Fahid Mohammed Aziz, Master of the *Star*, rang in the 'shut down' order to the engine room from the bridge telegraph, grabbed his cap and stepped out on the starboard flyway. Standing with a man he had never seen before, he recognized Ramon Vasquez on the deserted pier almost sixty feet below. "Qué paso, Amigos?" he shouted, while throwing them a sloppy salute.

"Welcome home, John." The two men on the pier laughed and Fahid grinned. Despite his distinctly far-eastern appearance, all his comrades and crew addressed him as such, homage he supposed, to the original name of his vessel. Somehow, he inherited the moniker when he took command. He couldn't recall, nor did he care, who originated the deceit.

Fahid strode quickly to the gangway, which was just being secured by two of the crew, bounced down it to the pier, then lazily strolled toward the waiting men. Even after twenty years at sea, it never ceased to amaze him how strange solid ground felt when first he set foot on land after a voyage.

"What's it to be this time, gentlemen? Guns to Lebanon, drugs to Miami or women to Syria?" While the *Star*, at one time or another, had carried all such cargo, she was most often legitimately laden. It made it that much easier for *Partidario* when she wasn't. Few ever suspected and, when and if they might, her cargo always had well documented legal cover. Fahid loved to bait his South American associates, and did so at every opportunity.

"Damn it, John. Watch your mouth. You never know who might overhear."

"Right, mi *jefe*. At 8:30pm, in the dark, on this insignificant excuse for a pier. You boys are too paranoid. Lighten up, Amigos. Seriously. What, to where, and when? Not soon, I hope. I desperately need to exchange some bodily fluids con mi chica." Fahid's reputation as a womanizer was legend in most of the *Star*'s many ports of call.

"Jacaranda."

"What?"

"Jacaranda and mahogany. At least that's what'll be on your manifest and visible in your holds," Vasquez said in a whisper, cautiously looking around.

"Who's the gorilla?"

"This is Jimmy, our inland go-between. Fortunately for you he doesn't speak much English. Excellent protection man, though."

"You look as much like a Jimmy as I do a John," Fahid said with an exaggerated smile, while shaking the other man's outstretched hand. He and it were huge and hairy. "Good to know ya, Jimmy."

They headed into the dilapidated warehouse contiguous to the pier. An overhead row of bare yellow light bulbs dimly illuminated the cavernous emptiness within. Other than the echo of their voices, the only sounds were their hollow footfalls, the muffled lapping of water on the support piers beneath them, and the *Star* groaning at her moorings.

"What the fuck is Jacaranda?" Fahid cursed loudly.

"Easy, John." Vasquez motioned for more quiet with two short, downward jabs of his hands. "Mahogany and Jacaranda. Hardwood timber for his royal highness, Crown Prince Saad al-Abdullah, Emir of Kuwait. Both grow like weeds about two hundred miles west of here. Very expensive stuff in the rest of the world. They're going to use it to build replacement furnishings in the royal palace. It seems the Iraqis burned the original during their short stay.

Probably cooked dog with it. Terrific cover for us. Our man from Baghdad will meet you offshore in the gulf to transfer the real cargo."

"Which is…?"

"Come. We'll show you," Vasquez playfully pounded the captain on the back and steered him toward a small office at the far end of the deserted warehouse. Jimmy lumbered along behind them.

Fahid's demeanor was calm, but his mind raced. *North up the South American coast, then to the Sargasso Sea. A right to Gibraltar, then across the Mediterranean. Through the Suez, to the Gulf of Oman. The straits of Hormuz then into the Persian Gulf. Nothing to it. Furniture. Riiiiight.*

36

The essence of stealth and silence, she crept across the rough-hewn floor. Her sensitive toes felt every sliver, every knot and irregularity in the wood, but her large black eyes remained glued to her unwary prey. The enveloping jungle night was alive with a cacophony of sounds, some incessant, some monotonous, others staccato and piercing. A few announced death while others celebrated success and the afterglow of satiation, yet she paid them scant notice. She was consumed by hunger. Arriving at a gap in the flooring, she judged the distance, and then effortlessly executed the sideways leap, landing fluidly with room to spare. The soothing sound of evening waves caressing the deserted beach only meters below the bungalow was very relaxing, yet her body remained taut with sensuous anticipation of an impending kill. The overhead fan wearily toiled in the heavy, moist air but offered little relief from the stifling heat of the calm night. Still, her target seemed unaware of approaching danger. Even for such a short time in this bungalow, she knew it like a lover knows the body of a mate. She had to. Familiarity with the terrain meant survival. Two more short, lightning quick dashes forward brought her within outer range. If she struck now, success would be reasonably certain. Miss, and there was still half the night left to begin anew. She never imagined herself to be a killer. She never imagined. For what seemed an eternity, she waited motionless. In truth it was less than a minute before she attacked.

Devoney watched this life and death drama unfold from the sanctity of her queen size waterbed. She never tired of watching these pale creatures, these geckos on their nocturnal hunting missions. Strange, pale creatures the shape and size of western fence lizards but with huge, wondrous eyes, finger-like toes, smooth pale bodies, and an insatiable appetite for insects. Just as well for the room was filled with all manner of them despite the protection.

Rolling to her side, she tossed the thin sheet completely off. Anything to better benefit from a chance stray breeze which might sympathetically find its way through the protective mosquito netting of her private bungalow. During the first days of her stay on *Pavao*, she spent most of the nights in Dominic's cottage. But as the project progressed, she found that she needed and enjoyed privacy and space of her own. She, Dominic and Cody were much the same in this regard, she thought. "When fully engrossed in a project, we all tend to put our personal and emotional lives on the back burner."

Silently, the bed rippled with her movement. To her incredulous question that first night ashore, Dominic explained that waterbeds were more resistant to the ravages of omnipresent, tropical moisture than more contemporary mattresses. She repositioned herself yet again, stretching her arms and legs to their fullest extent trying to avoid the heat of her own body. Finally, developing a comfortable contortion, she began to parade through her mind's eye the hectic events of the previous three and one half weeks on the island.

<h1 style="text-align:center">37</h1>

After surviving the storm, negotiating the tumultuous pass through the fringing barrier reef and tying the *Tambu* off at the pier, she was given the cook's tour of Dominic's island, *Pavao*. By definition, it was really an atoll; all that remained above water of a huge, ancient volcano, long since extinguished by time and the inexorable movement of tectonic plates. The circumference of the fringing reef measured almost thirty miles and incorporated only two tidal channels. The color change from the outer waters of the deep ocean to the interior tidal shallows was stunning. The depths of cobalt blue quickly gave way to an opulent turquoise that was staggeringly bright at midday. The west portion of the atoll where they docked was the only region that was habitable and was completely covered with heavy jungle. This raised arc of land described about three miles. Scattered over it were three primary structures, a number of smaller outbuildings and fifteen bungalows similar to Devoney's. One of the large buildings served as the dining, kitchen and meeting area. It, like all the others, was constructed entirely of tropical woods and indigenous materials. Completely open the length of both sides; it was strategically perched atop the highest point of land. The views from either side were sensational. Open ocean to the east and the interior of the lagoon to the west. For breakfast, you could catch a brilliant sunrise. From the opposite side of the large and comfortable rectangular room, one might languish with a beverage of choice in the early evening enjoying the ever spectacular display performed by the sun at its departure, all the while looking for the elusive, mystical green flash. A thick thatch of palm roofing overhung either side of the room by a good three meters and afforded ample protection from the multiple daily rain showers endemic to the tropics. Down the center of this long room hung a string of overhead fans lazily churning the thick, pungent air. On the east end of the room opposite the well-stocked bar was an open air, thatched cupola from which one could admire in comfort the changing tapestry of color imbuing the waters of the inner lagoon below. This structure catapulted out and over the jungled escarpment beneath, and in the afternoon provided the most sought after seats in the house. Devoney warmly recalled that she and Dominic had shared much of their time in this perch at the beginning of her stay.

To the north and just below the dining room were eight bungalows, and to the south an additional seven. All were approximately the same size and design. They were built far enough apart to be quite private, but close enough to the main buildings to be convenient and within walking distance. The main path to all the buildings meandered along the spine of the ridge eventually winding its way down to the calm waters of the lagoon and the dock. Each bungalow was accessed by a five meter long wooden span across the jungle and out to the stilted structure. They were designed and built to hang away from the ground in order to best benefit from natural air conditioning from all sides, most particularly from the ocean breezes off the water below. The access path was graveled with crushed coral, and at night was subtly lit with indirect floods ingeniously hidden in the lush jungle undergrowth. Each cottage had its own bath and shower, overhead fan, two queen size waterbeds and comfortable wicker furniture for lounging. Completely open on every side but the entry, and protected by mosquito netting all around, they provided comfortable, albeit rustic, accommodations for short or extended stays.

Well below the dining room and bungalows, even farther to the north, was the generator shack and communications station. The generator was a large, diesel powered monster that ran continuously. Because it was far enough away and downwind from the residence buildings, you couldn't hear its incessant operation unless you were within fifty meters. The communications 'shack' was anything but a shack. It was the only prefabricated building on the island, according to Dominic. "Hated to do it, but the demands of modern electronic equipment and soundproofing required that I fly it in pre-built modules," Dominic explained.

Devoney had only been in the COMM center twice. Once on the tour and the second time to call Laura. Nevertheless, she was astounded by the amount and diversity of equipment she observed. It reminded her of one of the computer labs in the tech center back on the Berkeley campus. "This is much more than a simple transmit and receive operation," she figured, fingering a state-of-the-art computer keyboard.

"Have to keep in constant touch with all my projects all over hell and gone, not to mention the weather," she was informed. She detected an unusual tone of admonishment in Dominic's voice. She made a mental note to return for a better look when Dominic persuasively held her elbow and guided her out of the three-room complex ending their perfunctory visit. She hadn't had the opportunity to get in again on her own due to the speedy arrival of the parts for their attempt to reconstruct *HAVOC*.

The last of the large ridge-top buildings, Dominic's residence, was hardly a bungalow. Devoney audibly gasped when first she saw it.

"You like?" Dominic beamed.

"Dominic...it's...it's..." she couldn't find the right words to finish.

Consisting of five rooms, three full baths and constructed using much the same materials as the smaller residence bungalows, the similarity ceased there. Cantilevered well out over the ocean side of the ridge, the dwelling was built around a circular deck creating a tropical atrium. One side was open and featured a magnificent ocean view. In the center and sunk flush with the floor decking was a spacious hot tub-spa. Each of the five main rooms opened to the atrium via sliding doors featuring etched glass, and each was separated from the next by ten meters of gracefully curving, thatched hallway. An exterior deck that funneled in either direction out from the entry bridge wrapped the entire structure. The master suite boasted a king-size waterbed and was appointed with an exotic assortment of marine artifacts, native masks and other tribal art. "Mostly from PNG," explained Dominic.

He watched as she slowly worked her way around the room carefully touching an item here and there as she passed.

"Definitely masculine tastes," she said, smiling at a display of penis gourds. She slowly turned her gaze from the gourds back to Dominic's eyes and then down to his lap-lap as if measuring him. "Hmm."

The tiled bath sported two large brass showerheads. "Convenient," she said.

"And economical," he added.

The room adjacent was obviously an office. In addition to the tasteful mahogany desk and credenza, there was a computer terminal with dual monitors, a SATNAV receiver similar to the one aboard the *Tambu*, three separate phones, a copy machine, big screen TV with attached VCR, a stereo tape deck and CD player and two large wooden file cabinets. On the wall, over a very large, very old captain's safe, was a Mercator projection of the world. A forest of multi-colored flag pins bristled across it. Most were congregated about the Pacific Rim countries. "Let's me keep location track of my ongoing projects at a glance. At least that's the theory. I must admit I'm currently a little behind."

"You are a very busy man. How do you ever find time to play?"

"For you, I'll make the time," he responded, kissing the nape of her neck while nudging her back toward the master bedroom.

"Finish our tour first," she said, making good her escape.

Two of the other rooms were exactly similar. "Guest rooms... for guests other than yourself, of course."

"I'm honored," she said, facing him with her hands folded in front of her. She bowed from the waist.

The fifth room was the largest, and by far the most incongruous with anything she had yet seen on Dominic's wondrous island. It was a library. Built into each of three walls was a floor to ceiling bookshelf completely filled with volumes old and new. One was entirely classics, the second fiction and the third, entirely reference. There were no windows in the room but ample natural light filtered in from an enormous skylight somehow built into the overhead thatching. On the fourth wall was another large screen complemented by a complete video and sound system. Four chest high square cabinets and four comfortable chairs comprised the rest of the room's furnishings. The cabinets all opened from the top and were filled to capacity with vertically imposed trays of CDs, tapes, microfiche and film. "I can call up just about any information I might need for background on a project from here," said Dominic obviously pleased with the look of astonishment on Devoney's face. "Suppose we need to know the guts of a ruby laser for *HAVOC*. I can access that information and have it printed out on the office computer from at least one of the sources in this room. Like I said, in my business timing is everything. If we need to know something in order to successfully complete a project, we need that information right now. I can't afford the time to call out to the mainland in most cases so I come here and can usually find it. I'm sure you university types know this, but very shortly all this will be obsolete. Soon, my desktop computer will be able to access data from just about any source, anywhere in the world for the price of a phone call. But, until then, this is our resource center."

"I didn't realize that being a facilitator and boat captain was so time critical," she responded.

"It isn't always. But sometimes an hour here or there may make a huge difference."

"Truly incredible, Dominic."

"Wait 'til you see what's down at the shore."

From the landing dock, the main path snaked along the shore of the lagoon in a northerly direction just above the high tide line. Where hardy mangrove thickets erupted from standing pools, sculpted plank bridges carried it comfortably above and across. After approximately 1,000 meters, the trail emptied into a very large, oval shaped clearing that served as vehicle storage and parking area. Here, a peculiar diversity of motorized conveyances was neatly stationed beneath a substantial concrete and sheet metal shed, which was positioned just into the jungle at the point the slope of the island met the coraled shore. Devoney was there when the first of the *HAVOC* equipment began to arrive. She was curious about the wide variety and number of vehicles Dominic kept ready on this seemingly insignificant speck of an island. It appeared that four-wheel drive ATVs were the carrier of choice. She counted at least half a dozen snarling around the staging area. She quickly noted that these noisy intruders to this paradise had a wheelbase that perfectly fit the width of the access path. "I usually discourage their use unless absolutely necessary," Dominic apologized as they watched a convoy of three disappear into the jungle.

A D6 Caterpillar bulldozer resided forlornly at the edge of the clearing next to a sturdy but obviously quite ancient dump truck. "We use those occasionally to maintain the runway," Dominic lectured, as they watched a Tri-Otter drop to just above the surface of the lagoon as it turned on final approach for the strip. A crushed coral causeway connected the parking arena to a 2,000-meter long man-made runway pushing out into the lagoon at a forty-five degree angle from the main section of the island. "Japs built this toward the end of the war as an emergency strip for their ferry pilots. Damn! Those guys are really good," he marveled, nodding toward the approaching aircraft. The plane gently kissed the far end of the runway and was nearly upon them by the time the small puff of coral dust announcing its touchdown had dissipated. Over the next two days, eight similar delivery flights would be made by a number of different type aircraft, each filled with the *HAVOC* parts from their faxed want list. "We use their underground storage bunker for our supplies, lab, and workshop," Dominic continued.

They hitched a ride aboard a medium sized forklift, which was stubbornly manhandling an oversized crate in the direction of the jungle edge of the clearing. The three powerful engines of the supply plane were already whining in run-up after the efficient unloading ritual was complete.

"So where are the locals?" Devoney shouted over the circus of noise engulfing the parking area.

"Killed off by our Japanese friends. There was only a handful though, as I understand it. Used this island as sort of a fish camp. You met some of the incredible fish population living around here on the way across."

They entered the thick concrete bunker after first transiting beneath a canopy of palms. The outer walls were at least one meter thick. The place was built like a fortress. "Those guys were always building to withstand the worst possible attack," commented Dominic. "Even way out here where the Allies wouldn't give this sand spit a second thought. Very cautious, those slants." Devoney winced at his cultural derision.

Once beyond the brooding entrance, they turned a ninety-degree corner and stopped in a large, well lit, 'L' shaped room. The air inside was comfortably cooler and noticeably dryer than outside. "Completely underground," Dominic proudly announced, jumping down from their ride. A low, distinctive hum of laboring HVACs breathed throughout the room.

"You or your associates must be very, very wealthy," remarked Devoney, taking in the stacks of newly arrived parts. A sudden wave of guilt washed over her when she realized the tremendous cost of their endeavor. "When we decided and agreed to do this and you volunteered to finance the project, I must admit I never gave the cost much thought. Rather typical of me, I suppose. Always substance over form, the end rather than the journey. Being a classic academic, I have long since stopped worrying about money and costs. Certainly naive of me in this case. We can still try for some university or government grants and subsidies, you know. I do have connections along those lines, but it might take some time."

"Let's not concern ourselves with that now. My bankers will let me know when I'm overdrawn. Remember, we agreed that you would help provide the technical expertise and I would provide the checkbook... at least until we make it rain." They both smiled for different reasons at that thought. "Financially, my friends and I have been fortunate a few times lately. Especially in some supply ventures in Asia. Timing is everything, as they say." Devoney was going to ask for specifics, but thought better of it when Dominic quickly turned away to supervise some of the unloading.

As near as she could tell, in addition to the crew of the *Tambu*, Dominic and herself, there were at least fifteen other men on the island. They all seemed to have specific jobs, treated Dominic with deference and all appeared to be in excellent physical condition. They ran the nationality gamut from African through a medley of Asian to European. Their common language was English, when they spoke to her at all, albeit haltingly in some cases. French was a close second and they seemed to prefer it when talking amongst themselves. *After all, it is his native tongue*, she reasoned.

In those first few days ashore, she rarely saw another person excepting Dominic. The crew seemed to be content aboard and occasionally she would see one of the *Tambu*'s Zodiacs speed away from the dock or observe it bouncing back across the lagoon. At meals, there was only a bartender who doubled as a waiter and cook. She recognized him to be one of the men who manned the pier when they landed. She and Dominic always dined alone. After two days, the rest of the men began to appear. "I requested the extra manpower to help with the project, in addition to the technicians and specialists we agreed we needed." Dominic noticed her watching all the activity in the bunker, and as he uncannily seemed to do with regularity, anticipated her question about the additional men even as it formed in her mind.

"Now just how is it that you successfully are able to read my mind so often?"

"Remember, I'm a facilitator... and lately a rather lucky and therefore rather successful one at that. I anticipate needs and do what's necessary to meet them. Mind reading is really a form of anticipation after all. Anticipation, timing and location are the keys to my success. By the way, do you have any needs that might require... filling?" he asked.

She grinned, and playfully punched his bare shoulder. Still there was a persistent nagging incongruity struggling for attention at the back of her mind trying to tell her that something was not quite right about all this. She dispatched the disquieting thought as they completed their inspection of the work areas.

"I suggest we construct the various components in here, then assemble the whole thing in the parking clearing. What do you think? Based on the *HAVOC* blueprints, I don't think we'll need a bigger spot. If we do, we'll just fire up the ol' D6 and clear some jungle."

Renewed excitement coursed through her with the notion of their impending project. With it, all other misgivings were soon forgotten. She couldn't wait to get started. "Let's check that inventory and do it!"

The distinctive chirping of the gecko, much like a horseman might make trying to get his mount moving, snatched Devoney back to the *now* from her mental vignette of remembrance. "I hope it'll work," she said aloud to the creature. "Still ... I'm scared and I'm not really sure why or of what." The gecko just stared.

38

After his initial anger subsided, a rush of loneliness enveloped him. Try as he might, Cody couldn't recall ever having been lonely or even lonesome, for that matter… until now. "It was more like a feeling of emptiness, or of being incomplete." He increased the tempo of his stride down the sterile, windowless hall as if to escape the emotion. But there was no evading it. Loneliness it truly was even to such an extent that he felt a real sense of being lost. "Lost is a matter of perspective," he reminded himself. "Damn! I sound like the company manual. I've never been, or at least admitted to being, lost."

His thoughts tracked back to terrifying nights streaking through the deadly skies over Vietnam and Cambodia, and then to a more recent mission culminating in fifteen dreadful days wading through the impenetrable jungles of Peru. *At least I always knew where I was. Or kidded myself that I knew. I was never afraid of being directionless, because I never really was. I was always in control. Self-sufficient. Always prepared, decisive and willing to make the move or to take the action... any action. Even if the doing involved huge risk. At least it was action. Direction.* Glaring at the security guards, he signed himself out of the headquarters building hoping that his countenance wouldn't betray the unrest in his soul. Emotionally he felt wrung out, and immediately recognized the irony. Rarely had he ever let emotion enter into any of his affairs, let alone control his actions. He had learned well. But none of his upbringing, teaching, training or experiences prepared him to deal with the raw emotions that now wrestled unchecked within him. *Must just be tired,* he tried to rationalize. *After all, it's been a long day with much to absorb.*

Finally responding to Conley's priority message after returning to the Pullman in Reno, he picked up a United Airlines red-eye to Denver and caught the waiting government Lear for the rest of the ride to Langley. "Shit! Only twenty-four hours ago I was hookin' lip with Jeremiah on one of the best trout lakes in the Sierra. Now I'm underground somewhere in the most secure building in the world surrounded by all the world's secrets. What a difference a day makes." He dodged through the early morning commuter rush on Taylor Road not really caring where he was headed. "Goddamn lost," he muttered.

The Director of the CIA, DDO Conley, the Secretary of Defense, the Chairman of the Joint Chiefs and all their aides and various department heads stood in silence when he strode into the situation room still wearing his Levis and Pendleton. No one offered him a hand or a verbal greeting. Previously, he would never have noticed whether they had or they hadn't. But the urgency and tenor in Conley's voice on the scrambler from Reno heightened his awareness. He slumped into the nearest chair and the assembled people took their seats. Conley's look was a mixture of concern and anger. "I'll come right to the point, Steele," Conley began. "We have proof that *Wolverine* is alive and active in the South Pacific."

Neither fact really surprised Cody. *Wolverine* had an uncanny knack for getting out of tough spots. And now, apparently, he'd managed resurrection. His main area of operation always was the Pacific Rim. Steele wondered whether the sudden jolt of adrenaline he experienced on hearing these revelations was from relief or anticipation. He put that decision away for later.

"But that's not the least of it," Conley continued, motioning for the lights and projector. What Cody witnessed on the screen chilled him to the bone. As the images slowly began to flash, unconsciously he stood, leaned forward on the polished table and mouthed, "NO! Impossible!"

"Sit, watch the rest, and then listen up, Steele. These came in two days ago via satellite feed from Guam. Our on-station operative has been following them for three or four days. Positive ID on the photos from the Israelis and our own slim data."

Cody stared in disbelief at the figures of the two people on the screen. Then his attention riveted solely on the woman distinctly displayed... Dr. Devoney Marsh. The series of crystal clear photographs were his worst nightmare come true.

"Definitely appears as if they like each other," someone commented from a corner of the darkened room. The casual remark intended as light humor, didn't play with any of those viewing, especially Cody. Once again, he slowly came to his feet, his hands clenched into tight fists. Conley waved him to his chair without a word.

"Lost contact with their boat in a violent storm in the sector just north of New Ireland. I put the *Corona* team on it over at NRO, and they'll let us know if they make contact again.

Cody knew this had to be big for Conley to call in the super secret *National Reconnaissance Office* personnel. Most people in the government, let alone the general public, knew nothing of this agency, or its highly developed satellite surveillance capabilities.

"So, Steele... what do you know about any of this?" The resonant voice of the Director cut through the darkness like a rapier.

Cody was at a loss; then he noticed the looks of suspicion on the faces in the room. The sensate part of his business was suspicion, and many had tried to get something on him for years. He was an outsider and a rebel to most of those working within the imposing gray and white structure. "I haven't a clue," he responded.

It had taken him a good half hour to bring the gathered officials up to speed concerning his whereabouts of late, and to convince them of his utter lack of complicity or knowledge regarding the events so vividly portrayed on screen. In addition to the images, each person in the room was provided a bound notebook filled with documentary, corroborative testimony pursuant to the situation. It had taken every iota of self-control to keep the gamut of his emotions from seeping through during the ensuing discussions in the briefing room. Shock, anger, disappointment and betrayal battled for control of his gut.

"The book says to follow precise operating procedures for getting to the bottom of a situation like this, so we'll run the standard routine for due diligence discovery through all channels and resources," intoned the Director. "We haven't got the assets to spare chasing around the Pacific right now looking for this guy, however. We're almost fully committed to mopping up in Kuwait, and will be for quite a while. So we'll wait until he surfaces somewhere, which we know he always does. One of our Pacific Rim agents will pick him up soon enough if the 'eyes-in-the-sky' don't locate him first. Anyway, he can't possibly do much damage out there in the middle of nowhere. Now that we've finally put a face on this guy, when he surfaces, we'll know it, and we *will* get him. By the way, this discovery process will mean a thorough check of Dr. Marsh by every department. Could turn up some nasty stuff. You in or out, Steele?"

"I'll do my own discovery, thanks," he responded bitterly, looking directly at Conley.

"Fine, Steele. But understand this. It's imperative we get *Wolverine*, and anyone working or conspiring with him. With luck: sooner rather than later. We want his organization taken down and dismantled. Smashed completely, for certain and for good this time. I'm certain you know how this looks to us," he said, tossing aside an implicating batch of photographs. "So don't be surprised if she gets snagged along with him. And don't, I repeat, do not get in our way. This is a government matter, not a personal vendetta. Besides, your past efforts with *Wolverine* don't seem to remain very permanent. If you want to work with us, Conley there'll brief you on what we have in mind, and what we want you to do. If not, stay out of the fuckin' way!" warned the Secretary of Defense. The meeting was adjourned.

In a fog, Steele hailed a cab. "Hampton, the Ambassador." Slumping into the seat, he thought back and replayed the meeting. *I suppose I can't blame them for being suspicious, even if their motives were to get a hammer on me rather than to get after the truth for the right reasons. After all, it was my operation that supposedly sanctioned Wolverine. It could have been a perfect inside double-cross, had I been the mole they supposed. Shit. My genuine astonishment alone ought to have convinced them. And I certainly do know Dr. Devoney Marsh,* he thought. *It has to be stupid coincidence. Incredible, but just coincidence.* This time, it was a rush of heat that coursed through him at thought of her.

Of all those present at the meeting, Conley had the best idea of what emotions Cody experienced when confronted with the evidence. DDO Conley was a fireplug of a presence looking like the short version of Mr. Clean in a suit rather than a T-shirt, and without the earring. However, his gruff manner and speech belied a brilliance that he had demonstrated time and again during his highly decorated naval career, an unteachable asset he brought to the intelligence community. His ability to work with and motivate people landed him his current position with the CIA. Once, over a bottle of Sake, Steele let Conley have just a flicker of his feelings for Devoney. Despite the potent rice wine, the DDO never forgot what was said, and the implications. "Probably won't ever do any better," Steele had understated. "Haven't a clue why she puts up with me." Anyone who knew or understood him would have read volumes in those two statements.

"Goddamn it!" Cody blurted.

"Excuse me?" said the startled cabbie.

"Nothing. Just thinking out loud." He thought, *Shit! How could a nation with the most advanced technology on the face of the planet lose a boat in an insignificant tropical storm? I know for a fact those NRO guys have spy birds that can read the paper over your shoulder in a fog from 250 miles up.*

As he left the conference room, Conley had taken him aside, and told him that *Aurora*, the latest generation of ultra-secret spy planes really a manned missile with wings had been engaged to do a fly over of the area and turned up nothing. "Thousands of islands out there. Off the record, they could be anywhere."

The cab screeched to a halt in front of the Ambassador Hotel ending Steele's musings. "Thanks, man," Steele said to the cabbie as he paid the fare. A uniformed doorman gave him a disdainful look evaluating his attire. He ignored the man, and rushed through the lobby. "I know *one* person who must know where she is."

After retrieving his address book, he dropped his briefcase, and dialed long distance, waiting patiently as routing noises clicked through the earpiece. He was at the end telephone in the house bank of ten. "Hi. This is Laura and I'm not in at the moment. But if you…" The message was cut short when he tomahawked the receiver against the lobby wall.

39

"Are you sure about this, Lew? I've known Molly and her family for years."

"No question, boss. Steve, our man at the Kavieng Club confirmed it. We've been suspicious ever since you picked up the boat and crew in Moresby last fall, and she started making calls every chance she got. The sheer number and consistency seemed unusual, particularly for someone like her."

Lew Sharpe flipped a typed transcript down in front of Dominic, nearly knocking over a cup of steaming coffee. He was a small, wiry man with a full, but immaculately trimmed, salt and pepper beard. His longish black hair always looked as if he had just used a full jar of Vaseline to plaster it back. A penchant for wearing mirrored sunglasses regardless of the hour, held in place by a distinctive hawk-bill nose, made for a very unctuous appearance. A gun-for-hire American mercenary and electronics genius, Dominic hired him away from the employ of the Libyans two years back. It was for his electronics wizardry that Dominic kept him very well paid, and the reason for his presence on *Pavao* at the moment. But he also had an unusual talent for eliciting information from the un-cooperative, sometimes using quite diabolical means. Sharpe relished this part of his job description. Dominic also made certain he kept this talent well honed.

"So, who's at the receiving end, and why haven't we got their total transcript along with hers?" Dominic thumbed through the file in front of him. They sat on the east side of the long dining area watching the morning sun free itself from the horizon.

"She's calling a stateside number in Houston. Its a sophisticated encoding scrambler, and the call is routed from there through God knows where, then to the receiver. If the code is randomly changed at the routing point we can't always break in between it and the other end. Besides, until you got hot on this weather shtick, listening in on her seemed low priority."

"*Partidario?*"

"Bet on it."

Dominic thought for a moment, looked out over the ocean, and then sighed. "Get what you can... however you have to. I'll tell her folks she was lost at sea in the storm. Don't let the Doc see or hear any of it though."

"Done. And my pleasure. I was getting rusty."

It was little trouble for Sharpe and a hulking, swarthy accomplice, known to the men simply as Baker, to convince Molly to join them in the Boston Whaler for a ride across the lagoon to the opposite side of the atoll. They pulled the sturdy craft to the side of the pier across from the *Tambu*. Molly usually slept out on deck when not underway, and the noise of the approaching Whaler's engine awakened her. It was well known by the shore staff that Molly knew the likely spots within the shallows where to catch the best eating fish. They told her that Devoney and Dominic had requested some for a late breakfast. She rubbed the sleep from her eyes, went below and threw on her swimsuit, grabbed her pole spear, and quickly joined them in the Whaler.

"Beautiful day. It's going to be a beeeauuuutiful day," Lew bellowed over the motor noise to no one in particular as they sped across the glassy waters of the inner lagoon.

It took about twenty minutes to reach the reef opposite the island.

"Okay, go left toward that pass there," Molly pointed.

Lew cranked the wheel hard right, throwing them all against the left gunwale.

"No! *That* way," she yelled.

"Keep your shirt on. I just want to check out the lean-to."

It was a palm frond structure used as simple protection from the sun by anyone happening to visit this otherwise vacant and very deserted stretch of beach. It really wasn't a beach, but coarse, crushed reef material strewn across the top of a barely raised section of the fringing shoal. The land area measured about eighty meters in length by fifty meters between the lagoon and the open ocean at low tide. At that time in the early morning, the sea was nearly as calm as the lagoon. The lean-to was at the highest point, and faced the shallows. The island from which they came looked tiny and distant.

Sharpe ran the boat right up on the beach, killing the engine the moment the hull began scraping across the coral. Molly was out before the craft came to a complete stop. She headed for the ocean side, figuring to beach comb for shells while the men did whatever it was they stopped here to do.

"Get her!" Sharpe commanded.

The big man intercepted the unsuspecting Molly just beyond the structure, seizing her arm in a vise-like grip, then swinging her around and to the ground.

"Hey! Let go," she cried in surprised alarm.

Baker ripped the pole spear from her and tossed it aside.

"The Man wants to ask you a few questions." He yanked her to her feet and half dragged, half carried the struggling girl to the lean-to where Lew waited

"Hands."

Immediately Baker bound the girl's hands at the wrist behind her back, adding a tight wrap at her elbows for good measure. The two men had worked together similarly several times. Just startled before, now Molly was truly terrified. She screamed loud and long.

Painstakingly, Sharpe cleaned his glasses with a sweat-stained bandanna, replaced them over his eyes, and then studiously adjusted them on his beak-like nose. "Pointless," he said as Molly gasped for breath. "Who the hell's going to hear you way out here?" He nodded once at Baker.

Grabbing the top of Molly's suit, Baker effortlessly ripped the flimsy material down and away, the motion throwing the frightened girl face down on the rough coral. Casually he stuffed the torn material in the pocket of his shorts.

"Get up, snitch," Sharpe growled at the whimpering girl at his feet.

Sniffling loudly, Molly rolled to her side and struggled to a kneeling position in front of her two tormentors. In a horrible flash of comprehension, she knew exactly what they were after and why.

"So Molly," Lew said sweetly. "Tell us about your conversations with Vasquez."

"I don't know what you're talking about," she cried. Her eyes darted wildly back and forth to each face glaring down at her.

"Sure you do...*Partidario*. C'mon honey. Just tell us and we won't hurt you."

Molly couldn't meet the mirrored eyes, so she looked down and tried to adjust her knees to a less painful position in the sharp coral. She wasn't an unattractive woman. Rather plain or nondescript, and a bit on the sturdy side. However, she never had any trouble attracting attention from men thanks to her very healthy chest. She shook her head in answer to his last question.

Sharpe nodded again.

Baker bent down and purposefully fondled Molly's large, quivering left breast despite her efforts to maneuver away from his insistent fingers. Suddenly, he seized a handful of her, and wrenched violently to the right in a twisting motion. She screamed in agony and once again fell forward on the sand shrieking, this time in pain. Baker began to unbelt his walking shorts, a malevolent sneer of lustful anticipation on his ugly face.

"Maybe later. Let's give her a nice necklace first and see what she has to say. After that, if she talks, you can partake," said Lew Sharpe.

Molly struggled again to her knees as Baker returned from the boat with an old truck tire used as a boat bumper, and a can of something. "Necklace?" she asked.

Sharpe looked down at the half naked form and slowly smiled, nodding. "Now think very carefully about this, Molly. What did you tell Ramon about us?"

"I...I..."

He slapped her sharply across the face with the back of his hand.

Together, they positioned the girl in a kneeling posture, and Baker threw the tire over her head and muscled its lower inside rim over her sweaty shoulders. They tied her to one of the lean-to uprights, securing her at the waist, chest, and neck so she wouldn't fall. Baker took full advantage in the process, excessively running his filthy, callused hands all over Molly's helpless body.

The tire rim chaffed into the girl's soft flesh, her knees were torn and bleeding from the coral, and her bound arms were losing feeling and beginning to severely cramp. Her head stuck almost completely out above the top edge of the tire. She tried to wriggle down and out of it, but the ropes securing her to the pole were too tight. She looked up at them totally bewildered. "What's this for? Please... please. I didn't do anything. Please don't hurt me. What are you going to do?" Fear silenced her sobs for the moment.

"Nothing, if you tell us what we want," Baker lied.

Molly wasn't a brilliant person, but she wasn't stupid either. She realized her only chance was to tell them just enough, something, anything. She understood the odds, and any hope she might be heard or rescued by someone from the distant island were zero. "I made two calls from Kavieng just to tell them what Mr. Dominic and the lady were doing. It was nothing, really."

"That's all? Just two?"

She vigorously nodded, the smell of old rubber almost gagging her.

Sharpe nodded.

Baker opened the can and screwed on a pour spout. Immediately Molly could tell it was gasoline, as the unmistakable smell overwhelmed the stench of rotting rubber. Unbelievingly, as if in a horrible nightmare, she watched as the big man emptied the can into the interior cavity of the tire encircling her neck and chest. Her struggles only served to slosh some of the dangerous liquid out. It stung her skin as it drained down her straining body. The fumes instantly brought a renewed flood of tears to her eyes and she vomited onto the tire. Through her tears of humiliation and pain, she noticed both men lighting big, fat cigars. Without waiting for them to ask again, she told them everything.

PART TWO

The Storm

40

"Good morning."

"Hey, beautiful."

It was the first time since they arrived on the island that Devoney detected a real sense of sincerity in Dominic's greeting. The interest he had shown her during those first days together had disappeared. A sort of complacency replaced the electricity between them once work commenced on the *HAVOC* project. However, every once in a while she could feel the heat flash to the boiling point. Like now, when she heard the interest in his voice. She flushed with the thrill of renewal despite herself. *There is definitely something about this guy,* she thought, crossing the room to join the two men at the breakfast table. She had spent many hours trying to understand her tumultuous emotions. *It all seems too easy. The boat, the island, the material, the technicians, all these bruiser types. Maybe he is just what he says he is. Maybe not, but so what? Nobody's been hurt, including me. How often does a researcher get a chance like this?* But yet, the only truth or consistency she could come up with was, *It's damn exciting!*

Maybe it was the hint of cruelty he brought to their lovemaking, shadows of disturbed emotions deep below the surface of a complex man. Possibly it could be the speed of her involvement, and the excitement of her infatuation. Indeed, he was charming, and apparently somewhat of an international scoundrel if only some of the many snippets of stories she overheard here and there on the island were true. *I'm certainly flattered by his attention. My friends are probably right, I am too uptight most of the time.* Maybe it was even the guilt she felt. *How can I be guilty? I'm not betraying Cody. There never really was a commitment.* Whatever it was, her intuition told her to be wary, but the rest of her was switched on. Dominic stood and held her chair, while the other man hardly raised his head in acknowledgment.

The morning sun, now 30 degrees above the horizon, burned the night's moisture from the surrounding jungle, causing mysterious wisps of steam to ascend randomly all around the dining structure. "It looks appropriately mystical," she observed.

Dominic was again seated, studying a list of some sort. He didn't even look up at her comment. "What's that, Babe?"

"Surreal. Mystical. Looks like I would imagine the earth to have looked during maybe the Jurassic period. Fitting background for the day man tries to harness the weather." She wasn't certain herself if she was serious, or just making a poor attempt at humor. Her wandering eyes were suddenly drawn to a thin column of dark, black smoke vertically blemishing the distant horizon. "What in the world is that?" She got up and spun the large brass telescope toward it. "It looks like its coming from the far side of the atoll."

"Bar-b-queing, I imagine. Great spot for it. Now that the crew is finished and with some time to themselves, they're probably cooking something up for breakfast. I saw a boat headed over that way earlier. Which reminds me, you better eat something now, as we've got a lot to go over before we turn on this atmospheric toaster of yours."

Devoney took a last look through the eyepiece and absently wondered what kind of material could possibly make such oily, black smoke.

"So how do you feel, Doctor?"

Devoney and Dominic stood in the center of the cleared parking area surveying an organized confusion of cables and equipment comprising the nervous system of *HAVOC*. In the center stood a ten-meter gantry surrounded by five concave, highly polished, metallic dishes, the dishes arrayed in such a way that their focal point was the apex of the tower. At the base of the structure was a super-conducting relay the size of a bus. Outward from it snaked masses of critical circuitry and seemingly random groups of machinery. "Like a mother about to give birth."

"Pretty short gestation period, I'd say. Only took us just over a month. Even with the changes and additions we've made and with all the modern technology, I'll bet this setup takes up more space than the original," Dominic commented. "No need for economies of space or size until we can demonstrate that it works. It only matters that we know where it all goes and what it's connected to. Those soggy old schematics were damn concise, yet I'm surprised it went up as fast as it did. Glad we had you and those two Chinese engineers helping. I bet those Germans and Japs would spin in their graves, or at the very least laugh their asses off if they could see this mess."

After breakfast they checked the latest SAT/NAV readouts from Dominic's office terminal, then leisurely strolled down to the shore for a last check of the circuitry and controls. By early that morning, Dominic had already reviewed the overnight intercepts from the NOAA weather station in Honolulu. Soon after his arrival on the island he arranged for a clandestine 'associate' to break into the downlink transmission from the ATS weather satellite. He and his conspirators tried to break into the closer station on Guam, but were thwarted by a watchful station apprentice. "No sense tipping our hand if we don't have to so soon," Dominic reasoned. "Besides, Hawaii is updated from Guam every six hours, and we know we can break in there. Let's leave it at that."

It was two hours before noon, the agreed upon startup time. They walked around the one hundred meter square cleared area where the solar collector panels lay glistening in the sun. Lew Sharpe and the two Chinese technicians were bent over a relay module in their center adjusting something. "Ready, Lew?"

The man in the mirrored shades stood, and thumbs-upped his affirmative response. "These should provide ample power to the cooker, at least until four this afternoon. We've used them to charge the hydroxide batteries inside the bunker, which will provide the necessary power source when the sun isn't overhead. Like the panels, we've staged them in series in such a way that we can more than quadruple the power output over that stated in the original specs," lectured Sharpe, pleased with his work.

"If we need them," added Devoney.

"How long do you think it'll take to know if it works?" asked Dominic.

"Tough to tell," she responded, watching the technicians. "I think we ought to at least have it on through a complete battery discharge. That will give us about eight hours of continuous on line time. We should notice something by then. That is, if this thing will hold together that long. If nothing happens after that, well…"

"It'll run that long, Doc. Don't you worry your pretty head about that. Just worry about the results."

"Let's run a final systems check," said Devoney, heading for the bunker entrance.

Gesturing toward the distant reef, Dominic shot Sharpe a questioning look. He ran to catch up after receiving a single, affirmative nod.

Their *HAVOC* command center was located in the deepest room within the old bunker. It was set up so the four main display terminals were aligned along one wall, and the operations control computer was on the right, perpendicular wall. In this way a single operator could facilitate the device's operation, while easily monitoring the equipment at the same time.

Devoney sat in the operator's chair and nervously brushed back some stray strands of her long hair. Her gaze fixed on the red button to the left center of the master control panel. Earlier in the week, she painted the start button a fiery red using a can of spray paint she found in the construction shed. "It's got to have a red button," she kidded the technician when the module was first installed.

"Let's do it," said Dominic, squeezing her left shoulder. He grabbed the portable PA mike with his free hand.

"Okay boys. Let's clear the area!" His voice reverberated through the structure as it echoed from the outside speakers.

She pounded instructions into the test computer. The bunker's interior lights dimmed slightly until the power surge suppressors came on line.

"Voltage spike inhibitors?"

"Check."

"Relay enable control?"

"Operable on standby."

"Power suppressors?"

"On-line."

"Data links?"

"Interfaced."

"Heat exchangers?"

"Up and running."

"Auxiliary power to control?"

"Standing by."

"Critical circuits?"

"All green."

"Panel on power grid?"

"On-line."

"Discharge suppressors?"

"Operational."

And so it went for over twenty minutes. Now and again they needed to stop and tweak one of the pieces of machinery before continuing down their list. To all present, their checklist run-through seemed to take twice as long as it had during earlier trials. Devoney let the computer do a self-test as the final check item, and when the display before her flashed 'ready', she slumped in her chair and sighed deeply.

"Champagne now or later?"

"What have we to celebrate now?" Devoney asked, trying to hide the concern she felt. "We've just spent I don't know how many gazillions of yours or your associate's money on a Jules Verne device that we haven't a clue whether it will work or not, and you want to toast. You, sir, are indeed a lovable rascal."

"Dr. Marsh, you're far too conservative. You've got to learn to push the envelope. Man has tried to do what we are about to attempt since at least the industrial revolution, and dreamt about it for God knows how long before that. Let's enjoy the process and see what happens."

Devoney closed her eyes, and for a moment Dominic's words seemed to be an echo of similar ones she heard many times from Cody Steele. She couldn't know that Dominic's hoped for rewards were 180 degrees juxtaposed to her own. She opened her eyes, smiled warmly at Dominic, and with a dramatic flourish, hit the enable button.

41

"Hey Earl! You'd better take a look at this."

Earl M. Semple, Chief of Station, put down his Coke, jammed the unused half of a dollar cigar into the corner of his mouth and ponderously lifted himself out of his chair to see what the hell his young native assistant was so bothered about. Their National Oceanic and Atmospheric Administration (NOAA) weather tracking station was perched atop the highest cliff on the southern most tip of the island of Guam in the Northern Mariana Islands. The station was directly down linked from one of the latest generation of weather satellites in geo-synchronous earth orbit some twenty-two thousand three hundred miles almost directly above them. Their hookup with the ATS satellite (Application Technology Satellite) allowed them a continuous feed to their computers or selective television, infrared or radar monitoring for specific weather patterns or anomalies. Their station's coverage area of responsibility was west to the Philippines, south to New Guinea, east to Hawaii on a good day, and north to Japan.

"We take care of one helluva tub of water," Earl was fond of saying.

For the most part, their area was outside the blue water sailing lanes and thus their primary function was to monitor the zone for disturbances which from time to time developed into population threatening weather heading in the direction of land masses at the extreme periphery of their coverage.

While Earl was closely studying his three-month-old issue of *Penthouse* magazine, Barry Umato, his nineteen-year-old apprentice, was following the progress and development of an easterly pressure wave. This particular event had begun in the area around Tarawa atoll less than sixty miles north of the equator and some fifteen hundred miles to their southeast. Barry had noticed the center of pressure change immediately at the commencement of his 6AM shift. For the past six hours he observed that the barometric pressure associated with this particular center was falling steadily as the wave moved steadily west.

"See if we can access yesterday's Honolulu read on this one."

"Already got it," responded Barry, pointing to a neat pile of high altitude photographs and plots.

"How far has it tracked?" Semple ran a dirty thumb back along a computer trace of the center's path.

"About 1200 nautical miles since inception."

"Estimated current winds?"

"Six knots gusting to fifteen at the surface, ten to twenty five aloft."

Kid's good, thought Semple, congratulating himself on his teaching acumen, even though his tutelage had little if anything to do with the young man's skill.

"Picks up cover and begins to circle just here," Umato pointed to a position on their locator map.

Both teacher and student knew that this type of pattern was relatively frequent in the tropics, particularly at this time of year when water temperatures were warmest. Both also knew that when the air masses in these pressure waves developed cloud cover and began to be drawn into a circular format as a result of the earth's rotation, the potential for a tropical storm increased exponentially.

"Okay. Let's upgrade to tropical disturbance and we'll see what it does when it hits the *Zone*. Put it out on the wire to all Pacific stations."

The *Zone* Earl referred to is the inter-tropical zone or point at which the prevailing trade wind systems from the northern and southern hemispheres converge.

"Where is it today?"

Umato's fingers danced over the keyboard of the constant-feed, update console, and seconds later the cursor on the monitor flashed at a point almost right on the equator directly south of their station. Wind speed range for the designation of tropical disturbance had to be between eight and eighteen miles per hour at sea level.

"Fuckin' middle of nowhere," muttered Earl.

"Nothing but a herd of fish out there to worry about. Blow itself out for sure by the time it gets anywhere near the *Zone*. Let me know if she ever hits forty mph."

Earl Semple lumbered back to his chair and resumed his pictorial fantasy.

256
ABPA 27 PHNL 135893
SUBJ/SIGNIFICANT TROPICAL WEATHER ADVISORY//
REF/NAVPACMETOCCEN WEST GU 1210PMLCL TUE AU 29 91//
TROPICAL WEATHER OUTLOOK
CENTRAL AND WESTERN PACIFIC BETWEEN 130W AND 180
NATIONAL OCEANIC AND ATMOSPHERIC ADMINISTRATION
GUAM

WESTERN AND CENTRAL PACIFIC AREA (180 TO MALAY
PENINSULA):
A. TROPICAL CYCLONE SUMMARY: NONE.
B. TROPICAL DISTURBANCE SUMMARY:
THE AREA OF CONVECTION PREVIOUSLY LOCATED NEAR O7N7
162E0 IS NOW LOCATED NEAR 04.6N1 146.9E3 AND IS THE
SUBJECT OF A TROPICAL DEPRESSION ALERT. THE CENTER IS
BECOMING MORE ORGANIZED AND HAS THE POTENTIAL FOR
STRENGTHENING. DEVELOPMENT WITHIN THE NEXT 24 HOURS
IS MARGINAL TO GOOD.
FORECAST TEAM: SEMPLE/UMATO//

42

Hurricanes are extremely intense tropical storms with sustained winds in excess of seventy-three miles per hour. They are the most powerful and devastating natural force on Earth. Responsible for over 500,000 deaths in this century alone, it is the storm surges — the water pushed before them, rather than their prodigious winds — which are the true killers. They have been described as being '...like an animal, vicious, out of control'; '...a monster.' Basically, hurricanes are a meteorological phenomenon requiring several, complex environmental factors: an easterly pressure wave passing through or occurring at or close to the inter-tropical convergence zone, and an influx of cool air usually from the polar region. Occasionally, masses of high altitude polar air mingled with prevailing westerly winds are drawn far down into the tropics. When these three main ingredients are present at the same place at the same time, the result can often be a hurricane. Usually the only difference in a harmless series of tropical storms and a devastating hurricane is the rotation of the later caused by the earth's spin, technically referred to as the Coriolis effect. At the equator this effect is at its weakest. But if these main ingredients are present and two pre-existing wind currents of different speeds collide, the stronger, faster one tends to curl around the slower. If these winds are strong enough and the Coriolis effect magnifies the spin, sometimes a dangerous storm can be spawned from a relatively harmless tropical depression.

A hurricane develops and operates on much the same principle as a steam engine. As the tropical sun beats down heating the surface waters of the ocean, warm moist air starts to rise. In essence, this causes vertical motion in an air mass or a vertical wind current. If westerly winds driven by an easterly pressure wave are drawn to or sucked toward this column in sufficient force and the resultant collision of air masses are given additional spin or 'voricity' by the rotation of the earth, a storm could be born. As the warm air in the column reaches the higher elevations of the atmosphere and collides with cool polar air and/or is naturally cooled by its expansion in the lower pressures of this high altitude, existing moisture is condensed, a process which in turn releases heat, which amplifies and begins the cycle anew. The greater the heat source, the greater the intensity of the potential storm. If a column of warm air in sufficient quantity could be artificially induced and maintained for an adequate period of time, and an easterly pressure wave with associated winds were to be drawn to or collide with this column, under the right circumstances, at least in theory, a hurricane might be created.

When Dr. Devoney Marsh hit the enable switch on *HAVOC*, seven hundred and fifty miles due east of the tropical depression being monitored by the NOAA weather station on Guam, it was with Dominic's, alias *Wolverine*'s, full knowledge and awareness of the potential trouble which might be caused by this potent, meteorological brew.

43

"You look like shit, Cody"

"And I feel worse than I look."

They sat in the dining area of Dr. Devoney Marsh's Mill Valley home working on the final half of a chilled bottle of California Chardonnay.

"So what the hell's going on? Where were you when you called?"

"Hampton. But you first. Where's Devoney?"

"The last time she called was about two weeks ago. Said she couldn't talk long. Something about having to sneak into a communications area to make the call. She was whispering and sounded very far away."

"Physically or mentally?"

"Physically. Lots of static. She seemed quite excited about whatever project she and this guy were working on, though."

"Did she say what it was?"

"Didn't have time to and I didn't ask. She did most of the talking anyway."

"As usual. Did she happen to say where she was?"

"Someplace called *Pavao*. She mentioned it the first time when she called to let us know she was staying over there. Some rich guy's island in paradise I take it. Said she's fine, but apprehensive about the success of the project."

"Did she mention when she might be coming back or when she would call again?"

"C'mon, Cody. You know her well enough to understand that she goes and does pretty much what she wants when she wants, and again I didn't ask. How'd you know I'd be here anyway, particularly when I didn't answer when you called yesterday?"

"Aren't you always here when she travels? Tell me something I don't already know."

"I do suppose it's about time I bought my own place," Laura Demming sighed. "I always seem to have someone else's place to take care of, and…"

"What?"

"Someone else's someone. So why do you look like you've been ridden hard and put away wet?"

"I thought you gave up that horse nonsense when you got your doctorate."

"You can take the horse away from the girl…"

"Yeah, I suppose so. I still fiddle with model trains, not to mention the real ones," he interrupted, thinking of the Pullman still in Reno. "In the last seventy two hours I've cheated death in an earthquake; almost was buried alive; been to Washington DC and the CIA in Virginia; gotten my ass chewed up one side and down the other by my sometimes employer, your Uncle Sam; drunk myself stupid in some fern bar in Hampton and finally dragged myself back across the country to seek your solace. Did she tell you anything else about this guy?"

"Name's Dominic and a real charmer I gather. I probably shouldn't be telling you this, but I think part of her is falling for him. It allows her to get back at you for always taking off. She was really pissed at you this last time."

"Yeah, I figured as much. And I shouldn't be telling you this either. His real name is Franz Toscana, and he's as dangerous as they come. A real bastard. A terrorist, an international criminal of the worst kind, a murderer for hire and God knows what else. Just her type."

"It's probably not the same guy."

"Trust me, Laura. I've got the best sources in the highest places you can imagine. Intelligence is much of what I do. Dominic and Toscana are one and the same and Devoney may be, strike that… *is* in real, life-threatening trouble by hanging out with that slime."

"Do you or your high placed sources have any idea where *Pavao* is, and what they are up to there?"

"Yeah," Cody blurted sardonically. "They've narrowed its location down to somewhere in the Pacific Ocean. What she's doing there, well that's another matter."

"Good. Now that we've got all that solved, how about another bottle?"

"Hey, c'mon Laura. It's 2am and I still have a serious overhang from last night."

"And with whom, may I ask, were you partying?"

"Myself."

"I can be much more fun, a far better conversationalist, and certainly more entertaining."

"I've always suspected as much."

"Besides, you've got to offer something for waking me up unannounced in the middle of the night. Why don't you try me and find out for sure?"

"The way things are going, I just might," Cody said, not really certain if she were kidding him as usual or truly encouraging him. "What would Dev say?"

"Probably she'd tell me to 'go for it' with her blessing." *Besides, who knows what she's doing right now?* Laura thought, *Or most probably, who she's doing right now.* She recalled the excitement in her friend's voice when Devoney gushed the highlights of her new romance in her first call home.

"Pour that wine, wench."

"By the way, my tired hero, in any of your latest adventures, did you ever find that lost gold mine?"

By the time they were halfway through their second bottle, Cody had outlined a plan of action for Laura in the event Devoney might call again. She would continue to housesit as usual, monitoring the answering machine and mail. If she couldn't warn her friend directly, she was to work a pre-arranged code word into their conversation. Steele confessed that he would bug the line in addition.

"Can you legally do that?"

"Do it... positively. Legally... Got anybody else you'd like to listen in on?"

"Maybe the head of my department."

He gave her his contact number at control through Langley in case she couldn't reach him through normal channels. "They like to think they always know where I am and can get me at a moment's notice. Sometimes they can, and in this instance I'll be good and stay in regular touch."

"What do I tell her if she does call?"

"Just tell her I have a crisis situation in which she is possibly involved."

"And if she doesn't buy it?"

"Just tell her it has to do with Sabaka."

"What in the world does your late cat have to do with this?" Laura asked incredulously.

"Well, when I finally admitted to her something about the nature of my work, we agreed on the name as the code word we would use in case either of us got in real trouble. She loved that cat, so I'm sure she'll remember if you have to use it."

"Do you think she'll still know to respond? What if she really is in trouble?"

"I honestly don't know. A contact with her should be enough to give us a start. If she does call, get as much as you can from her, and then get in contact with me as soon as you can. Be careful when talking with her, as I'm sure they will have their own lines wired as well. And you know how to reach me now."

"I wish I could."

During their conversation and the second bottle of wine, the left portion of Laura's bathrobe had gradually slipped down and off her shoulder. It was obvious she was naked beneath. Despite his best efforts to the contrary, his breath caught in his throat at the sight of her full breast almost completely exposed each time she reached forward for her glass. He felt the sudden, insistent, pleasurable pressure of physical need fill his groin. "Maybe you already have."

"What are you going to do in the meantime?" she asked. Cody rose to carry the empty glasses and the bottle to the sink in the kitchen.

"I'm going to see if I can find *Pavao*. If I can, I'll be taking a quick trip to the South Pacific."

When he turned back from the sink to face her, she stood directly in front of him. Her deep green eyes shone with excitement and anticipation, while the delicious woman scent of her enveloped him. He placed his hands on her shoulders in a feeble attempt to keep her at a safe distance. She firmly moved his hands to her hips, and with the motion her robe fell completely away. He gasped at the splendid sight of her naked.

"We both always knew that this was inevitable."

In one swift, sure motion he swept her into his arms, and moved toward the bedroom, turning off the light as he went.

44

At 6pm on *Pavao*, the *HAVOC* machinery was still in operation, and seemed to be running smoothly. The entire technical crew, including Dominic and Devoney, were gathered in the control room of the old Japanese bunker, monitoring a variety of readouts from the bank of screens. Despite five closed-circuit TV cameras strategically arrayed around the island just for the purpose, occasionally one of them would walk outside to observe the operation firsthand, and to take a look at the sky and sea, watching closely for any changes out of the ordinary. Dominic posted one of his men in the dining room at the large telescope, with instructions to report in twice each hour, even if there was nothing to report. The observer had instructions to scan to the east for any unusual weather. It was he who alerted them to the first, definitive visual signs.

"Okay. Let's get ready to switch over to batteries. We're losing output from the solar collectors as of about twenty minutes ago with the loss of sun angle. Lew, are you ready?"

"Anytime, boss."

"All stations?"

A chorus of 'ready' and 'online' responded to Dominic's question.

"Dev, watch the spike suppressors when we switch. I don't want to blow the damn thing out of the water in the middle of its maiden voyage. Now!" he shouted, pulling the crossover relays.

For a moment, nothing happened. Then, all at once, their screens went blank corresponding with a slight dimming of the overhead lights, then simultaneously everything came back up and began scrolling through self-tests.

"Back up with full power," Devoney called out.

A collective sigh of relief moved through the room.

"Well, at least we've definitely got wind. Whether *HAVOC* did it, or it is just an atypical summer's day is a tough call," reported Dominic.

Kevin Levy, stationed at the communications command module, waved at Dominic. "Two-way just came in from some of the boys fishing out on the reef."

Dominic gave all nonessential personnel the day off to pursue whatever they wished, but added a stern warning to retreat back to the bunker at the first signs of any unusual weather. Most of the men providing the muscle for Dominic and helping with the heavy construction phases of their project, absolutely doubted the practicalities of *HAVOC*, and despite Dominic's suggestion to stay on high ground during the test, went fishing.

"Get 'em back on the blower and put it over the internal loud speaker."

"Carlos, COMM 1 here. Do you read?"

"Loud and clear boss. Strange stuff going on out here."

"What's happening?"

"You must have noticed the winds already. It's the water that's really weird. Over."

"Where are you, and tell us what you see?"

All ears and eyes were glued to the speaker boxes on the walls.

"We're about six miles north of you on the ocean side of the shallow reef. We were trolling for grouper when we first noticed it. Over"

Devoney listened intently while her eyes scanned the meteorological readouts. She sat up when she saw the latest barometric pressure figures. She gave the computer three sharp raps as if to scold a misbehaving child, then punched in the backspace command on the previous read.

"Noticed what, and can the 'roger dodger over and out' stuff?"

"The reef top."

"What about the reef top, Carlos? Be very specific. Tell me exactly what you see in detail."

"Well, its not there any more."

"What do you mean it's not there?"

"I've been out here a dozen or more times now, you know, fishing this same spot, and have never seen anything like this."

"Like what? Get on with it, man."

Levy motioned to Dominic, at the same time pointing to the inter-island phone and mouthing the name, 'Akeem'.

"Tell him to stand by," whispered Dominic. Akeem was stationed at the telescope.

"Well, even at high tide, the tops of the reef are exposed by at least a good three feet. They're gone. They're totally underwater. We just pulled in the lines and came right across what should have been the highest point and still had two feet under the keel."

Devoney scanned the repeat barometric read, which was exactly the same as it was the first time, despite her knocking on the instrument. It showed 28.7 inches of mercury...a full inch below what it was when they turned *HAVOC* on.

"Okay, Carlos. Get your sorry butt back in here and tell the crew on the *Tambu* to tie her off securely on four points and two anchors and rig for heavy seas."

"You got it and out."

"All right, Levy. What's Akeem all steamed up about? Can we get him on the speaker?"

A deep voice, heavy with a mid-eastern accent rumbled through the room. "...squall line running parallel to the eastern horizon. Water in the lagoon is almost at the same level as the runway. High cirrus spreading over the entire western sky, and damned if those clouds don't seem to converge or begin directly above us." A low, persistent moaning could be heard punctuating Akeem's report.

"What's that background interference?" Dominic asked.

"Fucking winds been blowing steady like this through the rafters and trees for the last forty five minutes. I think we've angered Allah."

"COMM 1, Carlos, over."

"Stand by, Akeem."

"What is it, Carlos?"

"Waves."

"So what? You're on the ocean, remember?"

"There have never been waves like these in the lagoon."

"Describe."

They could all easily detect the fear creeping into Carlos' voice.

"Long, large and rhythmic."

"Well, they're obviously breaching across the submerged reef, so what's so unusual?"

"The rhythm, boss. I ain't ever seen such long, slow waves anywhere, and I've been fishing the ocean my whole life."

"What's that crashing noise in your background?"

"Lucky you called us back in when you did or we'd be shark food for sure on that reef right about now. These long, slow rollers are walling in the shallows on the ocean side and breaking at least fifteen feet over the reef. Hell, we could surf on these we're on right now and we're *in* the lagoon!"

"Thanks, Carlos. Carry on and don't forget the *Tambu.*"

"Gotcha. Over."

"So how about it, Dr. Marsh. What gives?"

"Barometer's dropping like a brick, winds are sustaining at just under forty knots and we've got a rain squall…"

She was interrupted by Lew Sharpe's loud entrance back into the command bunker. "You'd all better come see this."

"Not now, Sharpe."

"I'm telling you, boss. You'd really better take a look."

They all trooped to the entrance of the bunker, and were greeted by a spectacle that none had ever witnessed before.

45

"Now what are you up to?"

Earl Semple had just re-entered the NOAA weather station carrying a bag of aromatic burgers and fries from the local McDonalds. It never ceased to amaze him how the latest in technology and human development in any remote area of the world was usually preceded by a blizzard of fast food chains.

"Calling for a current picture from the bird," Umato answered, referring to the unseen ATS satellite thousands of miles overhead.

"Why not wait for the programmed transmit?"

"Because of these," he thrust a batch of computer readouts under Semple's ample nose.

On top of the pile of documents, with appropriate notes in Umato's precise hand, was the latest track of the tropical disturbance they had begun watching six hours previous.

"Thought you were supposed to leave early?"

"Yeah, I was. But this looked too interesting to pass up."

They each worked a twelve hour shift four days a week along with two other crews with similar workloads.

"Pressure down to 28.3 inches and its moved 750 nautical miles west in just over six hours."

"What?" Earl dropped his burger bag on the desk and plopped himself down in an ancient swivel chair directly across the desk from his young assistant.

"That's right, Chief."

"Impossible! Those things never move that far that fast."

"I thought so too. But as soon as this batch of high cirrus started forming around noon way to the east, it took off like a runaway bus."

"Damn," said Earl under his breath. He had big plans for the evening with one of the bar girls down at the Kit Kat Club. Now this event might force him to work much later than planned. "Look at that. Heading directly west with no northward movement. Man, that's really weird. Should've turned up hours ago. Current sustained wind speed?"

"50 gusting to an occasional 80 mph," responded Umato. "I upgraded to a tropical storm, and put it out to all stations while you were out getting the grease."

"Good boy," said Semple, thinking how fortunate he was having someone like Barry to cover for him. "What the hell's causing the disturbance to the west there?" He hoisted himself upright, and walked over to their wall map of the station's coverage area. "Looks like just a bunch of uninhabited little coral patches to me. No landmasses to speak of, and nothing on the computer generated models to indicate an unusual formation like this. That's the weather for ya."

"There are some inhabited islands and atolls in the computed convergence area," Umato looked up with some alarm in his eyes.

"No way to warn them though if this thing matures, particularly if it's moving as fast as it was. No big deal. Nothin' out there that matters."

Umato hated the way the American callously treated and referred to his countrymen and most natives, but he was the boss and controlled Barry's future so he swallowed his annoyance and fumed in silence.

The computer generated picture was just formulating on the down link screen to their left against a wall. Both men moved across to watch it materialize.

"Enhance this area," ordered Semple. He outlined a distinct patch of clouding west of them with a pudgy forefinger. When the enhancement process was complete, Semple again dropped into the protesting swivel to study the resultant image. "Damndest thing I ever seen. No reason in the world why these should be towering here."

"What happens if this tropical storm hits those formations?" asked Barry.

"Not very likely. The two events are still too far apart. One or both will certainly blow themselves out or away from each other. In any case, if they don't and they do collide, we've got one helluva hurricane. But, ain't nobody out there that amounts to much to worry about, and we can't contact them anyway. Most likely no radios, no phones or even electricity for a thousand square miles anywhere out there where this supposed event would happen.

Sure would be somethin' to see, though. Nothin' or nobody to worry about, kid."

Umato went back to his console inwardly raging, frustrated with the racist allusions and his inability to warn anyone, even if he could.

257
ZCZA 14 KHCN 0829042   TROPICAL   STORM   FORECAST/
ADVISORY NUMBER 2
REF/NAVPACMETOCCEN WEST GU 1849PMLCL TUE AU 29 91//
TROPICAL STORM OPAL - NEXT - CENTER LOCATED NEAR O3.1N
145.7E1 AND IS THE SUBJECT OF A TROPICAL STORM ALERT.
ESTIMATED MINIMUM CENTRAL PRESSURE 950 MB
MAXIMUM SUSTAINED WINDS 50 KT WITH GUSTS TO 80 KT
ALL SHIPPING IN THE VICINITY IS ADVISED OF HEAVY SEAS TO
THE POTENTIAL OF TWENTY FEET. ALL QUADRANTS RADII IN
NAUTICAL MILES. AT 12+ LOCAL CENTER WAS AT 04.6N1 146.9E3
REPEAT ... TROPICAL STORM ADVISORY - OPAL
FORECAST TEAM: SEMPLE/UMATO//

46

Tomast knew right away something was very wrong. Tomast also understood that when you live with the sea long enough, much like a woman, you think you get to know her every mood; the subtle nuances of her personality that tempt you to guess what she might do next, the minute changes in her that promise and inform of things to love and things to hate...things to beware of and things to embrace. Also like a woman, just when you think you know her well, the sea will do something totally and absolutely out of character with anything you might have expected or experienced before. All these thoughts flashed through Tomast's mind as he paddled across the deep outer reefs of his island that evening, headed for the sanctuary of his village, his home, and his beloved family.

He felt it first. The rhythm patterns of the waves changed imperceptibly. His body, seasoned and schooled by years spent aboard his dugout, intuitively felt the difference. What he didn't know and wouldn't have cared even if he did, was how the sustained winds of the fledgling hurricane to the east were pushing huge masses of water into monster swells and unleashing potential disaster in all directions. Almost imperceptible in deep water except for their slower speed, these swells could be murderous when they reached unprotected shallows. Next, Tomast noticed the unusual, high feather-like clouds forming on the eastern horizon shortly after he acknowledged the change in the movement of water beneath his boat. In and of themselves, the clouds didn't alarm him, but the combination of the two warned him of something definitely out of the ordinary. At about five o'clock, much earlier than normal, he dragged in his coral anchor, threw it in the bow with his daily catch, and pulled hard on his paddle for home. By the time he reached the channel passage through the outer fringing reef protecting his island, the sea had risen far above the normal high tide line. So high, in fact, that the long, unusually slow moving waves easily carried across the normally exposed, protective reef top and through to the shallow inner lagoon. Again, as he had done all too often that afternoon, he glanced over his shoulder at the sky. The clouds now had an ominous billowing texture, and strangely seemed to converge at a point just beyond the eastern horizon. By the time Tomast reached the channel he was all too aware that these slow, rhythmic swells and boiling skies portended something very, very bad.

He sweated profusely with the effort of paddling his heavy boat for speed. Instead of the usual calm waters found inside his island's fringing reef, he encountered big, open sea rollers when finally he made the inner lagoon. The normally calm water there was an oily black instead of its usual inviting turquoise. He saw the tiny figures of his village madly dashing back and forth across the beach less than a mile distant. His view was obstructed for about thirty seconds of every minute as each huge wave slid beneath him. His diminutive canoe seemed to slowly wallow backwards down the massive back of each wave, despite his efforts, the crest above the bow blocking his forward vision. Then the following wave would thrust him tantalizingly closer to his goal of shore, and had it not been for the extreme danger he felt, he might have reveled in the exhilarating thrill of speed generated by his craft surfing down each wave face.

Feeling terribly alone and powerless, he saw his people running wildly about. He couldn't reach them or yell to them as he normally did when he came home. The noise of the enormous waves crashing on shore drowned his frantic shouts.

Suddenly, he became aware of the color. Living in the tropics all his life afforded him the joy of witnessing many fantastically colorful sunsets and sunrises. But never had he beheld color like this, and this time it caused him no joy. The sky came alive with brilliant, huge reds and flaming deep oranges, much brighter than any he had ever seen before. His frightened, reeling mind immediately called up the thought of the fires from Hell. The dazzling evening sky, tumultuous overhead and reflected off the roiling waters of the lagoon, cast a blood red shroud over his island and his people. He felt as if he were paddling into ruin.

When at last he knew he was on the final wave that would put him ashore, he became aware of a new noise building to an intensity matching that of the pounding surf. A howling wind had arisen, whipping the tops of each wave into streams of white froth and bending the palms lining the shore nearly in half.

Tomast steeled himself for the crash he was certain would occur when this final wave met the steep incline of his home beach. Fortunately, the water had risen to such a height that his beach was almost completely submerged. To his astonishment, the wave deposited him harmlessly at the doorstep of his neighbor's house, well above and beyond the beach. He was able to simply step out of his canoe right onto solid ground. Kasha, the robust wife of his nearest neighbor and friend, stared wide-eyed at Tomast, pointed behind him, then screaming at the top of her lungs, disappeared inside. He spun around just in time to see the next mammoth wave marching across the shallow lagoon. Instinctively, he ran inland but was smashed face down into the coarse coral sand as the huge wave ripped its way inland. He was tumbled across the ground for about twenty meters before, gasping and sputtering for air, he was at last able to grab a palm, just as the wave ran its course expending its fury. He stood and looked at the spot where his canoe had come to rest. It, together with his neighbor's home, was gone. There was nothing there but for the hiss and swirl of receding waters. All he could see that remained of Kasha was her torn sarong caught atop some bushes far to his right.

Majanni. His only thoughts were for his wife and family. The chaos of wind, driving rain, waves, and screaming people receded from his mind as the safety of his family propelled him through the havoc. He ran up the slight rise separating his home from his neighbor's, the elevation, at least for the present, placing his house above the onslaught from the sea. As he ran he worried about the wind tearing the flimsy structure apart, and where he might safely protect his family if not inside the bungalow. "Tomast! What is happening?" she screamed. Through the wind, he raced up to their porch, panting with fear and physical effort.

Thankfully he saw that both his children were quietly huddled at either side of his very frightened wife. A blinding bolt of blue-white lightning split a palm less than fifty meters from his bungalow, followed instantly by a deafening peel of cracking thunder, the resultant concussion staggering them all. "I don't understand," he shouted. "I've never seen anything like this. My grandfather told me stories of a great storm he had survived as a young man. But that was on a fishing island far south of here. I just don't know. Quickly! Gather up some food and blankets and we will take shelter in the cave by the waterfall."

"What of our home, our things and our village?" she cried in alarm.

"There's no time. Get what you can ... NOW!"

As if in cosmic punctuation to his urgent demand, another tremendous bolt struck somewhere nearby, accompanied simultaneously by intense, pounding thunder. Without another word, Majanii hurried inside. Tomast took both of the children in his arms and turned toward the village and the lagoon. Flying debris filled the air. He scarcely could see either through the driving wind now whipping everything loose before it, its furious, angry roar deafening. Majanii reappeared just as their roof was torn away and smashed against a nearby stand of palms beyond what had been their beautiful garden.

They ran stumbling toward the inland cliff and the falls as the banshee wind mercilessly tore at them, nearly lifting them off their feet. Just when Tomast thought they might make the cave opening and its perceived safety, another huge surge of sea water from the latest wave engulfed and swept them toward the imposing, black rock face. Tomast tread as hard as he could in order to keep himself and his screaming children above the angry water. Other than cry out an unheard warning, he could do nothing for Majanii without sacrificing one of their beloved offspring. His hands and arms were full. He watched in horror as she frantically tried to swim against the driving current. Majanii, flailing valiantly, was crushed against the rock by thousands of tons of merciless water, and then swept into the cave entrance. The last Tomast saw of his cherished wife was her long black hair, wisping on the surface for an instant before being sucked out of sight and into oblivion.

At the instant before he too would have been smashed against the wall of rock, the water slaked. As it began to ebb back to the lagoon, Tomast found his feet, only to be thrown to the ground hard on his back as the rip of receding water carved away his foothold. The reverse flow began to sweep him and his struggling burden back to the sea. He tried to keep his feet up and out to protect them all from being smashed into any submerged objects still rooted. Suddenly, his right foot slammed into an unseen stump of a destroyed palm with such force that a splinter of his shin was split off and driven up and out through his knee cap. Even as he screamed out in agony, he had the presence of mind to straddle the stump momentarily halting their terrifying journey seaward. For a split second he grieved for Majanii, then struggled to the opposite side of the stump to brace for the next incoming wave. It hit them with the force of a pile driver, once again spinning them all toward the sheer walls of the rock outcropping. He held the forearms of his children, and kicked his left leg with all his remaining strength, to absolutely no avail. He slammed against the rock, spread-eagled backwards losing his daughter to the churning, unrelenting water with the impact. He and his son were shredded along the sharp rock face for what seemed an eternity to Tomast, until again he found purchase on a tall palm, incredibly still intact despite the water's onslaught.

"Why?" was just forming in his pummeled brain when they were instantly fried by a million volts coursing through the tree and their frail, conductive bodies.

47

The tumultuous skies enveloped them in a kaleidoscope of oranges, burnt sienna, and flaming reds. Isolated rays of the late afternoon sun spiked down on the lagoon and island in bolts of brilliant whites and yellows, causing the tropical foliage to reflect a surreal, almost day-glow green. Their hearing was assaulted by the rhythmic, slow pounding of a sea hurricane. It pummeled not the outer reefs as happened in normal weather, but directly against the breakwaters and cliff bases of the main island. A devil wind snarled through the gantry tie-downs, machinery, and overhead palms. They gathered in the parking area ankle deep in a white froth of wind-whipped seawater. But the most incredible sight by far was the towering, pure white cloud mass boiling directly overhead.

"Geezus! Is that us?" shouted Lew. He craned his head back and even removed his ever-present shades.

The columnar mass appeared to begin almost directly over the high point of the island. In actuality, it churned visible at about 5,000AGL where the artificially induced, warm, moist air pumping upward first encountered cold enough relative temperature to start the condensation process. This mechanism released heat adding even more intensity to the germinating phenomenon. It was beginning to feed and grow on itself. The column blasted straight up to a height of 50,000 feet where it finally began to dissipate, feathering outward in a huge, counter-clockwise spiraling formation. In the midst of this visual feast, it started to rain ... the deluge seemingly flowing from two completely different directions at once.

"You've been in the tropics a long time. Ever seen anything like this, boss?"

"I don't recall that I have, boys," Dominic replied, smiling with the knowledge of his creation. The deep red of the sky reflecting on his upturned face created wicked highlights, making him appear truly alien.

"Maybe it'll just top out and blow itself away if we shut it down," shuddered Devoney. She was more than a little frightened by the enormity of it all.

"Hey, gorgeous. It's your baby, and its just startin' to get exciting. Let's leave her on 'til the batteries go or the whole damn thing blows itself apart, whichever comes first."

"Hey. Its your toy on your island."

Trying to be heard, Dominic screamed into the two-way for Carlos and gestured wildly in the direction of the reef where the Zodiac should have come in.

"Carlos, COMM 1, Goddamn it! Come in, for Christ's sake! Where the hell are you guys?"

Entire tops of nearby palms were blowing completely away.

"I lost them coming across the lagoon," he heard Akeem's garbled transmit. "How about getting me out of this wind tunnel?"

"Stay put and keep us posted. We'll call you down if it really gets hairy. Better be working their butts off on the *Tambu*," he yelled at no one in particular.

They all stood, mouths agape, and gawked, for what seemed hours. Yet but ten minutes had elapsed since their opening the bunker door. In that time, the color of the sky deepened to an ugly blood red, and wind speed doubled. Wind driven rain, coming at them horizontally, drenched and stung their exposed skin. As they watched in awe, the lowering cloud column blossomed to the width of the entire atoll and lagoon, churning furiously all the while. The billowy soft, white texture dissolved into a menacing oily gray with little or no definition. Speech over the angry scream of the wind became impossible. As if rooted, still they watched, fascinated. It wasn't until they were assailed and completely enveloped in what seemed an enormous cloud of angry, stinging fireflies that they finally retreated back inside to what they hoped would be the relative safety of the bunker, bolting the heavy steel door with finality behind them. The *HAVOC* machinery carried on.

48

"Now, what the fuck?" Earl snatched his reading glasses from his nose, and dramatically tossed them a bit too hard against the plotting table shattering an eyepiece.

For two uninterrupted hours, they watched in fascination as the cosmic drama played across their monitors "This could be the super bowl, Barry m'boy!" He exulted, pounding his young apprentice on the back. The path of the growing tropical air mass had abruptly taken a highly unusual right angle turn, heading directly north.

"Shouldn't we broadcast a stage alert to all area stations?"

"Naw. Let's wait and see for a bit more. There's nothin' out there to worry about. Anyway, if these two events *do* collide, which I seriously doubt, the momentum will move the whole shootin' match into open ocean."

"I don't think...."

"I don't really give a shit what you think. I'm driving this bus, and we'll play it my way."

"But the procedures say...."

"Don't sweat the small stuff, Umato. No sense getting the brass all hot about a blow in the middle of nowhere."

"But this isn't just a storm anymore, sir. Take a look at these latest reads from the down-link." Umato passed a plotting transparency map and a printed readout across the chart table to his boss.

"Holy shit! Twenty eight years and I ain't ever seen numbers like these!"

"And check the wind speeds," prompted Umato.

Both the tropical storm and the unusual disturbance now directly in its path were registering abnormally low barometric pressures, and each boasted wind gusts over 100 miles an hour. Unsolicited, Umato was on the 'red' phone to NOAA's primary hemispheric weather headquarters in Hawaii. "Hawaii? Barry Umato, Guam. Upgrading the Malaysian bred disturbance we called in earlier to a full-scale blower. Identity '*OPAL*', next in name sequence. Wind speed, 85 nautical gusting to 110. Course now 00 degrees. Barometer 27.3 all still falling. And Hawaii, expect coincidence with the extreme, unusual disturbance in less than sixty minutes."

"That's a Rog, Guam. We've been watching the tails of it here. Had reports of swells to 50 feet from a Taiwanese fishing trawler off Yap, but couldn't raise him again to verify. Say again, barometer."

"27.3 and still falling... both areas."

"Mother Mary! That's no depression. Its a Godamn hole!" came the startled reply.

"Put out a full stage alert to the entire western Pacific Rim area, and do it yesterday!" the voice demanded.

"Pardon me, sir, but Mr. Semple wanted to wait on the alert because it's blowing north not west."

"Put that stupid sonovabitch on the horn, now!" Umato, with a theatrical flourish, handed over the receiver. "It's for you," he grinned.

"Semple... Goddamn it man. What's this bullshit about waiting? Looks to me like you guys got the blow job of the century about to happen right in your back yard and you're sittin' on your fat ass doin' nothing about it!"

"But…"

"I'm way ahead of you. And so's that kid, what's his name? And just what if it decides to go 270 degrees and take out the PI, Japan, or all of those Rim countries? How the hell are you going to rationalize that? Full stage alert, and do it now!"

"But…"

"Now! And see if we can get an airborne *STORMFURY* into the game."

Umato and Semple heard the distinctive, throaty roar of a Navy P3 Orion *Hurricane Hunter* depart from Kobler Field just upwind of their station. It took them a harried forty-two minutes to call out their alerts and to convince the base CO to let the bird go, as the mission was just at the distant edge of the sturdy turbo prop's operational safety envelope. But a chance to be on site for what looked to be the storm of the century, or at least the decade, easily persuaded the flight crew who in turn cajoled the base commander into acquiescence. In that time, the storm, now identified as *Opal*, merged with the unusual phenomena in the Bismarck Sea north of the Admiralty Islands.

The resulting coincidence of the two events spawned a super hurricane, or typhoon as they are called in the western area of the North Pacific. *Opal*, over the coming week, would wreak havoc like no other storm ever experienced in that quadrant of the globe.

"Winds, one five zero to... now off the scale. Barometer... 26.9 and still falling. Diameter at the center, best estimate, 600 nautical miles, but it's also off the scale. Forward speed unavailable. New course, two five zero degrees and steady. It has turned and is heading for shore."

Deflated, Earl Semple sat down hard on the straining swivel. He pushed himself across the room still seated in the chair to his now cold bag of burgers, put his feet up on a stack of satellite readouts, leaned back, rubbed his eyes, and muttered under his breath.

"What, sir?"

"Holy shit!"

286
ABPW10 PTWG 130683
HURRICANE OPAL ADVISORY/ NUMBER 1
REF/NAVPPACMETOCCEN WEST GU 2130PMLCL TUE AU 29 91//
HURRICANE ADVISORY FOR ALL WESTERN PACIFIC RIM AND EXTRA TROPICAL AREAS FOR THE NEXT TWENTY-FOUR HOURS. HURRICANE CENTER LOCATED NEAR 01.9N AND 143.00E AT CURRENT TIME. POSITION ACCURATE TO 60 NM.

ESTIMATED MINIMUM CENTRAL PRESSURE 920 MB
MAX SUSTAINED WINDS 120 KT WITH GUSTS OVER 150 KT
104 KT 25NE 25SE 25SW 25NW
91 KT 45NE 60SE 60SW 45NW
76 KT 60NE 100SE 100SW 60NW
30 FT SEAS 00NE 160SE 160SW 00NW
ALL QUADRANT RADII IN NAUTICAL MILES
REPEAT ... CENTER LOCATED NEAR 01.9N 143.00E
TIDES 12 TO 15 FEET ABOVE NORMAL LEVELS CAN BE EXPECTED NEAR AND TO THE EAST OF THE CENTER. THESE TIDES WILL BE ACCOMPANIED BY LARGE AND DANGEROUS BATTERING WAVES
REQUEST FOR 3 HOURLY SHIP REPORTS WITHIN 300 MILES OF 01.9N 143.00E

EXTENDED OUTLOOK SIMILAR ... USE FOR GUIDANCE ONLY ...
ERRORS MAY BE LARGE
NEXT ADVISORY ON THE HOUR OR AT MAX CHANGE
SEMPLE//
NNNNNNN

49

They lost the video feeds at midnight. Occasionally, someone outside would attempt a transmit, but the communications were never understood, as they came through laced with static and hopelessly garbled. At 2am the *HAVOC* master control panel warning lights and alarms went red across the board, then quite suddenly, the whole thing went totally dark. It was almost as if somebody simply pulled the plug.

The fifty plus year old bunker had been built to withstand everything but a direct hit from an Allied bomb, so those inside did have some sense of safety. But, just like the old steel walls, this sense of security was slowly eroding as well. Tremendous jolts shook the underground structure on numerous occasions throughout the night. They had long since switched to the internal generator for power, and its incessant throb offered some sense of confidence and a counterpoint to the drumming of rain, which sounded as if it were coming down in biblical proportions. The AC was working, albeit not as efficiently as it might, for it was somewhat hot and clammy throughout the subterranean chambers. Each of the three times they cracked open the entry door to see what was up outside, they were met with a gush of water accompanied by a tearing, screaming wind. It took all the considerable muscle of three men to reseal themselves inside. Dominic decided to leave any further attempts at outside exploration until sun up and busied the crew with the *HAVOC* control machinery, at least until the whole thing went down.

"No problem. We have enough food and water for a week should we have to stay inside for any duration," said Dominic to a thoroughly frightened Devoney. "I'm sure it'll have blown itself out or at least away by morning."

"What makes you think that? If in fact we did conjure up something, and the whole deal wasn't coincidence, how can we be certain it'll obey any normal laws of nature? I don't know why I ever allowed myself to get talked into something so hare-brained."

"Oh, c'mon now, Dr. Marsh. Use that pretty head and all that expensive training. All we did was prod ol' Ma' Nature just a bit. She'll have this thing on its way in no time. Remember... just remind yourself of all the potential good we might do if it did actually work. By the way, what in hell were those millions of blinking fireflies?" On purpose, Dominic pushed the one button in her that he knew would take her mind off her immediate situation and away from what he was sure was a successful *HAVOC* test. The teacher and scientist in Devoney at once kicked in right on cue, as Dominic knew they would.

"It's really a very simple phenomenon, but very interesting. Given the appropriate atmospheric conditions, such as a falling barometric pressure and ambient air with high moisture content, plus a predominance of positive or negative ionization caused by any number of reasons under the right set of circumstances, the friction caused by wind-driven sand particles moving across an expanse of like particles, in our case a beach, will sometimes cause an electrostatic discharge. Much the same as when you shuffle your feet across a thick rug on a rainy day then touch something or someone. If our rug is in a dark room, often you can see the static spark of discharge. The wind made the luminescent sand particles seem as if they were flying. They glowed in discharge for up to a few seconds at most until polarity was equalized. Only out there, there was a ton of particles and a ton of wind. Pretty wild, yes?"

Just then, another heart-stopping jolt made the bunker shudder violently. Tiny trickles of sand streamed from a plethora of cracks in the ceiling. Devoney couldn't help but think that the rusting interior of the old bunker was just what the inside of an old tomb would probably look and feel like. "What in the world is causing those? Didn't I tell you I was claustrophobic?"

"No chance. I was with you underwater inside those wrecks in Rabaul. Nice try. Probably just a tree. But I sure wish we really knew what was going on outside. Want to take a walk?"

The rest of the crew had become disinterested in attempting to reconstruct ties to *HAVOC* soon after the control board went south. They settled into small groups spread throughout the few, damp rooms, smoking and talking amongst themselves.

"We can…" Dominic cut himself short and motioned toward the generator room empty of any crew. "It even has a door," he said in a whisper. "I guarantee it'll take your mind off it, and make the night go much faster."

"You're incorrigible."

"Hey Lew. Got anything from outside?"

"Nothing. They must be dug in somewhere, and I think our aerials and dishes are all down so I'm not getting anything from the rest of the world either. Must be the weather," he grinned behind his mirrored glasses.

"Keep somebody on COMM watch all the time just in case, and keep trying to reach Carlos and Akeem."

"Gotcha, boss."

Just at 4:30am, Dominic shook Devoney awake from a fitful nap. She was curled up on the floor with her back to the main monitor table. "Let's see what's going on," he said, helping her to her feet.

She patted her hair in place and rubbed her scratchy eyes, all the while noticing something had changed. The deep drone of the pounding rain outside was gone. She couldn't put her finger on just exactly what else it was, but something was definitely different.

"Hasn't been a sound from outside for about forty minutes. Sure wish we hadn't lost the closed circuit so soon. See, I told you it would blow over."

"Are you sure? Remember what happened the last time we tried to go out?" She pointed at the two-inch deep pool still standing just to the side of the huge steel door.

Dominic spun the bolt lock wheel and cautiously pulled inward to crack the opening. Nothing. No sound, no water, no light, nothing. He strained the door open and disappeared into the early morning, and the eye of typhoon *Opal*.

50

Laura padded into the breakfast area wearing an old T-shirt which accentuated her figure, and did very little to hide any of it. Cody was wearing nothing but a telephone.

"What do you mean, all flights are canceled until further notice? What kind of airline are you guys running? What storm? No I haven't read the paper or seen the news." Noticing her approach, he nodded approvingly and spoke back into the receiver. "I was really busy this morning and didn't have time. Okay, I'll give them a try. Thanks."

"What's up, lover?" she asked. Nuzzling his neck from behind, her long, red hair cascaded down his bare chest.

"What would Devoney say?" He caught both her hands at his hips, and bit her ear.

"Knowing her, as I said last night, she'd love it, and would've probably wanted to watch." She tried to keep it as light as possible despite her deep feelings. "What's the matter? Felling just a tad guilty?"

"I'm not really certain how I feel. I'll... we'll have to sort all this out later. But I've wanted to do that for a very long time." Cody wrestled with his newfound emotions for Laura and his concern for Devoney. "Can you believe Continental has canceled all their flights outbound to the Pacific Rim countries? First time I've ever heard of such a thing. The guy was raving on about some super storm in the Pacific. Heard anything about it?"

"Yeah. Come to think of it, I did hear the weather guy say something about it on the radio yesterday afternoon before you got here. Something about Guam and how it came out of nowhere. Can't say as I was really paying much attention at the time, though. Where are you trying to disappear to this time? Devoney was always complaining about your taking off just when things would start to get serious between you. Now I understand what she meant."

"Oh. We're serious already. My, my. Don't you move a bit fast, Doctor?"

She moved to the window by the kitchen sink, her back to him and unconsciously smoothed the T-shirt down over her hips while she spoke. "I think I know what it was, Cody. And for me, it was *very* serious." She turned to face him.

"But, I'm not hoping or asking for anything more... at least for now. We've got some tangled webs to work out between the three of us, and it appears as if you are leaving me anyway. But, last night was pretty damn good, at least for me."

"Which time?" he winked while dialing a number in Virginia.

51

A strange and beguiling scene met Devoney as she scampered through the narrow opening, following Dominic after he cracked the iron entry door and exited the bunker. Strewn all around the site, despite its heavy steel cable stanchions and reinforced concrete foundations, the *HAVOC* machinery was tossed about as if the hand of a giant had toppled and cast it aside in a moment of agitation. The lagoon was flat-line calm, but menacingly hovered at a level well above the submerged surface of the runway. Mercifully, at least so far, the ground level of the bunker was still a good two feet higher than the level of the sea. Huge chunks and pieces of jungle shrubbery were indecently scattered everywhere, and with the exception of the D6 dozer standing stoically alone in three feet of water, all their vehicles were noticeably gone from the flooded parking area. But the eeriest sight of all was the developing scene in the sky above and around them.

The predominant and most unusual sensation for those observing on *Pavao* was a tangible and almost overwhelming calm. It belied and was totally incongruous with the ravaged and weather-shredded landscape surrounding them. The last of the evening stars twinkled in a clear, cobalt sky above, and mere wisps of stationary clouds smoothly gossamered the brightening ceiling to the east and north. A galleried bank of snow white clouds rose in a line toward the morning star, and ushered the first shards of morning sun across a dreary gray ocean. To the west and south, an ugly, vertical black storm wall rose and merged with the receding darkness that was the night sky. Its departure was occasionally punctuated by random flashes of silent lightning from well within the massive structure.

The clear air of *Opal*'s eye extended nearly seventy miles across as estimated by Dominic. However, in the vortex of the storm, the tropical waters

196

were churned to fury by unimaginably violent forces.

The rest of his team joined Devoney and Dominic outside, and began to spread out through the tangled mess of *HAVOC* when a sharp whistle from their leader brought them back on the run. The seemingly serene bank of clouds to the east came charging across the sea directly at them, heralded by a deep sloughing of powerful winds. When Devoney spotted the churning mass of water beneath the gray wall through her hand glasses, it didn't take much convincing whatsoever to get them all to retreat once again to the perceived safety of the old bunker. The ancient iron door was again slammed shut to a crescendo of howling wind, tearing at their old sanctuary as if in frustration, or as Devoney thought…in warning.

52

Richie Stevens was a wind groupie. If he had a home he would say it was Hood River, Oregon, or in 'The Gorge', as it is known to sail boarders the world over. An incredible slice of valley on the Columbia River east of Portland, and one of the most consistently windy places on earth. He came to the Philippines to sail, partially on a lark, the trip paid for by his girlfriend Marsha, whom he had met six months before at a board-head party back home. She had grown up in Manila, an Army brat of military family. She constantly preached to him about the Philippine Islands' (PI) warm, translucent waters, and strong constant winds, all recalled from her three years' residence at Clark Field, just north of Manila, five years earlier.

Richie was an accomplished sailor in high winds and flat-water chop, but was a relative rookie in the open ocean. He was intrigued and challenged by the uncertainties of wave sailing. After listening to Marsha's tales of paradise so often, he suggested they go, "If you could drop for the fare, babe." Fortunately for Richie, in addition to being spoiled, Marsha was also moderately rich, thanks to an inheritance from a wealthy aunt on her mother's side of the family.

That afternoon he was jibing the outside break off Dinagat Island, almost precisely 300 miles due south of Manila. He enjoyed knowing that his home was almost 7,000 miles of open Pacific away. The morning started clear and warm, with the usual onshore winds beginning to pick up about noon. He confidently cruised in with the shore break for lunch. They gave the quickly forming high overcast little thought, other than to note it made the exposed beach a bit more tolerable than normal. By noon, the overhead sun usually made lying on the sand feel like frying under a blowtorch. He never could figure out how Marsha was able to stand baking the way she did, but he relished the sight of her well-endowed, naked voluptuousness. *What a babe,* he thought when she sat up to greet him.

After lunch and a few brews, he lathered Marsha's back and thighs with sun tan oil, and launched his rig back through the rising waves. *Must either be high tide or a little weather, or maybe a bit of both,* he told himself as he worked his way back outside. The wind had risen markedly since the morning, and the skies were turning darker still. But, after three weeks in the country, Richie became accustomed to the common afternoon tropical squalls, and he hardly noticed these present changes. He concentrated on perfecting his duck jibing through the troughs of the growing waves, and his focus totally absorbed him. He biffed hard when his clew caught the water on a follow through, and as he struggled to set his rig in position for a quick water start, he glanced toward shore. What he didn't see made the breath catch in his throat. "Geez! All I can see is the back of these rollers; I don't remember them being so big out here before. Funny. They seem really slow ... big, but slow. Hmm. Must have been that third *San Miguel* I had for lunch," he thought out loud.

He muscled upright onto the board. Back in sailing position, he picked up speed so quickly he had to squat low bending his knees to keep balanced. He spilled air from his sail to keep from being catapulted over the bow of his board before regaining control, and finally hooked into his seat harness. Once set up and hooked in, he headed out perpendicular to the wave line, thinking that maybe he'd better make this his last run of the afternoon, or at least until the wind died, as it always did late in the day. From his position, cantilevered out from his rig, he could look straight out to the horizon. But strangely, the horizon line separating sky and sea didn't look to him as far away as it should. It seemed a black mass growing ever larger. He squinted his eyes against the wind-driven spray for a better view, but looked up when a flash of lightning distracted his concentration. It was then he noticed it was raining hard. Directly overhead the skies seemed to boil in anger. Strong, intermittent gusts tugged violently at his sail. Yet still he wasn't overly alarmed. "I've sailed stronger stuff in The Gorge," he reassured himself. "Really weird skies though, man. Shoulda put on my small sail at lunch."

He reversed direction, sculpting a clean jibe, and set his course diagonally for shore, or at least where he was certain shore ought to be, for all he could see in that direction were huge fountains of white water ripping off the tops of the slow moving waves. He took one last look seaward over his right shoulder, and that's when it came to him. "Holy shit! A tidal wave."

What he thought was the black line of horizon, was actually a sheer wall of water nearly twenty meters high. The configuration of the bay he sailed magnified the wave as it approached shore, and it grew ever larger by the second. He desperately pumped his rig for more speed, first thinking he might be able to catch one of the smaller ones before the rogue wave caught him. Then, in the cool insight of impending disaster, he reasoned that if he got inshore ahead of it, what then? Once his wave of choice ran out ahead of that monster, he was surely dead meat. "Shit. Man, my only chance is to try to catch and ride it out."

Ritchie felt his stomach leap to his throat as he turned back into the massive wave in order to set himself up. Adrenaline coursed through him with a rush as his body's systems went on overload. He could no longer see the wave's crest towering above him. He became aware of a sound like a freight train approaching, and the compressed air mass driven ahead by the mountain of water nearly yanked the boom from his clenched fists. Whether it was luck or skill, he would never know how he was able to hang on, but he did. Next, he felt a slow lifting sensation as tens of millions of tons of water welled beneath him like some giant presence. He tried to maneuver to keep himself down on the wave toward its trough, figuring if he could stay close to the bottom, and if it didn't break too soon, he might have a shot. But up its flank it carried him. As it forced him higher and higher, he could look inland and easily see over the tops of the waves lined shoreward in front of this moving behemoth. He could make out the beach and the bordering palms, and saw far inland as if looking down at some surreal model. By spilling nearly all his air, he found he could guide the board using his feet alone. A feeling of exuberance swept through him. *Literally surfing to death,* he thought.

Time seemed to slow to a crawl as the huge wave grew nearly thirty meters high, and was still building as it rampaged into shallow water. The deafening noise of the pressure wave was replaced by an eerie silence. The hissing of his board carving the face became Richie's only sound reference. He could literally 'feel' the ominous, throbbing presence of the moving black rampart behind and beneath him, and didn't have to look back to know it was there. "This is almost too easy," he swallowed.

He was locked into the wave about two thirds of the way up the face. It seemed that he was somewhat in control with the one small problem of not being able to get off. His only chance was to stay where he was and hope. Then, sound became an awareness once again. "Sorta like a waterfall," he imagined.

He looked back and up, and for the first time in his entire twenty-six year existence, realized that he really might die. The wave stormed into the shallows adjacent to the beach. The beach area sloped acutely to the water's edge, and in the shallows the monster wave could no longer support its height. It began breaking and breaking big. It lost one-third its height the second it crossed over the beach, yet still was so huge it maintained ten meters of water under it when it hit the tree line. Richie was forced to power his sail with air in order to maneuver lower on the collapsing face to avoid the hungry, cascading break churning above and just behind him. "It would be truly radical if somebody could see me now."

Only his skeg and the tail of his board remained in the wave, its speed and mass sufficient to hold him in place. He could tell he was inland. A roiling collection of debris began agitating in the trough just below his position. Adroitly, Richie slalomed around everything in his path, always mindful of the raging break just behind. Just when he thought it would never end, he sensed a slowing of the tremendous momentum all around him. Lightning lit the sky with multiple searing scars, pulsing a reflection off the dark face of the dying wave in all directions. Richie checked to the left to dodge an enormous tree trunk tumbling in the open trough, and the movement caused his skeg to pop free, the cavitation taking control of the board. Helplessly he slid sideways down the watery incline, frantically working his feet and hands in concert with his rig, still upright but with little directional stability or control. Just when he thought he might save it, he buried his port rail and was launched head first down into the churning abyss. Right before he crashed headlong into the debris churning in the trough, he caught sight of a familiar form being wind milled through the waters beneath him. His last earthly awareness was that he could recognize that lush body anywhere. In a horrible instant before the totality of eternal blackness, Richie Stevens realized that Marsha's voluptuous body had no head.

53

Typhoon *Opal* finally died two days after she hit the Chinese mainland. Robbed of her energy essence, moisture and heat, land friction gradually dissipated her winds and she blew herself out ten days after she spawned. But what an existence she had. *Opal* smashed a path of death and destruction three thousand miles long by 400 miles wide. Preceded by massive hurricane tides and followed by tumultuous seas, *Opal* blew havoc throughout the entire chain of the Philippine Islands. Hundreds of low-lying coastal villages and towns literally ceased to exist during her deadly onslaught. Her legacy was thousands of square miles of cropland underwater. After her forward progress slowed slightly crossing the Philippine mainland, *Opal* spread even wider, then swept north and west, inundating Taiwan and overwhelming some of the southern islands of Japan. Well over 20,000 people died during the first week of *Opal*'s Pacific Rim rampage and another 275,000 were left homeless. Countless boats and watercraft were sunk, and the property damage total went over 100 billion US dollars, even before the storm was officially declared over. The P3 Orion *Stormfury* was never heard from again, once successfully reporting back to base from *Opal*'s eye just south of Manila. The killer storm snatched seven other commercial aircraft from the sky as well. Even the higher elevations inland across her path were not spared. Tremendous loss of life and property were recorded in these normally safe regions, due to flash flooding and massive mudslides precipitated by *Opal*'s torrential rains. Winds in excess of 150 miles an hour destroyed buildings, hurled roofs about like Frisbees, and filled the air with trees, telephone poles, branches, cars and bodies, deadly missiles all for anyone so unfortunate as to be caught out in the open.

Devoney, Dominic, and those lucky enough to have been in the safety of the underground bunker on *Pavao* finally emerged for good three days after the *HAVOC* machinery first rumbled to life. The island took one hell of a beating, but remarkably, much of its infrastructure remained somewhat intact. Propitiously for them, *Opal* merely began her life of destruction over the small island blowing off and away to ultimately develop its full malevolence. *Pavao* was therefore spared the entire brunt of the storm in all her adult fury. They spent the better part of their first full day out just assessing the magnitude of damage and their situation.

It took an additional two days to dig through the destruction of their device, and to re-establish any sort of contact with the outside world, much to Dominic's displeasure. All of *Pavao*'s sophisticated communication equipment not protected in the bunker was destroyed, including the exposed overseas transmit antennae and satellite dishes. The bungalows were totaled and what little of them remained looked as if someone had taken a chainsaw to them. The main house was structurally intact, thanks to its steel anchor beams, but its interior was swept clean.

They found no sign whatsoever of any of the land crew. They did find the *Tambu* capsized and de-masted, floating in the lagoon. She lost one of her four point anchors and during the worst of it, must have spun crazily on the other three. "Hull's are completely intact. Once she was upside down the storm couldn't do much to her so long as she stayed afloat and fixed in the same position. Must have been one helluva wind to turn her over like that on half a naked mast," reflected Dominic.

After a fruitless search on land and in the lagoon for the crew of the *Tambu*, insisted upon by Devoney, a short service was held. She grieved for them more than she might have believed. For her, they were a connection to another, safer world; a link not there with any of Dominic's remaining men.

The east and gradual side of the island was totally denuded of vegetation, and the airstrip had some serious-sized chunks torn from its center. "Not a problem, boss," Lew informed Dominic. "It didn't blow the old D6 away. Shouldn't take us but a coupla hours to have her up and running, and we'll be landing 747s here in no time."

"Leave it for later. We have to get back on line with shore fixes first. Once we've re-established, we can always call in the little Martin amphib if we need to fly out in a hurry."

"Christ, Dominic. What's your friend going to say or do when he finds out we all but destroyed his island? I'm sure there's no such thing as insurance for this sort of thing way our here. And Geez. If *HAVOC* did this to *Pavao,* what did it do to anything or anyone downwind?" Dominic didn't respond, but turned away to hide his smile of satisfaction.

54

Carefully avoiding Conley's web of influence, but with sufficient juice of his own, courtesy of discreet, high echelon contacts within the Agency, Cody was able to negotiate a hitched ride east on a C-5A Galaxy out of Travis Air Force Base bound for Taipei. The military could and would fly through just about any weather. Once there, he hoped to call in some old markers from friends and beg, borrow, or steal an aircraft that would get him to the area in and around the Bismarck Sea. He figured he would begin his search at Kimbe, a pleasant town on the north side of New Britain Island, PNG. Once there he thought for certain he would be able to hire a chopper and the necessary equipment to locate Devoney, and this mysterious island nobody seemed to admit knowing anything about, including its location.

Once his ride was set, he spent the rest of the morning on the phone arranging for Harry in Reno and the Southern Pacific office to have his Pullman returned to Sonoma. He also spoke with Jeremiah in Hawthorne, and extended him the invitation to baby-sit his rolling home for the trip, or to use it should he ever find himself in the Bay Area and in need of a place to stay.

"Hey, man. How long will you be gone?" the Indian asked.

"Can't say for sure. But this shouldn't take long. Maybe two, three weeks at the most."

"Must involve a woman. Need any help?"

"Nah. I gotta do this on my own. Besides, I know the country, and this is a little out of your territory. But thanks just the same."

Cody was still amazed at how fast he had come to know and like this man. He intuitively understood that the Indian's offer of help was real and unconditional. Instinct, born from years of self-sufficiency somehow told him that he could count on Jeremiah for anything asked. It was a rare and warm feeling.

"Send me a postcard, and never, never underestimate me, white eyes. This has something to do with your Doctor, right?"

"Yeah, something," Cody said mostly to himself. "Something."

He never did tell her where he was going or exactly what he had in mind. Laura vociferously protested his leaving. After their night together, despite her arguments and assurances to the contrary, the change in her attitude toward him was obvious. He realized that she seemed almost...well, proprietary, a characteristic she had never previously displayed, at least around him. Giving it little further thought other than to realize the new bonds of their relationship certainly added further confusion to the one that existed previously between the three of them, he left. In the end, she kissed him long, hard, and passionately, then playfully pushed him out Devoney's front door. It took him the better part of an hour to begin setting aside the mental picture of her waving good-bye, totally naked.

After topping off the huge plane's tanks in Hawaii and six hours into the scheduled thirteen-hour Taipei leg, the uniform next to him unceremoniously shook him awake to tell him that they were putting down in Japan at Misawa Air Force Base. "Some sort of real heavy weather," the Major explained.

"What? You must be joking. Just crank this old bird up another ten grand in altitude and we'll be over anything."

"Apparently not this one. Some sort of highly unusual and definitely unseasonable disturbance. They don't want to queer this cargo. Sorry. That's all they told us."

Cody glanced at a huge pile of harmless looking aluminum cases just aft of where they were seated. He was going to ask, but thought better of it, recalling past, similar looking cargoes he had attended in his career, and easily imagining what clandestine mischief, or instant destruction they might contain.

The predicted quick stop for weather in Japan turned out to be an eight-day ordeal on the ground. Even their location far north of *Opal*'s path didn't spare the base from gale force winds and torrential downpours. It was closed tight and battened down hard for the entire week starting fifteen minutes after the Galaxy touched down. Cody sat helplessly watching Mother Nature at her worst out the window of his BOQ room. "Well, at least Dev's not going anywhere either during this mess. I'll just get there a week later if we don't drown here first," he mused, frustrated with his predicament. On the third day of waiting it out, he hammered his first through the bathroom mirror.

The base CO, learning of his status, assured him he would be able to arrange for a flight out to Hong Kong with a connection through Port Moresby once the storm let up. "There are any number of mining company choppers you can surely charter once you're in-country."

"Terrific. I could have swum there faster."

"Say, what happened to your hand, anyway?"

"Really bad hangnail."

55

Once they had the radios back up, it didn't take long to receive the big picture of *Opal*'s deadly path of destruction. They hauled the cots up to the main house from the bunker together with their food stores, and Dominic set up a 'situation room' in what used to be his office. They spread a map of the western Pacific over one wall, and used a magic marker to parameter the path of the storm based on the radio reports. During their first two days' listening, news was sketchy and scattered. In that time window, the storm-ravaged peoples of the Pacific Rim were just beginning to recover from the week of horror brought on by what network newscasters called 'the most devastating typhoon of the century'. Using all available sources for data, Devoney and Dominic plotted the pre-convergence of the two meteorological events that caused the super storm back along their respective paths. Without question, one of the events definitely began brewing very close to *Pavao*. Once the unique phenomena gathered momentum and united with the disturbance from the east, the seeds of disaster were sewn. To Devoney, the human toll was staggering. Even more so as she began to realize from their map that part of the thing traced directly back to them. *Without the HACOC influence, it might not have even been a typhoon. Almost unimaginable, but we probably caused it.* The gruesome thought turned her stomach.

The path of destruction traced across their map resembled a huge, reversed comma, its broad head circling the East China Sea and the end of the tail coming to a point right on top of *Pavao*. Dominic was strangely silent through most of the reports and plotting. Ultimately, she hoped he was as devastated as she with the realization that maybe, no probably, they did at least help create the monster. Little did she understand that his silence merely masked an inward glow of accomplishment, and hid a devious mind already plotting the next test.

That evening they dined in a corner of the empty room together, alone for the first time in over a week. Devoney gazed out over the calm lagoon, finding it hard to believe that only days before the still waters had spawned a horrible progeny. The only telltale signs of the recent devastation were the empty room, excepting their table, and the skinny trunks of frondless palm trees looking strangely absurd without their tops.

"What will we ever do?" she lamented, leaning her chin on her hands.

"Rebuild it, of course," Dominic replied, matter-of-factly.

"You must be out of your mind."

"Here. Look at these." He pulled out a Xeroxed batch of timed satellite images. "Lew got the fax and phone lines back up when we reconnected the bunker generator to the main house power leads. I called a buddy on Guam who is into meteorology and he sent these in this afternoon. Pay particular attention to the times and dates in the upper right hand corner of each." The twelve images tracked a developing pattern of clouds west across the Pacific. Each photograph represented a successive twenty-four hour period. "Notice that this disturbance way west of us was well on its way two days *before* we fired ol' *HAVOC* up," he said, pointing with his fork.

"Yes, but it looks like an explosion here on the third day, right over us." She was referring to a huge gray blot of cloud cover erupting from the center of the third image. "And that's just about the time we started."

"Could be coincidence, Doc. Aren't you guys the ones that are always crying for hard, empirical evidence before committing to anything? What if...just what if that disturbance, which you will certainly agree started way before we went on line, hit a similar disturbance of natural origins which just happened to occur right here, and at just about the same time we lit *HAVOC* off?"

"Well... I suppose that's possible." Devoney's mind ran through the scientific merits of his argument, considering the possibilities, wanting to be persuaded.

"Wouldn't you agree, especially given man's history of complete failure in this arena, that it would be highly unlikely that in this one isolated instance, we really could have set the whole thing in motion? At least agree there's room for doubt. Wouldn't you require further evidence, additional testing, and more hard data? What would your peers say given the same data and information?"

"They would probably say that they needed more proof. Or that there isn't enough tangible data, or that there is just too much coincidence and they probably would suggest that anybody was entirely foolish for even thinking of the possibility, let alone attempting to control the weather."

"Precisely, my dear, beautiful magician. We need another test."

"Now I'm certain you're crazy. You can't possibly be serious. It's too dangerous, let alone the expense. And the risk. Oh Dominic, be reasonable."

"How can we ever be certain? We now know many of the problems. We could streamline it. We could test it when we know there is no possibility of conflicting or interfering natural causes. Wait for a settled period of stable weather. No possibility of coincidence. Somewhere way away from any population centers," Dominic argued.

"What about all those innocent people?" she asked. World catastrophes always seemed to happen to someone else, usually far away. Until now for Devoney, it had been a feeling of comfortable insulation. Then she remembered Exxy and Gratvin.

"We could test in a different area. We don't have to run it 'til it croaks this time. Just fire it up for an hour or two and see what happens. You're the scientist. How would you go about a valid test?" Dominic persisted.

"Well we could…" she paused in contemplation. "No, I couldn't. It's way too soon. I've got to think about it for a while, study the data, and consult with my associates. If we're to blame for all that tragedy… besides, we'd have to rebuild it. We destroyed your friend's island at the cost of who knows what, and what about my career? There are too many unknowns, too much responsibility, Dominic." And for the first time in a long while, she thought, *And what about Cody?*

Dominic stood and walked over to the remains of the telescope stand. "Excuses, Dev. Nothing but excuses, and poor ones at that. I could have the material together in a month, easy. We have the know-how. Already proved that. What about all your dreams of irrigating the deserts, and feeding all the starving peoples of the world? You have to have dreams, kid. Without them, we aren't free."

"I'll need some time to think about it, Dominic. Too much has happened so quickly. I just need time to think."

He turned back to her, his face masked by shadow. "Fine. But just don't take too long."

Dominic had the bunker crew busily repairing the island. The *Tambu* was righted and thoroughly cleaned and refitted in preparation for receiving her new carbon fiber mast from Japan. Lew had the tractor working within hours of their final exodus from the bunker, and soon the airstrip was once again operable. Devoney had little to do during those ensuing days, and spent much of her time in depressed contemplation, walking the beach or snorkeling in the lagoon. She monitored the radio for news updates on *Opal.* As the final accounts summed up the big picture of devastation, she became even more troubled. Dominic was like a man possessed. He was constantly on the phone or fax ordering pieces and parts, or poring over the *HAVOC* schematics and operational readouts. They scarcely spoke to each other at all during the day, but dined together each evening. Their conversations touched mainly on the philosophies of the *HAVOC* concept, and the recent disaster it may or may not have precipitated, and always ended in the question of whether or not to rebuild it. He downplayed her troubled concerns. While she suspected as much, but wasn't entirely certain, Dominic had already made the decision for another test, and was well on his way to implementation. In his own mind, he hadn't decided whether Doctor Devoney Marsh held any further use for him from a scientific standpoint, and while he was still physically excited by her, the proximity of his crew, now all sleeping in the main house, precluded any intimacy. It was a desire fast receding from Devoney's own thoughts as well.

One morning, without saying a word to her, he boarded an outbound plane, which had just dropped off a load of supplies. He left her a crisp, hastily scrawled note, informing her that he needed to attend to some affairs in Japan, and he would return in a few days. She couldn't believe he would just leave her like that. Later, the same afternoon, using all her substantial powers of persuasion, she talked the two-man crew of a supply PBY flying boat into giving her a lift back to their point of origin, Guam. As ultimate coercion, she told them that she was running an important errand for Dominic.

The young-looking copilot transmitted to his pilot, "Don't want to piss off the boss." His observations were received on the inter-plane headset as they taxied across the smooth waters of the inner lagoon.

"Or especially his lady." The pilot fire-walled the old flying boat's dual throttles.

"I can think of a lot of other things I'd like to do to her, and pissing her off ain't high on that list," came the reply.

The two venerable Pratt and Whitney engines easily lifted the empty amphibian out over the cobalt waters surrounding *Pavao.*

That evening, Lew Sharpe got hold of Dominic at the Peninsula Hotel in Hong Kong. He told him of Devoney's abrupt departure. "I should have anticipated it. Damn! Did she say anything to you or anyone else?"

"Not a word."

"Did she call anyone?"

"Nope. Checked all the out-bounds just before I rang you."

"Did she leave any notes or anything for me?"

"Found it on your bed."

"Read it to me. No, better still; fax it. I have the portable machine on in the other room. Where's the PBY headed?"

"Guam. Boss... you sure you want me to fax this to you? I'll have to open it first."

"Yeah. No problem. And Lew?"

"Yes, boss."

"Find her and get rid of the bitch!"

"My pleasure. Do you want me to...?"

"Sure. You earned it. But only if you do the whole thing quietly, and make sure. We don't need her in this any more. No trails."

"You know me."

"Yeah, I do."

At the same hour of the same day Devoney's flight from *Pavao* touched down in Guam, Cody Steele dropped from the skids of a hovering chopper into the warm waters of *Pavao* lagoon, and began the long swim to shore. He managed to charter a PacificAir Mining helicopter out of Port Moresby after spending several hours talking to and bribing many of the local fishermen. Through them, he discovered the location of *Pavao*, the traditional name of the island, a name *not* found on any chart. The sun had just disappeared beneath the horizon, and their low lights-out approach was hidden by the far side of the atoll, any sound masked by the crashing outside surf.

56

"Where the hell have you been?" Laura's emotions ran a fast, emotional gamut after answering the phone and hearing her best friend's voice.

"Too long a story to tell you just now. I'm in Hawaii, and I'm going to spend a few days on Kauai getting my head back on straight. I'm exhausted. You wouldn't believe what happened," replied Devoney, pausing for breath.

"I'll bet. I'm sure it has a lot to do with that boat captain you mentioned last month," Laura said, searching.

"That's barely the half of it. Hear anything from our mystery man?" she asked.

Laura wasn't at all certain what to tell Devoney about Cody, if anything. She had given the matter unending thought, but hadn't expected to be confronted so soon. "Yeah. He stopped by here looking for you 10 days ago. But took off again after dinner," she responded, stretching the truth.

"Sounds familiar. Did he mention where he was going?"

"C'mon, Dev. You know what to expect when he gets that look in his eye. You've told me about it time and again over the past few years."

"Yeah. Nothing."

"I did overhear him on the phone with some military types at Travis, though."

"Well, that could mean anything. Oh well. It was just a far-fetched hope. I needed to run a couple of things by him, but now I guess I'll just have to deal with it myself. What else is new?"

"When will you be back?"

"I had tickets on this evening's United flight to SFO, but I decided to stay over here at the last minute, and just canceled. Should be home in three or four days. How's everything else?"

"With one exception which I'll tell you about when I see you, my life's status quo and boring next to yours."

"Well, hold down the fort and I'll see you sometime probably this weekend."

"Great. I'll look forward to it."

"Oh, and if Cody does get in touch, tell him I need to talk to him about Sabaka. Aloha." The connection went dead, replaced by the obnoxious sound of the dial tone. Laura stared at the receiver in shock. When she recovered, she cursed herself for forgetting to ask where Devoney was staying.

57

Cody came ashore on the low side of *Pavao* well before dawn. Quickly, he hauled in his floatable equipment pouch, and then made for the shelter of a huge pile of fresh debris inland above the waterline. "Must have been washed in by the storm." Instinctively, he breathed through his mouth to avoid the overpowering odor of rotting sea life and vegetation.

While he didn't expect anyone on the island to be in a high state of alert, he reminded himself to be extra careful. After all, he was dealing with *Wolverine*, and on his turf. He camouflaged the exposed skin of his face and arms with a layer of mud, and began to reconnoiter. Working along the shore on a line parallel to the airstrip, he stayed hidden in what was left of the storm-ravaged tropical growth. He came to the parking area across from the bunker, and noted its huge iron door standing wide open. But what really caught and held his attention was the confusing mass of mangled equipment and machinery strewn everywhere around the bunker. "One helluva storm to toss this heavy stuff around like that," he thought. "Wonder what the heck this thing was?"

Just then, he heard the sound of voices filtering down on a breeze from the structure clear at the top of the island. The distinctive throb of a generator firing up startled the silence of the morning. *Great,* Cody thought. *Coffee's on.*

By noon, he counted eight well-armed men working in and on various parts of the small island, but no sign of Devoney or *Wolverine*. He blended into the cover of a hibiscus thicket near the entrance to the main-house when the ninth walked by, less than a body length from his hiding place. The man turned in his direction and paused intently listening, then went into the roofless structure. Cody bit his lip hard in recognition. He knew the face behind those mirrored glasses. "I'll be damned! Lew Sharpe. I should just take him out now and be done with it. Could account for the kill as public improvement. Scum definitely attracts scum."

Cody waited a moment, and then scurried across the open pathway to the relative safety of the space beneath what remained of an overhanging verandah.

"When's the Otter due in?"

Cody could hear the conversation above as if he were standing right next to the speakers.

"We should see them any second, Lew," a second voice responded.

"They just reported at ten miles out."

"Good. Gas 'em up as soon as they're here. Maybe I can catch the bitch while she's still in Guam."

"Not likely. You really think she'll hang around there waiting for you?"

"She doesn't have a clue I'm coming after her, you idiot."

Just then, they all heard the high-pitched whine of a plane approaching the strip below. The characteristic pitch change in preparation for landing caught their attention, momentarily halting the conversation.

"Notify our people on Guam again, and have them check all outbound passengers, all airlines. If Dr. Devoney Marsh is on any manifest, let me know, ASAP."

Cody's blood went cold, and his heart leapt to his throat.

"You got it, Lew."

Waiting an hour and a half for an opportunity that never came to search the house, Cody worked his way back down the steep hillside and took cover in an overgrown area used primarily for a dump, across from the open bunker. He watched the unloading of the Otter while taking inventory of what he had learned on the island so far. *I'm sitting in and surrounded by a high tech pile of junk used for who knows what. Definitely the right island. No clue about Toscana. I've got to get out of here damn quick if I'm going to warn Dev. And I can't do that until it gets dark, unless I knock off at least nine well armed thugs plus two pilots. Then steal a plane I've never been checked out in. Other than that Mrs. Lincoln...* Thoughts tumbled through his brain, each following its own tangent. *I should also contact Laura and have her warn Dev.*

He watched the two Otter pilots supervise the refueling of their bird, and hunkered back into his refuge as they all sauntered by on their way back to the main-house.

"In the air well before dusk," said one.

"Did you check for rock pocks?" responded the other in a clipped British accent.

"Yeah. Just took a bit of paint off the bottom of the fuselage and prop. But no problem with airworthiness."

"Let's do another thorough walk-around before we get outta here just to be sure. Those coral pieces can chew the hell out of that bird, and I sure as tomorrow don't want to lose it over this God-forsaken stretch of open water."

"Right-o, cap'n sir."

The pilot's exchange gave Steele the idea. "I might not be able to overpower 'em all, and I probably can't stop 'em altogether, but I might be able to slow 'em down a bit." He screwed the long, thin Carswell silencer to the working end of his 9mm Browning Hi-Power, while he scanned the parking strip and bunker areas for other signs of life. "If I counted right, they all should be upstairs." He gauged the distance from his hiding place to the plane. Kneeling behind what looked like the remains of an oversized transmit dish, he chambered a round and wiped his eyes with the back of his wrist. Bracing both hands on the edge of the dish and taking careful aim, he held his breath and squeezed off a single shot. A small tuft of sand erupted just in front of the plane's nose gear. He waited a few minutes to make sure no one had heard the muted but distinctive discharge. Nothing. Repeating the firing process, he raised his aim a millimeter. No spout or telltale spray of sand this time. He took out his small binocs, focused on the plane, smiled, and began packing his gear. By the time Lew Sharpe, the two Otter pilots and two others returned to the plane, Steele lay securely hidden at the spot on the other side of the island where he came ashore.

"What the fuck?" swore the copilot.

"What is it?"

"Look at this, will you."

Lew Sharpe bent down and stared at the flattened left nose wheel of the plane.

"How'd that happen?" asked the pilot.

"I thought you said you took a look before we went up to lunch."

"I did. Must have been a slow leak. Those gravel fragments are murder."

"Coral," said Sharpe, still closely inspecting the flat. Slowly, he inserted a finger into a small, neat hole in the tire. "Coral," he murmured again, standing. "Might have done this." He carefully scanned the shoreline, and then whispered something to the two armed men standing with the pilots. They immediately sprinted for the shoreline path. "Well, don't just stand there. Fix the damn thing and let's get outta here!" he erupted at the startled pilots.

Somewhat relieved, Cody slipped back into the warm, tropical water just at dusk. He experienced no trouble avoiding the two, heavily muscled goons who woke him up as they crashed through the undergrowth well before missing his hiding place completely. As he stroked powerfully out toward the fringing reef and his rendezvous point with the chopper, he saw the landing lights of the Otter lift from the runway at the far end of the island. "Well, delayed 'em a bit anyway. Now at least I have a chance to get there the same day they do." A quick thought of Devoney raced through his consciousness immediately replaced by a devilishly smiling, mirrored glasses wearing Lew Sharpe. He filed both mental images away and concentrated entirely on his swim.

58

No matter how hard he tried or which strings he pulled, he couldn't get to Hong Kong until the following morning. There were no international, commercial, private, or military flights leaving Port Moresby until the next day. Steele burned up the phone and fax lines between PNG and a variety of high-placed US government sources spread throughout the Pacific Rim. He requested and begged for help, trying to persuade someone, anyone, for transportation out of PNG. Getting no assistance, he finally resigned himself to the reality that he would just have to leave when he could. Conley's people did allow as how they would keep watch in Guam, Hawaii, and San Francisco. For that he was grateful. He had swallowed his pride and contacted Conley, informing him of his latest efforts and current location. Then he asked for help. Because the Agency still had grave concerns regarding Dr. Marsh's involvement with *Wolverine*, they were happy to provide surveillance. For the third time he dialed Devoney's Mill Valley number, and for the third time got nothing but incessant ringing. "Laura must have forgotten to turn the answering machine back on after our night together." A night that seemed like it happened months ago. Given Laura's very ordered and efficient mind, he was willing to give her the benefit of the doubt. Any other explanations for his unanswered calls were all bad. He left urgent messages for both Devoney and Laura at their University offices. Finally exhausting all he could accomplish given his situation, he retired to the Port Moresby Travelodge. Before falling into a dead sleep, he figured he would at best be twelve to twenty-four hours behind both Devoney and Sharpe.

"Enjoy your flight, Mr. Smith," the attractive, blond flight attendant chirped. She smiled into the mirrors of passenger 2B's dark glasses.

Sharpe's timing was better than Steele's. He was airborne on a United flight direct for SFO forty-five minutes after his arrival on Guam. Even before the Otter's twin props had spun down to stop, *Wolverine*'s people provided him with copies of Devoney's flight itinerary together with her home address, and explicit directions from the airport to her house. However, the information did not include her unscheduled stopover in Hawaii. They didn't know. Sharpe requested a list of essentials he would need for the job, and was assured that all would be waiting in a secure rental vehicle when he landed in San Francisco, together with any updated information or changes. Using the seatback Airphone, he left a progress message for Dominic in Hong Kong.

"More champagne, sir?"

"Ahh. Nothing like going first class," thought Lew Sharpe, extending his glass for a refill. "What a great way to get to work."

59

After only one restless night of a scheduled four on Kauai, she had had enough. *Time to get back home and on with the rest of my life*, thought Dr. Devoney Marsh, as she thumbed through the local Yellow Pages.

Twenty minutes later she was furiously packing in order to make a connecting flight to Honolulu International in time to catch the redeye to Los Angeles. "You just missed the last nonstop flight of the day on any line to SF," the reservation agent informed her. "But you can catch Alaska Air to LA, then connect to SFO and still be there within two hours of the scheduled arrival of that last through flight you just missed. That's the best suggestion I can make, if you're really in that much of a hurry to leave paradise."

"After what I've done and been through these last few weeks, connecting through LA, and spending a few more hours doing it will be a piece of cake."

Waiting at all Hawaii arrival gates in San Francisco, neither Sharpe's nor Conley's people observed her coming up an entirely different concourse after deplaning from her LA connection.

Early the next morning, Steele caught Air Niugini's new Airbus 300 to Hong Kong. There, thanks to Agency intervention, he was VIP'd around the hectic and tedious gauntlet of check-in procedures, then quickly hustled aboard a nonstop Cathay Pacific flight bound for Los Angeles. As fate and luck would have it, his arrival in LA would be thirty minutes ahead of Devoney's. Neither had a clue of the other's whereabouts, yet they were just a few hundred yards apart, waiting at separate gates for a connecting flight to SFO, on different carriers.

Unfortunately, Lew Sharpe was ahead of them both at the SF terminal. He flew directly into San Francisco, arriving there several hours before either of them.

It was with mixed emotions that Devoney Marsh made the drive north across the Golden Gate Bridge, and through the rainbow-painted portal of highway 101's tunnel into Marin County, California. Despite the always dramatic and wondrous sight of millions of twinkling lights ringing San Francisco Bay to her right, it felt less like coming home than she would have hoped and imagined. Her adventure in the tropics seemed years removed, yet was only days passed. Parts of the laid-back lifestyle and stress-free existence she had recently experienced had taken their toll. She knew her home in Mill Valley would never again be quite the same sanctuary that it had always been prior to her trip. "God, what if we *were* truly responsible for all that destruction and loss of life. It *had* to have been pure coincidence. No way can man control or alter the weather. But still, the theory *is* correct." She wrestled and rationalized these thoughts and uncertainties all the way back from Guam. There it seemed, she re-entered the real world as if from a dream. Certainly she was looking forward to seeing Laura again, and her career did have some redeeming aspects. However, her whirlwind relationship with Dominic, the raw excitement and emotion of experimenting with *HAVOC* despite the apparent catastrophe, and especially the intangible lure of the tropics were siren songs all that would hauntingly sing in her brain forever *or at least until I make some serious decisions and changes,* she thought, as she exited the freeway at Blithedale Avenue. Five minutes later, as she turned onto her street, she got the first hint of trouble. A Mill Valley Police squad car and a California Highway Patrol unit blocked the entrance to the winding, tree-covered lane.

"Excuse me, ma'am, do you live around here?" asked a very large CHP officer through Devoney's rolled-down window.

"Right around the corner there," she responded, somewhat startled. It was quite rare to encounter such overt police presence in the small affluent community.

"Can we see some ID?"

"Officer ..." she began in frustration tinged with irritation. "I've flown halfway around the world packed like a sardine into an overbooked plane, waited an additional hour to get my bags off the flight, then fought rush hour traffic all through the City. I'm really tired and I just want to go home down the street there, take a nice hot bath, and get to bed. Now you want me to prove that I live where I live or whatever, while you guys chase around looking for someone's lost dog. What's this all about anyway?" Exasperated, she handed her driver's license up to the big patrolman.

The officer examined her picture, and then bent down and shined his flashlight directly on her face for what seemed way too long. Satisfied, he stood and handed the document to the Mill Valley cop.

"Dr. Marsh, you'd better come with us."

"Why? What for? What's going on, anyway?"

"Please, just get out of your car and come with us, ma'am."

Reluctantly, Devoney did as she was told. She carefully locked her vehicle before getting into the squad car. "That was pretty silly with all you guys around. No offense. Just a habit of mine. I work in Berkeley, you know. Got to lock the car there. Can't be too safe," she said to the patrolman.

"And a good habit, Doctor." He held the door for her.

They drove in silence. Rounding the familiar right hand curve just before Devoney's driveway, they came upon a scene that looked as if it were right on the set of a made-for-TV thriller. The house was bathed in glaring spotlights from at least half a dozen police vehicles. Two fire trucks and a paramedic van were parked helter-skelter across the front lawn area. Crowds of neighbors huddled in small knots here and there, while several local news wagons surrounded by a gaggle of reporters completed the incongruous scene. The entire yard and house were encircled with bright yellow plastic tape emblazoned with the words, 'CRIME SCENE DO NOT ENTER'.

"Oh my God, what in the name of…?" gasped Devoney.

"This *is* your house, Dr. Marsh?"

"Yes. Of course! But what…?"

"Do you know a Dr. Laura Demming?"

"Certainly. She's my best friend. But what's this got to do…?" Devoney stopped in mid-question, her mind scrambling for all the possibilities. Then an awful truth dawned on her. She bolted out of the patrol car before either of the officers could stop her. "Laura! Oh God!" Tearing through the warning tape, she dashed up her walkway toward the wide-open front door. There she ran directly into Cody Steele. "Cody! What in the world?" she stammered. She tried to push by him to no avail.

"Best not go in there."

"Laura?"

Steele nodded once, and folded his arms around the shaking Devoney. He directed her to the side as two detectives, cameras in hand, pushed by them.

"Worst I've ever seen," said one.

"Yeah. Tied spread-eagle to the bed like that, she didn't have a chance," agreed the second.

"She was a looker once, though."

"Was, is the operative word. Horrible."

"Marsh," the first cop motioned toward Devoney, holding a finger to his lips.

"Cody, what happened?" sobbed Devoney. "I tried to call her from the airport three times and she didn't answer."

"I know. I did too. When I didn't get her I called the cops, and got over here as fast as I could. Got here less than a half hour ago myself. Unfortunately, they tell me I was about an hour too late."

"Too late for what? What happened to her?"

"A guy by the name of Lew Sharpe apparently beat us all here," was all Steele offered in response.

"Lew. Lew with the glasses?"

"Yeah. That's the guy. You know him?"

"He works for Dominic," she blurted. "He's sort of an electrician, handyman guy. Very creepy too. But, what's this got to do with Laura?" She paused a few seconds. "Oh God, he was looking for me, wasn't he?"

Steele escorted her slowly down the walk, away from the house, one hand on her elbow, and an arm around her shoulders. Through a torrent of tears, she noticed they were headed in the direction of a tall, dark-looking man with a ponytail wearing a San Francisco Giants baseball cap.

"Yeah, 'creepy' is an understatement. He's one very bad man Devoney, and yes, I'm certain he was looking for you, under direct orders from his boss."

"You must be joking," Devoney spat. She attempted to jerk free of Cody's insistent grasp. "Dominic wouldn't... we were... they weren't going to..." The reality of what had happened, confirmed some of her worst fears.

"I think he was going to wait here, then surprise you when you came home, or just break in. Either way, he was here for you, Dev. Laura was just fodder. She was in the right place at the wrong time."

"Kill me? Not possible. How could you know that? And how could you...they know it was Lew?"

"One of your observant neighbors saw a fellow in the area, not near the house mind you, but close by. Wouldn't have said anything to anyone, but she thought the mirrored sunglasses were kind of strange, particularly at night. Plus he left a few partials. Fingerprints the police have already matched, courtesy of some high placed friends of mine and a portable fingerprint fax. He obviously left in a hurry before he could sanitize the place. The cops I called must have surprised him." He paused a moment while she wiped her eyes. "Dr. Devoney Marsh, I would like you to meet Jeremiah Wilkins," he said as they came up to the tall Indian.

"My pleasure. I'm sorry for these circumstances," Wilkins said.

In a nightmarish daze, Devoney took and shook his proffered hand. "Thanks. Thank you. Who are you, anyway?"

Two county coroners emerged from the house wheeling a spindly stretcher between them. Strapped to the stretcher was a black rubberized body bag, obviously occupied.

"Laura! NOOooooo!" screamed Devoney.

Wilkins caught up to her a half step ahead of Steele.

60

Doing a monotonous six knots, the *Star of India* churned steadily along through the Sargasso Sea. Her Master, Fahid Mohammed Aziz, aka 'John', lounged shirtless against one of four huge ventilators on the flying bridge. Even after a week of carnal passion, carried out in every conceivable position, he still became aroused when admiring the luscious form and shape of his latest 'assistant', Chantelle. She also lounged topless. However, Chantelle was in a low-slung beach chair discreetly out of sight from most crew members working on the decks below the bridge.

Chantelle's tall, voluptuous body was that of an Atlantic City showgirl, which she had been for three years before deciding to work her way to Europe and the Mediterranean performing aboard a cruise ship. Fahid discovered her in a bar in Casablanca. He had put the *Star* into the fabled port before heading back down and across the Atlantic to Porto de Santos, Brazil. There they would pick up the second half of their cargo. Deciding that he and the ship's crew deserved at least one night of celebration for successfully delivering the first half of their 'wood' to Iraq, he delayed their Atlantic voyage for a few days. The *Star*'s first delivery had gone just as Vasquez and *Partidario* had planned. The crew could afford a night or so of luxury. Fahid had twenty million dollars in uncut diamonds as payment for the first installment, locked in the Captain's safe. His and Chantelle's attraction was mutual and instantaneous. The first time that evening they consummated their passion quickly, albeit quite loudly in the men's room of the Talisman Bar and Dinner Club. After, he invited her on a tour of his ship. The tour got no further than his quarters on the boat deck. Following a night of insatiable lust, he asked her if she would care to join him and the *Star* for the journey to South America.

"Only if I get to see the rest of the ship," she responded.

Not one of the crew said a word after putting to sea and discovering their new shipmate. Chantelle was not the first assistant to cruise with their captain.

Fahid strode to the platform called the monkey island, and caressed Chantelle's full right breast in passing. She gave a slight moan of approval but didn't look up, instead remaining glued to her action/adventure novel. The *Star* was steered and navigated from this raised metal area. In the binnacle he checked the magnetic compass and the engine speed telegraph out of habit, even though he could tell from the early afternoon sun that they were headed correctly. From years of experience, he gauged their speed by the feel of the venerable old girl's engines throbbing beneath his sandaled feet. He rang for his first officer on the sound powered phone.

"Paul, get Derek up here on the QT, will ya'?"

"Aye, Captain."

The crew was a group of close knit, well paid associates, each with a variety of skills. On shore, most had trained together at one time or another. Some in Palestine with the Izz el-Deen al Qassam, the militant brigade of Hamas. The remainder in Pakistan or Afghanistan with al-Qaeda. Despite pledged allegiance to several extremist organizations including *Partidario,* all were radical Islamic Fundamentalists. All had long since abandoned nearly every Muslim diktat for the pleasures of capitalism and flesh. They had seen combat either with the PLA and Hezbollah against Israel, or as guerillas with the Mujahdeen against the Soviets in Afghanistan. Crewing the Star was a vacation by comparison. These were some of the most heartless, evil men on the planet. Their Jihad, or Holy War, was not in the name of Allah, but rather for their own sakes. Power was their motivator in the guise of religion, money their fuel. They would as soon murder in cold blood as have a beer. Not the least of their talent was a combined ability to efficiently sail a nearly fifty-year-old ship. However, despite their mutual camaraderie everywhere else, when at sea they treated Fahid with deserved deference. All had experienced him saving their butts with shrewd maneuvers in the old ship during many a foul storm. The entire crew was aware of Fahid's plan for stealing the payout for the second half of their delivery.

"Babe, best put a top on before Derek gets here. I want him to pay attention to what I have to say, and not have his interest wandering to my two wonderful playmates. This shouldn't take long, and then you can get back to your tan. You might even get a kick out of this."

"If you insist, Johnny," she said. Slowly she stood facing him. She stretched her arms over her head, and then slowly put on her shirt. "This better be good."

Five minutes later, Derek Powell, a tall, athletic youth of 26, stood next to Fahid and Chantelle as all three watched a pod of dolphin frolicking in the bow wave.

"Amazing creatures," observed Fahid.

"I think they're Bottlenose," said Derek.

"Very intelligent they say. Legend has it that they've even rescued a sailor on occasion. Quite protective of their own as well: which brings me to the reason I called you up here. Who was that guy you were talking with in Gibraltar?"

"What guy?" asked Derek somewhat defensively.

"The official at Port Authority. The crew was instructed to remain close by the pier, yet you wandered nearly all the way across the compound. Who was he?"

"I don't know what you're talking about, sir," stammered Powell, turning noticeably pale, despite his tanned face.

"Don't give me that crap, Powell. I wasn't born yesterday. Do you think I got where I am by being a blind idiot? Our people saw you talking with him, and we know who he is. The question is who the hell are you, and what did you tell him?"

Chantelle retreated a few steps at the sudden hard tone in Fahid's voice. She hadn't seen him get the slightest bit upset about anything since coming aboard. His unexpected anger caught her and Derek totally by surprise.

Realizing he was trapped, Derek went for the bluff. "I just wanted him to get word to my folks in Kansas City that I was OK, and not to worry."

"Nice try, kid. That guy is CIA all over. His name is Frank Parsons, and unfortunately for you, he's on our payroll. You told him about our cargo, our destination, our timetable, and God knows what else. Too bad for your folks."

With cat-like speed, Fahid stepped forward with his right foot to within inches of the startled man, but with his back to him. He cocked his right arm at 90 degrees, then spinning on that heel, precisely delivered a smashing blow to Powell's cheek with the back of his right elbow, breaking the fragile bone and splintering the nose as well. Derek Powell, gushing a torrent of blood and fibers from his ruined face, crumpled unconscious at Chantelle's feet.

"What in the name of...?" shrieked Chantelle.

"A bit of a traitor. Nothing to worry your pretty head about," said Fahid. He stepped over Powell, and led her by the elbow away from the mess.

"Why'd you have to do *that*? What's the problem? I thought you told me you guys were just delivering some furniture. Who are *you*, anyway?" Chantelle kept looking back over her shoulder at Powell.

"Just what you see, babe. A bunch of guys operating an old freighter trying to make a buck in a modern world."

"What was it you said about the CIA? What have they got to do with you?"

"Not a thing, babe. Not a thing. Let's get a bite to eat, and let the boys clean up this mess."

"What will you do with him?"

He smiled and said, "Oh, I think he'll have learned his lesson. We'll just put him off ship at the earliest convenience. He won't cause us any more trouble after this, I'm sure. You know kids nowadays. They learn fast. Paul! Come on up and take care of this, will you?" Fahid hollered down to the main deck where his first officer was waiting.

Soon after dark the same evening, Fahid quietly rose from his bunk and threw on his shorts and a T-shirt. He took a long look at the very naked, and soundly sleeping Chantelle before stealing out of the cabin. They had taken a quick lunch after the incident on the bridge, and then retired to the privacy of his well-appointed cabin for their 'dessert', as she had begun calling their afternoon lovemaking. Between sessions, she asked him again what he was going to do with Derek Powell.

"I promise, I'm not going to lay a hand on him again. I'll personally see that he leaves the ship alive, if that will make you feel better," Fahid responded.

"Thanks, Johnny. He seemed such an innocent guy. I thought for a minute you were going to kill him."

"I promise, I won't."

Then he explained to her about their clandestine delivery of wood, which was to be made into furniture for the Emir of Kuwait, leaving out the details of the shipment's actual destination and purpose. "The Crown Prince doesn't want the world to get wind of such excess, given the dire straits being suffered by most of his subjects at the moment. Understandable, I suppose under the circumstances."

"Why didn't you just tell me? And why such a cruel lesson for poor Derek?" she persisted.

"You never know what the world press might do if they got word of such goings on so soon after the war. Part of the arrangements in our deal is to keep a tight lid on the project, at least for now. The fewer people who know, the less chance of a leak: casual or on purpose. I had to show a firm hand to the crew by making an example of Mr. Powell. I was going to tell you about all this eventually, depending on what your plans might be after we get to Port Santos."

"We'll just see," she purred. Satisfied at last with his explanation, she snuggled back into him, molding her curves to his muscular contours.

Fahid worked his way to the stern section of the main deck where he met his first officer and three other able-bodied seamen. On the deck, in the middle of their circle hunched Derek Powell. He sat slumped; his face in his hands, dried blood caked down the front and sides of his shirt. Next to him was a five-gallon, metal bucket once filled with engine lubricant. Now it contained a length of heavy winch chain.

"Stand him up, boys," ordered Fahid. Powell moaned, but came upright with the help of strong hands beneath both his armpits.

"Open the safety wire." One of the men undid a section of the triple-cabled railing that outlined and protected the gangway entrances to all decks.

Fahid bent down and locked one side of a metal handcuff to one of Powell's ankles and the other through a link of chain from the bucket. He stood up and looked Powell directly in the eye. "*Partidario* does not take kindly to traitors, boy. And *I* can't stand 'em."

"I don't understand, Captain. What are you going to do?" Thoroughly scared, Powell eyed the handcuff on his ankle, then the chain-filled bucket.

"It's a nice night for a swim, don't you think Derek?"

"You're not going to throw me overboard, not locked to that chain?"

"I'm a very fair and sporting man, Mr. Powell. I'm not going to throw you anywhere." Fahid paused. "You're going to jump."

"And if I don't?" A last attempt at sounding brave.

"My comrades here will help you to the rail."

"I'll drown."

"Maybe, maybe not. Here's the key to the handcuffs." He held a small object up and toward Powell. "I could certainly tie your hands, throw you in like the garbage you are, and be done with it. But, as I said, I'm a sporting sort, so here's the deal. You jump, or we throw the bucket in and it'll pull you after. Either way doesn't matter to me. Save yourself a nasty scraping if you jump at the same time we heave the bucket, though. I'm going to give you the key just before you go in. I figure this chain will pull you down at the rate of, say about 200 feet a minute, so you'll have at least that much time to get the lock off. Much longer than that, and, well it won't matter anyway. Shouldn't be a problem for an athletic sort such as you. Be mindful of the pressure on your ears as you're descending now." The gathered knot of men chuckled a bit with their captain's warning.

"I know who and what you are and who you work for, boy. Have known all along. Just wanted to wait and see what move you'd make, and as it turned out, it wasn't a very effective one, now was it?"

Suddenly, Fahid nodded once and the small crush of powerful men moved forward forcing Powell to the open edge of deck. One grabbed the heavy bucket with both hands, and with one swinging motion, threw it out into the night. At almost the same instant, Fahid pressed the cuff key into Derek Powell's hand. The young man's body was viciously torn from the stern deck, and the splash it made in the *Star's* phosphorescent wake was barely noticeable.

"I promised I wouldn't lay a hand on him," commented the Captain to no one in particular as he watched the churning wake well below.

"I realize its highly unlikely, but aren't you worried even a bit about him possibly getting loose, what with the key and all?" asked the first officer.

"Even if he did, we're way outside the normal shipping lanes, and the water is over two thousand feet deep beneath the keel. There are probably sharks all over the place, and we're hundreds of miles from the nearest land. Besides…" he laughed loudly turning away from the stern, his thoughts returning to 'dessert'.

"Besides what, sir?" asked his number one.

"Wrong key."

61

"I guess we're ready for her memorial tomorrow. I still can't believe she's gone," Devoney murmured, staring out the Pullman window.

Steele glanced at Wilkins. Neither said a word. Wilkins had brought the Pullman down from Reno to Sonoma after receiving a call from Steele. Cody called him just before his departure for the Pacific from Travis AFB. He invited and encouraged Wilkins to stay as long as he liked, and to use the car as a base whenever he was in the area. Jeremiah obliged, and stayed in the comfortable coach while visiting relatives in the Cloverdale area. He had researched the burgeoning gambling industry on Native American reservations, and was checking out operating facilities throughout California and Nevada. Wilkins picked up Cody's urgent call one evening during his stay aboard the coach. They arranged to meet at the address in Mill Valley that fateful evening five nights previous. As luck would have it, they arrived on site at the same time. Unfortunately, there was nothing either could do. Before Devoney got there, Steele and Wilkins agreed that the Pullman would be the safest place for her to stay, despite the strained circumstances of their relationship. Following the nightmarish episode on the walk outside Devoney's front door, with Steele clearing the way, Wilkins had gathered up Devoney as she fainted, and whisked her to the back seat of his rented Land Rover. Checking their unconscious cargo every few minutes, the two men accomplished the one-hour drive back to Sonoma and the Pullman in hushed silence. The next morning they lounged in the parlor drinking coffee.

"Are you certain they won't try for her again?" Wilkins asked, purposefully avoiding use of the word 'killing' for Devoney's sake.

"Not a chance," responded Steele. "Sharpe knows we're onto him. He'll check in with his boss, and they'll decide she's too high profile. They'll get on with whatever they're up to. She's just an afterthought, no offense Dev. Something to do, even a macabre sport if you will. They would have eliminated you outright while you were still on the island, if they thought your survival would hamper them in the slightest. You were simply used, and when used up... There's too much at stake for them to take the chance on another try now that they've missed once."

"It's still hard for me to believe that he... they tried to kill me, after all we..."

Cody shook his head and smiled.

"What? What is it?" she asked.

"Oh, it's just that we've been trying to... *I've* been trying to catch this guy for years and..."

"Dominic?"

"Yeah, although he's known in the agency as *Wolverine*. I've mentioned this to you before."

Devoney was silent.

"And here you just happen upon him."

"Just lucky, I guess. Coincidence." Devoney closed her eyes and thought of Laura.

Steele looked at Wilkins who just shook his head.

"What about *HAVOC*? I know just about all there is to know. They wouldn't risk having all that exposed," Devoney said.

"And just what would you expose? The existence of some Jules Verne device that supposedly controls the weather? What proof do you have? Who's going to believe it? As you yourself stated, they have all the specs." Cody ticked off all the persuasive reasons he could think of. "Even if you did go public with it Dev, and if someone, or even most everyone, believed you. What then? What have they done or are they going to do that's illegal or that science hasn't been trying to do without success for hundreds of years?"

"Yes, but what about *Opal*? The world can't deny that."

"Correct, my dear Doctor. Talk about luck. *Opal* and *HAVOC* could have been the ultimate coincidence. *Opal* was an overgrown natural phenomenon. That's what the official word is, anyway. So where's the empirical data, or other proof that *HAVOC* had anything to do with it other than your say so? Put yourself in someone else's shoes, those present excepted, of course. Would you believe it had you not been there? Not likely."

"You guys believe me, don't you?" Devoney pleaded, almost in tears.

Cody looked at Jeremiah, and they nodded. Both men had grave reservations about the incredible story she told them several times over the last few days. However, where *Wolverine* was concerned, Cody had to accept and operate on the premise that Devoney's story was true. He couldn't chance it. It was *possible* that *Wolverine did* have an implement capable of mass destruction. Further, he would most certainly use it if indeed it were operable, as Devoney insisted it might be. And it *was* one helluva storm.

Silence again settled about them like a heavy cloak, each deep in their own thoughts. Steele looked furtively at Devoney. While they were sleeping in the same bed in his stateroom since Laura's death, it was as estranged roommates, and certainly not in the biblical sense. He comforted her in his arms as she cried herself to sleep on several of the past few nights, but any further intimacies seemed like pleasures of distant history. The death of their good friend drove a wedge further into their strained relationship. He wondered about times spent with her, and whether he should trust his memory of the good times. Of the times before she met *Wolverine*. Was he burnishing the strengths of their tumultuous relationship while ignoring the obvious imperfections? Was their relationship merely based on loneliness? And what of Laura? Should he confess the affair, or let it die with the loss of her? Memory embodies some sacred ground, and sometimes the silence of guilt guarantees its sanctity.

"Cody, you and your government guys have been after this bunch for a long time, right? Maybe we need a rabbit to draw out the dogs. Or a carrot on a stick, as you white folks would say," said Wilkins.

"What the hell do you mean by that?" asked Steele.

"Let's assume they're going to continue with this project. Offer them something. Make them think they need it for whatever their purposes might be with this *HAVOC* gadget. Get them to commit to a time and a place," responded Wilkins. He stood, and began to pace the length of the parlor.

"Just how do you propose that we offer them this carrot, JW? In the newspapers or maybe on TV?"

"Give them something that they think will enhance the performance of the thing. I dunno... a supercharger for the engine... a taller antennae... a gizmo that goes in the laser... you know, something they don't have but definitely think they need. You guys can certainly come up with something like that, I'm sure."

"Yeah, Conley could probably come up with something, but we'd need someone on the inside to get it to them. How do we know they're even going to try this again, anyway?" Cody wondered.

"Dominic ...or Franz ...or whatever his name is, told me so, several times," piped up Devoney.

"We still need to get it, whatever *it* might be, to them somehow. Right now, we have no idea where they are, or what they're up to."

"I might be able to contact them...him," said Devoney, very quietly.

Wilkins and Steele looked at her in disbelief.

62

After a quick walking tour of Praca de Indepencia, Independence Square, they boarded the ferry for the quick trip across the bay to the island of Guaruja.

"I think of all those huge statues, I liked the white lions the best," exclaimed Chantelle. She leaned on the rear fantail railing of the swift ferry, and gazed at the skyline.

"Yeah, everyone does," replied Fahid Aziz.

"Personally, I enjoy the gardens along the beach walk. Even though the sea is definitely my home, when I get ashore after a voyage it's always nice to smell the flowers."

In the early hours of the morning, after docking the *Star* safely in Porto de Santos, Fahid and Chantelle bid farewell to the crew and took a leisurely breakfast. After eating, they ventured along the famous beach walk bordering the waterfront before catching the ferry. Fahid made arrangements for them to stay at the Hotel Gavea on Guaruja, via his ship-to-shore the night before. Guaruja Island was quickly becoming an internationally known beach resort destination, and it was the ideal spot for Fahid to keep a low profile amongst the jet-setting crowd, while arranging for the second shipment to Kuwait. Additionally, Hotel Gavea has wonderfully large rooms with correspondingly large beds, and he looked forward to continuing his carnal pleasures with Chantelle in a larger playground than accommodated them on the *Star*.

"It's huge," commented Chantelle.

"Thank you," said Fahid.

"I meant the harbor," she gestured toward the harbor as its full size came into view.

"Largest in Brazil and Latin America. Rio is 400 kilometers that way," he pointed north to their right, "and Sao Paulo is 70 km in that direction, high up on a plateau inland."

"Rio." Exotic excitement conjured by the name made her cheeks glow. "You will take me there ...to Rio?"

"If there's time."

"What is so important you have to do, leaving me all alone here?" she prodded a finger into his ribs, pouting.

"Have to see to the cargo. As I mentioned on the voyage here, it's a very special wood that's needed for the Emir's furniture, and I have to be certain it's the right stuff."

"Why can't I go with you?"

"No whining, woman," he said. "I told you before, it's a difficult trip, and somewhat dangerous. We have to go inland a ways to meet the foresters, and its no place for someone so gorgeous as you. Stay on Guaruja. Enjoy the beach and the nightlife. I'll be back shortly, a few days at the most. Besides, you need to rest up. I think I've worn you out."

"Who's worn out?" She started rubbing his inner thigh.

"Not here, Chica. Too many tourists. Someone might see and get the wrong idea."

"Who cares? Nobody knows us. Why not? C'mon, Johnny. I need to play, right now!"

"Soon enough. There's hotel row just beyond the ferry landing."

She continued her deliberate, intimate massaging of his leg as the ferry docked.

Two days later and 200km inland from Santos, Fahid stood inside a nondescript warehouse with a group of about ten heavily armed men. All examined stacks of cut timber. There were four different piles of logs neatly arranged within the corrugated metal structure, which was tucked inconspicuously in the forest at the end of a tortuous dirt road. A portable Honda generator chugged a noisy backdrop to the scene, providing electricity for overhead lights. Three of the stacks were logs of large diameter, while the fourth consisted of rather anemic looking much smaller trees, by comparison. All the timber was cut to sixteen and thirty-two foot lengths, standards for all harvested wood the world over.

"Almost exactly the same quantity as in the first shipment," announced Ramon Vasquez, leader of *Partidario*. All present knew he was not referring to the timber.

"Tonnage should be approximately the same as well," he added, running a hand over the bark of one of the logs in the smaller stack.

"Let's see it," said Fahid.

"What's the matter, Aziz? Don't trust us?"

"Hey. I'm as much a *Partidario* supporter as any of you," Fahid lied. "It's just that my ass is on the line when and if I get stopped by the US Navy in the Gulf. I want to make 100 percent certain that this cargo looks, feels, smells, and tastes just like it's supposed to, if we get caught before Hussein's boys can get the stuff off." Thinking to himself, *Plus, I want to make sure it's here, cause that's why I get paid.*

Vasquez turned to Jimmy and asked, "Donde esta el borer?"

The big man quickly strode to the small, walled-in office at the left front corner and returned with several pieces of apparatus. Expertly, Jimmy fitted the four pieces of the device together and handed his boss what looked like a huge corkscrew. "This is an oversize Increment Borer," Vasquez explained to Fahid. "In the timber industry, smaller models are used to determine growth rate, tree soundness, and chemical penetration. They're all used to extract a wood core. We built this one specifically for our purpose. It has a hollow tube behind the hollow bit, which collects the core sample as the handle is turned driving the bit into the tree. Jimmy…" He handed the big man the device, and pointed to the base of one of the larger logs. As the beefy Brazilian drove the bit into the butt of the tree, Vasquez continued. "We drilled to the extent of the borer, approximately two meters. Then we remove the wood core from the device like this." Vasquez took the borer from Jimmy and pulled on the knob at the center of the turning handle, removing an inner stainless steel cylinder from the hollow bit tube. The cylinder was split its entire length on opposing sides, and with little effort Vasquez removed a core sample of wood and handed it to Fahid for examination. "After sealing the stuff in heavy-duty, leak-proof plastic liners, we roll them to a diameter just less than that of the core we removed. We cut just enough of the base of the core to make the rolled package and the cut core the exact length as the original sample removed. Then, using a steel rod, we insert the package into the hole and gently tamp it in as far as it will go. Finally, we insert the wood core plug back into the remaining hole, and tap it in as well." He demonstrated each step during his explanation.

"Ingenious," commented Fahid. "But how do you get rid of the outlines of this obvious plug? It has to be impossible to accurately line up the growth rings." He ran his finger around the very obscure but still visible outlines of the plug in the base of the log.

"Not really, my dear friend. Usually, just leaving them like this would be enough to fool even some trained observers, if ever anyone had cause to look. But we go one step further."

Jimmy returned once again from the office, carrying a well used, 61cc, Husqvarna chain saw with a 28 inch bar, pulling the starter cord as he walked. The efficient saw growled to life on the third pull, shattering the silence in the shed. Vasquez pointed to the log, and in seconds Jimmy cut a thin slice from its base. Silence once again returned to the warehouse excepting the ringing in everyone's ears.

"Now take a look."

Fahid squat down on his haunches and studiously examined the fresh cut for almost a full minute. "I'll be damned. Can't see anything but a cut tree. Strong work, Amigos."

"The new cut obliterates any trace of the plug and all we are left with is what will be itemized on your manifest, cut Jacaranda and Mahogany for His Royal Highness."

"Okay. So how do we, and most particularly Saddam's thugs, know which ones are carrying and which aren't? I didn't happen to be in the hold on the first delivery when they off-loaded the merchandise. I was too busy watching for those prowling Yankee patrol boats."

"Excellent question, Captain. Iraq's receivers have already been informed. Every timber company of any size throughout the world stamps its logo into the base of a tree cut for sale. Many even spray paint the imprint to make certain they get credit at the mills where they sell the logs. Note that the base of every piece we have here is imprinted with logging logos, usually initials. We used six different ones for this shipment. I took the liberty of having my own initials made on an imprint, only reversed. Any log imprinted 'VR' is literally worth its weight in gold. Cocaine is expensive stuff, *comprende?*"

63

"It's an entirely new technology, and the concept is just in its experimental infancy," explained Conley. "But they say it will eventually lead to an incredible power resource in the twenty first century. At least that's what the boys at Lawrence Livermore are claiming. I had to threaten them with a pull of their major government funding in order to get this thing, but once they found out it might actually go into use outside their lab, they complied willingly. I think they are dying to find out how it actually test drives." Conley paced the parlor area of the Pullman explaining the details of the indirect drive fusion ignition device to his three-person audience.

"So we... they aren't certain that it'll really work, then? Is that correct?" Steele eyed the written material Conley had spread all over the dining table.

"Oh, it'll work all right. They assured me of that, given its correct installation into this device of yours," he said, nodding in Devoney's direction. "But to what extent and with how much control, is anybody's guess at this stage in its development."

"Well, won't it be dangerous then, given all those unknowns?" asked Devoney.

"The LLNL boys don't think so, Dr. Marsh. Particularly given the size of the units they are going to provide, and the small amounts of fuel in the fusion capsule or target. The obvious selling point to the bad guys is its conveniently small size, which makes it easily transportable. These schematics and charts will convince even the most ardent detractor of the heat source potential, given that person has any degree of technical smarts."

"Some of these guys have that in spades," commented Devoney. "Especially the Chinese." Steele nodded his head in agreement.

Steele had contacted Conley at the 'Farm' in Virginia, and after suffering the obligatory five-minute tirade and tongue-lashing for his recent, unauthorized Asian adventure, explained the outlines of their idea to his occasional boss.

"Well, if she really knows where they are or at least can contact them, why doesn't she just call them up, set up a time and place for the meet, and we'll be there with the cavalry to snag the whole bunch of them?"

"C'mon, Chief. We've been chasing these guys around the world for years with no success. Do you really think they'd let us, that is Dr. Marsh, just waltz in without some form of guarantees and protection?" It wasn't the first time in his years of association with the CIA, that Steele wondered about the cowboy mentality of government agencies, but he kept the thought to himself. "This is a real opportunity if we do it with patience and planning. Remember, it has to be operable, at least to some extent, to provide them with something they couldn't possibly get anywhere else. Plus, we'll need all our resources to be certain Devoney's kept as safe as possible."

"Yeah, I suppose you're right for a change. I'll see what I can drum up with the techies. If I get lucky, I'll call you back in 24 and arrange to meet you out there. For once, stand by and answer your phone… please?"

Steele grinned and hung up.

Three days later, after briefing Conley on *HAVOC*, and describing their plan, Wilkins, Steele, and Devoney received a crash course in *Inertial Confinement Fusion* (ICF) aboard the old Pullman. Conley, after being introduced to Wilkins, surprised the hell out of both Wilkins and Steele.

"It's an honor. Your reputation precedes you, Sir, " said the CIA Deputy Director, warmly grasping Wilkins outstretched hand. "Green Beret, two silver stars, a bronze, and a bunch of purple hearts wasn't it, Captain? Thanks for your help over at the special weapons facility in Hawthorne, and for helping us out here. Welcome back to the war."

Steele, speechless, looked wide-eyed back and forth from his friend to his sometime boss.

64

27,000 feet AGL and three hours out of Beijing, Franz Toscana had his second Sapphire Bombay martini. He was headed back to Hong Kong aboard the leased Gulfstream III. He looked over the set of instructions and bank drafts given him by his Chinese counterpart, when the call came through from the cockpit.

His short meeting in the ancient Chinese capital had gone pretty much as he expected. The Chinese government 'officials' wanted an astronomical return on their money this time. No more experiments. No more excuses. No more anything after this. "Now it's time for payback, and don't bother trying to disappear if this doesn't work," they warned.

"Sounds just like another bad line out of another bad gangster flick," he thought at the time. "Always interesting how life truly does mimic art."

In his best salesman's approach, he reported his 'success' with the initial *HAVOC* trial, rationalizing the tremendous expense, while embellishing his part as he described the potential for the device. "You gotta be a little bit of everything in this business," he smiled to himself on the completion of his report and subsequent request for funds. "Salesman, terrorist, charter boat captain, everything." His Chinese benefactors, 'sponsors' as he liked to think of them, took less than two hours to come to a decision concerning his latest funding request. More than anything, he realized they wanted the device, which he promised to provide, only after a select number of worldwide 'demonstrations'. He had little doubt that he could easily elude any Chinese assassins in the event he was not able to perform. However, he didn't want to have to deal with the ongoing consequences of failure the rest of his life, given such a large and potentially dangerous 'client'. As always, there were ways to skim from any patron, and he was a master in that arena. So even if he did fail, he would succeed. But with enough money behind him, failure was an unlikely possibility. Especially with something as fat as the *HAVOC* device could be, if indeed it did work. He left Beijing with drafts on Chinese Swiss accounts in amounts more than adequate to rebuild *HAVOC*. "If only it were mobile," he wished. "It would be my sword, the world my Damocles."

"It's for you, baby," cooed the tall, athletic Malaysian 'cabin attendant'. Molucca was the only other occupant of the luxuriously appointed Gulfstream's cabin. Toscana grinned, mentally thanking his good fortune for finding this exotic beauty in Bali three years ago, and enlisting her talents when and as he required and/or needed. He paid her handsomely for being 'on call' from time to time, but her many 'services' and exotic 'talents' were well worth the money. She asked few questions, and seemed as hungry for him as he always was for her, though he knew his money helped fire her appetite. Fortunately, her most recent 'service' had just been completed prior to the making of his second martini. The rented cockpit crew seemed not to notice anything unusual in either of their appearances, save their satiated smiles when the copilot came back personally to tell them of the call.

"Boss, Sharpe here." The voice on the scrambler sounded as if it were coming from next door, as opposed to three thousand miles away.

"Tell me some good news this time, Lew."

"Hey, man. It wasn't my fault she wasn't there. You know as well as I that those things happen in this business. Besides, if she does talk, no one will believe her anyway."

"Yeah, I know Lew. Just making sure you're paying attention to the details. I hear you had some fun with her roommate."

"How'd you know?"

"Saw it on the news in Hong Kong. Looked and sounded like some of your best work. You know how the Asians love violence. The report showed up on the local CNN channel. Left the scene sterile and sanitized, I trust."

"Clean as new fallen snow in Tibet."

"Good. So what's so important you had to call me here?" Toscana knew Sharpe had no idea where 'here' was, given the random routing of the call through at least a dozen ground links and half that many satellites.

"Believe it or not, that Marsh woman called *you*. Left a message with one of the secretaries at our shell corporation in New Zealand. See, I told you she had no idea it was us after her."

"Maybe…" Toscana thought for a moment savoring his cocktail, as he watched Molucca reapply her makeup.

"What'd she want?"

"Didn't say, other than she asked you to contact her at her Berkeley office. Said something about reconsidering your offer, whatever that means."

"Hmm. I guess I must have something good she wants, or... needs," *Wolverine* said into the mouthpiece, and to the Bali goddess smiling seductively at him.

65

"It's as if any youth and innocence I had left was ripped from me with Laura's death. I just don't know, Cody." Steele lay naked on their stateroom bed except for a bath towel wrapped around his waist. He watched a disturbed Devoney Marsh pad barefoot back and forth across the deep pile, burgundy carpet at the foot of the bed.

"How can I ever hope to pull this off? Knowing he killed Laura, or at least gave the order. I'm loath just to hear his name, whatever it actually is. Hell, I want him dead. How am I supposed to deal with that, let alone work with the guy?"

And possibly sleep with him, Steele shuddered to himself knowing Devoney most certainly had thought of that possibility as well. *What macabre twists of fate,* he thought. *Typical when dealing with* Wolverine. Steele ran the entire plan through his mind at least three times after Devoney had placed the call, leaving the message for Dominic to call her in Berkeley. Conley told them he could have the ICF apparatus within twenty-four hours if need be. After all, Livermore was only two hours away. He lectured them all on the technical details, but focused most of his attention on Devoney. He explained that the learning curve for operation wasn't steep at all.

"Once you have the hardware, driving it is supposed to be a slam dunk. Anyway, you say you've already built and proven this *HAVOC* thing with that cumbersome gear you described. Toscana's got the laser technology, or at least you say he had it. This ICF device is just Wilkins' 'carrot', or bait in our case, that will complete the package. The technology is being researched in order for the US to come up with viable, clean energy sources that are alternatives to oil. It has unlimited heat energy production capabilities, but it's in its infancy relative to large scale production. All you'll have to do is convince

244

him, or at least whoever is supposed to rebuild it, that the ICF will be easier for them, that's to say you, to use. It should be much more efficient, and most importantly easily mobile, given its relatively small size. Any one of those arguments should do it." Conley left the Pullman, begging off Steele's invitation to spend the remainder of his stay in the third stateroom aboard.

"Nah," Conley waved off the offer. "Always wanted to pamper myself over at the Sonoma Mission Inn. It's just ten minutes away, they tell me. Make sure you keep the call forward from her office engaged in case he calls right back. That trace apparatus I left is state-of-the-art, and maybe we can nail him through it straight away. Glad she's willing to step up and help us with this, Steele." He stepped off the rear platform of the old railroad car, and headed for his vehicle and driver.

"Suit yourself, Chief. There's certainly better company here and at least as much ambiance."

"Yeah, but I'm sure you guys don't give massages."

"Hell, Dev. You've already taken the first step by leaving that message. That alone took guts. The rest will get easier, I promise. Just keep focused and you'll do fine. Besides, we'll be right around the proverbial corner. Between Conley's guys and me, we've got all kinds of reliable gadgets to keep track of and listen in on you, so we'll be with you the whole time and on the spot should you need us. Know that your actions will avenge Laura's death. That should be more than enough motivation to get you through. Believe me, I want him just as much as you do, and what happened with Laura is just the final straw."

Devoney stopped pacing and looked at him skeptically. "So what happens when I do connect with him? You're not going to let him… er, us, actually rebuild *HAVOC,* are you?"

"Not a chance. As soon as we know that he decides to stay or that you can keep him in one place long enough, we'll drop by and pick him up."

Or… Steele thought silently *…take him out once and for all.*

"Well, it sounds OK, I guess, " she allowed. She came around to the side of the bed, dropped the white, terry cloth robe to the floor, and snuggled under the down comforter next to Steele. "Get under here, my hero," she murmured. "And turn off the lights."

Steele did as he was told, depositing his towel next to her robe before crawling in under the covers. "I would never let anything happen to you, Baby," he whispered in her ear, taking her in his arms.

At first, their embrace was somewhat formal. Guilt was an unseen, uninvited third party there with them both: Devoney's for sleeping with Wolverine, Cody's archrival, and the one responsible for Laura's death; Cody's for sleeping with Laura, who was killed because Devoney slept with Wolverine. It was crowded in that bed, for resentment shared it with them both. Ultimately, loneliness and need won out.

The soft chirping of Steele's bedside phone rudely interrupted their rediscovered passion.

"It's really not that difficult a concept, Dominic," Devoney did her best to sound calm, given the imprudent interruption in her love life, and the subsequent flurry of activity in the small bedroom.

Immediately realizing who was on the other end of the call, having taken the 'person-to-person' request from the overseas operator, Steele dashed into Wilkins stateroom to wake JW, and have him man the tracing instruments set up in the parlor. "Put some cloths on, white man." The Native American grinned at Steele's nakedness, after sitting up and understanding the nature of his friend's urgency. Steele laughed softly and put a finger to his lips, indicating the need for silence before hustling back to his own stateroom and handing Devoney the portable mouthpiece. Only after the conversation had begun did he throw on his robe. He headed back out to join Wilkins by the speaker and trace gear in the parlor.

"Where are you anyway? Not in your office at this hour, I'm sure. And I'll bet that wasn't your secretary that answered." Dominic sounded as if he were right down the street.

"I'm staying with a friend. That was her husband you woke up. A robber tragically killed Laura, my best friend, a few nights ago in my house, and I haven't been able to bring myself to stay over there just yet. I always try to leave my call forward on at the office. That's how you happened to get me here."

"That explains why your home number wasn't answered. I was sure I would catch you there this late," said *Wolverine*. "I'm terribly sorry about your friend. Did they catch the guy yet?"

"No.

"Well, they say America is truly a most violent society. I hope you're OK, and I'm glad you've decided to come back. As before, I need your help. I can assure you peace and quiet after we put *HAVOC* back together again, and you already know the wonders of *Pavao*."

"I know, Dominic. But I think work on the project right now will help take my mind off what has happened, and I'll look forward to spending some time there with you after," she lied. "Where are you?"

"In Australia, and I miss you, " He matched hers with his own lies. "I'm really sorry I had to leave you and *Pavao* so abruptly, but my money lenders needed to be reassured, and I'm sure you can guess how much our project cost. So, go on about this new concept of yours, we can talk about 'us' when I see you."

"Well, I've had a lot of time to think lately, and after I decided to take you up on the reconstruct, I did some research into heat source technology. I was hoping to make the apparatus easier to move, while also refining and increasing its core concept of generating and focusing the heat source. I spoke with a variety of specialists and experts in laser and energy technology. Then I stumbled on this. The research development is still brand new, but the concept is literally as old as the sun." Leaning her head out the stateroom door, Devoney could see Cody signaling her to keep talking by wheeling his index finger.

"Sounds great. I hope you haven't spilled the beans to any of your fellow academics that are driven by the needs to publish stuff like this? Let's make certain that it works before we tell the world."

"No, I just mainly talked theory with them. I didn't specifically describe the final use, just the concept."

"This guy's really good," whispered Wilkins to Cody. They watched the trace lines flicker and connect between locations around the Mercator projection of the world on their monitor. "We should've had him in the first two minutes. He's either on to us, really careful and very good, or all of the above." Steele nodded, tweaking the brightness control on the display. The lines were beginning to localize in Asia and Oceania, rather than randomly stringing all over the map.

"The sun is driven by fusion," Devoney explained. "The process is a reaction which fuses elements into different and heavier elements, and in so doing releases tremendous amounts of energy in the form of heat."

Steele and Wilkins both urgently signaled her to continue. The trace intercept lines were all red now indicating a fix location within thirty seconds. They were bouncing between China and Australia.

"Sounds very complicated. Are you sure this is something simple enough for the likes of my crew to put together? I don't want to have to bring in any more outsiders until we know we have a working finished product."

"Sure. I think we can do it. I just wanted to make you aware of the process and the benefits."

"Well, so long as you are certain that it'll work like it did before. We could always just redo it just the way we did it the first time."

"I think this will be much more effective Dominic, because we can control the output, where before we didn't have a clue and were at its mercy. If not, we can just do it like we did on *Pavao*. But I'm really concerned that something terrible might happen again if we try it like that."

"Now that we know the end result, in any event, we'll just turn it off earlier. Why don't you hold off on the rest of the technical details until we can sit down with the crew, and you can teach us all?" Dominic eyed the passing seconds on his watch, keenly alert to the elapsed time of the connection.

"Don't you want to hear the rest?" she asked.

"There's something here that requires my attention." He leered at Molucca who leered back.

"But…"

"I'll send you details and tickets to your office tomorrow, and we'll pick you up when you arrive. Until then, sweetness."

"Dominic, I…" The monotony of the dial tone abruptly sounded in the receiver.

"Lew, we're on with *HAVOC*. Do we still have access to that small, isolated private cay off Anguilla in the Virgin Islands?"

"Believe so, Boss. Why?

"Get in touch with the boys down there and tell them to prepare it for a visit. Secure the area out to at least a five-mile perimeter, and do it subtly, my friend. Then get me some serious details on the area just north of Sacramento, California. I need aerials, topos, demographics, and especially ten-year historical rainfall and river flow data for this and next month; if you can get a weather model for the next six weeks from our meteorological friends; that would be helpful as well. Next, arrange the usual pickup routine for our beautiful friend and helpful accomplice, Dr. Devoney Marsh. And finally, if you don't know, find out where *Partidario* is now, and where the main men will be in the next two weeks. I understand from my deep cover sources in Porto Santos that the brain trust may be getting ready to launch that rust bucket tub of theirs for yet another trans-Atlantic crossing soon."

"Sacramento?"

"Yeah, Lew. Sacramento."

"So, she couldn't stay away, eh? You da *man*, boss. Where and when do you want to make the grab?"

"Make arrangements for coverage and the switch at Phoenix in two days. I'll have her own, private flight attendant meet her," *Wolverine* nodded toward the exotic beauty sitting across the cabin from him.

"Vasquez has yet to leave Brazil, and word has it that most of the rest of them are in Sao Paulo. I feel payback in the air, right Boss? Haven't heard from our lady insider for a few weeks though. I'll do some research and have that info for you when I see you. When will that be, by the way?"

"Meet me at the usual spot in the BVIs in four days. Ciao, Lew."

"About time you got off the phone, lover," purred Molucca. She took the handset from *Wolverine* and unplugged it.

66

Driven by the jet stream careening around thirty thousand feet above the Earth, all weather is ultimately forced east. The jet is not a gentle phenomenon. It is a huge mass of upper atmospheric cold air constantly in motion in the form of winds. Like a raging river running an irregular course, these winds collide with, and their directions are altered by, mountain ranges the world over. Like a flood, they can and will build momentum across unencumbered flat landscapes. The jet is anything but one-dimensional. The aberrations in it caused or enhanced by massive geographical features create surges and gyrations that can and often do suck huge chunks of cold air south and ultimately east from the Arctic. Occasionally, under just the right circumstances still well out of the predictability models of modern meteorology, when one of these colossal cold air 'fronts' hits less dense warm air over land or larger lakes, an undulation in the jet will spin off its Arctic air in the form of a storm. Just such an event was spawning over the northern portion of the Bering Sea as Devoney boarded the Southwest Airlines flight 438 from San Francisco bound for Phoenix, Arizona.

At 2:00pm the afternoon following their call to *Wolverine*, a special air courier dropped off a package of instructions and tickets at the Berkeley office of Dr. Devoney Marsh. Two of Conley's men, posing as University administrative staff, received the package. One tailed the courier, and the other alerted the Pullman of the parcel's arrival. He was instructed to bring it up to Sonoma ASAP. The tail on the courier ended at the legitimate offices of the delivery service, where an examination of the waybill indicated the original pickup came from Mexico City.

Wolverine's instructions to Devoney were brief, and offered little in the

250

way of information. She was to fly to Mexico City from San Francisco, changing planes in Phoenix. The brief, handwritten note enclosed with the package encouraged Devoney to bring the ICF equipment, and that Toscana's 'HAVOC team', as he referred to them, would meet her when she arrived in Mexico.

"Damn! That doesn't give us a whole loft of lead time," Conley swore after rereading the instructions. He and they arrived at the Pullman simultaneously. "09:35 at SFO tomorrow. OK. Let me use your blower, Steele. I've gotta build a fire under these folks, and make sure they're ready at all these ports, in addition to prying that gear loose from Livermore." When Conley got excited, the old Navy oozed out.

"Aye, aye, Captain." Steele offered a salute, while giving Conley his telephone.

"Now remember, should anything, anything at all go wrong, and I assure you it won't, if you get worried hit those switches on the face of the ICF vessel in the sequence we gave you, and we'll send in the cavalry. It works just like an EPIRB."

"What the hell is an EPIRB? And what're *they* going to say about those switches?"

"Emergency Position Indicating Radio Beacon... EPIRB for short," responded Conley. "We've connected them through the temperature sensor and only the correct sequence will engage it. They'll think, after you tell them, that it's all part of the heat monitoring process, which is basically true. However, activated in the correct sequence, the switches will employ the internal transmitter, which only you know is there. It's built right into the sensing device, and it's the smallest and most powerful unit made. It will broadcast on channel 16 or 2182 kilohertz, which is the bandwidth monitored 24/7 by the Coast Guard, and all ocean-going vessels. We installed it as an integrated part of the ICF, and nobody but you should be the wiser. There is absolutely no reason for having to take the containment vessel apart, and therefore no way that the beacon will be found. Anyway, we'll be close enough to you to figure out what's going on ourselves, but... just in case..."

"The ICF components are onboard, and your guys say everything is in place in Phoenix and Mexico City," Wilkins reported. He joined them at the entrance to the boarding walkway. "Hell, at least he could've sent you on United or some other carrier where you could go first class."

"Let's just see this through his way, for now. No slip ups this time, " retorted Conley. "I wonder where he's going from Mexico City? Could be either the right or left oceans from there. Either way. Not a problem. We'll be on it the whole way. One of our guys is already on board. You better get on too, Dr. Marsh."

"I'll be there before you, Dev," said Cody. He took her by the shoulders and whispered in her ear. "The Company jet is waiting, and we'll be airborne before *Southwest* even has your doors closed here. You won't see Jeremiah or me unless you need us, but we'll be there the whole time. Here's a last ditch, emergency number in case all this hi-tech stuff doesn't work."

"Oh, that makes me really confident," responded Devoney pulling away. "Don't forget, I'm only doing this for Laura. You guys worry about saving the rest of the world." She locked eyes with Steele, then turned and disappeared down the ramp.

Devoney arrived in Phoenix right on time, and headed for the International concourse on the west side of the airport complex. She had until 2:30pm to catch Aero Mexico flight 479 to Mexico City, so she had plenty of time to kill. She browsed and window-shopped her way toward the international gates trying her nonchalant best to spot her protectors in the bustling crowds, but to no avail. Catching sight of herself in a pub mirror as she passed made her decide a makeup re-application was desperately needed. *Man, I look beat and I'm just starting this ordeal*. Deliberately, so that her unseen entourage could easily observe and understand her intentions, she strode toward and into the women's washroom, located just before the entrance to the international concourse. While combing out her hair she glanced to her right and caught the reflection of a tall, quite stunning Asian woman heading for the stalls directly behind her. *Strikingly beautiful*, she admired to herself, hearing the stall door slam. She continued with her makeover. She barely had time to feel the cold wetness of the damp cloth as it covered her lips and nose before her world went black.

"It's been almost ten minutes." Agent Bonner spoke into the microphone in his cuff. To anyone watching, agent Bonner looked and acted just like one of his Treasury Department brethren working the Secret Service. Most agencies and services of the government used the ultra-light transmitting and receiving apparatus popularized in countless film enactments. Bonner's mannerisms fit these characterizations perfectly. However, at the moment he wasn't the least bit interested in whether he was attracting attention or acting a part. Rather, his concentration was riveted on the doorway to the women's washroom where his tail had yet to re-emerge.

"Is Luana in the vicinity?" Bonner heard Conley's amplified voice charge through the receiver in his ear.

"Affirmative, sir. She's right here with me." Agent Luana Larson nodded silently as she listened on the same frequency.

"Good. Larson get in there and find out what the hell's she doing. And Larson..." commanded Conley. "Watch your six."

"On my way, sir."

Agent Larson strode purposefully into the women's washroom, one hand in her purse tightly clasping her Glock 40 caliber semi-automatic. Once through the tiled entrance she kept to the wall opposite the mirrored-facade over the row of sinks. Quickly she surveyed the interior of the room via the mirror. Seeing no one, she dropped silently to her haunches and peered beneath the enclosed stalls.

"No one here, guys," she reported on her cuff-mike. A loud chorus of "Shit!" came back at her through her earphone.

Quickly, she ran to the far side of the washroom where a service door occupied most of the exposed wall. She determined it was solidly locked when Bonner and three other agents flooded into the room.

"Damn, damn, damn! I can't believe how fifteen of you guys, supposedly highly trained agents, and ten *Radio Shack*'s worth of high tech electronics could let her slip away like this," Conley fumed.

"What happened to the tall Asian broad that went in right after her?"

"No trace of her either, sir. Obviously one of the perps."

"What about her transmitter?"

"Still dead," answered a voice from within the van.

"Where're Steele and Wilkins?"

"They went down to the *Southwest* freight handling area to check on the ICF gear," responded Bonner.

"Why the hell can't I raise either of them on any frequency?"

"You know how Steele hates to wear wires," responded the agent manning the microphone in the van.

"Goddamit!"

After Sharpe unlocked the service door in the women's room, he and Molucca hastily dragged the unconscious body through the cluttered service vestibule and out into the adjacent maintenance corridor. He ran a portable all-channels receiving device over her form and quickly found and disabled Devoney's transmitting earrings. He locked both service doors before they lifted her limp body into a large, wheeled carton container. Molucca quickly donned dark blue overalls matching those already worn by her accomplice. With their *Federal Express* baseball caps firmly in place, they pushed the *Fed Ex* package mover through the long service corridor and out onto the Phoenix tarmac. The turboprop Gulfstream I, emblazoned with the *Federal Express* logo and colors was already warming up on the north side of the concourse. The smaller plane was surrounded and dwarfed by its larger, similarly painted, jet-powered cousins. In the frenetic activity whirling around the cargo carriers, no one seemed to notice two more uniformed workers load a variety of cartons and one canvass wrapped body into the open rear hatch of the Gulfstream.

"How'd you know which bathroom she was going to use?" Sharpe asked as Molucca closed and latched the full-sized cargo door.

"Women's intuition. I saw her check herself out in the pub mirror, and I knew she would head for the nearest facility after that. Exactly what I would've done. That's when I called you on the radio."

"Lucky thing she picked one with a service entrance."

"Plan A. All washrooms have them in this concourse. Makes them much easier to clean from the maintenance area. That's why Dominic picked Phoenix. We would have gotten her anyway in one of the others, sooner or later. If not, we did have a few other backup plans. Did you have any trouble with airport personnel?"

"Money always talks," smiled Sharpe. "Told the three assigned to that area to take an expense paid, early coffee break. By the time anyone checks with those guys, if they bother to, we'll be long gone.

Molucca admired the naked form of Dr. Devoney Marsh stretched across the cabin couch. *Maybe there will be time for us to get intimately acquainted later.* This provocative thought caused a wicked smile to trace across her classic features.

Devoney moaned, but remained unconscious. The hard looking man with the mirrored glasses rolled her onto her back after very carefully and thoroughly checking every inch of her while she was on her stomach. He handed Molucca the earrings containing the tiny transmitters. "When we're in the air, turn these back on and get rid of them. Have the flyboys up front toss 'em out over downtown." He did the same unconditional examination of her front, taking even more time, letting his hands slowly wander. "You look like you want to help out," Lew Sharpe sneered up at Molucca.

"We're just supposed to make sure she's not wearing any bugs. I don't recall instructions about giving her a physical."

"She had more electronics in her luggage and those cartons than those two guys have up in the cockpit. Lucky for us those agency suits always use the same frequencies. Didn't take me but fifteen minutes to find 'em all. I see why the boss wants a second go at this one, though," grinned Sharpe. His hands were still busy.

"That's enough, Sharpe! At least for now. Put this blanket over her and buckle her in. She'll be awake soon."

"OK girls and boys. This is your Captain. Just got clearance. We're outta here." The pilot's voice crackled over the cabin intercom as he firewalled the two throttles of the older Gulfstream.

Wilkins and Steele puffed up to the G-men grouped around Conley. "Tell me some good news, Conley." Steele shot the words at the Deputy Director.

"Gone."

"Jeez! I can't believe they got her by all you guys? What about her transmitter?" Not one of the agency men or women looked him in the eye.

"It's down. They must have found it, but we're still monitoring for a signal. Let's remember now, it's not over," Conley instructed. "We've got cover in Mexico, and here on every flight out to Mexico City leaving today."

"What if she's not going to Mexico? Or what if she's not going by air. Or what if she's going via another destination first? C'mon chief, tell me you guys have all that covered."

"Take it easy, Steele. That's why we've got electronic surveillance on her, in her luggage, and on the ICF cartons. Speaking of those, what did you find out?"

"The *Southwest* ground crew had them unloaded and transferred to the *Fed Ex* terminal just like you ordered."

"*Fed Ex*? Shit! I didn't order that. What the hell are you talking about?"

"The crew chief said he had orders to remove the cartons and forward them to Mexico on *Fed Ex*. We figured that was your gambit to control the merchandise, " Wilkins explained. "*Southwest* said those orders came down from command which is you, Conley."

Conversation was interrupted for a few seconds by the throaty roar of a twin turboprop *Federal Express* Gulfstream leaving the runway.

"Not a chance in hell. Don't you think I would've told you? Bonner, Larson, get down there and see where the fuck those cartons are, or where they went. Thomson, Flaherty, bring that crew chief up here on the double. Maybe he can shed some light on these orders, or give us a description of who gave them. Swartz, Taylor, get me a manifest and destination for every *Fed Ex* flight out of here for the next 24 hours, including that one that just left. Scott, what have you got on her luggage and those cartons?" Conley asked the one lone man still sitting within the darkness of the van and seated at the deck of consoles and monitors.

"Ident indicates they're all where they're supposed to be, sir. Right on board *Aero Mexico* 479."

"Where does it say she is?"

"Downtown Phoenix."

Steele pounded a fist into the side of the van. "Yeah, sure."

"Gulfstream FX two niner lima x-ray, Houston, you're cleared to land. Ground 121.9er. First taxiway to your right. Have a good day, sir."

"First taxiway right. Roger that, Houston. FX two niner lima x-ray."

The little Gulfstream touched down with a screech as both the wing gear greased the runway simultaneously. The pilot held the yoke in his gut as long as possible. When he felt the plane's weight transfer from its wings to the main gear, he slowly eased backpressure on the yoke and the nose gear settled gently onto the tarmac.

After contacting ground control, they requested and received permission to taxi to a private hangar opposite the field from Houston's main terminal. Once parked and shut down, they efficiently shuttled the ICF cartons and an unconscious Devoney Marsh to the newer, turbo-jet powered, unmarked Gulfstream III waiting beside the hangar. After the transfer was complete, the turboprop was tractored into the interior of the building where it was washed clean of its false logo. The two sliding hangar doors were closed and locked behind it.

Molucca shook her head in appreciation. "That man Dominic. He sure has a lot of contacts."

"You bet," agreed Sharpe. "These planes and that hangar belong to an oil tycoon client of his. The boss did some extraction work for him a few years back, and the guy owed us a favor or three, big time."

"Extraction? What do you mean? Oil extraction? I didn't know Franz was into oil."

"Not oil. You know, extraction. Removal."

"Oh. What did he remove?"

"The guy's wife."

Thirty minutes later they were straight and level at thirty-five thousand feet over the Gulf of Mexico, headed for the British Virgin Islands.

67

October 20, 1991
The Honorable William H. Todd, Governor, State of California
State Capitol
Sacramento
California 95814

Dear Governor Todd:

As flood season rapidly approaches, we are certain you have given a great deal of thought, not to mention time, money, and effort, to the protection of the people and property of the great state of California. We know you know how vulnerable your state truly is: particularly the area around Sacramento. We also know that none of your efforts at flood control can mitigate a 100-year flood, a fact clearly demonstrated by the catastrophic events of 1982 and 1986. Californians love to live and work near water, and there is nothing you can do.

This is to advise that unless we receive fifty million dollars, US, delivered at a place to be identified later, on or before November 20, 1991, we will unleash a flood on your state that will indeed be of biblical proportions.

I realize how preposterous this may sound. But, I ask you to review events and disaster totals from the storm OPAL in the Pacific but a few months ago for verification of our capabilities. OPAL was our creation. In the event this evidence is not satisfactory inducement enough, please pay close attention to all unusual weather related disasters in the western hemisphere within the next few weeks. We will be responsible for their creation. They will be a warning demonstration for you!

Fifty million dollars is mere change relative to the potential cost in human lives lost, economic production decreases, and infrastructure damage as a result of a flood of this magnitude. I urge you not to be remiss in giving this demand your utmost attention. We will be in contact.
Cordially,
The Weathermen

Toscana laughed to himself as he read through his rough draft. "Man, if I were Governor and I received this, it'd be in the lunatic file in a heartbeat. Well, if he does cough up the demand, so much the better. But, I seriously doubt it. However, this and the Atlantic test will give us a chance to fine-tune the beast before we seriously take some state or country to task. At least the California thing will put them on notice that we can do it where and when we say. They'll have to believe then. Too much empirical evidence for mere luck or coincidence. Plus, my Chinese sponsors will love this, and it'll prove that they are about to get their yen's worth."

The couriers and faxes were on their way. He reread the original draft once more, then lit a match to its corner and waited until the paper was but black ash in the porcelain bowl of the toilet. With a flush it was gone.

"Just like California," thought the *Wolverine*.

PART THREE

The Dam

68

Millions of years ago, before the majestic Sierra Nevada mountain range was volcanically thrust up and out from the earth's mantle of primordial ooze, a great, meandering river many times the size and width of the modern Mississippi covered much of the northeastern portion of what is now the state of California. In many places its massive banks were miles apart, and its bottom gravels hundreds of feet thick. Settled at the base of these gravels, where river channel met bedrock, were vast fortunes in placer gold. Following the violent birth of the Sierra, this river system ceased to exist, but for the remnants of its bottom channels now suspended atop, astride, and through the fledgling mountain range.

Beginning in 1850, following the discovery of gold in California, bands of tough, adventurous fortune-seekers followed the watercourses of existing rivers and streams into the Sierra. In the process of their determined search, theses hardy souls discovered the ancient riverbeds and recognized them for what they potentially contained ...gold! From 1850 until 1883, wherever the old river channel cut through the slate and granite bedrock of the Sierra, gold camps and towns sprang up like weeds. Springs, creeks, lakes, and rivers were diverted to these rustic encampments, where their waters were used to wash the rich gravels through crude but effective sluices, twenty four hours a day. Diversion ditches, or flumes as they were called, were hastily dug by hand, carrying water from a source to the very top of the gravel channel, then directed through a series of piping that was reduced in diameter as it fell toward the base of the 'diggins'. Thus, by the use of gravity, a powerful stream of water could be blasted out the nozzle of the pipe, known as a 'monitor'. The resultant jet of water from these monitors was so great that it could knock a two hundred foot high hillside down in a matter of minutes, or cut a man in two should he absentmindedly venture into the water jet. In this manner, hundreds of millions of cubic yards of channel material were processed, and ultimately washed from the Sierra mountainsides. The dregs and silt of this material, called 'slickins', found its way into the streams and rivers of the region, and eventually was carried into the watercourses that fed the rich farmlands of the central valley of California. These lands were experiencing a gold rush of their own which directly corresponded with that in the mountains, a cause necessitating the result in order to feed the hundreds of thousands of fortune seekers streaming into the new state in search of instant wealth. When the flow of these rivers could no longer sustain the residue, it settled to the bottom of its host. Over a few short years, the prodigious tonnage of silt deposits in the valley-rivers significantly shallowed their normal channels, which began to cause yearly spring flooding to the rich farmlands adjacent to the rivers, much to the despair of the struggling farmers. As surface mining became less productive, more gravel and dirt had to be moved and processed in order to expose the gold, further exacerbating the downstream flooding problems. After several ugly confrontations between a growing number of disgruntled farmers fed up with the building of new levees every year, and a decreasing number of desperate miners, the California State Legislature passed the Anti-Debris Act in 1883. This legislation basically outlawed most hydraulic mining in the Sierra, and was the death knell for many a gold rush community.

Measured in terms of GNP, California would be the seventh largest producing country in the world. Situated at the north end of the great central valley of California, its capitol of Sacramento is within miles of the confluence of four of the state's largest rivers: the Feather, the Yuba, the Sacramento, and the American. All four drain the Sierra gold country. United, they flow through the downtown area of the city and beyond as the Sacramento River. As it flows through the city today, the Sacramento's bottom is seventeen feet *above* the downtown business and political districts!

69

Completed in 1956, Folsom is actually the second dam with the same name attempting to harness the mighty American River. It, like its predecessor, is located 16 miles upstream from downtown Sacramento. The brothers Livermore constructed the original out of cut stone in 1852. It was meant to serve as a flood control measure for downstream farms and the burgeoning population of the new capitol of California. The earlier dam builders, while certainly visionaries, were not nearly as aggressive in their thinking as were the hydraulic miners working just miles upriver from the dam project. Consequently, as a flood control measure, the first dam was soon overwhelmed. Levee building, once again, quickly became the primary method of water control for the city of Sacramento, and its rich agricultural basin. Subsequent to the continuing downstream water problems, the Livermores' dam became a water quality and distribution means.

Folsom dam today towers 340 structural feet above the river. While not as visually imposing or as spectacular as many of its contemporaries, because it is built across the broad shoulder of the Sierra foothills as opposed to an acute, rugged and rocky canyon, its capacity is dramatic, nevertheless. Its top width is thirty-six feet, with a maximum base width of 270 feet. It has a crest length of 1,400 feet, flanked by long earth-fill wing dams extending from either side and abutting its massive concrete spillways. The total crest length, including the earth-fill sections, is an impressive 26,670 feet: all this to hold back 1,010,000 acre-feet of American River water from the 2,000,000 plus downstream inhabitants of Sacramento. The modern visionaries who engineered and built Folsom realized water demands and flood control would soon outstrip the dam's capacity just as they did its predecessor's, so an even larger upstream project was designed in conjunction. However, the location of the proposed upstream Auburn Dam is directly over an active earthquake fault and consequently the project's functionality, safety and future are still in heated debate. This leaves Folsom Dam as the sole stopgap for a drainage area consisting of 1,888 miles of Sierra streams and rivers.

Engineers incorporated very sophisticated equipment in the construction and ultimate operation of Folsom, and currently use computer technology to create flow models for planning water storage and release. But, when Folsom was designed and built, those technicians did not anticipate and/or underestimated two very significant variables. Unbelievable as it seems, the first was the weather, and its effects.

The dam has five, massive 42 by 50 foot, radial, steel spillway gates, with an additional three for emergencies. By design they are known as 'tainter' gates. Each one is accessed and controlled from the top of the dam by hydraulic motors, which require the simultaneous, manual turning of two separate keys for operation. These gates, together with the dam's three gigantic 15.5 foot in diameter penstocks, and eight 5 by 9 foot outlet conduits, can easily control and release an outflow of up to 130,000 cubic feet of water per second (c.f.s.). In an emergency, with everything wide open, the dam's engineers and designers claim it can withstand a prodigious outflow of over 500,000 c.f.s. in theory. However, and unfortunately, over a sustained period of time, downstream flood control measures in the form of gates, smaller dams and levees on the Sacramento and lower American Rivers can only deal with a maximum of 115,000 c.f.s. Exceed that amount of release, and over one hundred and seventy square miles of heavily populated areas are at risk. With a shoreline of 75 miles and average inflow of 2,731,000 acre feet of water per year, it was thought that these control mechanisms would be more than enough to harness the American River as it flowed into the reservoir known as Folsom Lake. Upon completion in 1956, it was also envisioned that the reservoir would take two years to fill. 1956 marked an occasion when it rained continuously for 100 days in northern California. At times during this record deluge, flow on the American River exceeded 300,000 cubic feet per second. Folsom Lake water ran through the top of the new spillway gates in a mere *3 days*! Once again, during a February storm in 1986, the dam was staggered by the weather. Inflow into the already full reservoir exceeded 300,000 cubic feet per second and, for a few frightening hours, outflow gushed through and over the dam at a dangerously high 180,000 cubic feet per second or almost 40 percent over the maximum sustainable outflow built into downstream flood control safety specifications. Fortunately, that storm was short-lived.

The second thing the engineers failed to anticipate was highly sophisticated sabotage.

That evening, back in Sonoma, California, Steele and Wilkins pored over maps and charts spread over most of the parlor furniture in the Pullman.

"How do you know for sure she'll be in this hemisphere?"

"It's the beginning of storm season, especially in the central and northern Atlantic. I'm guessing that *Wolverine* is most likely going to use *HAVOC* to augment or piggyback existing or prevailing weather patterns," reasoned Steele.

"Makes sense, but this is still a lot of world to cover." Wilkins waved his hand over the charts. "Why *not* Mexico?"

"That whole deal was just a red herring to throw us, or anyone else after him, off the track. Not enough opportunity or history for large weather disturbances there or in central America this time of year."

"Who the hell else is after him, my new friend?"

"Well, *Partidario* for one. Remember that warehouse in Ireland I was telling you about? If *Partidario* wasn't convinced they got him there, they still might be in the picture here. I'm sure they have or had moles inside *Wolverine*'s organization. If they do, they'll be tailing Dev as well. Hell, those guys have been after each other almost as long as I've been in the hunt. The good guys would be better off leaving them alone and letting them take care of each other. I don't think, or I sure as hell hope, that Toscana isn't onto Devoney by her connection with me, or she's in a lot more trouble than she is already."

"So why didn't we just stay in Phoenix? Seems like it would be that much closer to the action, wherever it's going to be."

"Conley and his pack of Agency bureaucrats had it under control, at least as much as they could get anything under control. I don't like to have to work confined by team players, as I'm sure you've already gathered. Besides, we have all the communications access technology we need here, plus sufficient resources to map our own course. I've linked all my monitoring gear to NOAA and NWS, so we get real time down-links of all the latest weather data to be had." Steele nodded toward the bank of computer screens scrolling columns of numbers, glowing from the right inset wall of the Pullman. "Conley is too good a Company man to not keep us in the loop if his minions get onto something, or if Devoney trips the transmitter. The guy covers his bases. Plus, he's got

Crystal watching from upstairs. You remember the *Keyhole* cameras on those archaic satellites in *Corona*? Well, now the CIA boys call their imaging satellite program *'Crystal'*, and the latest generation KH11 cameras can read the paper over your shoulder from 250 miles up at night in the fog. Anything unusual, he'll call them in and we'll see it. In the meantime, we may be able to find her, er, them, before they do."

"You've been in the spook business too long, my friend. You sound just like one. And if we do find her first, are *we* going to tell *them*?" grinned Wilkins.

"Depends on where we find her."

Equatorial trade winds are normally uniform. That is, unless some phenomenon causes a strong enough influence to create a variance or disturbance in their otherwise orderly and usually uneventful east to west journey across the Atlantic. Embryos of these winds are born as the sands of vast Sahara heat during the day. Cooler upper level air rushes in across the desert, replacing massive quantities of rising hot air. As the resulting river of air begins its charge west, thanks to the spin of the planet on this October 1991 day, it collides with a huge stationary mushroom of cold air erupting just offshore from Dakar in Senegal. An unusual cold-water upwelling creates this incident. The immense cold air mushroom, some ten miles in diameter, causes a bend in the otherwise straight flow of heated desert air. As a result, the Trades begin to curl, and in so doing begin to draw up even more warm, moist air from the surface of the ocean. A *Tropical Disturbance* is born.

70

Devoney became conscious grudgingly. Through slit eyelids she noticed the white muslin curtains to the left of her bed, dancing about prodded by a gentle breeze. The distinctive tang of ocean air tingled her nose, and she could hear the rattle of palm fronds just outside the window. Without moving her head she surveyed the room as best she could, discovering it to be done in tasteful pastels, and somewhat Spartan rattan furnishings.

"Ah, welcome back, gorgeous."

Her lids flew open, and she sat bolt upright. She immediately regretted the quick movement, as a headache exploded in her temples like a jackhammer on overdrive. "Dominic, it's you," she responded, dropping back onto the pillow.

"Who were you expecting, Doctor?"

"I'm not sure. I was… I'm just not…" She rubbed her eyes hard with her thumb and forefinger while she tried to grasp her surroundings and likewise her predicament. "Do you suppose I might have a glass of water, please? Where am I… er… are we?"

"Certainly. At your service." He handed her a tall glass tinkling with ice cubes. "We're in the Caribbean for all practical purposes. Close enough anyway. Welcome to *Langosta Cay.*"

"Sheesh, Dominic. Yet another island." She struggled back to a sitting position and inhaled the water.

"Yes, yes. But I love the water, don't you know?"

"So what happened? I thought I was supposed to meet you in Mexico?"

"A slight change in plans was required, my dear. Now tell me what you'd like for breakfast, and then we can talk about these wondrous devices you brought with you."

Just then a vaguely familiar, tall, striking Asian woman entered the room behind Dominic.

Rising warm air in the fledgling tropical disturbance near Africa vacuums up prodigious quantities of warm ocean, then thrusts thousands of feet straight up until it reaches a height at which the temperature is insufficient for it to hold its trapped moisture. Enormous cumulous clouds balloon through the cooler upper atmosphere, jettisoning untold millions of tons of condensed water in the form of sheeting rain. The cycle is self-sustaining, so long as there is warm water to drive the engine. There are thousands of miles of it between this point and the Caribbean. Most often these disturbances will blow themselves out over water, and don't amount to much more than a spectacular heavenly show for anyone lucky or interested enough to witness it. However, this October phenomenon is different. The hot river of desert air blasting west collides head on with the towering line of thunderstorms and bounces around the more dense vertical columns of squalls. The dynamic of the collision forces the entire air mass to begin a slow rotation, spawning a growing vortex at the center. Even more volatile hot air is sucked skyward. *Grace.*

Langosta Cay is a nearly flat, semi-arid parcel of sand and coral perched on a massive underwater shelf, just under 100 miles northeast of the island of Anguilla. Locals call it and similar nondescript islands, '*cays*'. Hundreds of similar islands are scattered about the Caribbean. Many uninhabited. Typical of most land masses in this part of the Tropical Atlantic, given a bit of fertilizer and fresh water, one can grow just about anything. Dominic's caretakers had done just that. The interior of the two-by-five mile spit of land now boasted acre upon acre of resplendent palm orchards where, prior to *Wolverine*'s stewardship, there had been nothing more than wind-swept rock and sand. Bougainvillea in explosions of tropical color highlighted the walls of the fourteen structures scattered about the island. Interspersed throughout the mature palms were an occasional mango tree, a few banana trees, and a few tamarinds. Along the shores where the orchards weren't constantly tended, the insatiable cactus wrestled grounds keepers for their indigenous right to the land. While not nearly as sumptuous as those on *Pavao*, Devoney soon discovered that *Langosta*'s improvements lacked little in the way of comfort. All the structures were connected by paved walkways lined with indigenous stone. Each of the bungalows serving as living quarters enjoyed a filtered view of shore and sea and was protectively nestled in the trees. The palms served as shade, but most importantly provided a canopy of protection, to some degree, from hurricanes. *Langosta* and all the other islands in this area of the Caribbean are dead center in the infamous Atlantic hurricane corridor. A two story tile roofed structure, the largest building on the island, served as the dining and communications center. Its roof was the highest point above ground on the island, if you didn't count the antennas. Across the curtain of palms, magnificent views in all directions could be enjoyed from its spacious balconies.

"So why did you leave *Pavao* so abruptly? The least you could have done was to tell me 'good-bye'," glowered Devoney, as they strolled barefoot along the water's edge in the early afternoon sun.

"I'm sorry for that, babe, truly I am. I'm sure you were aware of the enormous costs of our project. You even mentioned your worry to me in that regard on at least one occasion, remember? Anyway, I got a call from my investors, shall we say, wondering about the expense. It was an explanation that demanded my immediate and personal attention, and you were sleeping when the call came in."

"Who are these 'investors' anyway? And why did they become involved so suddenly? You assured me that money was not an issue?"

"It wasn't until I put in a call for additional funds to rebuild this beast," Dominic swept his hand across the installation being prepared inland of their walk. "Plus, there obviously was not going to be any return *on* their original investment, let alone return *of* capital given the events of *Opal*. I needed to plead a case for additional money and time."

"Because the costs of our original effort and this, it became necessary to present my, excuse me, *our*, case for immediate additional funding to my wealthy friends in person."

"Obviously, you were successful," noted Devoney. "The rebuild looks much more efficient than our first attempt and it appears nearly finished. Boy, did you get it back together in a hurry."

"Very observant, Doctor. We were able to streamline much of the construction based on what we learned on the first project. Indeed, by tomorrow morning the fusion unit will be ready to take out for a test drive. That is, assuming your ICF modules can be modified and calibrated to fit our original heat source generating equipment from *Pavao*. Your classroom technique this morning with the engineers was brilliant in its simplicity. I might even be able to install it myself." Dominic chuckled as he encircled Devoney's waist with an insistent arm.

She felt a sudden icy chill flash up her spine at his touch. "It shouldn't be much of a problem as I explained earlier. It is really a simple concept, and these units were designed to be assembled and disassembled quickly and easily. Tell me again why you had to kidnap me."

Dominic ignored her question.

Their exploratory stroll took them by the transmit dishes, towers and control structure which would again serve as the focal point of the new *HAVOC* machinery. They continued on around the north end of the island to a long pier, extending some two hundred meters out into the cobalt blue waters. All the while Devoney did her best to memorize the layout and find where her best chance for escape might be, and most importantly, where she might have the best access for communications out to the rescuers she hoped were nearby.

"What's with the shark cages?" Devoney asked. On the near side of the pier sat two, shiny aluminum cages, each about six feet on a side.

"When we don't occupy *Langosta,* sometimes it's leased by the operators of an exotic dive tour outfit out of Houston, I think. Part of their program is to run shark-feeding expeditions out at the edge of the drop-off. These are state of the art cages, they tell me. Nothing can get in. The edge of the Cayman Trench is right off the end of the pier. At least the beginning of it anyway," Dominic explained. They traversed the warm sand to the solid structure. The pilings and horizontal joists of the pier were metal I-beams supporting a wooden walkway about twenty feet across.

"One of the deepest sub-sea faults in the world," responded Devoney. "I dived the middle of it from Little Cayman a few years ago. Bloody Bay Wall, I think they called it. We were anchored only thirty meters from shore. On one side of our dive boat you could jump in and only have three meters of water. Jump off the other side and you had 2,000!"

"Not quite as dramatic as that off the end of the pier here," said Dominic. "However, the depth is more than adequate for our small, coastal freighters to maneuver in and out with the heavier equipment we require. You probably noticed that I tried to streamline the whole setup this time. The ideal, given your, er... *our* goals, will be the ability to easily disassemble and transport *HAVOC* to areas of the world requiring our service, if you will."

"If it really works, Dominic. If it works."

"Oh, it'll work. We witnessed that on *Pavao.*"

"What's with the pipe lines hung under here?" asked Devoney.

"You said we needed to test the thing before we left it on for any length of time. So I arranged to have ocean water pumped into a containment vessel around the heat generator, just like you asked. We circulate it via these pipes. The cold intake comes from about 30 meters down off the end of the pier, and any hot water is pumped out the second line to about 100 meters. We can bleed off any heat the test or actual operation may generate if we have to. Piece of cake. The whole thing will perform better than it did on *Pavao*. I know it."

"But we need control, sir. If it truly does function, the key for world acceptance and use will be our ability to demonstrate that we are capable of limiting our 'successes' to a large extent. We can't go around killing hundreds and leaving thousands homeless as was the case with *Opal,* just to end a lousy drought or two. We need to be able to shut it down on demand. Once the fusion process begins we can't stop it until the fuel is exhausted. That's why this coolant shunt is so critical. Candidly, I couldn't live with a disastrous repeat of our last outing. Now why *did* you have to kidnap me?"

"Truthfully, because you were being followed. My investors require absolute anonymity, at least until the apparatus is proven and operational. Failure is a loss of face for them, and part of the funding requirement is that I keep all trials and details absolutely secret. I'm sure you can appreciate that."

"I suppose so," said Devoney skeptically. "But we're not terrorists building a bomb here, you know. Wouldn't your investors appreciate being associated with one of the greatest achievements of our time, at least potentially? And, by the way, though I expected they might, I had no knowledge that I was being followed." Another chill coursed through her with the lie.

"Indeed they would and will. However, as I said, there is the potential of failure, and to these folks that is definitely *not* anything they would wish to be tied to. Therefore the cloak and dagger routine in Phoenix. I didn't think you knew about your 'shadows'," Dominic grinned. His piercing eyes seemed deep brown pools of danger.

"Why didn't you just say so, and maybe I could have convinced *my* benefactors to leave us be until we have it working?" Devoney looked away from him, not trusting her eyes not to betray her thoughts.

"Think about it, Dev," said Dominic. "Do you really think they would have let you come alone with a multi-million dollar piece of untried, government-owned equipment to someplace totally beyond their ability to monitor and control? Highly unlikely. If it weren't for your academic credentials and our success the first time, I doubt if they would have let you come at all, let alone given you their expensive toys. Must have been quite a story you laid on their table to get them to trust you with these gizmos. Your shadows had government written all over them. Plus, isn't it more exciting this way? Doing it totally on our own."

"I told them the truth about everything we did and didn't do. I finally convinced them that months, maybe even years of development time might be saved if we could marry their ICF modules with your existing *HAVOC* equipment from *Pavao*. I recalled enough of our empirical data, and was able to reproduce an adequate amount of the original schematics to make the case. They did take a bit of convincing to let it happen in the private sector, without their mid-wifing, so to speak. Besides, based on my experience with you, I didn't think I could convince you to take your stuff to *their* playground," she said.

The truth is certainly easier to sell, she thought. *It certainly is more exciting to do it alone. But not exactly the kind of excitement that I would choose given any options.* Devoney continued out loud, "Well, yes. I suppose you're right about them wanting to monitor what we do with the fusion modules. It's Lawrence Livermore gear, by the way."

"Ha! I knew those guys on you were government. Better still, " Dominic shouted, clapping his hands once. "It'll work for sure if those white-coated boys designed and built it."

"This stuff has been in development for tens of years, Dominic. You can hardly blame them for being just a little proprietary."

They had reached the end of the long pier. Just as they turned to retrace their steps back to the beach, a familiar figure in mirrored sunglasses trotted out to intercept them. "What's happening, Lew?" A lanky figure came abreast of them.

Devoney was certain she saw a nod of knowing acknowledgment in the cryptic leer Lew Sharpe broadcast down at her.

71

"It's Conley," Cody said to Wilkins. "That's just great," he said into the mouthpiece of the portable phone. "Keep us advised." He slammed the phone into its cradle on the end table. "Well, it appears America's finest have hit a dead end. They haven't found a trace of her or the crates."

"What'd you expect?" asked Jeremiah.

"Nada at the terminal in Mexico City. Zip on *Fed Ex* Gulfstream 29LX, the flight the crates were supposedly transferred to from *Southwest*. It just disappeared and *Federal Express* said it doesn't even have a bird with those tail alphas. FAA says their IFR flight plan filed out of Phoenix was for Mexico City via San Diego, but the pilot canceled and went VFR to Houston once he reached 10,000 feet. Claimed he had a re-route order from his Atlanta headquarters. The last anyone heard of him he was on final, and instructed to contact ground control once wheels down there. The good guys didn't discover all this until *after* the plane was down. No one has seen it since, and Conley's Houston boys can't even find a similar bird anywhere on the field. It just vanished."

"Well, at least we know that the slime has her."

"Great, just great," Steele repeated.

"Not that bad," reasoned Wilkins. "They need her to install those fusion units, and until the thing works, or doesn't, she's reasonably safe. That'll take at least a few days, and given what Devoney explained to us relative to the process, they'll have to try it out at least once before activating it fully. There's our chance as the heat signature from the test should be quite substantial. Remember those *Crystal* cameras can now pick up infrared as well. Maybe we can get them to try out that new *Millstar* system Conley was raving about, that allows those babies to transmit real time."

275

"Yeah, but where do we tell them to focus?"

"Like you said, it's storm time in the Atlantic."

"Okay, cast off lines fore and aft!" Fahid bellowed from the flying bridge. "Number One, goose her the hell outta here on a course of 090."

"Aye, mi Capitan!"

The distinguished old Liberty ship *Star* lurched a bit, and the crew felt a vibrating rumble under their feet as the faithful single shaft began to rotate the huge screw driving the ship out of Santos harbor. Chantelle waved at the departing harbor tugs, then joined the captain on the bridge and was ignored. She noticed that, since his return from inland, he seemed much cooler toward her. Their lovemaking sessions had gone from almost an hourly crusade to an infrequent and far more subdued ritual. She decided this was due to his preoccupation with their loading and departure details from Brazil, and resolved to do everything she could to change his attitude. She was amazed at the speed and efficiency with which the cargo of fine hard wood was loaded aboard, two days after 'Johnny' returned from the hills west of Sao Paulo. Obviously, the *Star*'s ragtag crew was far more experienced than they appeared on the surface. The ship was re-provisioned and made seaworthy in a matter of hours, once her lover returned and informed her that they needed to leave. While she was disappointed at not getting the chance to see Rio, she did have that extra ten grand waiting for her on her return to the States.

"Just another $10,000 phone call," she smiled to herself, as she watched the busy port facility recede behind in their wake.

"All right, now. Let's be gentle with these. They're only worth several millions of dollars, and on top of that, they're loaners," said Devoney. *Wolverine*'s workmen and technicians gathered around her. Carefully, she positioned several tiny fuel capsules within the generating module. "As I told most of you yesterday, this concept has been around in theory for many years. We just didn't have the technology to develop it economically until recently."

Get on with it, woman, Dominic thought.

"What we are hoping to do is fuse together the elements within these small fuel chambers. That's where the acronym ICF comes from, *Inertial Confinement Fusion*. They call these capsules 'targets'. The fusion, hopefully, will be 'confined' within the target capsules. If we can fuse the substances inside these targets we will create a heavier element. In this case, helium.

"What's in these things?" asked Lew Sharpe. He turned one of the small cylindrical capsules around in his hand. It was about the size of a dime.

"A mixture of tritium and deuterium," Devoney answered. She did not look at him.

"Never heard of 'em."

"I'm sure you have in another form, Mr. Sharpe. Both are hydrogen isotopes. We call them *'heavy hydrogen'*."

"OK. Why do we call 'em targets?"

"That's precisely what they are, and I'll get to that in a second, if you don't mind. The fusion process releases vast amounts of energy in the form of heat, which as you all know, is what we are after with *HAVOC*. It requires extreme conditions of pressure and temperature," she continued. "The reason these fuel cells are so tiny is for a control factor. Once fusion begins, we will have a far easier time, focusing and controlling the heat dynamic within the process, given the relative small amount of our fuel. Additionally, being so tiny, in the event we need to terminate the process, the relatively small amounts of fusion fuel can be exhausted in a reasonably short period of time."

"This stuff looks like gold," said Sharpe.

"It is, Mr. Sharpe. In order to effectively interact with the fuel, the material the fuel container or capsule is made from needs to be a substance with a high atomic number such as lead, or as you correctly identified in this case, gold."

"So why do you call it 'inertial'?" asked one of the brighter technicians.

"The premise of ICF relies on the inertia of the fuel to permit conditions necessary for fusion within the confinement of the containment capsule."

The technician looked at her blankly.

"Now, we need an energy *driver* to begin the fusion process. In order to achieve critical mass, we need the heat energy generated from within the capsule by our fusion elements to *exceed* the energy applied onto the containment vessel required to start the show. In this case, that *driver* will be a laser, similar to what we used on *Pavao*. These cylinders are called indirect-drive targets. Ones that are direct-drive are usually spherical. The laser is focused directly on the sphere, which heats causing compression and huge pressures within. In our case, the gold of the containment vessel will convert the driver beams to x-rays. These will compress the fuel capsules, and that pressure creates extreme internal temperatures igniting the fusion process. The indirect-drive method is far more economical, and easier to manipulate.

"Will there be a quiz?" chuckled Dominic.

Devoney completed the target installations, and with the eager assistance of three technicians and Dominic, finalized the precision aiming of their ruby laser driver. She stepped back, receiving a hearty round of applause from her helpers. Despite her frightening predicament amongst these hardened mercenaries, she smiled and bowed her acknowledgment. "Let's light this candle and see if the damn thing works," she said.

Dominic threw the engage levers powering the laser.

72

The term hurricane originates from the Spanish word *'huracan'*, translating as evil spirit. Even though October is usually the tail end of hurricane season in the tropical Atlantic, the National Hurricane Center (NHC) and the Tropical Prediction Center (TPC) in Miami remain open and active through the end of November. Occasionally, a rogue weather system has been known to have just enough strength to do serious damage to landfall even late in the seasons. On this date, both were monitoring a developing *Tropical Wave* off the western coast of Africa. The observing NOAA satellite did not provide real time images or data, and the weather techs in Miami did not immediately see nor anticipate the weak area of low pressure forming at a point just off the west coast of Africa to amount to much. Their last evaluation showed it without a defined or closed circulation, and it was thought that it would simply dissipate in a matter of hours. In fact, *Grace,* as this truly evil spirit would come to be known, was stewing a witch's brew of trouble. She was far more intense than those defining a *Tropical Wave,* and winds within were actually approaching hurricane speed of 73 mph sustained. At that moment, *Grace* was far from someone's afterthought, as her elements fit the classic hurricane parameters. She was forming 6 degrees north latitude of the equator over a sea whose surface temperature was 82 degrees. The latter ingredient the perfect input for storm energy. A high-pressure area over the riot of cumulous clouds churning at her crown and brow was also a fundamental element in *Grace*'s development. It allowed mass to evacuate from the growing storm. She inhaled huge quantities of warm water from the ocean's surface and spilled it back out in torrential downpours over a rapidly expanding area in excess of 300 miles across. Counter-clockwise winds spun her vortex ever tighter, serving to exponentially increase her appetite, and consequently her rate of growth. The faster the interior winds, the more warm air is forced up the center. As the rising air condenses it produces heat, forcing it to rise even faster. Air is forced from the top of the storm just as if it were some sort of meteorological smokestack. As more air spills out the top, more air has to fill the void at the surface, and the ocean begins to lacerate and flail as the storm starts feeding on itself. Combine all this with the westerly influence of the temperate *Trades* and the spin of planet Earth, and the Caribbean plus the east coast of the United States will soon be in for a huge surprise. Normally, a storm such as *Grace* would forage its way across the Atlantic in a somewhat northwestern direction following the warm surface currents, which provide fuel for such monsters. Indeed, *Grace* began her epic path of misery thusly. The burgeoning storm might have stayed true to historical track models had it not been for events in the northeastern Caribbean that began the very afternoon of her graduation from the category of *Tropical Storm* to full-fledged hurricane.

"Enter!" commanded Fahid in response to the double rap at his cabin door.

"But Johnny, I'm not…"

"Silence, bitch!" he spat. The Captain of the *Star* remained seated as his XO entered. Naked, Chantelle knelt between his spread legs.

"Excuse me, sir. I can come back."

"Not at all, Number One. Nothing important was happening here. What's up, and pardon the pun?" Fahid Aziz stood, stepped over the embarrassed girl, tucked himself back in his shorts, and faced his first officer.

"Well, you told me you wanted to know when we turned north on the 34th," he said referring to longitude line 34.

"Yes, I could feel your turn to port a few minutes ago, but I was… involved at the time," said Aziz. He glanced at Chantelle. The flustered girl was still on the deck behind them trying to cover herself with not enough hands.

"Get this traitor whore out of my sight."

"What?" she screamed.

"You know damn well what I'm talking about, bitch. You didn't think I'd go off and leave you unattended without having some sort of checks on you, did you? I know the manager of the Gaveo Hotel quite personally. I've provided him entertainment much better than you over the years, so he owes me. I had your room bugged before we even checked in. I've got tapes of the call in and your subsequent return call out. What'd you tell Siedlemann's, or Toscana's goons, or whatever the fuck he's calling himself now?" Chantelle was up on her feet cowering against the cold steel wall on the far side of the cabin, still unsuccessfully trying to conceal her nakedness.

"I don't know what you're…"

Aziz's lightning backhand slap struck her open mouth, its force knocked her face down onto the Captain's bunk. He was on her immediately, grabbing a handful of long blond mane, twisting her head toward him.

"It doesn't matter. They have no clue where we're sailing. All you could tell them is that we were there. It will do them no good whatsoever. What'd they pay, anyway?"

"I… I…" A strong knee in the center of her spine gave Aziz leverage, and he slowly pulled her lovely head back.

"What'd they pay?" he demanded again through clenched teeth. He increased the pressure on her spine and neck.

"$10,000," she sobbed.

He let her go, throwing her face hard against the bed. "Take her and give her to the crew."

"Our pleasure," grinned the XO. The big man manhandled Chantelle to a standing position despite her struggles, and moved for the door. "Any particular order you might have in mind, sir?"

"Whatever works. One at a time, all at once. Doesn't matter to me. I'm through with her."

"Much appreciated, Captain. The boys and me have been admiring this piece ever since you snagged her. Been wonderin' how good she was. What do you want to do with her when we're through?"

"When you're through? Take her again. Then let me know. If there's anything left, we'll figure out something appropriate. Now get on with it. After you've had your turn, meet me on the bridge. I want to go over our course and strategy."

"Aye, Captain. We'll take good care of her." He left, dragging the screaming girl with him.

Aziz heard the echoes of Chantelle's desperate cries fade into the bowels of the old ship. He grinned.

High above the Caribbean, a *Crystal* satellite's cameras were brought to bear on an area of interest twenty kilometers square. The NRO, as the imaging surveillance arm of the government intelligence gathering agencies, had been instructed days earlier by Charles Conley to keep a literal eye out as it swept the Caribbean. This was not an uncommon request. Frequently, the NRO resources were called upon to do special clandestine searches of all manner by various agencies. Particularly often, those requests came from the operations side of the CIA, responsible for intelligence gathering and 'hands-on' functions in the field.

"What are we looking for?" asked the image interpreters.

"Anything unusual," responded Conley. He examined the batch of images just received via special courier.

"Oh, that really narrows it down."

"Just let me know if that *Vega* bird of yours catches anything way out of the ordinary." *Vega* was the most recent code name for image collecting satellite intel in the *Crystal* program.

Late that afternoon, local Caribbean time, *Vega* picked up an unusual heat emission. Its normal swipe or path of inspection covered a strip of the earth some 100 kilometers wide. Conley was notified. Ninety minutes later, when the satellite was again over the target, digitized instructions were transmitted to its microprocessor brain commanding it to focus its cameras on the area of interest just northeast of Anguilla. The highly sophisticated and extremely classified lenses aboard *Vega* have the capability to read newsprint from space. However, it wasn't news that interested Conley.

"It's a developing science," apologized the interpreter.

"C'mon, guys. I know you're saving all the bells and whistles. I also know what you boys did in *Desert Storm* using *Millstar.* Those field commanders were getting real time intel right on the battlefield. Why can't I?"

"Well, this is as close as you're going to get on this pass. We've analyzed both the high and low resolution passes of your target from the past several days, and all we can see unusual is some sort of construction towers and dishes going up. For all we know, it's some rich guy who owns the island getting set up for some better TV reception."

"So, why'd you call?"

"Because, on the last pass we noted an unusual 'hot spot' on our infrared bandwidth," said the technician. "You requested unusual."

"It wasn't some motorized activity or a high power generator, was it?" asked the DDO, thinking about residual heat.

"Nope. We've programmed the satellite to ignore those, people, animals, and most other normal heat signatures. This was a burst of high intensity, coherent heat energy unlike anything I've ever seen before."

"Maybe your bird hiccupped," said Conley.

"Not a chance, Director. This was definitely a definitive high energy, short burst of heat. As you can see, it's gone on this pass, and we aren't even getting residual from anything on the island, except…"

"What?" shouted Conley into his speakerphone.

"There is an unusual aurora of heat glow coming from the water just off the end of the long pier servicing the island."

"Keep me in the loop, guys. Run a narrow swath search on each subsequent pass and do it full spectrum." His intuitive internal voice, successfully honed over years of experience, told him he was onto something. Conley pressed the disconnect, and then punched in a 707 area code. *Maybe I ought to call in some favors over at NSA and get Echelon involved*, he thought.

73

"Up and running," said Lew Sharpe. He washed down a last bite of bagel with a swallow of steaming coffee. He and Dominic were seated on the second floor, east-facing verandah of the communications and dining building. "Up with the techs at 2am to start the test procedures, and it was on-line with heat output by 4. Fired right up just like the Dr. Babe said it would." The two men watched as the morning sun poked a crescent above the eastern horizon, amidst a colorfully spectacular display of unusual cloud formations. The spreading fingers of high feathery clouds were stained dazzling red and orange, and seemed to converge at a point just beyond the horizon.

"Red sky in the morning, as they say," grinned Dominic. "Any problems?"

"Sailor's warning," responded Sharpe. He positioned his trademark glasses on his hawk-beak nose to shield his eyes from the rising sun. "No problems whatsoever. The heat output should easily exceed what we produced on *Pavao*. We should start to see some serious changes in those clouds very soon, if it works."

"Great. I hope so. That should make our Chinese friends happy. Put a video on it ASAP, and we'll send them a tape along with the data we're keeping."

"Why didn't they just buy it straight away?" asked Sharpe.

"No one would, given the questions about our first experience. There wasn't enough certainty before. *Opal* was too much of a proximity coincidence."

"No way. We had vortices, cloud formations up the ying yang, winds all to hell and back. Our own cyclone for sure, way before *Opal* decided to join the show."

"Yeah, but we can't prove it. My fault. I was too taken with the potential, and didn't record everything we did and what happened. At least not in a way that I could make a positive sales pitch. I guess I was surprised the damn thing really did work. It's just as well, though. We'll get substantially more this way," said Dominic. "They want us to show that it'll create distinctive weather patterns or definitive changes in existing weather over sea *and* land before they buy. But they were interested enough to bankroll us for this effort, I'm happy to report."

"That's why you wanted that California info. Like I said, you da man, Boss."

"Thanks, Lew. For our investor's sake, we'll just call the new little storms we create 'trials'. If we show them empirical data that indicates our ability to control and increase the heat output… Well, they should be able to figure out the potential from there. Plus, they can see the actual results on CNN or the weather channel. We'll just take our $100 million finder's fee and go on to the next project. That should cover our out-of-pocket expenses. By the way, remember I told you that those *Partidario* zealots might be on the move?"

"Yeah. You said they were in Brazil, I think."

"Right. Well I just heard they put to sea and guess where they're headed?"

"Haven't a clue." Sharpe's eyes were on an expanding mountain of clouds spread across the eastern horizon.

"Due north. That should put them right in the middle of our little test, if I've calculated correctly, and the gods are with us."

"That's why you didn't want us to turn it on until this morning. You're a clever one, man. I love this job!"

Dominic smiled. "Have you seen Dr. Marsh around this morning?"

"I thought you spent the night with her."

"She claimed exhaustion. Said she wanted to go over the new ICF schematics once more to be certain the modifications were right before you fired it up at 2. I let her get away with it, just in case we need her to tweak some of the rigging today. I want to be sure the mechanics of the device are totally operational before we punch her ticket. I posted two men at her bungalow, just to keep her honest. Obviously she's onto us, based on all the hardware you took off her. I'm just not certain how she'll try to contact the cavalry, or when. Anyway, I'll make sure she's long gone before any help arrives. Count on that!"

"You sure you're up to it, Boss? I know you had somewhat of a thing for her for a while there. I'm happy to take care of it," said Sharpe. He tried to sound disinterested.

"No. I'll deal with it. I might ask you to watch, though. Just to make certain," Dominic laughed. "Plus, you might learn something. And Lew…"

"Yeah?"

"I've got Molucca to keep me company."

Sharpe grinned, "Nice backup. Well, I owe you for the screw-up in Mill Valley."

"We'll deal with Dr. Marsh shortly. Did you get all those letters out?" Dominic stood, and walked to the railing of the balcony.

"Went out to all parties yesterday via courier from New York. They'll never be able to run a trace back from there, 'cause the couriers are clean. Think we'll get any responses?"

"Not a chance. Would you bother if you got an extortion letter threatening the wrath of God in the form of weather?" Dominic turned his back to the sun, and faced Sharpe.

"I guess your right, as usual," Sharpe responded.

"The head guys will turn the letters over to their various agencies. *Those* guys are just stupid enough to believe someone could control the weather without any evidence. But none of them will know for sure if *The Weathermen* are for real. They won't do a thing. They'll just sit on their hands and wait. Even if they do, there are too many potential target areas for anyone to cover. Convincing any one of them is a *huge* 'if'. The Feds may take a close look at *Langosta* because of the ICF and Devoney, but they won't find enough to cause us any worries. We'll be long gone as soon as we're certain about that weather coming at us from the horizon. Let's take a look at the stuff you've got on Folsom Dam."

During moments like these Fahid Aziz was most content. Though his ship was old, she was sure and sound, and definitely his home. Headed into the open Atlantic from an exotic port in command of an ocean going vessel had always been his dream as a child. While skilled in negotiating, and adept socially, he reveled in the solitude of the sea. The bridge was pleasantly warm, and the electronics hummed reassurance as they monitored his ship's vital functions and the state of the sea ahead. Alone on the bridge, he was master of all he could see. A touch of his hand on the helm and his charge and crew would respond to his every whim. The empty, warm, open ocean beckoned, as did the riches he would gain once the load in his hold was successfully delivered in but a few weeks. Celebrate? Of course! What then? Maybe a bigger ship, though he admired the old Liberty for her perseverance and reliability. Maybe not. Women? Certainly! A different life? Never! He grinned as his ship rose over yet another oceanic roller.

"So where are we, Captain?" the XO asked.

"Just west of *Fernando de Noronha Island,* that slash of brown off the starboard bow." The *Star* lumbered along at nine knots in building seas. "We'll stay on this course until we get just southwest of the Azores. That'll keep us out of most shipping lanes, and away from the blue-water sailing types. Should take us under two weeks, wind and current depending. Gotta keep an eye on this weather, though. Barometer's dropping like a rock, and I'm sure you noticed the seas."

"Well, to tell you the truth, I haven't noticed much. We've been busy with the 'entertainment'," Number One grinned. "Any marine weather notices other than that disturbance way northeast of us?"

"None. They say it's supposed to blow itself out long before we get in the area. How's it going with her?"

"She's a strong and feisty one built for sex as I'm sure you know. Stayed conscious for the first ten guys or so. But who's counting? Had to throw water on her to get her through the rest of the crew. Damn girl kept passing out on us."

"Where's the action?" asked Aziz.

"We had her on a mess table so two guys could hold her down for the third. Nice body, eh?" Fahid just grinned his agreement.

"Any further thoughts on what we should do with her, after?"

"Put her in the meat locker 'til we get two or three days north of the equator then throw what's left of her over with the garbage."

"Great. No worries. It'll give the off duty boys more time to play and something to do. Should we worry about someone finding the body?"

"Not likely. Besides, I hear sharks love naked blondes too."

Tropical storm *Grace* flirts with Cape Verde for about ten hours before she turns west northwest at about thirty miles an hour, and with vengeance. As her winds build to hurricane speed, she pushes huge amounts of water in front of her in the form of waves and surges. Wave size is basically determined by the speed and duration of the wind, and the amount of open sea the wave has to build. Mariners refer to this distance as 'fetch'. The fetch *Grace* enjoys is the width of the Atlantic Ocean. In the time it will take her to reach the *Tropic of Cancer* at 20 degrees north, her waves will have burgeoned to what is known as 'fully developed seas'. These will reach as high as the physics of wind and water will allow and they will be ship-eating monsters. As the storm voraciously feeds on the warm ocean surface, a cold-water upwelling is created. The colder, deeper waters rise to fill a natural void. These are nutrient rich, and they bring the deep-water food chain to the surface. Baitfish feed on plankton, blue water fish such as snapper and tuna feed on the baitfish, swordfish and dolphin feed on the smaller species, and sharks clean the table. In the wake of the storm, sea birds dive for the scraps that float on the surface, signaling the location of the upwelling. The temperature variance from the water at the leading edge of the storm's eye and the center of the vortex is a thermometer busting 40 degrees. This in a distance of but three short miles.

74

"I just got off the blower with the imaging boys over at NRO. They've got a huge, unknown IFR heat signature in the east portion of the British Virgin Islands," Conley paused. "I hate to admit it, but I guess you were right about her not being in Mexico." Cody listened to the slight buzzing static in his phone earpiece as the scramblers at both his and Conley's stations waited for the next voice activation.

"Specifics on location?" asked Cody. Jeremiah Wilkins entered the parlor from the galley of the old Pullman when he heard Steele answer the phone. He carried a plate of turkey sandwiches, which he placed in front of his friend. Cody switched the receiver over to 'speaker' so he could grab a sandwich.

"One of a gaggle of small sand-spit islets that litter the area east of Anguilla. We're trying to trace ownership as we speak, but it looks like our spot. Heat source output nearly blinded our eye-in-the-sky. Top-ended the IFR register. Interesting that it was just a one shot deal, though. No continuity like we expected from the device as Dr. Marsh described."

"She's testing it," offered Wilkins.

"After they are sure they've got the new adaptation right for the ICF heat, my guess is they'll probably turn it on full tilt sometime today," agreed Conley. "I convinced the JSOC (*Joint Special Operations Command*) to let us take in SEAL Team Six. They're on stand-by alert out of Virginia, and I can back them up with just about anything we need to overrun the place. I wanted you boys there to go ashore with them, if that's all right with you?"

"Rhetorical," blurted Steele around a mouthful of sandwich. "But, we've got to be certain that Devoney is all right. Let's not go charging in without a care. What have you got that can get us there yesterday?"

"Get to Travis and there'll be a Company Lear waiting and warmed up. You'll rendezvous at St. Martin, and I'll figure out transport from there by the time you arrive."

"Any idea on the number of 'unfriendlies' who'll be waiting for us?" asked Wilkins.

"None at the moment, but we're working on that with *Vega*. That thing is amazing. It'll do both high and low rez scans in the visible and IFR spectrums. The computer evaluation will eliminate all heat sources *except* the humans we don't see and count on visual. We should have an accurate number by the time you're wheels down on St. Martin. And oh, by the way, listen to this." Conley read the text of the letter received by the Governor of California from *The Weathermen*. "Governor Todd's aide brought this into the Sacramento office yesterday. He said the Governor received it in the afternoon mail. They get crank stuff like this all the time and just turn it over to the FBI as a matter of course. I ended up with it because I briefed the FBI Director about our ongoing situation two days ago, telling him as little as possible. However, I did mention that the investigation had potential weather implications. Being a bright guy, even though he *is* an attorney, he got a copy of it to me straight away. Think it's related?"

"Rhetorical," Steele said again. "Weren't the Weathermen a bunch of radical zealots working out of Berkeley in the 70s? Interesting choice of names."

"Yep, they were. And listen, it gets better, or worse, if you think *HAVOC* will actually work. Not only did Governor Todd receive this letter, but there were several others sent out as well."

"Go," said Steele.

"The Presidents of Venezuela, Mexico, Argentina, Spain, and France."

"Damn. What now?" Wilkins eyed Steele.

"I'm not through. The Governors of the states of Washington, Oregon, Missouri, Mississippi, Texas, Louisiana, and Florida also got basically the same letter. Who knows how many more will be reported in the next 24."

"What's the good news?" asked Steele.

Conley responded, "The mail isn't delivered again until tomorrow."

"OK…" Steele paused, thinking. "Let's concentrate on what we know with some certainty, and that is, there's something definitely going on in the Caribbean. As far as we know, NRO surveillance hasn't picked up any other 'hot spot's around the globe and nobody's reported anything else unusual, right?"

"Correcto," responded Conley.

"See if you can get *Vega* and any other NRO assets to concentrate their search on that list of targets. Any unusual heat signatures matching those we have on file should send up some red flags."

"Already on it with NRO and I think I've cajoled NSA to involve *Echelon* as well," said Conley.

"*Echelon*? Can't place it right off. You?" Wilkins turned to Cody.

"Vaguely. Some sort of super secret listening factory or something, I think."

"Close enough," Conley interrupted. "The National Security Agency has listening posts, stations, factories, whatever you want to call them all over the world. Every conversation transmitted electronically anywhere in the world can be and probably is recorded. Code name, '*Echelon*'."

"That's reassuring," commented Wilkins. "Whatever happened to the rights of privacy?"

"All in the name of national security," responded Conley. "They program their Crays up in Virginia to monitor and kick out recorded conversations based on key words, phrases, phone numbers, or just about anything they want to detail. I've got them 'listening' in our target area. They're complaining about high static, due to storm interference on all bandwidths, but promised to alert me if anything comes through. It may be a long shot, but you never know."

"Well, it would seem we've got the whole alphabet soup of secret agencies involved. The more, the merrier. I hope the right hand knows whose pocket the left is in."

Conley laughed, "That's my job. I'm supposed to be the coach of this team."

"OK, coach. We'll get a move on up to Travis as soon as we hang up. I'm sure that Lear is fax-capable, so why don't you get us copies of all those letters and we'll strategize in the air. I'm assuming you noticed the NHC updates on that tropical storm off Africa."

"Yeah. We're monitoring it. Looks like it's tracking north of our target area if it stays true to form. Plus, the weather gods are telling me it's unlikely to make it to hurricane status this late in the season. Anyway, it's too far to the east to be much trouble right now and it's almost certainly of natural origin, given its position and current status."

"Well, stay on it and get us any updates if anything changes. If Devoney was only half right in her descriptions and stories about their collaboration with *Opal,* we'd better be prepared for the worst," warned Steele.

"That's being a good Scout, Steele. Bring your umbrellas and get your butts to the Tropics. I'll keep you advised." Charles Conley hung up before Wilkins or Steele could say anything further.

At the same time *Grace* attains hurricane status in the Atlantic, arctic air funnels through the Bering Straight faster than the main body of the jet stream rushing along high above. In this region, opposing landmasses create the necessary components to form a huge venturi. The jet is pulled east over Alaska, where lower portions of it are again funneled between the majestic Brooks and Alaska Ranges, before heading out across the vast Yukon Territory. The air slamming into these huge geographic obstacles forces the jet to gyrate, twist, curl, and surge. As it begins its southwesterly charge over the western Yukon, state-sized undulations, formed by its passage across Alaska, cause juxtapositioned chunks of air within it to eddy and whirl. One of these masses is the super-cooled Arctic portion of air, which spins out from the leading edge of a forward wave in the twisting jet. It is spun off in a clockwise direction, opposite to the winds common in an ordinary low-pressure system. Nothing noteworthy normally occurs during this phenomenon until or unless this cold front collides with warmer air.

75

Devoney intercepted Dominic and Lew Sharpe just as they were stepping out of the communication rooms, situated on the ground floor of the large two-story structure.

"Good morning, Doctor," grinned Sharpe.

"Morning, gentlemen. Did I miss breakfast?" Devoney tried to get a good look inside through the doorway behind them. She had little opportunity to poke around all the facilities on *Langosta* subsequent to her abrupt arrival. Dominic had her 'schedule' booked solid with ICF instructions, modifications, installation and testing. She hoped she might have a chance to somehow get a message out through normal channels when everyone was busy with the *HAVOC* start-up, instead of having to trigger the EPIRB. "Those two big bruisers you left to protect me, wouldn't let me out to take my morning spin around the island, Dominic. What's the matter, don't you trust me? I'm certainly not going to swim away. Particularly before we are underway."

So far, Devoney's short stay on *Langosta Cay* had been an adventure in the bizarre. At least mentally. She had a much more difficult time than she ever expected, rationalizing the reasons for her presence amongst this mercenary band of terrorists and killers. If half of what Cody had told her about these guys was true, she was in deep yogurt. Yet, her right brain was definitely soothed and lulled by the encompassing warmth and seemingly slow pace of the Caribbean. The empirically trained left portion was excited with the prospect of once again attempting to create something no scientist had ever successfully fabricated in all of history before. However, the rational side of her, the little angel that sat on her shoulder, the tiny voice in the back of her head, constantly warned her that she was helping build an incredible weapon, one that could truly wreak unthinkable havoc, not some useful tool.

Further, she was painfully aware that at least one of her collaborators, the one in those sophomoric mirrored glasses, would just as soon kill her on the spot as offer her greetings in the morning. He had already demonstrated his sadistic killing abilities on her best friend, a reality so horrible even looking at Lew Sharpe made her nauseous. She knew her ex-lover, the mastermind and leader of the whole debacle, could probably be just as deadly. Yet, the night before, despite her best efforts to the contrary, she was once again attracted. "Must be the thrill factor, or something biological. Damn these hormones," she cursed herself. "Why am I so incredibly weak, not to mention gullible? And damn you Cody Steele!"

"It's not that I don't trust *you*," Dominic lied. "It's the rest of the crew around here I'm worried about. I've been working them pretty hard these last few weeks getting everything ready, and they haven't had any R&R lately, let alone seen any women as lovely as you scampering about. I just wanted to make certain you weren't 'bothered' by any of my more amorous associates, given that none of the bungalow doors have locks."

"What about that Molucca woman? Protecting her, as well?"

"She's just one of the guys. What's the matter, a bit jealous, Doctor?"

"Just asking. Well, all that protection is very thoughtful of you," she said, forcing a smile that all three knew was fake. "I thought I'd check on *HAVOC*'s progress in the control center. I stopped by there on the way over, and I understand we've been on-line since early this morning. The techs wanted me to find you first before we started any 'tweaking', as they called it."

"Correct. Started her up at 4am," said Sharpe. "And it appears we are having some success, as well." The man in the mirrored glasses pointed out toward the eastern horizon where a high band of dark clouds could be seen boiling skyward, even from their distant vantage point.

"Good, good. Now let's not get too carried away. We don't want a repeat of *Opal.* We must be prepared to go off-line or shut down completely if that frontal system gets beyond *Tropical Disturbance* parameters. Remember, we discussed this at length yesterday, and that was our agreement."

"Don't worry your pretty head, woman," laughed Dominic. He took Devoney by the elbow and turned her away from the communications room and aimed her at the entry door.

"Anyone care to join me at the control shed to go over the output numbers and take a look at the meteorology readouts?" Devoney flipped through the pages of her clipboard.

"Lead the way, Doctor."

Once inside the control center, a concrete tilt-up affair with a heavily insulated metal roof, Devoney and Dominic quizzed the technicians monitoring the *HAVOC* read-outs and gauges.

"No. No unusual spikes in the heat ranges or overloads in the generator this time. Everything is nominal and in the green," responded the man watching a vast array of instrumentation on an angled panel that ran half the length of one wall. "But, this is kind of interesting." He pointed to a video monitor at one end of his panel. Dominic and Lew Sharpe joined the technician, and all three bent closer to the screen in question for a closer look. Devoney held back a few steps and pretended to record some of the gauge readings on her clipboard. "This is the live video feed from our eastern patrol boat. Right now they are about twelve miles out, just as you requested," said the man, nodding at Dominic. "They called in about forty minutes ago and reported that the seas had gone unusually calm, all of a sudden. Bob, can you read me? Pan on the ocean surface." Immediately, the three men observed a view of a very calm, turquoise sea on the monitor. Devoney checked to see that the men were totally absorbed with the picture.

"So, what's so unusual about that?" asked Sharpe. "It looks green like it always does."

"Ten minutes ago, that same patch of water had a ten knot breeze rippling it. Even boasted a white cap or two." All three checked the screen again. The ocean was dead flat calm. Devoney quickly flipped a series of switches on the master ICF panel in the sequence she had memorized. No dial even so much as wavered. She heard absolutely nothing other than the monotonous hum of the HAVOC machinery. "Now look at the horizon. Bob, give us a wide angle shot to the east." A wall of black cumulous clouds materialized on the screen. Their tops were flattened and spreading ominously in the direction of the camera. The cameraman zoomed in on the summits of the clouds, where a solid vertical sheet of gray could easily be observed above and to the left of the billowing walls. The midsection of the cloud mass seemed as if it were erupting.

"Looks like torrential rain to me," said Devoney joining the group.

"Sure does," agreed the technician. "An awful lot of energy exchange happening in there."

"How long after we fired this thing up did that storm front begin to develop?" she asked.

"About three hours," a big burly fellow in a black T-shirt yelled the response to her from the other side of the room. He monitored the plunging barometer and NOAA weather satellite intercepts from his station against the opposite wall.

"Sounds about right," said Devoney. "If our heat output has been constant for that long, and everything is working correctly, we should have started to see results from that direction in that time frame. I never thought they would be quite as dramatic, though." She leaned between Sharpe and Dominic to take a closer look at the video screen. "Looks like a pretty nasty little storm, gentlemen. We better think about shutting down, before too long." She wondered if an EPIRB made any noise.

Bob, the boat driver twelve miles east had just reset his video camera on its stationary bow mount when he heard the distinctive 'pinging' of a rescue beacon. Like all good sailors, he was monitoring channel 16, the marine emergency broadcast frequency.

The most common storm track for a late season hurricane like *Grace* follows a course between 280 and 300 degrees magnetic from the west coast of Africa to the east coast of the United States. This bearing observes the hosting current of warm surface water almost exactly. It is theorized that when this repetitious current finally plays out its warmth, it absorbs colder north Atlantic water, which contains a greater percentage of salt. Since saltier water is denser, its mass sinks deeper on the return journey south, forcing a corresponding increase in the flow of warm water north. As a result, the north Atlantic is warmer than usual this October 1991. All this principle will do is to add power to the killer storm now known as *Hurricane Grace*.

True to form, *Grace* plows along a bearing of 280 degrees magnetic until she reaches the 18th parallel north of the equator. Abruptly, and quite uncharacteristically, she begins tracking due west at forty miles an hour as if inexorably drawn by some unseen cosmic magnet. Her turbulence spans over 600 miles of open ocean. The new path allows her ample opportunity to graze warm, tropical surface waters even though she has moved off the northerly streaming current. Heat energy is her heartbeat and her reason for being. As if cognizant, she forages west toward a new heat source, one that is man made.

76

The ghost-gray little jet with the sleek lines gradually turned on final low over Simpson Bay Lagoon. Steele could see the lights of Marigot, St. Martin's capital, as they rounded Paradise Peak, nearly in the center of the small island. He watched the blue runway marker lights of Princess Juliana International Airport seem to rise up, spread apart, and then straddle the aircraft just as the wheels squeaked acquisition to the ground. It was just before midnight when Steele and Wilkins exited the CIA Lear, its turbines still spinning down. DDO Conley was on the tarmac waiting for them together with a very fit looking service type. They spotted two waiting Humvees just off to the side of the taxiway. An insistent blast of hot wind kicked up all manner of paper trash and gritty dirt carrying it across the length of the parking area.

"Welcome to paradise, gentlemen," Conley shook both their hands with vigor. He wore a loud Aloha shirt, sandals and white tennis shorts. "This is Captain Younger, CO of SEAL Team Six." Younger shook hands with both the older men, his grip vice-like.

"I thought Six was no more?" said Steele.

"That's what you're *supposed* to think, sir," smiled Younger. SEAL Team Six had been the Navy's best-of-the-best SEAL units specially trained in anti-terrorism techniques. They were highly visible in the Grenada and Panama campaigns, but dropped from operative roster service, at least in the public eye, for a number of mostly political reasons shortly thereafter.

"We're keeping a low profile lately," understated the six-foot tall, sturdy young officer with a southern accent. "We did manage a few successful 'hot' encounters in the Gulf War though."

"Still out of Little Creek, VA?" asked Wilkins as they walked toward the waiting Humvee.

"Yes sir. Home sweet home. However, some of our SBUs are training out of Pensacola."

"Did you have a chance to review those extortion documents?" Conley climbed into the shotgun seat of the lead vehicle. Wilkins and Steele piled into the high-riding Hummer through the rear two doors. The driver, also a SEAL, wasted no time gunning his charge directly across the active runway and out a back access gate. Captain Younger and one other SEAL unloaded the Lear, and were quickly in pursuit in the second vehicle.

"Sure did. They did a good job of spreading their options. Any one target would take a whole regiment to police it, if that were how you chose to proceed. Nice shirt, Chuck."

"Thanks, Steele. I get way too much of that coat and tie routine every day in Washington. Besides, this is St. Martin, you know, paradise. We're not going to do anything about the letters at this point. Conventional wisdom from the think tank at the Pentagon is that it's a huge bluff, probably trying to buy time for what they're up to down here. First things first. We've got to get the ICF components and Dr. Marsh back in our hands. After that we'll worry about *The Weathermen*. I think we can all guess who's behind the letter writing campaign, and it's sure not a bunch of thugs from the 70s. By the way, she tripped the EPIRB."

"Damn! That means she's in deep shit. I told her to open that transmit channel only if she felt life-threatened, or if she wasn't able to get through using normal resources. She's inventive, so I presume the former is the case. You haven't heard anything else from her have you? Did the eye-in-the-sky spot her? Where the hell are we going, anyway?"

"Haven't heard a peep. *Vega* did spot two very feminine types on several high rez passes. One is a tall, leggy brunette. Stunning. Doesn't even come close to looking like our Doctor. The other is a blond. No facial features, unfortunately. She, we are presuming it is Dr. Marsh, was looking down at what looks like a clipboard for the entire sequence. We're headed for Orleans, that little fishing village on the east side up by the border." The French and the Dutch administer St. Martin. It is the smallest island in the world to be so divided and controlled. The divisional border runs approximately east and west through the center, with the Dutch administering the southern portion. "There will be fewer prying eyes there, especially at this time of night."

"Especially in this weather," added Jeremiah Wilkins, as a powerful gust rocked the brawny Humvee.

"Hurricane *Grace* they're calling it. Supposed to track north of here by all expert accounts. That was until about six hours ago when she took an unscheduled turn due west. Guess she didn't consult the 'experts'. Now the weather gurus aren't at all sure *which* way she's going. At present, she's headed straight for your target."

"Well, I guess weather prediction still isn't quite rocket science. What time did *Vega* pick up *HAVOC* on-line full time?" asked Steele.

"About twenty one to twenty three hours ago," Conley responded. "The disparity in precise time evaluation is due to the ninety-minute orbit period of the satellite. Either way, it puts *HAVOC*'s influence in the realm of possibilities for affecting the radical movement of the storm. That's one helluva heat source they've got. I hate to admit it, and it's certainly hard to believe, but your Dr. Marsh may just have a functioning instrument."

"She's far from mine, and I wish she *did* have it. Unfortunately, I think our boy *Wolverine* is controlling the performance."

"That's why I brought along these reinforcements for you," said Conley, patting the driver on the shoulder. "You've got about twelve to fifteen hours to go in and get her before *Grace* hits that island full force. Weather's predicted to deteriorate drastically starting now, if you haven't noticed." As if to emphasize Conley's information the Hummer was rocked by another powerful gust. "The photo analysts tell us that it appears *Wolverine* has twenty two men on the island. In addition, there are at least four patrol craft offshore circling, each with a crew of two."

"That's thirty, plus the two women. How many more are there that you and the 'analysts' aren't sure about?"

"The thirty doesn't include Dr. Marsh. She's supposedly on our side."

They passed through Orleans, and stopped just north of the picturesque village at a pier in desperate need of some serious maintenance attention. Secured to the end of it was a long, low, lethal-looking craft attended by four, just as lethal-looking SEALs. Four more SEALs surrounded a third Humvee at the shore end of the decrepit dock. No one else could be seen, and there were no vehicles moving through the area, although the sounds of lilting music and libatious activity drifted up the shore side boulevard from one of the numerous local bars.

"Well, I count twelve of us," commented Steele after Captain Younger made introductions all around. "We've got them definitely outnumbered. Maybe they'll just surrender."

"Not too far from the truth, given the assets we've assembled," responded Conley.

"So why don't we just fly right in, rock 'n roll, and be done with it? I'm sure these fellows have the appropriate air 'assets' for the job?" asked Wilkins, nodding toward the SEAL Team.

Conley replied as he unfolded a nautical map, laying it on the hood of the nearest vehicle, "All the reasons are too numerous to mention, but these are some of the highlights. First, we don't have updated, good intel on the island." He pointed to *Langosta Cay,* as one of the SEALs shone a hand-held spot on their chart. "Most of it's covered with mature palms. Our IFR imaging didn't pick up anything unusual in there underneath the canopy, but you know *Wolverine.* Second, we've got to take the ICF components and the *HAVOC* machinery intact if at all possible, not to mention getting Dr. Marsh out safely. Now that we're relatively certain that it is truly a functioning device, all sorts of government agencies will be dying to get their test tubes on it. Three, there's a better chance they might hear us coming by air than by water, which would compromise the success of number two, to say nothing of your health. I don't want you guys flying into to the teeth of a hurricane, which is number four and assumes that *Grace* will continue on her present course. The additional reasons get somewhat redundant and tedious from here on out, so I'll spare you. Besides, that baby out there can do the job nearly as fast as air, with damn good fire support." They all looked at the dark craft impatiently pulling at her moorings. The seas began to churn even within the confines of the protected bay.

"This is the *Mark V,*" instructed Captain Younger, as they all gingerly made their way down the rickety wooden pier. "82 feet of pure muscle powered by two gas turbines. Fully loaded, she'll do in excess of 50 knots with a range of around one fifty. Basically it's the Navy's answer to Cigarette boats."

"Impressive," admired Steele.

"Last I heard you guys were using HSBs," noted Wilkins.

"Higher top end, less range and lower load capacity," responded Younger.

"Besides, all the High Speed Boats are on the west coast. This rocket was in Florida and ready to go. It took me a bit of string pulling with the Special Boat Unit personnel to let it go and without a crew, though," added Conley.

"We might even know how to drive her, despite what the SBUs will try and tell you," chuckled the young SEAL Captain. "In her normal configuration she'll carry sixteen of us, two crew, all our gear, and two Zodiacs. However, we've got extra fuel tanks for the mission tonight, so it'll be kinda cramped with the twelve of us, plus gear. Y'all can water ski over if you'd like. It'll give us a bit more room," encouraged Younger.

"Not at 'in excess of 50 knots' I'm not."

"I didn't know Paiutes knew how to ski," said Steele. He jumped onto the sloping aft deck. The two SEALs on board looked at each other with eyebrows raised. Earlier in the evening, the DDO briefed the SEALs about the two new team members who would join them for this mission. He told them both Wilkins and Steele were more than capable of taking care of themselves, both were service, special forces trained, and that both had seen combat in Vietnam. This later tidbit duly impressed the young SEALs. This would be the first 'hot' sortie for four of them. Conley didn't mention that one of them was a full-blooded Native American.

"Welcome aboard, sir. The deck is sloped like this so we can make insertions and extractions while fully underway. We've got five deck mounts for weapons back here as well. Based on the intel DDO Conley provided, and given the weight and space envelope, I've decided to go with two M2 .50 caliber Heavy Machine Guns, plus one 7.62mm Mini Gun in addition to our personal kits," continued Captain Younger. "The Director tells me you guys want to go in stealthy so I guess we won't need anything too much heavier, 'cause we ain't gonna be standing off lobbing heavy fire at the beach. At least that's what the action plan, such as it is, calls for at the moment."

"OK. Let's get you guys under way. We figure it'll take you an hour to an hour and a half to reach *Langosta*, not counting the weather and recon before you land. It looks like the south end somewhere is the best ingress area, but it's up to you to decide when you get there. Remember, the two primary objectives in the COA (*Courses of Action*). If you happen to wax a few 'unfriendlies' in the execution, I'll just have to live with that," Conley smiled, summing up. He handed the charts and maps to Wilkins. "The contact frequencies are all there, plus a timeline. We've got two MH-60s standing by. One's a *Pave Hawk,* and the other's a Special Ops bird, but don't count on them for backup or egress due to weather, as I explained earlier. Steele, Wilkins… Captain Younger is OIC (*Officer in Command*). Younger, these two guys are some of the best in the business, so don't hesitate to take their advice. Everyone put your egos on hold. Those guys on the island are all experienced pros, so all of you pay attention to your butts."

With amazing agility for a big man, Wilkins jumped aboard. His graceful leap didn't go un-noticed by the SEALs still on the pier who followed closely behind. Five minutes later the menacing craft eased away from the dock, her engines growling in aggravation at the slow speed the pilot employed, as he guided her out of the bay. Conley heard, rather than saw the MK-5 get underway, as the slate gray vessel disappeared into the night with a powerful throaty roar.

77

An eerie calm settled over the Leeward, Windward, and Virgin Islands. The normal trades disappeared. Shore and land birds sensed a change in pressure long before any weather showed itself, and they hunkered down in hiding and waited. The absence of their raucous calling added to the aberrant quiet pervading the area, sometimes referred to as the *'Indies'*. The leading edge of hurricane *Grace* was still hundreds of miles east of *Langosta Cay* as the MK-5 sliced the building swells, which portended her advance. The brute waves were driven by winds in excess of 150mph within the storm. 200 miles west of the front, those faced by the SEALs plus two were one third of that, but increasing steadily. Still, for all aboard, despite the individually padded compartments with hydraulic shocks in the seats, it was an unpleasant journey.

The capsule of arctic air blows into a low-pressure wave. It collides with a huge mass of subtropical air sucked in from the central Pacific, southwest beyond Hawaii. The disharmony of the two masses intensifies into a serious winter storm. The disturbance meanders southeast across the Yukon, and then dips into British Columbia via the Gulf of Alaska. The normal storm track for a disturbance such as this is generally east. This one seems to stall for a relatively long period almost directly over Juneau, as if deciding on which way to go next. Unseasonably hard rains pound the west coast of BC as the storm finally begins spinning south, following the Coastal Mountains into the continental United States. Like its cousin almost half a world away, it draws sustenance from the relatively warm waters of the coastal Pacific, and continues to consume and inhale hemisphere-sized masses of sub-tropical air. Powerful winds sweeping down from the cold front between the warm and cold masses signal big trouble to meteorologists watching its development.

It is the sixth in a series of storms, which have saturated the northwest in the month of October 1991.

For the next three days, the storm meanders across central Washington, then into Oregon at a leisurely twenty miles an hour. Once again it stalls. This time on the border of California and Oregon, and for the following three days, its overwhelming size and capacity drench the coastal and mountain regions in record amounts of rainfall. Supersaturated, the ground no longer can hold or absorb the prodigious quantities of water, and it begins flooding off the land into streams and rivers, ultimately either flowing back into the sea, or inundating quickly rising lakes and reservoirs. Many of these reservoirs soon exceed their design capacities and water managers, in order to save their dams and with little choice, are forced to dump outflow at over maximum, which in turn will stress flood measures downstream. Flood warnings are issued all over northern California. But the worst is yet to come.

Heat and moisture drive the storm engine. Suddenly, for no apparent reason, it gains furious momentum burgeoning upward and galloping southeast across the splendid Sierra Nevada, as if drawn by some unseen force. This unusual up-thrusting characteristic doubles the size of the monster storm within hours. The void created by rising warm air, the essence of the beast, is quickly filled with more fuel. The cycle feeds on itself. The storm's ravenous hunger for sustenance continues to siphon warm tropical moisture from the Pacific into its mechanism, increasing the deluge and the danger for those unlucky enough to be in the path of its easterly exodus.

On the bridge of the *Star of India*, Fahid Aziz braced himself against the polished wood of the ship's wheel as another unseen mountain of water passed beneath the keel of the venerable old Liberty. Both had experienced and weathered horrendous weather before, but only the human was concerned. No matter how experienced the sailor, when the weather gets mean he still worries, for he knows that only his skill and the strength of his ship stand between him and eternity. Sometimes, often in a hurricane, skill and strength are not enough. Aziz knew the gale, as they were calling it when last he was able to hear anything on his radio, was coming. It was the ominous static layered across all bandwidths that was the tip-off. For six hours the *Star* ran its bow into the building seas. When it grew dark and the crew could no longer see the furious water surrounding them, they foretold the imminence of the storm's approach by the rhythm and feel of their vessel as she pitched up the crests of the mountainous seas, then plunged down the stomach-swallowing inclines that inevitably follow. A wallow in the trough and the frightening sequence would repeat again and again. Any sustained, normal shipboard activity was impossible, least of all sleep. At 9pm, waves began breaking high over the *Star*'s bow and forward deck wells. Fahid saw a cauldron of foaming white water all around as his ship shook herself free, emptying angry seas back through the scuppers. The last VHF report he was able to copy was from a ship miles to their northwest. She broadcasted on the marine emergency frequency of 2182 kilohertz. They reported ten-meter swells and warned that they were turning west to run with them. Fahid steered a course due north and was getting smashed head-on. Based on that final report and his present predicament, he rightfully concluded that his adversary was a full-blown hurricane.

"These have got to be close to twenty meters," he thought. Glancing starboard, he didn't see the black wall approaching dead ahead…its frothing summit well above his eye level. Sometimes, storm waves stack when they catch up with pre-existing ocean swells that can originate outside the storm. Often, these are so steep and immense that even a large ship cannot possibly ride up and over. Such was the case with this rogue wave. The *Star* sliced through the wave's gut, and as the tough old vessel passed though, tons of water hammered the glass windshields on the bridge. Fortunately they held. Fahid was knocked off his feet as the *Star* was instantly slowed by millions of gallons of seawater walling before her. Then, miraculously, she passed completely through the monster, shook herself from side to side ridding herself of the wave's death grip, and slid down into the following trough. In somewhat of a daze, Fahid struggled to his feet amidst all manner of debris, broken loose by the concussive force of the wave. Rumbling crashes echoed throughout his vessel, mostly from the stern compartments. He rang for the engine room, and thankfully, got an immediate answer. He stared out into the night, trying to see if there was a following sister to the calamity they had just survived. The *Star* continued on undaunted, riding the growing sea waves with precarious ease. "That was thirty meters if it was an inch," Fahid Aziz swallowed hard.

"What time did you first pick up that transmission?" asked Dominic.

"Right after you guys had me imaging the horizon, around 9:30 or 10:00 this morning," Bob the patrol boat captain responded.

"Well, why'd you wait so long to say something, God damn it?"

"How was I supposed to know the signal was coming from right on the island? We don't carry localizing gear out there, boss."

Following the end of his shift at four that afternoon, Bob and his partner walked from the dock to the dining room via the communications areas. Transferring their gear from the speedy patrol vessel and turning its control over to the next shift, they warned their relief of the quickly deteriorating weather and heavy seas coming in from the east. They reported the emergency transmissions to the duty personnel in communications, and were just finishing their early dinner when Sharpe and Dominic found them. Louvered metal wind protectors had been lowered to shield the open air eating area from the rising winds, swirling in from the east. The first sustained rains rattled against the metal fixtures, just as they finished eating.

"That signal could have been coming from anywhere from any number of sources as far as we could tell. It *was* on the strong side, now that I think about it."

The communications team tuned into the VHF transmission and quickly triangulated the origination of the signal. The headman called over to the *HAVOC* control center on the landline asking for Dominic. "Why are you guys broadcasting an emergency on an open frequency over there?" the comm chief queried his boss.

"What the fuck are you talking about?"

"We've localized an emergency transponder beaming from your 20," the technician reported using CB speak.

"What?"

"Guess that means you don't know anymore about it than we do," chuckled the tech. "Come on over and I'll let you see and hear for yourself."

Five minutes later, Lew Sharpe and Dominic shouldered their way into the cramped Comm center. Five minutes after that they were upstairs interrogating Bob and crew. Receiving little further information than they already had, Dominic led Sharpe out into the wind-driven rain heading back to the *HAVOC* 'shack', as the crew now called the command and control center. Any discussion en route was impossible, as the wind driving through abundant palm fronds created a cacophonous clattering, which in combination with the roar of heavy surf pounding the eastern shore of the cay, was nearly overwhelming. The two men crashed into the control room amidst a swirl of water and gusting wind, slamming and bolting the sturdy metal door behind them. Sharpe carried a hand-held device, which looked much like a common metal detector. To the amazement of all present that stopped to watch, he began sleuthing around the control and display units, slowly waving the unit back and forth over the equipment. "Here!" he announced triumphantly. He stood directly in front of the ICF temperature sensor, precisely where Conley's team had installed and hidden the tiny EPIRB. Lew Sharpe looked slowly around the room. Dr. Devoney Marsh was nowhere to be seen.

US Bureau of Reclamation engineers monitoring inflows to Folsom Lake did so from a concrete command center, buried deep within the bowels of Folsom Dam. Though somewhat concerned with the total amount of runoff from the foothills of the Sierra so early in their 'collection year', the men making the flow decisions were confident of the facility's ability to deal with the abnormal quantities of water generated from multiple October storms. Calculated reservoir capacity at that moment was just over 750,000 acre-feet, or about 75 percent of availability. The lake was currently collecting runoff from the tail end of the latest storm. Water was cascaded in torrents off super-saturated ground throughout the drainage area, and inflow was at a manageable 30,000 cubic feet per second, but that number was increasing. Even operating their three penstocks and other intake conduits below maximum-rated outflow capacities, it would be weeks before the tainter gates would come into play, if they relied on current absorption statistics. Nothing to worry about. The likelihood of additional back-to-back powerful storms this early in the season was statistically improbable. Current outflow, coordinated by the California Department of Water Resources Flood Control Division, was running at a conservative 10,200c.f.s. Once runoff from the current storm receded, the engineers knew that a carefully calculated program of releases would reduce the lake's capacity to about half in anticipation of further late fall and winter storms. They always tried to maintain 400,000 acre-feet of storage for flood control throughout the season. Once it was available again, their comfort level would be restored.

78

"Jesus, sir!" exclaimed the XO as he struggled to slam shut the companionway door to the bridge.

"Yeah. Before it's all over, we might need his help as well," said Aziz through clenched teeth.

The wheelhouse was a disaster. Charts, pencils, rain gear, and a variety of tools and instruments were strewn all over the deck. Pieces of Fahid's coffee mug crunched underfoot. The *Star* still maintained a steady though plodding course north, encouraged by masterful seamanship at the hand of its Captain. Aziz was doing his best to wrestle the helm, appropriately trying to anticipate the direction of the next killer wave. While reliable, the nearly fifty year old, three cylinder, reciprocating triple expansion steam engine did not provide the ship enough steerage to make swift directional adjustments, so intuition was key to the effort. A quick glance at the gimbaled compass housed in a brass binnacle directly in front of the wheel station showed both sailors that the waves were beginning to come at them off their port bow. The captain compensated with rudder and engine speed to keep the ship headed into the worsening weather.

"Did you check the…?"

"Yes, sir. The cargo is secure. I dogged down the slack in the chains myself," interrupted the XO. They had sailed enough together that they thought nearly alike. At least when it came to matters of the sea.

"What about that noise aft?"

"Portable generator broke loose and did some serious damage to an interior bulkhead. It wasn't structural, and nothing that'll sink us. Four of the boys wrestled it back where it started. It won't budge again."

"I'm considering coming about and running with these seas until daybreak."

"Not a bad thought, but the turn'll probably kill us," countered the XO. "Then we've got to deal with trailing water over the stern and into the engine compartment. Would've been a no-brainer if they'd built these rust buckets with the bridge aft."

"Another screw and triple the horsepower would be nice, as well," Aziz added. "If she lies down in the turn, I don't know if she'll come back. We've only bent her over to about 50 degrees that one time in the Indian Ocean. But I don't think she can take another direct hit from another one of those rogues."

The big First Officer had never seen or heard his boss and friend quite so obviously worried. "Your call, boss. Shit, would you look at…" The XO's expletive was cut short by the bridge windows instantly imploding, the broken shards followed by thousands of gallons of seawater. The wheelhouse went immediately dark. Wind shrieked through the blown out windows. For half a minute, Aziz and the XO literally swam inside the bridge compartment inundated by the breaching sea. The *Star* rocked violently from bow to stern, then abruptly yawed to starboard. The bridge finally began to drain and the drenched seamen struggled to their knees, holding onto anything that wasn't torn away by the relentless water. Shorting electronics sparked and zapped sporadically all around them. Jolts of crashing and clanging thundered throughout the hull, as a variety of equipment and tools tore loose and careened around any open space. Finally, battery-operated backup emergency lighting kicked in, illuminating the calamity in a ghostly red luminescence. Wind-blasted rain and sea spray peppered them in stinging fusillades. Two crewmen could be heard yelling frightened obscenities outside in the companionway. They burst onto the bridge, and were stunned when they saw the wreckage and their dazed disheveled commanders.

"The starboard flying bridge is gone, Captain," one of them finally stuttered out a report. "It's nothing but a mangled snarl of steel."

"Not important now. Check the main deck and bridge house windows," yelled Aziz. The high pitch of his voice necessary to be heard over the shrieking wind and the red wash of the emergency lights cast Aziz in perfect caricature of a demented sea captain. Despite the growing debacle, the two crew and the XO stood as if rooted, and stared as their wild captain waved his arms, shouting. "Chase down and stow all that loose gear. Number One, take two men and let's get some plywood up over these and any other forward breaks. If she takes water down below we'll lose her for sure. I've gotta come about, like it or not. Get that wood ready and we'll bolt it on in the troughs," ordered Aziz, knowing the effort would border on suicidal. Finally, the other men came alive to their hazardous reality and moved in response to his orders. *If we live through the turn*, he thought.

"All right. Don't panic. She's not getting off the island. We can find her at our leisure. I want verification that we've got a hurricane tracking this way. At least we can demonstrate we've directed and intensified it, even if we didn't start this one. Then I want these elements of *HAVOC* disassembled and ready for transport." Dominic handed a one page, single-spaced list to the head shift technician. "Is the radar hot?"

"Up and active. No targets since we called in the patrols. However, we're getting surface interference on the long range settings east, due to the huge swells."

"Not a problem. Anyone coming in is likely to approach by air and it won't be from the east, particularly in this weather. Keep a sharp eye west. Lew?"

"Yes, sir."

"Are we set up for intruders?"

"Yep. I've got men on the upper deck with night vision goggles. You don't think they'll come in just for her?"

"Maybe not just for her. But the *HAVOC* package is a mighty inviting target. We've probably got the weather on our side. Chances are they won't make any attempts until after the hurricane passes. By then, we'll be gone. But keep those guys alert and let's put some people on the perimeters, now that the sea patrols are in. Best guess on where she went?"

"Probably north. That's the area she knows best. She'll head for the pier. She may think that it's the logical rescue point."

"Any good hiding spots along the way?"

"None that I don't know better than she," Lew Sharpe grinned.

"Take what and whoever you need and go get her. Keep me advised on the two-way and I'll meet you when you find her. And Lew…"

"Yeah?"

"Don't kill her. I've got something appropriate in mind."

"You got it, boss."

Devoney sprinted through the undergrowth on the east side of *Langosta*. It was pitch black and everything seemed totally unfamiliar. She thought she'd been along the unpaved trail she found herself on, but couldn't be certain. "I've got to get away from these trails and over to that pier," she told herself. "Damn. I wish I had my running shoes and a flashlight." She wore nothing more substantial than a T-shirt, shorts, and sandals. Keeping the ocean on her right, she worked through the border row of palms and undergrowth about 50 meters from the beach. She heard the rhythmic pounding of surf over the wailing of an incensed wind. Twice, she thought she could hear muffled yells of someone well behind her in toward the center of the island. "Maybe they weren't on to me after all," she concluded. Stopping to concentrate, she heard nothing but the cackle of palm fronds agitated by the pandemonium of the increasing gale. "Better that I left anyway. God knows what they would've done had they caught me. Cody said that he'd come as soon as I flipped that beacon on. I wonder how far away they are?"

Keeping up a steady pace, she ran in the open, walking quickly when going through dense cover. Lightning illuminated her intended route in split second, intermittent brilliance. After nearly 30 minutes, she came to a fenced clearing. From behind the trunk of a giant palm, she watched. After a series of lengthy stitches of lightning she was certain the enclosure was deserted. It appeared to be cluttered with all manner of discarded equipment, casings, wooden and cardboard crates, junk. She recalled Dominic mentioning a disposal collection area during their walk the day before. "Must be the place. He said they burned the paper and wood products, and bulldozed the metal into the underwater trench." It looked as if the enclosure took up about an acre, but she couldn't be sure, given the unreliable nature of her light source. She scaled the cyclone fencing and dropped heavily onto the sandy soil of the interior where she froze, waiting for her pounding heart to subside. Gingerly, she picked around the larger discards, mindful of the razor-sharp metal strapping which seemed underfoot everywhere, until she found a huge wooden packing case open on one end. She scooted inside, just as a noisy squall featuring torrential rain swept the end of the island. "Hope I'm the only one in here," she shuddered. With her back pressed against one wall, she slid to a sitting position. Despite the desperation of her situation and even though fueled by adrenaline, she felt bone-weary tired.

Aziz verified he still had steam up and associated power. His engineers were a tough bunch and had been through many storms, but this time over the blower they sounded truly scared. Apparently, they were thrown around rather severely, but the moment of swing in the engine room was far less than on the bridge, so down below they recovered quickly with less damage. The captain gathered a small cadre of officers for a brief strategy session in the mid-ship deckhouse, while one crew back on the bridge tried to hold the old ship steady.

The wheelhouse was still a catastrophe, and coherent discussion was impossible over the devil wind clamoring through the broken windscreens. He addressed a thoroughly frightened and bedraggled bunch.

"Here's the deal. I'm going to try and turn her 180 degrees so we can run with the seas and weather. I need everything movable stowed, dogged, nailed, bolted down, or thrown overboard. Yes, I'm aware that we may take water into the engine room with trailing seas. But we're being buried, taking water everywhere as we speak, trying to hit the bastards head on. We'll either short everything out and she'll electrocute us all, or we'll lose power and capsize if I continue on this course. I'll ring for full power astern, and keep her bow on to the seas in reverse hoping for the best opportunity. Wave periods are running about 15 to 20 seconds. Just after we nose over one of these mountains I'm going full right rudder, and hope that we don't get caught at ninety degrees to any crest at any point in the turn. Might take us five or six wave cycles to get past the critical angle and I'm sure it'll be chancy. With luck, she won't go all the way over and not recover. I'll attempt to use the force of the wave on the starboard bow to help throw us around. If we don't try this, we're going over or under anyway. OK, that's it. I'm open for suggestions."

Little conversation followed, and all nodded a half-hearted assent. Aziz had saved their bacon before, and they all ultimately trusted his judgment. What choice did they have? "We're not done yet, boys. We'll turn this rusted crate around and be countin' our money before you know it." Aziz was aware that it was up to him to leave them some hope. "Once we're running downwind and stern to, things should get less crazy. Number One, make sure your plywood team has everything they need to put cover on the bridge windshields. We'll install in the protection of the troughs. You and your guys will need to hang on over the tops, 'cause you'll be fully exposed to maximum gusts."

Aziz headed back for the bridge to a chorus of 'aye, ayes'.

79

"Have a nice nap, Doctor?"

Devoney awoke to a shaft of light painfully assaulting her eyes.

"Nice of you to stop and wait for us here."

She squinted trying to focus, but couldn't see anything except two dark silhouettes behind the dazzling beam. However, the mocking voice was unmistakable. Lew Sharpe. A chill of dread shot through her as her heart pounded into overdrive. She started to rise, but a forceful backhand blow to her left cheek sent her crashing toward the darkness at the rear of the crate. She scrambled to her feet, only to be struck down yet again. The metallic tang of her own blood burst across her taste buds. In a fetal ball, she hugged the back corner of the carton wanting to scream out, but knowing the futility of it. Determined not to give her tormentor the satisfaction of hearing her terror, while still cowering in the corner, her hand came across a section of loose metal strapping. Heedless of its sharp, edges she grabbed it tightly and again began to rise. Anticipating the direction of the next blow perfectly, she ducked to her left, spinning on her right heel, then reversed her spin, and simultaneously lashed out with the metal band aiming low for her attacker's shins. She was rewarded by a roared curse, followed by an animal-like yelp. Sharpe dropped his flashlight, and reached for his wounded legs with both hands. Fueled by the pent-up fury and plain old terror, Devoney struck out again. The assassin tumbled forward in agony as the strapping dug deep gouges of raw flesh from his forearms. She dove for his light, then dashed for the opening and would have made a successful escape had the second assailant whom she had forgotten in the melee not tripped her. She tumbled face first onto the rough sand just at the entrance to her wooden haven. A strong, lithesome presence was immediately upon her, and despite her frantic efforts, she could not shake the second attacker from her back. Finally, exhausted, Devoney gave in and lay still. It was then she first noticed the fragrance of exotic perfume.

Disengaging herself from the prone victim, Molucca sprang to her feet. Devoney painfully rolled over onto her back, spitting sand from her bruised mouth. She started to sit upright, freezing motionless, when she saw the remorseless dark eye of Molucca's semi-automatic Glock poised inches from her forehead.

"Slowly, very slowly, my beautiful Dr. Marsh."

Just then, Lew Sharpe staggered from the carton, bellowing like the wounded bull he was. In the luminescence of Molucca's light, the two women could see blood streaming down his arms and lower legs. With one swift motion, the Balinesean woman ripped Devoney's T-shirt from her chest and handed it to Sharpe.

"Here, Lew. Wrap your arms with this."

Sharpe ignored the bandage, instead lunging for Devoney's neck with both hands, only to be thwarted by a sharp blow to his damaged arms. Molucca stood poised to swing her heavy light again. But Sharpe crumpled to the sand in a heap, and keened a strange animalistic howl.

"Now, now, Mr. Sharpe. Remember what the boss ordered. We're not supposed to kill our guests. At least, not until he's here to supervise. Get up and shut up. You need to call in and let him know she's taken. Now wrap up those arms. You're bleeding all over my sandals."

80

The eye of a hurricane is generally a calm area near its center surrounded by towering, solid, vertical walls of clouds. Located within these cloudbanks is the energy core of the storm. Clouds and rain in the form of *'rainbands'* spiral inward toward the eye. These narrow, long strips of intense rain can begin and extend hundreds of miles away from the center of the storm. The rotation of the earth precipitates an inward spiraling phenomenon (the Coriolis force) toward the storm center and these rainbands form path indicators for winds carrying warm moist air, which feed the storm. As the rainbands approach the eye they intensify and ultimately become a solid, churning, massive wall. It is within this interior partition surrounding the eye that the highest wind speeds are usually recorded and also where the hot moist air gathered from the ocean's surface finally towers upward dramatically creating the mechanics which drive the hurricane. These towers are often referred to as *'chimneys'* for obvious reasons. The higher the air ascends, the lower the atmospheric pressure acting upon it. This lower pressure allows the air mass to cool by expansion. As it cools, moisture is condensed releasing heat to the heart of the storm basically intensifying and regenerating the dynamics of the process. In the upper atmosphere, sometimes in excess of 50,000 feet, where the air becomes much cooler, it ultimately begins to sink causing lower pressure toward the center of this cosmic chimney than that on the outside. These pressure differentials create more wind, which further allows the storm to feed on itself.

At the outer reaches of an approaching hurricane, most particularly at its leading edges, rainbands will erupt in intermittent, though often torrential, downpours. A period of relative calm, then high winds, followed by cascading rain, often in heroic proportions, will signal the storm's approach. The more frequent the downpour, the closer the storm center. Usually, a storm like *Grace* will sustain gale force winds inward to about ten to thirty miles of the cloud wall. From this distance in to the chimney, hurricane winds in excess of 74 mph can exist. It is within the vertical wall surrounding the storm's eye that winds averaging over 150mph might occur. In the eye, wind speeds drop dramatically to dead, flat calm. It is the eye where definitive cold-water up-wellings are pronounced; the warmer surface waters having been stripped away by the feeding frenzy of the storm's mechanism.

Despite the sensational press and drama afforded to hurricane winds, it is storm surge or the hurricane tide, which is the most devastating result in such a storm. The resultant flooding is the major cause of death, destruction and injury in a hurricane. While not truly a tide by definition, the surge is an abnormal rise in coastal waters over and above what would exist in the normal, periodic tide. The surge is caused by the build up of water pushed along by a storm's winds over many hundreds of miles of ocean, compounded by the action of waves. Depending on the size and severity of the storm, these hurricane tides may gradually begin hours before the arrival of the storm and sometimes last for hours after, adding sometimes as much as twenty feet to the normal high tide line.

81

His Doppler radar showed nearly solid masses of rainsqualls coming at them from their port bow. Unbeknownst to Aziz, the most intense quadrant of the storm was already upon them. His sole, occupying concern was for holding the *Star* into the oncoming behemoth waves. He had to time the period of the wave from crest-to-crest as best he could, in an attempt to gauge the precise moment to begin his fateful turn. They successfully reversed power to full astern, yet still held their bow on to the waves. Even though they were running at four knots in reverse, as opposed to nine ahead, there was absolutely no perceptible difference in motion, relative to the onslaught of the waves. The old ship rumbled beneath Aziz's feet as if sensing her precarious predicament. Wind-driven rain and stinging ocean spray slashed through the shattered windscreens, drenching him and the two crew in the wheelhouse. A quick glance at them in the glow of the emergency lights showed the frightened faces of two otherwise extremely tough individuals, their eyes wide as they all watched the next mountainous sea explode over their bow. His XO manned the engine room, and stood by at the other end of the blower.

"Don't worry, boys. Piece of cake," he hollered. *Vasquez shoulda made the trip with us after all*, he thought. *And he thinks our cut's too big. After this, I should ask for more!* "OK, XO. Give me everything we've got! I'm turning this baby on a dime." Swallowing hard, he said to himself, "Possibly a quarter… I hope."

Just as the *Star* bottomed through the next abysmal trough, Aziz put the helm hard astarboard and braced himself. As the ship struggled up the forward wall of the next gigantic wave, he could feel her vibrate even more, but with no perceptible change in direction. As the foaming crest shattered over the bow and they began their heart-swallowing plummet down the back of the wave, he felt the beginning of a list to port followed by a noticeable turning sensation. Accumulated water and debris in the bridge was swept against the port wall. Still, he held the helm over, losing his footing to the swirling water, but maintaining his leverage by grasping the compass binnacle with his free hand. The needle on the gimbaled dial within was clearly swinging. They rode over another crest, feeling its enormous power compress their bodies as the ship's bow swung skyward. Over the top, one third of the *Star*'s keel thrust completely free of the sheer back side of the giant black wave. They crashed back into the furious sea, water cascading well over the gunwales, burying the foredeck. She wailed a torturous, metallic moan in protest, but yanked buoyantly free. As their turn tightened, the port list grew to 30, then 45 degrees. Still, Aziz held the wheel over against its stops, despite the frantic protests of the two crew. He could hear a chaos of crashes from within the tortured hull, and hoped that none were the result of anything vital wrenching free. By the next wave crest, the *Star* was nearly right-angled to the direction of the wave. As she rose up toward the perilous apex, for a few anxious seconds, her list orientation to the horizon was well beyond ninety degrees, and her list angle to the wave was over forty. Only the raw power and sheer forward momentum of the gargantuan wave kept her from rolling. Thousands of tons of water at the crest swatted the exposed starboard bow of the *Star*, her own 10,000 plus tons mere flotsam. Fortunately, the wave's powerful blow assisted her turn by immediately adding an additional ten degrees to port, taking her through the critical right angle moment. A split second after the strike, Aziz heard a rolling thunder come from the forward cargo hold. It was an ominous rumble, as if the Gods were throwing bowling balls below deck. Instantly, he knew that their precious cargo had broken free. An inch thick link in a chain securing the aft end of the logs parted, and was stretched straight by the enormous strain of weight and gravity releasing one end of the log deck. The majority of logs, still secured at one end, swung like colossal pendulums, crashing into the port side of the vessel with a sickening crack. The butt end of the largest log struck a steel hull plate with such force that it caused a huge dent and a small fracture crack in the metal. As the *Star* wallowed down the aft side of the mountainous wave nearly sideways, Aziz frantically muscled the helm completely over to port, a madman spinning his wheel of fate. Simultaneously, he yelled into the blower at the top of his lungs for all ahead full power. Slowly, the *Star* came about, slowly righting herself in so doing, her countering roll to starboard not nearly as acute as the port list in the midst of the turn. The logs careened to starboard but with nowhere near the force or momentum as in the first pandemonium. By the next trough the *Star* was stern to the onslaught, Aziz getting maximum forward spin on his screw. The logs were apparently at rest once more, for the bowling sounds seemed to have ceased.

"Number One?"

"No, this is Sampson. The XO is headed your way with the plywood crew," came a tentative response from the engine room.

"Everyone survive down there?"

"Well, we've got one man with two broken legs, and two with a broken arm apiece. Cuts, bruises, and scratches for everyone. Other than that, we're ready for the dance."

"Nice work, Sampson. Any mechanical trouble?"

"The pumps are just staying even with the bilge water, which is over our ankles. We're desperate to change the fuel filters because of that broach and flop over we did. We can't see a bloody thing 'cause only two of the emergency lights work. The generator's intermittent, if you haven't noticed. It's hotter than hell down here, and we've got pieces and parts of crap all over the compartment. Other than that, everything's just dandy, thanks for asking."

Aziz laughed hard. So long as the crew demonstrated even a slight sense of humor, albeit of the gallows variety, he knew they would perform.

"All right, steady as she goes. The comfort level of the ride should improve some now that we're straight on to the seas again." The XO stumbled onto the bridge, bleeding profusely from a nasty gash to his forehead. "Get those filters changed ASAP. I don't want to end up dead in the water in the middle of this. Trust me. You don't want to see these seas." The bridge crew watched stunned, as another brute wave burst around them from behind, its crest well above the wheelhouse.

"Shit! That's another one thirty meters at least! Number One. Find three or four guys who are still able-bodied, and secure that timber forward before it takes us over on our side. And stick a cork in that bleeder on your head."

Sharpe reported in on his radio, after crudely bandaging his wounded forearms with strips of cotton material torn from Devoney's T-shirt. Dominic ordered them to stay put and wait for him. Twice more, Molucca had to forcefully warn Sharpe not to attack their cringing prisoner. Devoney watched and listened in horror, afraid to move a muscle. In the reflected beam of Molucca's light, she could see Sharpe's agitated countenance twist into a red mask of fury. Lowering his face to within inches of hers, Sharpe cursed vehemently; informing her in explicit detail of all the hideous things he was going to do to her body. His disgusting spittle sprayed her face and when she attempted to turn away he crushed her jaw in his rough hand and forced her to hear him out, eyeball to maniacal eyeball. Molucca laughed casually in the background. Heedless of her semi-naked chest exposed in a half-bra, with brute strength and hatred he spun Devoney over and forced her face down. Course, wet sand ground into soft skin when Sharpe wrenched both her hands behind her back, and bound them securely at the wrists. A tie at her ankles completed her incapacitation. For a measure of revenge, he also tied three wraps around her elbows and drew the rope painfully tight. She tried not to whimper in agony. Rain began to cascade on them in a ceaseless downpour, rather than in bursting squalls. Sharpe and Molucca sought shelter back inside the large crate, leaving Devoney hogtied outside on the sand, struggling not to inhale the quickly pooling water.

Five minutes later a lone, ghostly figure dashed out of the palm orchard, head angled forward against the slashing rain. Dominic arrived running. Sharpe hailed him from inside the protection of the crate. He strode right over Devoney's bound form to join his associates out of the rain. Then shouted out to her.

"Well, babe. Guess we both knew it would end. I just didn't think it would be quite like this. A disposal site, how ironic." Water pounded over Devoney's mouth, and she needed to struggle to an uncomfortable position on her side to keep from drowning.

"They're working on packing up the *HAVOC* components right now," Dominic explained to Sharpe, panting to catch his breath. "Should be ready in about thirty minutes. Take Molucca and get to the compound. Then have the two choppers loaded and ready to move."

"We're leaving in this weather?" Sharpe asked.

"We can't take the chance on waiting around for the good Doctor's friends. I think we'll be OK. Those Bell Jets are tough birds. I've flown one in pretty marginal weather a few times. What's the matter, Lew? A little wind and rain got you spooked? We'll pick up the Gulfstream in Florida and be in sunny California before anyone knows it."

"What about her?"

"I'll take excellent care of her, my friend. Count on it. I know you wanted to assist, but I need you at the center. I'll tell you all about it in detail on the plane."

Despite the pounding rain, the clamoring wind, and the serious pain in her bound limbs, Devoney heard every word.

Nearly two hours after surviving her harrowing turn, the *Star* maintained a reasonably steady course due south, despite the frenzied and erratic seas pushing and pulling at her. Captain Aziz really couldn't care less about their direction. Rather, he was pleased that the old ship, though battered, was still afloat and had power. Shattered windscreens were covered with plywood, the main generator was back in action, and his precious cargo was once again secure in the forward hold. He was content to run out the hurricane in this direction. He knew that storms in this latitude normally would track north and west so he figured correctly that all he was losing by staying his course south were the few hours it would take for the storm to pass over. The time lost was nothing compared to having his life and the riches hidden within the complement of logs in the forward cargo hold.

Aziz corrected course and adjusted power by feel, as he could see nothing around him, thanks to the plywood bolted over the bridge windows. He steered in such a way as to maintain an upright attitude relative to the forward motion of each giant wave, and could only hope that the vessel wouldn't loose purchase on her rudder and keel skidding down the forward slopes of the mammoths. He and his XO were almost thankful they *couldn't* see out, for the sight of twenty meter waves rolling under their insignificant ship would certainly frighten the most courageous and experienced seaman, no matter the size of the vessel.

Damage and injury reports flooded into the bridge. Nearly every one of the crew had been injured. The worst was to the engine crewman who suffered breaks to both his legs. A heavy tool cabinet came loose and pinned him to the oily deck. His injuries were painful, but not life threatening. Gamely, the rest of the crew worked through their myriad wounds, understanding that their ship required the most care and nurturing if they were to survive. At least until the storm ran its course. No one thought about or bothered to check on Chantelle in the meat locker. It didn't matter, as the entire crew was far too occupied to enjoy, or even contemplate her services, had she still been alive to provide them. The first and most vital order of business was to wrestle the logs back to their stowage position. This was a most dangerous process, as the hold was dark, and the free ends of the logs tended to roll menacingly from side to side with each wave. Until this lateral motion could be stayed, the momentum and weight of the logs jeopardized the *Star*'s upright angle.

She would tend to list precariously to the side the logs would tumble, only to lamely struggle back upright, thanks to the skill of her captain countering with power and helm. The repair crew had to be nimble to avoid being crushed to death by the log's deadly swath, as they pendulum-ed to and fro. One by one, they were repositioned to the center, and then blocked in place by oversize wooden wedges until they all could be chained to the deck once again. The XO found the dented hull plate, and reported to his captain that the damage, while severe, was not overly critical, for the harm was above their waterline, except when listing to port. In the gloom of the hold, he did not notice the hairline crack near the outer edge of the dimpled plate. The pumps in the engine room still only kept even with the insidious water, gaining on it by a few hundred gallons on the upslope of the towering walls, then losing it all back on the downside. With each successive assault, small oily waves of bilge water under the engine room floor grates mimicked those of their huge cousins, scouring the exterior of the *Star.* If they could only break free of the storm, or if the wave size would decrease by a few meters, they might get ahead. Fortunately, no wave had yet broken over their stern subsequent to their turn; the occurrence Aziz feared most.

"Captain! Look at this!" shouted the XO. He pointed at the glowing green monitor of their Doppler weather radar. While the ship was old, thanks to the profits from her occupation, her equipment was state-of-the art. The range of the display varied between ten and 200 nautical miles. The current setting was on fifty.

"Damn lucky we've still got the mast," commented Aziz. He craned his neck around to see the small screen.

"And power to operate it," responded the XO.

"I'll be damned."

"Yep," the XO concurred. They both stared at the area in the right center of the screen. It indicated a circular region devoid of clouds and precipitation. "It's got to be the eye."

Aziz did the math, "About thirty minutes off our port bow on this heading. We should be able to hold on 'til then."

"At least," agreed the XO, still grinning.

"Bound to be dicey until we break through the eye wall, though. But can't be much worse than we've already weathered."

The *Star* suffered through the eye wall and burst through to the relative calm and serenity of the lower left quarter of *Grace*'s eye. Continuing on their same course would take the vessel back into the least violent of the storm's quadrants. *Grace* had burgeoned to a behemoth nearly eight hundred miles across at her north south axis, well beyond the range of the *Star*'s radar to comprehend. Unfortunately, the point at which the old ship broke into the hurricane's eye was also the coordinate experiencing the greatest surface temperature deterioration, due to massive cold-water upwelling. In a matter of less than three and one half miles, the hull plates of the *Star of India* experienced a thirty five degree degradation in water temperature to just under 44 degrees Fahrenheit. In the midst of their mutual congratulations for surviving the hellacious hurricane, Aziz and his Number One heard a thunderous crack reverberate throughout their ship. It felt and sounded as if a bolt of lightning had struck their foredeck.

Dominic waited until Molucca and Sharpe disappeared into the darkness of the plantation, and then ventured out into the storm. He bent over Devoney and swiftly cut the rope from her ankles, then lifted her to her feet by the tie at her elbows. She cried out in pain.

"I'll bet that *does* hurt," he yelled over the crashing rain, admiring her bare chest. "Too bad you chose the wrong side, Dev."

She looked into his steely eyes and saw no hope or compassion. Her tears of pain and fright washed away in the rain. "What're you going to do?"

"About what?"

"Me?"

"Oh. Thought you were asking about your device. You and I are going for a walk. *HAVOC*'s going for a little cross-country flight. One more demonstration like this and I think we just might cash in and head for the sunny tropics." Roughly, he spun her around, and shoved her ahead.

She tried to think of something she might say or do to stall whatever it was he had in mind. At the same time she furtively glanced around, looking for possible escape routes. She knew that on her own it would be impossible. She needed to buy time that didn't seem to be for sale. "You know they'll be coming. They're probably on their way right now," she said, hoping. Her voice sounded desperate, even to her.

"Not likely. Look around. We're in the middle of a hurricane in the middle of the night, if you haven't noticed. Any rescue team won't be stupid enough to risk it until this breaks or passes," he assured her.

"I know Cody..." she said, and then stopped abruptly.

"What did you say?" He yanked her to a stop and swung her around by the shoulders to face him.

"Nothing. I didn't say anything."

"Wrong. You said something about Cody. There's only one Cody I know who could possibly be mixed up in this, and that's Cody Steele."

Devoney just stood there in wet, painful misery. *Wolverine* searched her face for what seemed like hours, but was no more than seconds. Then a look of understanding flashed across his face. "You're Steele's Doctor. Now it all starts to fall into place. We knew he was involved with someone on faculty at Berkeley. At least off and on over the years. Never was worth me pursuing for the leverage against him. You don't seem like his type. Then, I suppose he doesn't have a type in his line of work."

Devoney's chin dropped to her chest, and her shoulders slumped in resignation at the truth in his words.

Dominic smiled a slow evil smile. "So Steele will be in the rescue effort. Almost makes me want to stay and take care of a few outstanding debts he still owes. Almost, but I've a few other items of business which are much more important than Steele at the moment. Keep moving," he laughed as they continued on through the night and rain. "Cody Steele. I'll be damned. Well Dr. Marsh, I don't believe in serendipity. Perhaps your showing up in PNG was a set up. However, the intensity of your passion though...hmm. That's hard to fake. You're either a great actress, or *really* confused." His thoughts trailed into silence as they blundered on through the night. "*Pavao. That* was very real," he reasoned. "So, possibly our introduction to this whole affair was on the up-and-up. No way you, he, or they could have known," he concluded. "See, Devoney, this storm will keep your hero grounded for at least a few more hours, even if they were bright enough to pick up your tiny signal. If not, it won't matter after that anyway. At least, it won't matter to you."

"You're going to kill me."

"Me. Nah. I'm a civilized man. You know that. I won't. But ... *HAVOC* might. You're lucky I sent Sharpe out on other errands. Now there's a fellow you should worry about."

They struggled through the driving rain for another twenty minutes. Dominic's light was but meager help, and Devoney stumbled nearly every other step, her bondage contributing to her lack of balance. Quickly, she became totally disoriented as her sense of direction relative to the sound of the surf was destroyed, lost in the lament of the gale-force wind driving the big seas against all sides of *Langosta Cay.* The sound converged on them from every bearing. Finally, they broke out of the palms onto a beach about 200 meters south of the pier. They could see it brilliantly outlined by the flashes of almost continuous streaks of lightning. She observed huge waves bursting over the far end, the solid pier breaking the crests into long veils of wind-driven, flowing foam. He picked up their pace to almost a jog by grasping her elbow with his free hand, and literally pulling her along with him in the direction of the pier. On one side, the four patrol boats strained at their moorings, slamming a torturous tattoo against the pilings. On the other, the buoyant shark cages were securely chained top and bottom, not moving an inch. The clutching seas reached about a third of the way up their aluminum bars.

"OK, Doc. This is your new home." Dominic was up on the pier, and he opened the top hatch on the nearest cage. "Hope you like it."

The wind blew spray all around him. Thunder rumbled and crashed continuously. Lightning stitched the roiled sky. The sound of it was overwhelming. Absurdly, it reminded Devoney of something out of Disney's *Fantasia.*

82

The need for speed to produce quantities of Liberty Ships during W.W.II resulted in a production line effort where various compartments and components of each ship were pre-fabricated then mated and welded together. This technique was a significant departure from the time consuming method using rivets. Over 5,000 of these ships were mass-produced in this manner; often some were completed keel to launch in a matter of days. Normally, steel plating such as that used in the building process of these ships will yield or deform to a certain extent when high stresses are placed upon it. The 'yield strength', or the point at which the metal will start to bend or stretch under stress, is approximately 50% of its 'tensile strength'. Under nominal conditions at stress loads up to its maximum tensile capacity, such metal will deform or stretch to between 25% and 40% of its length before ultimately breaking. In engineering jargon, this flexibility or pliance is referred to as 'ductility'.

In 1963, the United States Naval Research Laboratory published a study describing what is referred to as the 'Nil Ductility Transition' (NDT) temperature phenomenon. This occurrence has subsequently been referred to as 'brittle fracture'. The Navy's publication was the first scientific research addressing and quantifying the temperature at which the molecular dynamic of steel under stress changes from ductile to brittle. The driving force behind the fifteen-year study was the significant failures suffered by over 20% of the Libertys during and after the course of the war, some 1,200 vessels in all. In the later stages of the war effort, at least three of these ships literally broke in half, one while actually tied to a pier in Boston. After a thorough examination of the two halves and the origination of the break, it was determined that the plates and welds failed at the yield rather than the tensile

326

strength of the metal. They literally shattered as if brittle glass, the crack instantly running the entire circumference of the hull. It was determined that the catastrophe was caused mainly by the 35 degree temperature of the harbor water and precipitated by a stray arc welder's strike. This event led the Navy to contemplate how many of the losses of these ships in the North Atlantic were due to action by the enemy as opposed to the temperature of the icy waters where they sailed. Further study brought up the disturbing suggestion that many of the Libertys, which might have survived an initial assault, may have been lost when they shattered due to NDT temperature phenomenon. The culminating evidence came when comparing the failure rate of ships in the North Atlantic, which was substantial, versus that of those operating in the warm waters of the South Pacific, virtually zero.

The Navy's research detailed that metal plating could be successfully loaded or stressed to its maximum tensile strength above the NDT temperature. However, below that critical temperature, when the same plate is loaded to only its yield strength (about half that of its tensile capacity) it will shatter like glass, the crack continuing until it runs out of steel, runs into a piece of ductile metal, or until the stress load is alleviated. The propagation of this event results at temperatures lower than the NDT temperature of the steel plating and a precipitating point of origin such as a pre-existing crack or heavy blow to the metal. The average NDT temperature for the steel of the 5,000 plus Liberty Ships, including the *John Nash* AKA *Star of India,* was determined to be a water temperature of 50 degrees Fahrenheit.

Aziz and all the rest of his crew regardless of where they were stationed were thrown violently forward, then immediately wrenched back and pounded against aft walls and bulkheads. For an instant, all momentum ceased. It was as if the *Star* has run hard aground, though the depth beneath her keel was well over five hundred fathoms. Then, almost instantly, the ship lurched bow-up at 60 degrees. Except there was no bow anymore. At the speed of sound, the brittle fracture ran the circumference of the ship beginning from the crack in the forward portside cargo hold hull plate. The *Star* clam shelled open and split completely apart. The forward third of the ship sank in five seconds, taking most of the cargo with it. The logs not pulled beneath the confused seas spilled out onto the surface, except for one whose tie-down chain caught in a jagged tear sliced into a hull plate in the section still afloat. It swung outboard of what once was the port section of the main deck area. The bulk of weight in the remaining aft two thirds of the stricken vessel centered in her submerged engine compartment, a lucky break for those not thrown immediately overboard. They had a few more precious moments to contemplate their fate. Unfortunately, what was left of the *Star* still afloat was open to the elements, like a ripped open tin can tentatively bobbing in a maelstrom. Equipment and machinery rained down on the trapped crew, killing many, and burying several beneath tons of debris. Aziz lived through the ferocity of the first catastrophe, and struggled over the mangled body of his dead XO, out his ruined wheelhouse, and onto the port flying bridge. Crawling along a catwalk wall, now his floor, he peered over the side to the churning water 75 feet below, wondering what happened and what to do next. Straight above him, sixty feet up, was the sliced open remains of the main deck. He called out in vain. No one was there and he received no answer. The hulk began to cork in the confused winds of the hurricane's eye. His ears still ringing from the splitting concussion of his ship ripping apart, he didn't hear the clattering of the one remaining jacaranda log tolling ominously against the torn hull as the ruined ship porpoised back and forth. The huge boiler wrenched free in the bowels of the stricken vessel far below; and crashed the vertical length of the engine compartment, puncturing the submerged stern. Water blasted like a geyser up through the rent in the old plating. The remains of the *Star* started their final journey. Vertical and one way. As she began to settle, the weight of her massive screw caused the wreckage above to swing in a counter direction. The captured log swung outboard in a deadly arc. Aziz contemplated his options, and thought of abandoning ship. He didn't see or hear the 1,000-pound club whistling toward him in the dark. Answering a chill of premonition, he rose up and was swatted off his perch like an insignificant bug. He was dead before the ruins of his mutilated body struck the surface of the angry sea.

83

Just before 2:30am, the Mark-5 struggled to maintain position off the south end of *Langosta Cay*. The approach had gotten progressively wilder as they closed the distance with the leading edge of hurricane *Grace*. Four to eight meter seas rolled under the keel, and it took both pilots working in concert to keep the sleek craft steady. The occasional conversation had to be screamed over the whistling wind and the constant modulations of the whining gas turbines. They held 200 meters off a potential landing area. Cautiously, they ran two complete circuits of the small island, noting the four patrol craft recorded by *Vega* weathering the enormous swells, somewhat safely tied to the lee side of the long pier at the north end.

"At least the storm is giving us a few breaks," Cody yelled. He handed the field glasses back to Captain Younger. "You look a little green, Jeremiah."

"Don't get much chance to surf like this in Nevada," the Indian grinned.

They hadn't seen a soul so far, but did catch an occasional light glimmering through the palms when the wind ripped apart their tough fronds.

"OK. Here's the COA the way I see it," shouted the SEAL Captain. "We'll take 'er into the east side of that beach to dismount. We've got to leave two with the boat, so Robinson, McCarthy, Jones, and Wilkins will be with me. We'll work our way up the east side and filter in toward the central area where the equipment is supposed to be, according to the satellite intel. Steele, you take MacPhee, Parker, Gunnery Sergeant Dillon, and Jameson up the west side, and visit that two-story structure with the antennae. I want suppressers on until the bad guys start shooting, if they get the chance. Game plan is, don't let 'em. We'll rendezvous back here on or before 0330. Stay off your radios at all costs. The DDO tells me these boys have all the latest hi-tech gadgets, and any transmissions might alert them. We'll get the hard goods. Steele, you save the Doctor. Questions?"

"Yeah," responded one of the younger looking men. "When's breakfast?" Younger ordered the Mark-5 crew to take the vessel out and stand offshore a safe distance, in case they needed out or heavy fire support from the fixed .50s and the minigun. They made a mad dash into the beach in the highly maneuverable Zodiacs, timing their landing to coincide with the rolling surf. Four SEALs bolted to the edge of the vegetation where it intersected the beach to secure the area. After four signaled 'clears' from the sentries, each team pulled its sturdy little craft up into the underbrush off the beach area. It would take someone either stumbling over them or to be specifically looking for the inflatables for them to be discovered. The teams were clothed completely in black, including blackface and black watch caps. Individual armament varied according to personal preference. Steele's command carried three M-16A2s with attached 40mm grenade launchers and two H&K MP5N 9mm assault rifles. Three of the five holstered Berretta 9mm handguns, while the remaining two sported the famous Colt 45. Each man was wired with a voice activated, hands-free microphone, connected to a multi-frequency transmitter capable of communicating man-to-man or back-to-base. Each carried a variety of grenades, including two flash bangs, and small quantities of packaged C4 explosive with detonators. *Starlight* light enhancement goggles rounded out their kits, although their use was questionable. The approaching storm was announced by stitching bolts of lightning, making the use of the night vision instruments hazardous. A unanimous command decision was made not to bear in sniper rifles, relying instead on speed and surprise to achieve their ends. They hoped to be in and out with a minimum of confrontation. In the event they found themselves in a firefight, a sniper's rifle would be of little use. The fact that Devoney tripped the EPIRB troubled Steele. If *Wolverine* discovered the transmitter she was in more trouble than she knew. Dominic's men would be expecting them, and be that much more alert. He informed the gathered team of his concerns. Fading into the covering palms, the two patrols separated just off the beach.

The ferocity of the wind grew by the minute. Appropriately, motion detectors didn't worry Steele, as they would be useless, given the amount of debris being kicked up by the gale. This left any defense of the island in the hands of humans, and even the most alert would be distracted by the gathering elements of the storm. He had the utmost confidence in his own and his team's ability to overcome and defeat the mortal obstacles. Briefly, his thoughts flashed to Wilkins, who would be in his element. Long-range recon patrol on seek and destroy missions had been his specialty in the distant jungles of Nam. Steele grinned, thinking that the SEALs with the big Indian would probably learn a thing or two. He and his team diffused quickly into a skirmish line about 75 meters long. They worked quickly from palm to palm, silently hand-signaling each other when to cover and when to advance. The first structure they came to was a small fuel storage shed, open to the elements on one side. No one was around. Fifty-gallon drums of what looked to be diesel fuel were neatly stacked in three double rows within. He motioned the closest SEAL to him to come join up inside. They molded a slice of C4 around the base of one of the drums in the bottom row, attaching a length of measured Primadet cord and inserted a blasting cap. The SEAL set a miniature timer at eight minutes, and pulled the safety.

"The hell with stealth. We're outnumbered and we need a diversion. I figure this shack is about a good five minute run from the main working area. The explosion should give us just the time we need to get in and grab the goods. We'll be there when it goes. When they find there's no one here they'll stampede back. That's ten minutes. If we can't get it done in ten…well… By then we'll have a good head start back to the beach. Contact Younger, and give those guys the timing."

"But the CO said no…"

Steele interrupted, "Yeah, I know. No radios. Sometimes you've gotta break the rules and take a few risks. Let's go!"

From the deck of the pier Dominic stuffed Devoney through the small metal hatch at the top of the shark cage, dumping her into water over her knees. He jumped down into the water after securing the hatch with a chain and lock. She slumped against the bars in utter defeat.

"Don't worry, beautiful. You'll still be here when Steele arrives after the storm. Well, at best your lovely body will. The least I can do is make your last few minutes comfortable." He withdrew a lethal-looking knife from a sheath on the inside of his left calf, its razor-sharp blade slicing easily through the rope at her wrists and elbows. She immediately pushed with all her strength against a pair of the cage's bars, ignoring the sharp pain of blood rushing back into her numb hands. "With luck, it'll be over quickly when the first storm surge rushes through. At worst, you've got an hour or so until high tide, and you'll drown very slowly. Don't waste your effort trying to force the bars, they're titanium. You'll need to save your strength for holding your breath." He laughed again and was gone.

Steele and his team had just secured behind the periphery of palms at the edge of the two-story structure, when the shock of a tremendous explosion rocked the area. Two mushrooming fireballs erupted above the palm canopy, only to be quickly dissipated and doused by the torrential wind and rain. Shouts of alarm echoed through the building, quickly alive with light in every window. Steele's team watched a heavily armed line of men pour out the main entrance, then duck for cover as they fanned out in the direction of the explosion.

"Stupid," Steele muttered. "We could pick them off like ducks at a shooting gallery. *Wolverine* needs to train these guys better."

They counted seven opposition. Steele waited forty seconds, and then motioned to his team for cover as he advanced toward the entrance. He could almost feel the sights of his squad sweep protection all around as he crouched low to the right side of the door, listening to the humming whir of an electric generator coming from close inside. He froze when the sound of an urgent voice chattered to life, coming from the room just adjacent to the door. Someone was on a radio. Arming a flash bang grenade, he bounced it in the direction of the voice, turning his eyes from the entrance. Almost instantly the doorway burst into brilliance, and a rush of gaseous smoke blossomed out into the night. Seconds later, Steele dove through the opening, rolled twice, and came upright directly in front of a stunned communications technician, his weapon fixed inches from the man's nose.

"Where's Dr. Marsh?" he shouted. The man looked up in an uncomprehending daze. Steele grabbed him by his shirt front with one hand jerking him to his feet, shouting his question again, the muzzle of his gun buried in the man's throat. The tech blubbered something unintelligible. Steele deposited the small man in a heap on the floor, just as two more of his team spun through the entrance. "Watch him," Steele ordered. "I'll check upstairs. Frank," he motioned to the second SEAL, "Secure the rest of the rooms down here."

Steele ran the interior stairs to the second floor. Carefully, he followed the barrel of his weapon low into each of the unoccupied rooms. *Good,* he thought. *The rest of the bad guys headed for the explosion. But no sign of Devoney.* Out on the balcony, he could see the fading glow of the burnt-out fuel shed, but could hear nothing save an angry wind spitting rain directly in his face. The grounds below were empty. Retreating back to the communications center, Steele mentally ran through his next move. The tech was still cowering on the floor.

"We're clear in this building. Destroy this equipment and tell Younger we're closing on his flank."

"What about…?"

Steele struck a vicious chop to the back of the whimpering man's neck. He puddled unconscious to the floor.

"Guess that answered my question," the young SEAL grinned at Steele.

"Younger says Conley has called in the choppers. Says the weather guys are showing a huge storm surge ahead of the hurricane, and he's worried about the MK5 surviving. Air support should be here in thirty."

"OK," acknowledged Steele. "Let's see how he's doing with *HAVOC*."

Just then, a line of splinters flew all around them as a burst of automatic weapon fire detonated from the surrounding trees. The SEALs dove out the door, rolling to opposite sides. Cody lay down a long return volley of covering fire, which was immediately answered threefold. The doorjamb burst into kindling just as he lunged behind a communications console. Two quick shots to the ceiling extinguished the overhead fluorescents, leaving a dull green glow from the computer's monitor the only illumination for the room. He heard exchanges coming more rapidly from outside and correctly feared that the numbers were quickly mounting against them. A deep breath as he dashed up the stairs, once more shooting out the lights before him. Out the back of the darkened upstairs kitchen he found a metal fire escape, and without thought or hesitation slid to the ground, his hands and insteps controlling his descent down the slippery wet railing. Thumbing his weapon to the three shot selection, he circled through the palms behind the raging firefight. In the eruptions of muzzle flashes the marksmen from both sides could easily be pinpointed. Recognizing the distinctively brilliant muzzle signature of the AK-47, a weapon not carried by any of his crew, he put down two quick fusillades at each of two targets. Both went silent and dark. He moved further around behind the shooters and whispered his intentions to his guys, via his sound-powered mouth mike, hoping he would be heard rather than shot. At insanely close range, but protected by the cover of palms and the discord of the raging storm, he efficiently took down two more of *Wolverine*'s men. The fight quickly diminished to sporadic single shot exchanges, then nothing. He checked in after two minutes of silence.

"Everybody OK?" he called over the howling gale. He received two 'hoo yaws' in response.

"Frank's down," came a third. "Took two in the leg and one in his foot. I think he'll make it."

"Shit yes, I will," gurgled Frank Jameson in obvious pain.

"We've got to get him out, though."

"Dale, you and Parker get Jameson back to staging. MacPhee, let's move toward the control building."

"Call me Mac, sir. I'll meet you there."

"There's a tool shed or something about fifty meters out behind it north. Be there in five."

"On the way."

Wolverine, sprinting back from the pier through the palms, pulled up short when he heard the explosion, which was his fuel storage shed blowing up. He crept through the trees, light extinguished, experience and familiarity with the surroundings guiding his way. The staccato bursts of automatic gunfire coming from the direction of the *HAVOC* command building and cottages again forced him to a cautious halt.

"Steele," he cursed. "We're too much alike. Nothing much stops me either." He changed direction heading for the sound of the fight, when he heard a second battle erupt in the direction of the two-story. He spat into the radio Sharpe left with him, "What the fuck is happening?" Receiving no immediate reply, he crept from tree to tree in the direction of central control. Arriving at the perimeter of the *HAVOC* compound, he watched his men exchanging fire with five commandos. His mercenaries had the intruders pinned down between three of the cottages used as personnel quarters adjacent to the center. It appeared they held an obvious edge in numbers, and were tightening a deadly ring around the besieged intruders, though it was obvious by its intensity that the fight was far from over. Just then, his radio chirped.

"Yeah, go."

"Boss, Sharpe here. We've got the choppers out of their shed, and I'm checking them out as we speak. We can lift off in five, and none too soon by the sounds of the excitement in your direction."

"Looks like we've got 'em outnumbered here," responded Dominic. "Have you got *HAVOC*?" He watched two of the black clad intruders disappear into Molucca's quarters. "Into the spider's lair," he grinned.

"Bingo. Got the lasers and the computer discs. Grabbed enough of the ICF fuel to ruin somebody's day as well. Stowed and ready to go. You want some help back there?"

"No. We'll leave these guys to fight it out. That's what I pay 'em for. I'll be right there. Molucca with you?"

"She's in the fight. Last she said was that she was going to her cabin for her knife and weapons. Said something about 'kicking butt'. I can call her in if you want."

"It's her choice. She knows what she's doing and where we're going. Stand by."

Reluctantly, Dominic took a last look at the furious battle and slunk back into the interior of the plantation. He would have liked to get in a few licks himself, especially now that his enemy had been identified. "Time enough for that later."

MacPhee and Steele were at the shed when Younger and Wilkins' team were ambushed from the control center.

"They must've had a contingency plan in case there was shooting," offered MacPhee.

The two men worked their way in the direction of the action, and arrived at the opposite side of the compound perimeter about the same instant Dominic departed. All of a sudden they heard Younger's strained and hollow voice on the radio.

"Call it off guys, they've got us nailed." Steele and MacPhee looked at each other questioning. It was totally out of character for SEALs to simply surrender.

"And that was an order," a female voice immediately followed on the same frequency.

Their Captain's admission and the female voice with the exotic accent stopped the SEALs in their tracks. Steele just reached the entrance to one of the besieged bungalows with MacPhee covering, when the command repeated over their frequency. He dove through the open doorway rolling into the interior of the cottage. He was startled to see a very beautiful woman holding a small but deadly looking knife to Younger's throat with one hand, and a Glock 36 aimed directly at him, held steady in the other. Wilkins was also present, his hands grudgingly raised. He gave Steele a sheepish look.

"Drop your weapon," she demanded of Steele. "Now, or your Captain won't be singing in the choir any longer."

Even in the dim light, Cody saw blood oozing at the point where the woman held the knife against the young Captain's throat. He also noted dark red rivulets dripping from the back of the Captain's right hand, hanging limp at his side. Reluctantly, he did as he was instructed.

"Hands behind your heads, fingers clasped," she ordered. "You young men should know better than to enter a lady's bedroom unannounced," she grinned. "One at a time, maybe, but not all at once."

Younger's knees buckled, and it seemed all he could do to stay conscious. Steele heard the sound of the gun battle fading in and out in the yard area. Though outnumbered, he knew the SEALs wouldn't just give up unless unequivocally ordered. Again she spoke on Younger's headset.

"Put 'em down boys, or your man's dead, NOW!" The sound of gunfire ceased.

Just then, the distinctive throb of two powerful turbines undulated over the storm noise. Instinctively, Molucca looked up. It was all the time Wilkins needed. Reflecting back later, Steele couldn't remember if his friend made one move or three. The entire sequence seemed a single blur. In the instant the woman looked up, Wilkins withdrew a huge knife from the small of his back, flipped it over in his hand in the same motion, and threw it by its point. The perfectly balanced blade rotated once in flight and struck home one half inch to the right of where the Indian intended. Younger and the woman collapsed in a tangled, bloody heap. Steele was on the pair an instant after the knife struck its target. Separating the wounded Younger from the very beautiful but very dead woman, he snatched Younger's headphone from her in the process. He alerted the SEALs that all was under control on the inside of the cottage, just as the distinctive thunder of a .50 caliber minigun erupted outside. Together, Wilkins and Steele laid the wounded Captain out on a single bed to one side of the cottage, cleaning and field dressing his serious shoulder wound as best and as quickly as they could. They scuttled back over to the fallen woman. The black hilt of Wilkins' knife protruded from her forehead.

Wilkins kicked the dead woman's stiletto to the side of the room. "Now *this* is a knife." He removed his weapon by placing a boot on the woman's chest, and pulling on the handle using both hands.

"Haven't seen anything like that since the first *Rambo* film," grinned Steele, watching the big Indian wipe the blade clean on the pant leg of the dead woman. "With an arm like that, maybe you could be a short reliever for the Giants."

84

The MH-60K Special Operations aircraft and the MH-60G *Pave Hawk* are both derivatives of the classic Sikorsky UH-60 *Blackhawk* helicopter. Each has basically the same airframe, with only a small differential in interior configuration. Built to deliver a small cadre of troops just about anywhere in any kind of weather, day or night, Conley knew that these two would be stressed to their limits flying into the teeth of hurricane *Grace*. He really had little choice. As he watched the progress of the growing storm from his command center at Princess Juliana Airport on St. Martin, it became obvious that storm surge, tremendous waves, and the wind elements within the hurricane itself would put the MK-5 in serious jeopardy during the return voyage. If Steele's team were to get off *Langosta* at all during the storm, it would necessarily have to be by air. There was a very real possibility that the team might perish, along with any other souls on the island if forced to remain ashore and face the insidious surge. Each of the two crew on both choppers were advised that the probability of making a safe round trip mission, given the advancing weather, would be little more than 50%. Less the longer they waited, as *Grace* bore down at them with a vengeance. All four crew volunteered without hesitation. Weather reports from NOAA satellites and oceanic stationary weather buoys positioned throughout the Atlantic indicated an enormous surge leading the storm. Combined with a high tide at 0330 hours, the entire cay was likely to be underwater at some point. If they were going, they had to leave now!

Both helicopters launched, after topping off their main and exterior auxiliary fuel cells. Each was configured to transport fourteen passengers and two crew: the thought process being that all could make it back in one aircraft if the other were damaged or lost. Without their interior aux fuel tanks, and with

337

the burn-off of fuel to the half-way point in the mission increasing their payload capacity, it would be a cozy ride for all in one. Each carried a Lockheed Martin *Hellfire* anti-armor missile, and each was armed with two .50 caliber, belt-fed mini-guns mounted on fixed, swiveling pedestals on either side of each chopper. Their Forward Looking Infra-red Radar systems (FLIR) allowed them to easily access island waypoints en route and their final target destination. FLIR also provided the pilots the frightening picture of the monster storm, which was about to swallow them. Even though the helicopters were built for low level flight, the two aircraft commanders prudently chose to fly in above 200 feet AGL rather than risk losing their craft to wind shear, or even rogue waves at an altitude any lower. They would have to chance detection by surface scanning radar, but those were the breaks. Any radar coming from the direction they were flying would hopefully be rendered unreliable, or totally destroyed, by the horrendous elements from within hurricane *Grace*. Conley instructed them to contact the Mark-5 with intent, five miles from 'feet dry' on *Langosta*.

"So how'd she get the drop on you anyway? I thought you SEAL guys were supposed to be sneaky?"

"We were working our way for the control center through the palms behind these cottages when all hell broke loose. You guys must've tipped them off somehow," responded Wilkins to Steele's questions. Both were crouched to either side of the doorway weapons in hand, trying to pick out targets in the brilliant flashes of .50 caliber steel hail raining down from the MH-60 right over the control shed. The chaos of firepower, wind, rain, and thunder was confusing at best.

"Wasn't us. We told Younger about our little diversion. Maybe they picked up the incoming on radar. That building at your eleven o'clock." Steele directed the chopper's fire on anything that looked at all suspicious via his mouth mike, in the course of the discussion with Wilkins.

"They just opened up on us all of a sudden."

"Come to think of it, I did see two guys with night vision gear around their necks charge out of the two story when we lit the charge in the fuel shack. Knowing now how truly sneaky you aren't, they could've spotted you guys from the balcony up there. Probably even without the night vision," Cody chuckled. Younger moaned and moved behind them.

"I dove through the back window and Younger came busting through the door like John Wayne. Didn't even see her. She shot Younger in the back and had me dead-to-rights just about the time you rolled in. It must be her cottage by the looks of it. I admit we didn't check too carefully to see if anyone was home after they started shooting. We were a bit preoccupied with the action outside, and trying to get cover. I noticed you weren't exactly takin' charge in here until those fly boys showed. Two guys running east."

"Let 'em go. We need to get out of here, and I didn't find Devoney. Hold fire and stand by, *Nemo* one."

"Roger."

"*Nemo* one, sheesh. Who comes up with these handles?" Wilkins just shook his head.

"*Nemo*s one and two. Works for me." Steele grinned again as the shooting ceased. "OK, let's see what we've got."

The two teams gathered cautiously outside the *HAVOC* center. Besides Younger and Jameson, Jones was also a casualty, but ambulatory. His weapon took a direct hit in the firefight and he lost three fingers on his right hand to shrapnel as it disintegrated.

"We need to get Younger back to base and care as quickly as possible. Jones and Jameson, too. Plus, I don't think this storm is getting much better." Steele could barely be heard above the roar of the wind and the noise of the chopper. "*Nemo* one, can you put her down anywhere close by?"

"Negative. Too much wind for minimal clearance in any LZs of opportunity."

"Standby"

"OK, McCarthy, you and Parkinson take Younger back to staging. I know that bird can set down there."

"*Nemo* two is down there already," MacPhee piped in. "They called in the MK-5 on Conley's orders, and are waiting for us to decide what next."

"Jones, you hand gun capable?"

"Yes, sir." Steele saw the pain in the young man's eyes, but heard solid determination in his voice.

"Take point ahead of Younger's group. Get these guys back to the beach in one piece."

"Sir!"

"Gunny? You're the OIC. Get these men to staging, pronto!"

"Roger that," replied Dillon.

"Jeremiah, you and MacPhee search these buildings. See if there's anything left of *HAVOC*. My guess is they destroyed it when they discovered we were here. Check it out anyway. Let's meet back at staging in say thirty, on my mark... now." They all set the bezels of their watches accordingly. "*Nemo*. Are you FLIR capable?"

"Negative. Normally it's standard equipment along with AM and FM on these flying jalopies. Mine must've blown a circuit on the way into this mess. What'd you have in mind?"

"Wanted to check on unfriendlies and other buildings in the area."

"Visual, no aids, I can see three down and not moving to your four, five and seven o'clocks on the ground just in the trees."

"Good enough. Thanks for your support. See you at staging with the rest of our crew in twenty-nine. Out." The whine of the twin GE turbofans powering up from stationary hover drowned out even the fury of the storm for the few seconds it took the chopper to disappear.

"That's it then. I'll check their casualties and hope I can find a live one who knows where Devoney is. Let's move."

Steele watched Wilkins and MacPhee dash across the compound to the entrance of the control building. Curtains of rain in cascading sheets obscured them off and on as they bent sideways into the wind's savage assault. He lowered his covering weapon only after Wilkins waved, and followed a stun grenade through the open door. He ran for the palms indicated by the MH-60 pilot, worrying to himself about the length of time it took to cover the distance. Recalling his recent endurance run in the Sierra, he muttered, "I'm no sprinter. Never was. Never will be." Finding the downed men where the *Nemo* pilot indicated was easy. Finding one who would talk was a different story. All three were quite dead, their bodies literally shredded by the mini-gun. Dropping the lifeless shoulder of the third, he caught a brief flicker of peripheral movement, but way too late. The heavy downpour played hell with his vision. A blow to his back and right side crashed him face down in the mud, his weapon lost in the sprawling fall. Instinctively he rolled sideways three revolutions. He sprang to his feet to face his stalking attacker just ten feet away. He was black as ebony and huge. "Damn!" Steele reached for his holstered Browning 9mm, stopping short when his adversary shook his head emphasizing his wishes with a wave of an AK-47.

"Goin kill you with my hans, mon," the big man smiled, his face all gleaming teeth. "You military fools ruin ma guud gig here."

Cody swallowed hard. "I'm too old for this shit! My rotten luck. A Jamaican on steroids with an attitude. Well, the bigger they are, the harder they hit you."

The big man flicked his weapon to the side like a used toothpick, moved into a centering crouch, and advanced. A line from the *"Butch Cassidy and the Sundance Kid"* film flashed through Steele's worried mind.

"Rules!" he shouted.

"What, mon?" A look of surprise crossed the Jamaican's intent face, the unexpected outburst stopping his deadly advance just long enough for Steele to take a giant stride forward with his left foot and savagely kick a boot in the man's groin with his right. The giant doubled forward at the waist, grabbed his testicles, but didn't go down.

"Gotta get the rules straight," Steele puffed with all his strength, ripping his left knee into the lowered chin of his opponent. The blow might have prostrated any normal sized human, but it merely staggered the Jamaican back on his heels. A white-hot stab of pain burst across Steele's consciousness. "Damn! Hafta get these knees fixed." He clapped both hands simultaneously hard to the ears of the reeling black man, grimly acknowledging to himself that he may be lucky enough to possibly survive this encounter. Soccer style, he swept his right leg across the back of the staggering man's lower calves and the big man went down like a giant oak, still holding his groin. Cody drew his handgun and pounced on the supine giant, sticking the business end of the weapon in the man's left ear.

"Seven feet?" he yelled, noticing the trickle of blood draining out the ear, evidence of a shattered eardrum.

"Whaaa...?"

"Just checking to see if you could still hear me. You're seven feet if you're an inch, big guy. Where's Dr. Devoney Marsh?" He twisted the barrel of his gun deeper into the man's head.

"Whaaa...?"

"You heard me, where is the Doctor?" Cody hissed.

"I doan know, mon," the Jamaican moaned.

Without hesitation, Steele turned and fired a round through the man's right kneecap. The Jamaican's pained bucking reaction almost threw him off his perch on the immense chest.

"You OK?" came Wilkins' immediate question on his headset.

"Yeah. Just asking a few questions of one of our friends," he responded. "Where is Dr. Marsh? I've got more shells left than you have important bodily targets. If you don't want to sing soprano, tell me where she is... now!" He gouged his weapon into the man's already ruined groin for emphasis, while holding the big Jamaican's neck tight with his free hand.

"Doan, mon. Doan shoot. Mon, I dunno for sure. They caught her north. Maybe roun dee pier. I doanno, mon." He groaned in agony, feebly trying to brush Steele aside with a huge muddy paw of a hand. Steele shot him in the other knee, leapt up, retrieved his rifle and headed north at a slow steady jog. "Mon, I sure ain't no sprinter."

Dominic arrived at a clearing on the east side of *Langosta,* just as Sharpe had the first of two Bell JetRanger III's main rotors spinning in startup. The two sleek craft had been stored in an underground bunker whose doors, when closed above, were flush with the surrounding surface, and camouflaged accordingly. The choppers were flown directly into their snug, concrete hangar, and then wheeled to either side to make landing space available for the next craft. When the double overhead doors were in place, detection from the air or by satellite was next to impossible. Four of his men readied the second JetRanger.

"How's it going back there?" Sharpe shouted.

"Hard to tell. Either way, we've got plenty of time to get out of here before anyone notices. We shouldn't have too rough a trip. The last info I got from the weather tech in control was that the hurricane went right angle due north the minute we shut *HAVOC* down."

"Good news," responded Sharpe, flipping switches on the aircraft's overhead display panel. "Dr. Marsh?"

"Went for a dive, I believe. Inside a heavy cage with no air tanks. Wonder how long she held her breath?" *Wolverine* laughed and ducked around the chopper to enter. He settled into the pilot's seat vacated by Sharpe, fastened his shoulder belts, checked the *HAVOC* gear tied down in the cargo bay behind, then positioned the collective. "OK. Let's go to California."

Dominic's chopper lifted into the stormy night, eight minutes ahead of the takeoff by the second JetRanger. The SEALs at the south end of the island heard the roar of its engine seconds before the nimble helicopter sped overhead.

"Shit! Where'd that thing come from? I didn't think that sounded like the *Pave.* Call Conley. Tell him we've got a bogie headed their way. Maybe we should launch number one here in pursuit?" the young SEAL boat crew asked no one in particular, pointing to their own ship.

"Belay that," barked Gunnery Sergeant Dillon. He watched the chopper disappear into the blackness of the night and storm. "This bird stays put until number two shows. Parkinson, man one of those 50s on the boat just in case." He pointed to the bow of the beached craft. "I want this perimeter secure just the way we've trained. No air pursuit until we get the whole team accounted for."

Parkinson had just swung himself into position behind the lethal minigun, when the second JetRanger appeared over the palm canopy. Dillon pointed and nodded. The belt-fed .50 roared to deafening life. Parkinson walked his line of tracers across the tree tops to the right of the speeding chopper and directly into its fuselage where he held his and his gun's focus, as the white and blue craft screamed past low overhead. The helicopter was beyond the SEAL's beach perimeter in an instant, and out over the black water gaining altitude as if nothing were wrong. Then seemingly in slow motion, it twisted to it's right, losing the tail boom in the process, and started spinning end over end. A tremendous explosion rocked the night, lighting the beach area for a brief instant with the intensity of a noonday sun. The night vision of those watching was ruined. Once the eyes of the SEALs readapted to the darkness, the Bell Jet was gone. Half of its main rotor was all that remained, stuck in the sand just at the surf line. Parkinson grinned from ear to ear as adrenaline coursed through his system.

"Nice shootin', Tex!" yelled Gunnery Sergeant Dillon.

Ten minutes later, Steele was three hundred meters from the ruined pier, approaching from the west side. The wind whistled a hollow wail through the ravaged palm plantation and the sea was a meteorological disaster. The waves had ripped the deep end out of the pier, and curled it back on itself like the spine of a used sardine can. The bow of one of the four patrol craft was all that remained of the *Wolverine*'s Atlantic navy; the other three vessels were pounded to kindling. The shattered scrap of bow, still moored to what was left of the shore end of the dock, was crashed up on the sand, then pulled back into the shallows in sequence with each wave. The seas hit the pier perpendicular from the east. As Steele got nearer, he noticed the level of the sea was nearly over the top of the pier in the wave troughs, and it was totally submerged in the body of each as they passed over. When only ten meters from the shore end, he heard a high-pitched keening, which came and went in time with each subsequent wave. Rounding the end of the ruined dock, he saw what looked to be an aluminum grate, disappear under another huge ocean roller breaking in the shallows. As the wave subsided, the top third of a shark cage appeared beneath its grate-like hatch, only to be swallowed again by the next onrush of churning water. It was during the respite between each wave that he recognized the frantic voice of Dr. Devoney Marsh.

Understanding that it would be suicidal to try and help from on the pier or in the water, he stood uselessly rooted to the beach shouting for all he was worth between each wave, attempting to encourage the desperate, drowning woman imprisoned within the doomed cage to hold on. His mind raced, searching for alternatives, always returning to the hopelessness of the predicament. All he could do was helplessly watch.

"*Nemo*, this is Steele. Get up to the north end ASAP. I've located Dr. Marsh. We won't be able to make the rendezvous at your current position as previously planned. Pick us up here on your way out. Acknowledge."

"Roger that, Steele. We'll be airborne in five minutes, if you call flying in this soup air. Say again, off in five. There with you in ten. We'll only have one chance to get you because the storm wall is coming in fast. We need to evacuate the area with haste. Copy?"

"Affirmative. Ten minutes." He did a quick spin, searching through 360 degrees, and realized that there was no safe landing zone (LZ) for the chopper. The aircrew would have to try and pick them up on the drop wire, then winch them up.

At just about the moment Steele decided to do something foolish and go into the water, the sea did something incredible. The storm continued to build from all sides, its fury dumping prodigious quantities of rain driven by winds in excess of 120 knots. Lightning flashed with increasing frequency providing strobe-effect visuals, accompanied by continuous detonations of deafening thunder. Yet incredibly, the sea began to subside. At first, subtly. The deck of the pier became visible and accessible. The waves continued unabated, but they retreated, and broke further and further out from the beach. Cody stood amazed. His reverie was shattered by a gurgling scream from Devoney Marsh.

"It's the storm surge, hurry!"

Steele bolted into the churning surf up to his knees, and in seconds was inspecting the chains holding Devoney's shark cage prison to the metal pilings.

Happy to see her alive, though obviously traumatized he tried to calm her as bet he could, given the immediacy of the situation. "You all right?" he asked, examining and pulling at the lower fastenings.

"How do I look? What took you so long?" she coughed.

"Held up in traffic. Seems there's a storm coming. And it's good to see you too. We'll get you out of here." The cage was secured to the pilings by anchor chain, made up of one-inch thick links. Seawater continued to drain from the shallows, exposing the last of the remaining pilings of the decimated pier. "How long do we have?"

"Maybe five minutes at the most. Depends on the size of the initial surge wave," Devoney choked, spitting water. "You've got to get me out of here, now!"

"I'm working on it, Baby. Hold on." Steele swung himself to the top of the cage and pulled at the hatch. He immediately noticed the substantial dead bolt mechanism locking the access. It would do a small bank's vault proud. He hurdled back onto the soggy sand.

The water receded nearly to the end of what remained of the pier. A strange, surreal quiet enveloped them in a partial, heavy silence. Though the elements of the storm continued to pummel and lash, the sea sounds ceased. The quiet was eerie and unsettling. Something momentous was about to occur. They could feel it. Devoney looked over Cody's shoulder and gasped. He spun to see what it was. Out as far as they could make out on the horizon was an immense black wall, flaunted and defined by the accenting brilliance of reflected lightning. No telling if it was two miles away or twenty. Distance was impossible to judge, given the circumstances, and their relative positions. Devoney screamed, long and loud. Cody ran for the beach.

He stumbled back to the cage with his kit bag, fumbling two flakes of C-4 out of their wrappings. He stopped, eyeing the dark sky for the chopper, the distinctive whining of its turbines a sound of reassurance. Devoney shook the bars of her prison in frustration watching Steele plaster a handful of explosive on links of both the top and bottom chains.

"Blow the lid, Dammit! Blow the lid!" she wailed.

"No good, kiddo. The amount of this stuff it would take to blow it would kill you in the process. Gotta try and take out the chains."

"Then what?" she cried. "How am I supposed to get out?" She eyed the horizon apprehensively and shook the bars again. The stench of exposed sea bottom assaulted their noses.

"I'm still working on that part." The MH-60 materialized out of the night right above them, its NAV lights adding another dimension of color to the already bizarre light show in process.

"Dev, you've got to get to the far corner of the cage to your right, turn your back and cover your ears. This may burn a bit. If I figured correctly, at least we can get the cage free and go from there."

"Then what?" she sobbed.

"Then we'll get you out somehow. Would you rather stay and drown?" He started to get rattled, not knowing his next move, pressured by the fast approaching black wall roaring in from the horizon, and the panic of the frantic woman.

"Steele?" came the call on his headset.

"Yo! Drop the down line on the winch after you see two explosions. I'm attempting to break the cage free of the pilings. Move off about 100 meters. I've got C-4 blowing some chain down here in… 10… 9…" The whine of the turbines faded to the south about five seconds.

The two shocks of explosion were nothing compared with the continuing din issuing forth from the storm. Steele checked his work, pulling the ends of the chain free from the piling. The MH-60 was back on station just above them. An ominous hissing grew louder and saturated their hearing. Neither needed the look they both took anyway to know that the surge was rushing toward them, a black flowing doom cloaked in windblown foam.

"Drop that jump line, now!"

They heard the whine of the big turbines fluctuate as the pilot massaged the power settings, trying to keep the craft on station directly above them, despite the violent winds pummeling his ship.

"C'mon, Cody. Please hurry! O God, hurry!"

He wrapped the sturdy climbing line around an upright support at the corner of the cage, just as the dark water rushed above his ankles. Devoney cried and screamed at the same time. He concentrated for all he was worth, focusing to make certain that the line was securely tied in a bowline around the support then wrapped over, around, through and hooked to a separate cage upright. If one gave, at least they might have a chance with the second. The onrushing seawater was not coming in waveform. More like a tidal flow occurring at warp speed. He called the chopper as the water rose above his knees.

"Get us the hell out of here, now!"

They felt a quick tug as the pilot took the slack out of the line and a sideways jerk as the wind buffeted the powerful aircraft. The pilot fought to keep the chopper directly over the pier, lest the lateral motion of the wind cause the dangling cage to smash against it before he could get altitude. Cody hopped onto the cage and locked both arms around two of its upright bars in a stranglehold worthy of the WWF. The MH-60 is a powerful craft, but it was at its redline lift-weight capacity with half the SEAL platoon aboard, plus the added weight of the partially submerged cage and its two grim occupants below. The extra water weight and suction created by the surge compounded the situation. The straining rotors convulsed for what seemed an eternity. Wilkins was at the open hatch above, hand on the down line, watching the drama unfold below. He saw the cage disappear totally in the dark storm surge, only to piston partially free as the chopper held a steady up angle. Finally, the cage and its reluctant passengers popped totally clear of the black water, which was now well above the pier and moving inexorably inland. The copter shot up fifty feet the instant the cage came free of the water. The pilot managed to arrest his sudden lift, but not quickly enough to disallow bounce. Unfortunately, as the wire down line stretched on the downside of the boomerang, the shark cage smashed back into the sea on its side. When once again it came free, Cody Steele wasn't on it.

He imagined himself in an acceptable dream, neither happy nor sad, but a dream nevertheless. The darkness was fluid and infinite. Coincident with the initial shock of the cage slamming into the mounting storm surge, the air was smashed from his lungs. The heavy weight of the cage together with its downward momentum, forced him deep under water. The instinct for survival is absolute however, and somehow he fought his way to the surface in a thrashing frenzy. The cage and the chopper were gone. Bicycling his legs treading hard, gasping and coughing, desperate to fill his shrieking lungs with precious air, he tried not to panic. His eyes stung from immersion, and the salt spray driven into them by the screaming wind. The helicopter, Devoney, *Wolverine,* or the mission, never crossed his mind. Nothing, other than survival. Just when he figured he might finally be composed enough to get a full gulp of air, a huge wave hammered him under once again, its velocity and direction pulling him shoreward. Years of experience in water taught him to relax rather than fight. Yet his brain and system were starving for oxygen and receiving none. He had to do something, and do it fast. Layers in a surge wave move at surprisingly different speeds. That next to the bottom moves the quickest, trapping and tumbling flotsam along with it until the wave has run its course. Such would have been the result for Steele, had he not been slammed against the shore footing of the disintegrating pier. This interruption in the fast moving bottom layer of surge lasted just long enough for Steele to cork free, and in one last desperate effort, struggle for the surface somewhere above. Darkness rushed in before he was able to make it. Then nothing. His next cognizant thought was one of confusion. He knew he must be alive, for the pain in his back where he struck the footing was as if he had been hit by a bus. He spun completely around in the water, looking. There was nothing but black water laced with white streaks of wind blown foam, black sky, and the totality of the raging hurricane. It was if the island simply ceased to exist. *Either I blacked out for so long I've been swept past, or… No, that island couldn't be completely submerged.* He wrestled with the unbelievable thought as he removed his boots. With no point of reference, he wasn't able to tell if he was making lateral movement in any given direction, though there was certainly motion. Waves roller-coastered him up and over their towering crests, then plunged him deep into cavernous troughs. He wasn't at all certain if these were truly waves by definition, or simply the tops of enormous ocean swells being ripped off by lashing wind, breaking upon themselves, rather than falling of their own weight as they ran to the shallows crashing on some shore.

Suddenly, he felt a presence in the water just at his left thigh. A rough skin brushed against him and reflexively he kicked at and away from the creature. His heart leaped to his throat, "Shark!" While searching the water all around, he unsheathed the survival knife from the pocket on his right leg. He knew from experience that the weapon would be of little use on a predator of any size. Particularly one he couldn't see. But still he felt better having it in hand. A bump on his right foot. He spun to face his adversary, expecting to see or feel a gash of teeth. Certainly there would be the dreaded telltale dorsal fin. Black water, nothing more. "Just testing me, huh?" he shouted, his yell lost in the tumult of wave and wind. For seconds that seemed hours there was no further contact. Then, for some reason he knew it was there behind him. Slowly he finned his hands to turn himself. *No fast motions. It's just curious,* he wished to himself. Once turned, he couldn't believe the anthropomorphic smile on the face of the curious creature confronting him not three feet away. He burst forth in a roar of relieved laughter, startling the animal and swallowing a pint of seawater in the process. Within seconds, the Atlantic Spotted Dolphin was back within arm's length, head out of the water, curiously surveying this strange intruder to its domain.

Later, Steele was unable to recall how long he talked to, or at the dolphin. He would swear that the animal listened and seemed to understand the whole story, which he confessed to telling it. "What the hell else was I supposed to do? There was no island, at least that I could see. You guys weren't anywhere close by. I didn't have anything else to do, and certainly nowhere else to go. After a while I started to get enormously tired, exhausted really. I reached for it and he didn't move, but let me hold his dorsal. Didn't seem to bother him in the least. He or she must have started to swim with me hanging on. I don't remember being swept or dragged along in the water. There was no sensation of forward movement. How could I tell, with the wind and surge what it was.

The only sensations I had were of relief for a handhold, and amazement for how strong and graceful it was. It seems like he shepherded me along for at least twenty or thirty minutes, but I have no clue. I didn't even think to check my watch. The only thing I remember checking for at some point was my throat mike, which was gone. I'm sure it was lost when we got dumped into the water on that first bounce. The force impact was too much. I just couldn't hold on. Anyway, there I was just hanging on to this friendly dolphin, talking my fool head off in the middle of a hurricane, in the middle of the ocean with no land in sight, and the next thing I know, we're hard up against the antennae on the *Langosta* two-story. He swam us right up to it, stopped as if to say, 'end of the line', waited 'til I let go of him and had a death grip on the tower, smiled, went up on his tail in reverse, clicked and whistled good-bye, and was gone. End of story. Next thing I know, the water is receding, I can see the roof of the structure, and you guys are blinding me with that million candle power spot you've got."

The four SEALs, Jeremiah Wilkins, and Devoney Marsh just grinned and nodded condescendingly at him as the MH-60 dropped on final for St. Martin.

"What… you don't believe me?"

On a rotor and a prayer, the two SEAL helicopters made it in safely back to the relative shelter of St. Martin. Three wounded SEALs were triaged at the local hospital. After being treated and stabilized, despite marginal weather, Captain Younger was immediately flown to Bethesda and the Navy's top-of-the-line treatment facility on the Lear. The two other wounded men remained with their unit on request. Sequestered in a group of suites in the Hotel Mont Vernon, courtesy of the CIA, the rest of the team rode out *Grace*'s onslaught. The hurricane's wrath was nowhere near as devastating to St. Martin as it was to *Langosta*. The storm center turned directly north shortly before the SEALs hit its beach, thus reducing catastrophic damage to landmasses due west of the tiny cay. They spent three hours reviewing the entire mission, examining every detail, from the wild ride in on the Mark 5, to Gunny Dillon's shooting of the lock on Devoney's shark cage with the big .50 cal. while in flight. "Shit. I had to do something dramatic and fast. The weight of that cage was making the helo unstable, and I wasn't at all sure that drop line would last the whole flight. I knew it was risky, but we didn't have a choice. So I just had Gunny shoot the damn lock apart. I reached in and pulled the Doc out, then cut the damn thing loose. Besides, she wasn't too happy dangling down there in thin air over open ocean in a hurricane. We were five minutes beyond the chopper's 'fail/safe' fuel level when we finally found you," recounted Wilkins. "I had to gently encourage the pilot to continue his search. Lucky thing his GPS unit was working, and he had a waypoint on the compound entered in the memory. We ran five-minute radials outbound from there every twenty degrees. Found you on our next to last effort. You're one lucky fellow, white guy."

Following their morning debrief, they would have had a bird's eye view of the hurricane surge lashing up the incline to their hotel, had they not all been obliviously fast asleep, the events of the early morning and the adrenaline drain leading to exhaustion. Conley, however, was wide-awake, and he busily monitored all message traffic dealing with the states targeted in the extortion letters. For the time being, he gave little credence to Dr. Devoney Marsh's arguments that California was the next strike for *HAVOC*. She had as much trouble convincing Conley as Steele did extolling his rescue by the dolphin. The US experienced periods of horrendous weather in three distinct regions, the northwest, the northeast, and the Great Lakes area. All incorporated states targeted by *The Weathermen*. Carefully watching from alerted satellites, after twenty-four hours, there did not appear to be any peculiar 'hot spot' signatures prominent in any of the affected areas. After a hearty round of back slaps, high fives, 'hoo yaws' and heartfelt 'good-byes', the remainder of SEAL Team Six hopped a C-130 back to their base. Conley recalled the Lear arranging for Devoney, Wilkins, and Steele to be transported back to Travis AFB in California a day later.

"I'm staying here for awhile. I like it," he informed the three as they boarded the little jet.

"Gotta get your money's worth out of that shirt, I'll bet," chuckled Cody. "Also bet you could sell it to JW. You guys have similar taste in shirts."

"That, and I have my suite set up with all the bells and whistles I need to keep an eye out for your friendly *Wolverine* and his remaining crew. Besides, we're sending in a 'mop up' team to *Langosta* as soon as the end of this storm passes, and I want to be there to see what they find."

"Based on the wild ride we had in our MH-60, and *they're* built for tough weather, maybe he went down in the JetRanger. I'm sure you have the word out all over to be on the lookout for it."

"Correct, but with no luck at all so far. Hey, there's a gadzillion little islands all over this area and he could have put down on any one of them. Remember, the guy's very resourceful."

"And lucky," added Wilkins.

"He's a devious, vicious, murdering asshole," spat Devoney.

"That, and a whole lot worse, I'm sure," laughed Cody. "We'll be back in Sonoma, and we'll sit tight until we hear from you, one way or the other. If it *is* California, we can be there on the double."

"What makes you think I'd use you guys again?" asked Conley.

"You can't afford not to. Besides, you owe it to the lovely Doctor here. You dragged her into this party, and now she's got a rather large score to settle."

85

Late evening in Sonoma, four days after their wild escape from *Langosta*, Wilkins was in the parlor of the Pullman on the phone dealing with details of his tribal responsibilities. Devoney and Cody sat on the outside rear step, watching and listening to the unseasonably warm rain.

"You abandoned me," she said softly.

"Excuse me?"

"Not just on *Langosta*, but time and again over the course of our entire… our entire… whatever it is… was."

"What brought this on?" He turned to look at her. She continued to stare out at the drenched landscape softly illuminated by the interior lights from the Pullman.

"You left me to fend for myself."

"Gee, I seem to recall bustin' my ass to save you from that wonderful, exciting storm surge," he tried to keep it light.

Devoney sighed and turned to face him, "Not just there, over and over again. Nearly every time Director Conley called, you would just leave. Good friends, let alone lovers, just don't do that to each other. I had hoped we were at *least* friends. If it was another women, it might be easier for me to understand. Instead, you're off tilting at windmills, trying to prove something to God knows who."

"That's kind of unfair. We've talked about what I do several times."

"I've had a lot of time to think about things…us." She ignored his last response. "I've come to some rather startling conclusions about our so-called relationship. Jeremiah knows more about what's going on in your life than I do, and you just met him. Don't get me wrong; I really like him. Not to mention the fact he saved my life."

Cody knew she was right, but nevertheless tried to argue his case. He was quite aware that this casual discussion was turning out to be much more. He knew what he said in the next few minutes might determine whether their relationship would endure, a result he always avoided considering in the past. "You know I can't tell you most of the details."

"I'm sure you slept with Laura while I was away. And I'm glad you did, for her sake."

He fell further behind her fast moving train of thought with each revelation.

"She didn't tell, but I could tell by the elated sound of her voice. Intuition, I suppose. She adored you like a brother *and* a lover. I'm happy that at least part of that adoration was consummated.

"Baby, I…"

"I need simple things. Basic things. Someone I can count on, knowing they'll always be there for me... no matter what. Someone to take care of me... first. Even before themselves. Someone who is complete because I am in his life, and loves me for being there. Most importantly, someone I can trust unconditionally. These are the things that are basic to a committed, lasting relationship... at least to the one I want. I gave all that to you. That your father never told you that you were worthy in his eyes was his fault, not yours. And certainly not mine. This was probably our last chance. What happened to you, Cody? Where did you go?"

"I thought we had all that." He looked out at the huge stand of eucalyptus trees lining the rail siding. He knew he didn't have the answers, and was afraid of the questions.

"Not close. You and Laura shared more intimacy than you and I."

He thought for a moment, and considered the turbulent emotions wrestling their way to the surface. "I guess the reason I never committed to anyone before is because I thought I might fail the tremendous responsibilities that go with any successful relationship. It's hard for me to imagine someone counting on me when I have a difficult enough time counting on myself. That fear of failure is a driving force in my life, as I know you're aware. It's a worthiness issue. On the other hand, I'm afraid of being alone. A real conundrum, I admit. But I never dreamed I'd find a woman like you. You are everything I've always wanted in a relationship except I never really felt we were partners. We've somehow missed that important… very important part. The sharing of, and striving for mutual goals. The commonality of interests. You've struggled for acclaim and approval in the academic world, and have been tremendously successful. Likewise I have in my world as well. My efforts, though, are in a totally different arena, in very different direction. Ultimately, we've both tried to make the world a little bit better by these efforts, to the detriment of our personal relationships. A week or so ago, right here in the Pullman, when we were planning the capture of *Wolverine* and the return of HAVOC, was the first time in our… relationship that *I* felt we were a team, united in the pursuit of a common goal for the right reasons. It felt good, really good. It made me happy. I thought and hoped it would be grounding for the kind of lasting relationship you so eloquently describe. I had these hopes even knowing that you slept with Dominic, *Wolverine,* and might even again before the operation was over. I didn't like it. I hated the idea! But I was OK, knowing we were investing in an emotional partnership. Plus if it all worked, we'd be that much closer for going through it all."

"That's all very touching, Cody," she said with a note of sarcasm. The use of his name instead of calling him 'Baby' their common pet name for each other a definite signal that she was *very* upset. "It's about time that you decide about your own worthiness. By your measure, not anyone else's. Until then, I have to know and feel in my heart that you are all those things I need, we need, the relationship needs. Right now, I'm sorry, I just don't feel that way.

They stood in silence, the Pullman wrapped in a cloak of incessant rain, each pondering an epiphany from the discussion. Wilkins stuck his head out the etched glass doorway and broke the mood. "Am I interrupting anything?"

"Not much, evidently," answered Devoney.

"Conley's on the line."

"Steele."

"Get out your maps of northern California."

"And it's nice to talk to you too, Chief," chuckled Cody. He switched the conversation onto the speaker. "Having a nice Caribbean vacation?" Devoney unfolded the Forest Service maps over the coffee table in front of the sofa, where all three gathered.

"About thirty six hours ago, *Vega* recorded a suspect heat signature identical to those we spotted on *Langosta.* It might be *HAVOC*, only this event is much smaller, but more intense."

"Easily accomplished using the ICF modules, Director," Devoney said.

"It was a random pass," continued the voice from the speaker. "It took us about four additional hours to reposition the satellite, stabilizing its trajectory over the target area. In the meantime, we picked up an encrypted UHF signal with *Echelon*, and have narrowed its transmission to within one mile of the heat source."

"Which is where?" asked Wilkins.

Conley continued without missing a beat, or addressing the question. "This is highly sophisticated gear they're using. Top of the line."

"Sounds like *Wolverine*," added Steele. "Nothing but the best."

"Our cryptographers are working on the decipher as we speak. Interestingly enough, whoever it is got a response on the same frequency within ten minutes of the transmit, from China, also encrypted."

"China?" chorused all three.

"Yep. Should have guessed they were involved in something like this. We were able to get a positive ID on the IFR source, once we got the eye-in-the-sky in the right place on the very next pass. That was about thirty hours ago. By the next orbit, it was gone. Coincidentally...or not, it was just about that time, noon yesterday local, that the little thunderstorm, dumping all that rain on you and the northwest over the last week, finally decided to move east."

"What's so unusual about that?" asked Steele, pretty certain of the answer.

"Well, while you were cavorting around the Caribbean, that weather system has been stationary for about three days. Now all of a sudden, it decides to move east. You figure it out."

"*HAVOC*," Devoney piped up. "It *does* work, I'm sure of it."

"Anyway, the weather team tells me that the storm center passed directly over the co-ordinates of the heat source. Sure would seem like our boy's at it again. I ordered in SEAL Team One from southern California, backed up by the Marines. They should be reporting in on site any minute. All this is happening in and around a little semi-ghost town north of you called Michigan Bluff. It's on the north fork of the American River."

"Going in without us?"

"Nobody for you to rescue this time. But I need you guys somewhere else."

"Where?"

"Don't get your knickers in a knot. It gets better. Do you know that area?"

"Been through there on a dirt bike years ago," said Cody. Devoney rifled through the maps, looking for the right one. "There are some killer trails up in that area. It's wild country, very remote, and full of old mines."

"That's just exactly what the brain trust at the 'Farm' figured. *Wolverine*'s got the thing squirreled away in an old mine tunnel somewhere. Less than twenty four hours ago, Governor Todd of your great state received another demand letter threatening death and destruction if a wire transfer, in a very significant amount, to a Swiss account, wasn't executed within the hour. A copy is being faxed to you as we speak. Needless to say, he didn't send the money."

"What was the threat?" asked Devoney.

"Bad weather," croaked the voice from the speaker.

"That's original," laughed Wilkins.

"Really bad weather. Less than three hours ago, the dam at the *very* remote Hell Hole reservoir was mysteriously blown. It's on the Rubicon River, in case you're following along." Conley, thousands of miles away on St. Martin, heard the distinctive sound of maps being shuffled in Sonoma, California.

"The Rubicon empties into the middle fork of the American River. The dam at Hell Hole failed in 1964, dumping its entire capacity of 200,000 acre-feet of water. Unfortunately, it was full this time as well, thanks to that little rainstorm I mentioned, and the one you are probably enjoying at the moment. Notice anything interesting or unusual here?"

"Folsom Lake. All the storm runoff will end up in Folsom Lake." Cody traced the American River down his map.

"Including the Hell Hole flood, plus all the additional rain the storm will drop on the watershed as it traverses east," Conley added. "The experts calculate the Hell Hole flood will get there in just over two hours. The two dams are 68 miles apart. Sources from the Bureau of Reclamation that manage the reservoir at Folsom tell us that the lake is over 75% of capacity. If it were lower, as it normally would be this time of year, there wouldn't be a problem. Unfortunately, again thanks to this storm and a very wet October, it's going to be pushed to the limit."

"So? What's that got to do with us?" interjected Wilkins.

"Well, where's the weak link? Where would you go if you were going to wreak havoc, pun intended…if you were the bad guys?"

"Folsom dam!"

"I've got a California Highway Patrol chopper en route to pick you up. It was the only transportation around on short notice and the fastest way to get you boys there. You're the closest assets we've got, and you know what we're up against. The cavalry will be there close behind you guys. I hope I'm wrong, but if I'm not…"

Devoney talked at the speaker, not wanting to look Cody in the eye, "I'll stay here to monitor the communications gear. Plus, I need to put in writing as much of the *HAVOC* data as I can before I forget it, in case we don't recover the device."

The sound of a helicopter overhead interrupted any further conversation.

The CHP pilot put them down in the center of a landing circle, just west of the powerhouse at the base of Folsom Dam. They were led up to a landing, into the dam and through its length along a subterranean tunnel, to the control room deep within the structure. Four Bureau of Reclamation engineers nervously worked their respective positions in the large room, monitoring inflow and outflow gauges, talking on the phone with upstream reservoir managers, running different outflow scenarios and models on their computers, and swallowing prodigious amounts of bad coffee. The shift manager brought them all up to speed, using a narrative laced with statistics and definite concern. The bottom line distilled to the simple fact that Folsom reservoir was too full. Too much water was coming in, and not enough could be let out to compensate the over-matched, down-river levee system.

"The Hell Hole runoff is just affecting inflow volumes and reservoir totals as we speak," a flow engineer said. "We had just under 250,000 c.f.s. coming in with existing runoff and this current rogue storm, until now. We'll be capacity at over one million acre-feet within hours when all that release gets here. That's why we had to go to 150,000 c.f.s. on the outflow side. What happened up there on the Rubicon anyway?"

"We'll have hell to pay with the downstream population when the levees go. Maybe one of these VIPs the Feds sent knows what happened." The shift manager nodded at Steele and Wilkins.

"Yeah, well let's see what the good people of Sacramento have to say if the dam goes 'cause we can't contain it all without the extra discharge," responded the first engineer. "Water will be lapping over the crest if this keeps up."

"Now what? Who the hell are they?" The safety supervisor pointed to a screen in his bank of video monitors. Two dark figures were seen at either end of a grated catwalk, which was cantilevered out over the dam face and directly above the spillways controlled by the eight massive tainter gates. Mercury vapor floodlights distorted their shadows into grotesque caricatures against the backdrop of the massive dam. Steele, Wilkins, and the other three men in the room crowded around the displays to get a better look.

"Anyone supposed to be up there?" asked Steele. "Especially now?"

"Nope. As soon as we go over 130,000 c.f.s. discharge, we close Folsom Dam Road on either side back a ways, and clear all the tunnels and accesses to the dam face as a safety precaution. The accesses to that catwalk are always securely locked. The only personnel authorized to be there would be the Bureau folks adjusting the flows, and they need to be cleared through me first just to be up there."

"And that hasn't happened, right?" interjected Wilkins.

"Not since midnight when we last opened the gates a bit to increase the outflow."

"*Wolverine*!" blurted Steele.

"With Sharpe most likely," added Wilkins.

"What's the fastest way up to the catwalk from here?" asked Steele.

"Use the interior elevator out that door to your left. It goes up through the heart of the beast. Punch the 'SL' street level button or the car will take you to the top of the observation tower. Turn right from the roadway exit door, then over the parapet and down to the spillway catwalks. There's a stairway down to each gate's control motor and mechanism. But I've got the elevator shut down now."

"Well un-shut it *now*, unless you want to end up in San Francisco Bay when the dam blows!" Steele dashed for the indicated doorway.

"And boys," added Wilkins, "I'd think seriously about getting to high ground if I were you." The four engineers didn't need to be told twice. In seconds they were up, and sprinting for the powerhouse exit.

The two-minute elevator ride up to the roadway seemed an eternity. Steele looked at Wilkins who watched the elevator level display flash overhead. He grinned and laughed. "Bet you never figured you'd be chasing bad guys around an old dam in the middle of the night, in the worst rain storm in over 100 years, when you first met me."

Wilkins nodded, but said nothing.

"Well, I appreciate your involvement JW, not to mention saving our bacon down in the Caribbean. I don't think I thanked you for that yet."

"Well then, you can buy breakfast this morning… after. Besides, I wasn't too keen on being a gambling promoter anyway." He sighed deeply just as the elevator car jerked to a halt. "But, as soon as we clean up this mess, I've got to address that situation back with the tribe. Maybe I'll ask you to stop by and tell a story or two. We could sell tickets."

"Done." They stepped out of the elevator building into the raging storm, but were still somewhat protected from the torrential deluge by the overhang of the building's roof.

"My guess is they're going to try and open the gates all the way, or disable them completely so the reservoir will overflow. Either way, it's not a good thing. You're faster. Go for the far stairway at the last emergency gate, and I'll try and head them off via the first one over there. Will pinch them in between," Steele pointed to the barbed wire fence with the red 'Authorized Personnel Only' sign. "Be careful, Amigo."

"Always. Keep your powder dry." Wilkins ran out into the storm, and disappeared down the middle of the deserted roadway.

Steele was at the first stairway gate seconds later. The wire cyclone fence was cut, and the normally locked gate was smashed open. The sight of the boiling water at the base of the enormous dam hundreds of feet below, took Cody's breath away. The sound of water exploding out the partially opened spillway gates reminded him of jet a blast, loud memories from his days on an aircraft carrier. "How do I get myself into these things?" With both hands on the pipe railings, he hurried down and out onto the catwalk above gate number 1. The wet grating underfoot was like ice. Not sure what he was looking for and not seeing anyone, he approached the control shed housing the engine that operated the massive gate. He could see the machinery from his vantage point on the catwalk. The lighted interior space was far too confined to conceal anyone. An open door banged against its jam, driven by the wind created by the cascading jet of water just below. He recalled the recent lecture they received from the Bureau manager that the electric motor controlling the hydraulics operating each gate required two keys, turned simultaneously by two individuals from either side of the ten-foot long shed. "No way they're going to have keys, and we saw them on opposite ends of the catwalk, about four or five hundred feet apart. Must be planting explosives," Steele reasoned. Leaning out over the handrail, he tried to see if there was anyone down on the steel girders that formed the 'V' of the pivots, on either side of the huge curved gate. Nothing. He dashed back up to the roadway, and down the second gate's stairway. Its gate also had been forced. "Probably done and gone by now. Wonder if Wilkins is having better luck." Just then, a figure climbed up onto the catwalk from the far side of the control shed. Obviously absorbed in the effort, it didn't notice Steele standing forty feet away, exposed by the bright light from the roadway floods above. There was nowhere to hide, and no time to run. The powerful lights illuminated the walkway, the street above and the top part of the enormous dam. It felt to Steele like he was on a bizarre stage. He drew his Browning and hollered, "Hold it! Stop where you are!"

A report like that of large fireworks sounded over the consistent, thunderous din of rushing water. Then a long deep, metallic moan wrenched the air, followed by a jolt. A turbulent explosion shook the metal catwalk. The rush of escaping water through destroyed tainter gate number 2, shot well over three hundred horizontal feet from the breach out into the night, before mare's tailing down into the river bed. The concussion and shock wave knocked Steele against the near handrail, then shook him off his feet and over the outside railing. He dropped the automatic, and desperately grabbed for the grate of the catwalk as he was somersaulted over and out into the black void. The clutching fingers of his left hand barely managed to snag a claw hold around a floor support as he tumbled over, the effort rotating his body almost 360 degrees, and swinging him in toward the dam face. A wrenching pain in his shoulder nearly caused him to let go. As his body rebounded back out in an arc over the void, with a last Herculean thrust, he was able to gain purchase around the support with his right hand. Knowing full well the resolve and resiliency of his adversaries, he moved fast, kipping up over the floor of the catwalk onto his stomach. Immediately he rolled to his back. The first thing he saw was the unblinking, black eye on the working end of an AK-47, inches away.

"Up!" commanded the black-clad figure, his down-turned face in shadow. "You've a very nasty habit of showing up in the most unusual places at most inopportune times, Mr. Steele." Cody complied.

"Back off three paces, hands locked on top of your head," the man yelled to be heard over the tumult of the spewing cascade below them, waving his weapon for emphasis.

Again, Steele did as he was told. He looked for any opening to attack or an escape route at all. Neither was available. In addition to the very conspicuous weapon, he noticed the man carried a climber's rope looped diagonally over one shoulder and across his chest, its end trailing off somewhere down below. When the man turned into the light, Steele saw his distinctive hawk-beak nose. "Sharpe. Wilkins was right on." Another tremendous jolt threw both men off their feet onto their backs. The warning signature sound of the explosion was lost in the thunderous roar from below. Neither man was ready. With a deep guttural wail, gate 3 wrenched free from one of its destroyed pivots and swung away useless. Steele gained his feet a split second before Sharpe, who grappled after his dropped weapon. Seeing his disadvantage, Sharpe spun on his hands, swinging both feet in an arc inches off the grate, upending the charging Steele. Both men slowly got to their feet, eyeing each other for an opening. Sharpe swung first, a short, right-handed jab. Steele stepped forward and inside the attack, and looped his left arm completely over the top of the shorter man's right shoulder, locking his forearm under the assassin's armpit. He followed through in one continuous motion, hammering his right elbow into the man's surprised face. Sharpe grunted and fell back from the force of the blow, still locked in Steele's sure embrace, blood coursing from his ruined nose. Instead of landing flat on his back, he let his momentum carry him over backward. The rolling move freed him from the arm lock, and brought him back to his feet above Steele. He lashed out with a quick kick that connected with Steele's forehead, splitting open an eyebrow, and snapping his head back. The power of the strike spun Steele over toward the open edge of the catwalk and the abyss. He managed to clutch a railing upright, just before his momentum would have carried him over the side. Sharpe followed with a second kick aimed for Steele's exposed midsection. It was meant to be more of a final shove. Steele was able to catch and lock Sharpe's ankle in the crook of his left arm at the second of impact. He grasped the railing at the same time with his other hand, and pulled himself upright. Still holding Sharpe's right ankle and the railing, he spun a roundhouse kick across the back of his opponent's only supporting leg, crashing him back onto the catwalk. With all his strength, Steele twisted the ankle with both hands, spinning Sharpe to his stomach. Holding onto the metal grate in a pushup posture, Sharpe pistoned back with his free leg, catching Steele square in the chest, forcing him to release the ankle and stumble over on his side. Panting hard, both men cautiously crouched to their feet once more, backing away from each other a few paces.

From somewhere out in the black night, both men heard the distinctive 'whop' 'whop' sound of a helicopter approaching. Neither looked away. Both strained to see the chopper peripherally. Sharpe spit out a mouthful of blood, wiped the back of his hand across his smashed nose, eyeing Steele all the while, hate burning in his stare. Suddenly, a powerful spot illuminated the dam face from the south as a chopper dropped over the roadway and down to the level of the catwalk. It hovered some two hundred feet above the American River far below. Its beam searched along the walkway in an area two spillways over from the combatants. Two immense geysers spewed parallel columns of snow white water from the breached gates out into the black void, their size, the prodigious rain, and the position of the chopper, prevented those aboard from spotting Steele or Sharpe. Brightly illuminated by the lights above, the chopper inched closer to the dam, right over spillway 4. The two men saw the markings of a local TV station emblazoned on its side in big blue lettering,

KSAC. The beam of the spot jerked erratically up and down, exploring along the empty walkway, then swung in their direction. Its searching stopped when it caught Sharpe's profile. Steele saw a cameraman with a video unit lean out the open doorway, one foot on the skid of the chopper. "Crazy fools." He watched the craft maneuver closer to the far side of the water columns. Steele hoped Sharpe would turn to look directly at the light source and be momentarily blinded. He planned his move accordingly, when a third, much louder explosion announced another breach, this time at gate number 4.

The power of water released at about 60,000 cubic feet per second was more than enough to shred metal, let alone flesh. Especially from within three hundred feet of the breach. The news chopper was about one hundred and fifty feet from the dam face, hovering right over the spillway, when gate 4 exploded. Almost spellbound, Steele watched the massive geyser reach out and engulf the helicopter, snatching it as if it were some insignificant bug. He saw it crush from the middle, and be spun over on its side, its main rotor flail, then disappear in the enormous water shaft. The deadly white column carried it and its occupants out and down, into the merciless black below.

The last explosion weakened the center support of the metal catwalk just above gate 4, causing the entire walkway structure to suddenly twist and bend. Steele and Sharpe each grabbed and held the metal pipe handrail. Their collapsing perch bucked beneath them, staggering them to and fro with its wild convulsions. Each had a difficult time maintaining balance, constantly readjusting footing to compensate for the erratic movements. During one dramatic lurch, as he shifted his feet, Sharpe unknowingly stepped in an errant loop of his climbing line. The thirty five year old support finally gave way. It crashed into the water column at gate 4, and took the center section of the catwalk with it. Before the metal beam separated, it dragged the end Sharpe stood on down with it. The incline went from level to fifty degrees down angle in an instant. Because Sharpe faced Steele, he couldn't see the last gate breach, and the consequences of its destruction develop. He was therefore unable to adjust his stance and grip fast enough to keep from falling. The speed of the walkway failure caused Sharpe to loose his temporary hold on the handrail. His feet were jerked out from beneath him. As it dropped away at a crazy angle, Sharpe's end of the catwalk pitched him face down onto the slippery, inclined grating. He clutched for a handhold, trying to arrest his slide, but couldn't get enough fingers through the square holes in the grate. Clinging to the handrail by wrapping it under his right armpit, and locking the grip by grasping his hands, Steele watched in fascination as Sharpe's feet-first slip gradually picked up speed.

"Steele, help me!" he screamed in panic. Then he was gone.

Everything happened so fast it seemed surreal. Steele wiped blood from his torn eyebrow and looked around, trying to grasp his situation, and decide what to do next. Waiting for the convulsions in the walkway to cease, he noticed a section of climbing rope wound around a handrail upright, and snagged in an angled crevice in the floor grating. It wasn't moving, and was under obvious tension. On his stomach, he inched his way down to the break, and cautiously peered over. There, some twenty feet below and directly over the roaring white water, dangled Lew Sharpe, head down, snared by his ankle in the rope. The sound was overwhelming, the speed and uniformity of the escaping water mesmerizing. Steele was certain the terrorist was yelling his bloody head off. "Hang on, Sharpe!" He knew there was no possible way the man could hear. Hell, he couldn't even hear his own shout, the roar of the water was so overpowering. "I don't know why the fuck I'm even thinking of saving the bastard." Again, he locked his right elbow through an upright. He was about to try and corkscrew his free wrist through the line where it angled across the break, when it suddenly lashed through its temporary snare. The flailing Sharpe dropped another few feet closer to his destiny before the line caught once again. There was little purchase or friction between the nylon rope and the wet metal. Steele saw Sharpe pathetically waving his arms, as his fate rushed by just below at almost 60,000 c.f.s. With each movement of his body, Sharpe caused his lifeline to twist, and each twist changed the tension and purchase on the line. As Steele took another look over, he felt rather than heard a 'zipping' sound as the rope ran its final course across the squares of the metal grate. Steele watched in horror as Lew Sharpe disappeared within the massive shaft of surging water, pulverized into a tiny pink puff that was swallowed in an instant.

Steele lay on his belly for a moment, and watched the deadly white-water column rush out into the night, engulfed in its deafening roar. He shook his head in disbelief, then carefully got back on all fours, and began the slow process of working his way up the bent and twisted catwalk. Once back on the few remaining feet still intact, he noticed the overhead floods reflecting off something caught in the grating just where the last section broke away. He approached, then stood over a pair of mirrored sunglasses, one earpiece of which was caught through one of the floor's metal squares. Deliberately, he crushed a heel down on the dark reflecting glass until he felt it shatter and crunch under his foot, its shards tinkling away through the grate. "That's for you, Laura. Rest peacefully now." He felt a slight thud underfoot, turned in alarm, and came face to face with what first he perceived to be a ghost. There, but ten feet away, stood a black-clad figure, wrapped in climbing rope. Only this one was holding a Glock .357 Sig. in one hand aimed right at his heart. "*Wolverine!*"

"So that's really my code name." The black-clad figure laughed. "I rather like it," Toscana said. "Somewhat appropriate, wouldn't you agree, Mr. Steele?"

Cody ignored the question, wondering how to avoid being shot. His wrenched shoulder ached severely, his head pounded, and he could felt warm blood mixed with cold rain dripping from his chin. "I didn't think terrorism for the sheer act alone was your style, Toscana, or whatever you're calling yourself this week. Where's the Machiavellian angle in all this?" Steele glanced at the railing, and then quickly back over his shoulder down the ruined catwalk. No way out. His foe was too far away for a quick move, and the only avenue of escape would mean an instant death similar to Sharpe's.

"*Wolverine* is fine for the few moments you have left on this good earth. Oh, there's a political *and* a money angle, don't worry about that. Too bad about Devoney Marsh, Steele. She was good, in the biblical sense."

"Why don't you tell her yourself? I'm sure she might have a few poignant things to say to you, as well. The last time I saw her was just a few hours ago." He saw a perplexed look flash across *Wolverine*'s face, and figuring it might be his only chance, tensed for a quick move toward the terrorist.

"Ah, ah, ah. Not at all a healthy idea, Steele." *Wolverine* shouted over the thunderous din of water blast, sensing as well as seeing the move. He deliberately cocked the hammer of the Glock. "Either there's a wonderful story here, or you're trying to distract me with fables. I haven't time for either, I'm sorry to say…and your time is up, my unworthy Cody Steele." *Wolverine* slowly raised the pistol, taking dead aim for Steele's forehead. In the same instant, the two men both saw the tiny red laser-aiming dot materialize on the barrel of the pistol.

Neither heard the shot. The deadly weapon was blasted from *Wolverine*'s hand by the force of impact, flinging it out over the outside handrail. The assailant shook his hand once hard, surprise and pain evident on his face. Steele started toward the man in a centered crouch, only to come up short when he heard a shrill whistle from above. Both men looked up for its source, keeping each other in the field of vision all the while. Wilkins, standing directly beneath a floodlight up on the roadway, waved once and was gone. Steele smiled and turned back to the difficult situation at hand. In the time it took to look up and turn back, *Wolverine* was over the side of the railing, and disappearing down the face of the dam. When Steele reached the spot just vacated by his adversary, *Wolverine*, attached to his climbing line, swung across the steeply angled dam face one hundred feet below. He used a side-step running motion employed by climbers to relocate their horizontal position on a mountain face. "Must have tied the end off somewhere by the control shed," Steele reasoned. The tiny black figure was at the powerhouse level far below almost before the idea to cut the line reached Steele's brain. He watched *Wolverine* sprint toward the Highway Patrol chopper, as the explosive charge on gate 1 detonated.

Steele was hammered to his back again when the entire gate assembly ruptured from its massive pivot bolts. It crashed down its spillway to the river with a series of shrieking clangs. The entire catwalk over spillway 1 was torn from its supports along with the tainter gate. Even though each gate control mechanism had to be accessed from its own stairway and separate section of catwalk, the entire walkway for all eight spillways was interconnected structurally. Was. As the catwalk section above gate 1 tore down and away, it wrenched and destroyed all but one support on section 2 where Steele lay clutching a handrail upright. Number 2's stairway was wrecked, twisting and banging in the water column. At first, he didn't dare move, fearing any change in weight distribution might complete the disaster and seal his fate. Dragging himself tentatively to his feet, still maintaining a stranglehold on the handrail, he surveyed the impossible sight surrounding him. The roadway floods illuminated the entire devastation. He stood on the only section of catwalk still intact. Those over gate 1 and 3 dangled uselessly below. Spillways 1 through 4 were wide open, their gates destroyed by the terrorist's explosives. "Wonder what's up with 5 through 8?" Steele pondered. Over 240,000 c.f.s of water smashed down the American River watercourse far below, at least double what the levee system downstream was designed to handle. It was only a matter of time before much of Sacramento would be underwater. Ten feet in three directions from his precarious perch was abyss, while twenty feet of airspace separated him from the rain slick, nearly vertical, dam face. When he turned to look up at the roadway, the grating below him quivered and bucked, creaking in protest. That's when he saw a huge metal hook attached to a thick cable descending slowly down toward him through the pounding rain.

Without hesitation, Steele stepped onto the giant ball hook when it stopped inches to his right. It was at least two feet wide at the maw, and if he had wished, he could easily have stood with both feet inside the bottom of its arc. As it was, given the unsettling events of the recent half hour, he stood with his left foot on the hook and wrapped his right around the hook cable, locking his ankle through an additional turn for good measure. The view was staggering. As the unlikely elevator began to rise, it swung out and away from the catwalk, affording its rider a stunning panorama of four horsetails of cascading water feathering out from the dam and down, dropping nearly the height of a thirty-story building. Just as the hook assembly approached the roadway, gate number 5 destructed. Steele watched captivated, as the one hundred ton tainter gate ripped off its pivots and tumbled into oblivion down the spillway, pummeled as it fell by a fifth cascading water column of reservoir water erupting from the dam face.

"Welcome back, white man. Hope you had a ticket for that ride," the shout from above wafted down to Steele through the drumming rain.

"Where the…?"

"Up here. You didn't think this thing would drive itself now, did you?"

Steele squinted up through the rain and finally spotted Wilkins leaning out the port control cab window of the huge construction crane some hundred and fifteen feet above. "Hang on, I'll be right there."

Steele watched in amazement as his friend wound his way down a series of exposed metal stairways within the superstructure of the monster crane. Its gantry tapered from the roadway to the cab on four spindly-looking legs.

"Damn, I'm sure glad you know how to drive one of these things," with a wide grin, he slapped the big Native American on the back. Wilkins winced noticeably.

"You must be joking. I haven't a clue. But, hey. How hard could it be? On, off, start, stop, up, down. All I had to do was figure out which knob or lever did which. By the way, you look like… well…shit. Forget to duck?"

"Thanks. You don't look so good either," he eyed the bleeding wound in Wilkins' right shoulder.

"Those bad guys sure like their cutlery." He reached into his jacket pocket and withdrew a deadly looking Italian throwing knife. "Your friend *Wolverine* left this in me over at the emergency gates when he found me spoiling his fun. I got lucky and saw him plant those satchel charges on the gate pivots. I waited until he was working on the second, figuring the first wouldn't be set to go until he had time to leave. He left a nice convenient climbing rope down to number 8. I used his line, and basically just went along behind him, pulling the detonators and tossing the charges down the river. Unfortunately, ol' *Wolverine* doubled back for something, the rope probably, and caught me in the act. I didn't even see him until it was too late. He must have some Indian blood. I guess he left his gun in his pack up above, or he'd have had me easy. As it was he made an amazing throw of about twenty-five feet with this thing," he gingerly rotated his wounded shoulder and grimaced. "Lucky for me your buddy was on the move when he threw, or I might have been in *real* trouble."

"Did you pull it out?" Steele asked, already knowing the answer.

"Yeah. Not a lot of other folks around to help. It was sorta getting in my way."

"Geez! You're lucky you're not bleeding to death. *Are* you?"

"Nah. Stuffed a hanky in the hole. It only hurts when I laugh, or rappel."

"Why didn't you just shoot the bastard back there when you had the chance?"

"Maybe that's what I was trying to do and missed."

"Doubt it. I've seen how accurate you are with a knife."

"But I've got a bad wing. I thought you noticed?"

"Nice try. You're left handed."

"Throw right, shoot left. Well, I thought I'd let you take care of him after I leveled the playing field a bit. I remember the stories you told me about all the years you chased the son-of-a-bitch, and how frustrated you were. I didn't want you to miss out on the thrilling climax after all that. And, having seen you in action, I was certain," Wilkins winked, "That you could take care of yourself. 'Closure', is what everyone is calling it nowadays, I believe. Besides, I had to figure out some way to save your sorry butt, given the fact that your end of this dam kept exploding out from under you."

"Thanks for the vote of confidence, but he's still with us somewhere out here. He did a dive over the side on that climbing rope. Wilkins?"

"Yeah?"

"To hell with closure. Next time, just shoot the bastard. We've got to get you some medical attention, soon," said Steele.

"I think we'd best do something about the big leaks in this dam first. Then we'll worry about the little one here in my shoulder."

They moved over to the parapet above the dam face, and watched thousands of tons of reservoir water being blasted from the dam at over

300,000 c.f.s. The massive structure vibrated, resonating with the changing pressures throughout. They scurried back to the shelter of the tower roof to get out of the ceaseless downpour.

"I don't think that's in our job description, even though…" Steele stopped in mid-sentence deep in thought. "It might be too late anyway, but, we could…" again he trailed off.

"I'm starting to recognize that look, my friend. Every time I've seen it lately we're off on some wildass adventure, leaping tall buildings in a single bound. How are we going to save the world this time?"

Steele ran to the reservoir side of the roadway, then went left about two hundred feet to the north. He was back under the shelter moments later, dripping wet, but grinning from ear to ear, panting hard.

"So, about how much weight do you think your little toy can handle?" He looked up at the giant crane.

"Well, it's on permanent rails in the roadway, and I think I recall the Bureau folks mentioning that they used it to replace the heavy equipment down in the powerhouse. I'd guess, from the size of it and the gearing, maybe one hundred tons," responded Wilkins.

"You know…? It sorta reminds me of those old forest service lookouts, except for the arm. Think it can pull a barge?"

"A barge?"

"That whopper just over the other side there," Steele pointed north in the opposite direction from the gates and spillways. "They must've used it to repair something on the reservoir side, or to float in some of that heavy machinery for your crane."

"All well and good, but what help will towing a barge be in stopping that outflow?"

"I didn't say we were going to tow it. I said 'pull'."

"Still confusing me white eyes."

"Underwater. We're going to pull it underwater," grinned Steele. "At least part of it, once we get it over the gates. It looks long enough to cover at least three of the openings. Let me show you what I've got in mind."

The two men just broke the cover of shelter, when the black and white California Highway Patrol helicopter roared up to the parapet level, its canopy only yards from the startled pair. Automatic weapon fire erupted from the open pilot's side window showering concrete divots in all directions, and adding a distinctive staccato to the riotous noise already enveloping the dam.

Steele dove and rolled for the parapet to his right. Its top was about three feet above the roadway and offered protection only so long as the chopper remained where it was on the outside. He caught a glance of Wilkins vaulting over the reservoir edge, and hoped water level was only a reasonable drop from the top. The helo pilot hugged the dam for a few seconds, and then pushed the nimble craft up over the parapet, barely clearing it with his left skid. The shooting ceased as soon as the craft began to move, convincing Steele that the pilot was its sole occupant. "Lucky for us that the guy can't fly and shoot at the same time…at least accurately. Hasta be *Wolverine*." His suspicion was confirmed when the chopper came around in a tight left turn, its Plexiglas canopy penetrated by the illuminating floods, revealing the pilot. Steele was certain he saw the man at the controls point at him. *Wolverine* brought the craft to a stationary hover perpendicular to the roadway and about ten feet above it. There were no shadows or nooks and crannies within which to seek cover. Other than to go over the dam face, Steele had no choice but to jump up, and sprint for the shelter of the tower entry thirty yards away. It was the longest thirty yards of his life. A fire line of lead chased him to the tower; the concrete fragments it chewed out of the roadway peppered Steele's back, and nicked the exposed skin on his neck and head. "Better concrete than the real thing." Crashing through the self-locking glass door of the elevator tower, he dove into the relative safety of the darkened interior. "Shit! He knows I'm unarmed. But he also knows Wilkins is carrying." The helicopter danced sideways to its right, and the pilot flipped on its powerful spot. "Confirming Wilkins' position," Cody knew instinctively. "Exactly what I'd do given the same circumstances." He scanned the sparse interior for something, anything. In a corner, he noticed two aluminum stanchions used to direct people touring the dam. Each was about three feet high. He snatched one up, testing its heft. Satisfied, he searched the room again. Nothing. He found what he was looking for outside the right hand, heavy plate glass window on the walkway. *Wolverine*, evidently satisfied that Wilkins was no longer a threat, maneuvered the patrol copter back over the roadway, and sprayed the tower entry with a full magazine from his 9mm MAC-10 on auto. He paused to reload, holding the collective between his knees, and emptied a second fusillade into the shattered foyer. Steele saw the move, and rolled to the relative safety of the concrete wall adjacent to the elevator. He covered his face and head with both arms for protection from the shower of flying glass. His light leather jacket was jerked about as it shredded, yet it did offer a layer of protection. The nerves in the flesh on the back of his legs screamed in pain, as glass sliced through his pants. His Levis were no match for the razor sharp edges of flying shards. Waiting for the reload interval, he calculated his odds of success. They were way too small. When the pause came, Steele erupted from his pile of glass gripping the metal pole under an arm, jumped out on to the sidewalk through the shattered window, and grabbed the climbing rope. *Wolverine's* rope. *Wolverine* saw Steele move, cursed and jammed the collective back and to his left, spinning his craft out over the dam face. The main rotor just missed Cody's head as it whirled by. Steele tied a quick bowline through the welded metal loop at the top of the stanchion, then scurried over to the destroyed cyclone fence, which once protected the gate to spillway 1. There he tied the other end to a metal upright imbedded in concrete. *Wolverine* saw Steele moving along the roadway, and massaged his controls to position the helicopter for the optimum kill shot. The two men were less than twenty feet apart when Steele, using a sideways hammer throwing motion, pitched the heavy stanchion over the parapet directly at the exposed canopy of the helicopter. It shattered into a spider web of tiny cracks, but didn't break. *Wolverine's* reflex reaction was almost instantaneous. Seeing the unlikely missile in the split second before it struck, he forced his machine over to its right. The weight of the stanchion caused it to drop straight down between the fuselage and the left skid. *Wolverine's* aerobatics maneuver spun the metal pole back around the climbing line in two deadly loops to the outside of the skid. His lateral visibility to the left destroyed, *Wolverine* initiated a short radius climbing turn in Steele's direction, his purpose to put the craft down on the roadbed and finish the encounter once and for all. He had position, opportunity, and firepower. Just as the helicopter reached the apex of its turn directly over the parapet on the dam side, the rope stretched tight. The sleek craft jerked to a halt, its lift interrupted, and crashed its skids onto the concrete rampart. Immediately, *Wolverine* applied full power and reversed direction. He slammed the collective full right to get away from the dam face trying for room and altitude. The 3,000-pound test climbing line stretched but held just long enough, snapping the craft over sideways. The fence upright exploded from its concrete foundation, and banged down the spillway as the helicopter fell away. Steele heard the whine of the turbine straining for purchase as the stricken craft disappeared down into the blackness of the riverbed canyon. The last he saw of it was when its spot winked out seconds later.

Steele found Wilkins hanging by a hand on the mid-section of the forward hawser that secured the barge to the reservoir side rampart.

"Well that certainly was refreshing," bellowed Wilkins. "Didja cut yourself shaving? You look like a goalie in a dart game. Hope the other guy looks worse."

"There's a ladder into the water off the front. You'll have to swim around to reach it," Cody motioned with his hand.

"Swell," muttered Wilkins. He let go of the rope, and dropped back into the freezing water. A minute later he stood shivering on the thick wood decking of the construction barge.

It was about two hundred feet long by fifty feet wide, and decked with well-worn, oil-soaked 4x12"s. Its hull was metal, and it drafted a shallow three feet unloaded. It was secured both fore and aft paralleling the dam, about 100 meters north of the first gate. Basically, it was little more than a large, rectangular metal box covered by wood.

"Must've used it to transport large or unusual-sized parts over to the crane for the powerhouse down below. Probably couldn't make the final sharp turn on a truck, if they were too long," observed Wilkins. The two men walked the length of the vessel. "What happened to our friendly Highway Patrolman?"

"Last I saw, he was in a dive for the river bottom, dragging part of the fence with him. With luck, they may find him, or at least a few pieces, downstream in a few months. I didn't see or hear an explosion. But hey, I can't hear much out here anyway."

"Couldn't have happened to a nicer fellow. Next time, I will."

"You will, what?"

"Just shoot the bastard!"

They both laughed. "With any luck, this *is* the last time," chuckled Steele.

"OK, what's the plan, genius?" Wilkins massaged his damaged shoulder.

"We're going to tow that barge in place over gates 2, 3 and 4 with your crane. We'll anchor the far side securely to the dam. Then we'll drop a length of chain over the near side and it'll be sucked through the middle gate. We'll snag the chain on the spillway side with the ball-hook, winch it in and pull the barge vertically down over the openings. No worries."

Wilkins rolled his eyes. "You've *gotta* be kidding. The barge can sink or break up; we've little chance even seeing the damn chain in the spillway let alone hooking it, *if* we can get it sucked through, and I doubt this tinker toy crane has the horsepower to pull that barge under, given the unlikely event we succeed with one and two. No worries, my ass. How about a better plan, white guy?"

"No time left, and I'm too tired to come up with anything else other than running for it, and I'm way too tired for that. Besides, all you have to do is drive that thing. I have to be the bait on the hook."

They quickly went over Steele's idea in detail, touching mostly on the shortcomings and unknowns. Wilkins pounded him on the back and laughed. He then climbed the crane gantry, and began the slow process of moving it down the dam. Steele, moved onto the barge, and untied both mooring lines. He attached a section of stern line to the hook and ball from the crane's arm that Wilkins obligingly swung out and over the reservoir side before moving the equipment. The massive crane easily pulled the empty barge, although the process was frustratingly slow, due to the gantry's huge size. While they inched along, Cody located a long section of anchor chain in stowage. He wrestled the heavy links to the center of the barge, and then dragged an end fore and aft. He secured the two ends to mooring points at each outside port end of the barge. By the time Wilkins had the crane and barge positioned directly over the reservoir side of gate 3, Steele had a second length of chain attached to the middle of the first. During their short journey down the roadway, both men were concerned when their convoy approached, then passed above the first two gates. There were serious whirlpools above both, indicative of the amount and force of the water being sucked down, and then blasted out the gate openings twenty feet below. However, the buoyant barge easily floated into place. They positioned its midsection directly over the surface of gate 3. Wilkins saw all five floodlit water plumes as well as the raging river over four hundred feet below his lofty perch. Next, Steele moored the barge to the dam with hawsers. Wilkins met Steele on the roadway to finalize their strategy.

"You're sure this will work?"

"You must be joking," chuckled Steele. "I haven't a clue, and I'm certainly open for suggestions."

"We could just leave before the whole things collapses." Both men felt strong vibrations course through the concrete roadway, caused by the enormous volumes of water jetting through the relatively small gate openings.

"Ri-i-ight," returned Steele, sarcastically. "You couldn't look at yourself in the mirror if we didn't try."

"Possibly die trying," corrected Wilkins. "You don't *want* to look at yourself, my friend," he laughed. "You're the true definition of a bloody mess! At least my swim stopped *my* bleeding. Maybe you should take a dip before we start. It hurts just to look at you."

"Unfortunately, I'll get my chance." Steele watched number 3's water column shoot out the length of a football field before dropping away. "Let's get these chains ready. Now comes the interesting part."

"You're sure the force of the water through that gate will be strong enough to suck this anchor chain through?"

"Nothing to it. That's the easy part. Hell, I just saw these geysers eat a helicopter, and turn Sharpe into a pink grease spot. It's snagging the chain with your hook that's going to be tough. Just give me enough slack to swing it, once I'm down there. Think you'll be able to see me?" Steele pointed to a spot far down the spillway below the spouting water.

"Piece of cake. I could see the lights of downtown Sacramento easy from up there, if this damn rain would let up. Let's get on with it. I'm freezing." The big Indian turned, and started another long climb up to the cockpit of the crane. "When we get through with this, I'm going to suggest they put a heater in this buggy," he yelled over his shoulder.

"When this is finished, *if* I live through it, I'm taking a three day nap. I've had it," Steele muttered.

About ten feet of clearance separated the side of the dam and the near side of the barge. An opaque glow radiating up through the black water directly over the submerged gate caught his attention. He guessed it was the floods reflecting off the water column on the other side. That's where he lowered the end of the pile of chain. Hand-over-hand, he dropped in the first twenty feet. The chain seemed unaffected by the sucking current, and dangled straight down. Steele shook his head in disappointment, thinking his plan might fail. Suddenly, he felt a tug as if a giant fish had taken the end. He let out another five feet or so, and the drag increased. Winding two turns around a stanchion, he still was scarcely able to hold its weight against the additional pull. Throwing caution to the wind, he let the whole thing go, and had to dance out of the way as the entire two hundred feet of rusted links rushed over the side and out of sight. A tremor shook the barge as the last of the chain streamed over, yanking the length of sister chain to which it was attached into a vibrating bow. The old barge listed slightly toward the dam. Steele pumped his fist, and waved up to Wilkins.

"See anything yet?"

"Standby." Wilkins shouted down. "I think so," he yelled. "It's hard to tell 'cause the spillway's dark, and I don't have much of an angle. But I think I see movement down there."

Steele waved, and headed back over to the roadway. Wilkins moved the crane back to a point between gates 2 and 3. Once it was settled in place, he winched the ball hook over to the dam face parapet. Steele reached the top of the rampart at the same time. He took a few deep breaths, looked down the almost vertical concrete wall of the dam, stepped up on the hook, and signaled his readiness. Slowly, Wilkins took tension up on the cable, lifting the hook and rider off the parapet and out over the abyss. He maneuvered his charge about fifty feet horizontally out over the face, before gradually lowering him down between the water columns. Dangling some fifty feet out and two hundred feet above anything solid, made it difficult for Cody to concentrate. Once between the two giant waterspouts, man and equipment were blasted by an icy wet gale spawned at the gate by too much water being forced through too small an orifice. The openings acted like huge nozzles under immense pressure. He was soaked through to his skin; the exposure to freezing water and wind caused him to shiver violently. He hoped his hands wouldn't become so numb that he couldn't maintain a grip. His swallow was dry and he focused on just clinging to the slippery cable as it began to pendulum during the plunge further into the maelstrom. Noting the swing, Wilkins decided to increase the descent speed hoping that Steele could survive any impact, and knowing full well he could not, if the ball hook curved into either water column. Steele positioned himself on top of the ball. The hook smashed hard on the raised buttress separating the two spillways, then slid ten feet over the side into number 3, before the stretch slack played out. The whole show came to a halt in two feet of cold, rushing water. As he rolled down into the spillway channel, he somehow maintained his death grip on the cable. Wilkins carefully coaxed out the slack, lifting ball hook and rider back a few feet above the buttress.

"Well, at least I won't be killed in a fall from here. I'll have a nice slide to the bottom, then be crushed in the river course." Steele waited for the cable to stop its jerking bounce, and tried to orient himself. On either side above, two massive waterspouts blasted horizontally, and thundered away into the night. An enveloping mist drifted beneath both, opening and closing at the whim of the wind. Unusual shadowing added to Steele's difficulties, as he was well below and away from the lights. However, it was a changing shadow that helped him spot the anchor chain. When the mist wandered just so, he thought he could see a black line running down spillway 3 just off center. It was about thirty feet away, and the shadows came and went as the chain twirled and bounced. Small geysers would spout here and there, as the links undulated in the rushing water. Getting the crane's cable to swing was the centerpiece of their scheme. They knew they had to take the hook under the water column, or risk instant disaster by moving the cable closer to, or even into it. If the water caught the cable, Steele would be whipped up into it, or thrown off. Either way, he was history. From over three hundred feet above, Wilkins twitched the crane arm a fraction, transferring a much greater movement to the end of the line down below. Like a kid on a swing, the idea was to have Steele use his weight to increase the distance of the arc. The ball hook jerked up, swung about ten feet back over spillway 2, and then began its arc in the direction of 3. The lumbering weight of the heavy ball caused it to bounce and scrape across the water channel. In the middle of each swing it crashed into the separating buttress, then lurched over and into the adjacent spillway. After the third full swing and crash, Cody considered attempting a horizontal running maneuver while hanging onto the hook, like the one executed by *Wolverine* earlier. Quickly he discarded that thought, knowing his hands were too cold and the hook too wet and slippery. He settled on a sort of hopping move.

"I only need a swing of fifty to sixty feet. These main spillways are only fifty feet across, and the damn chain isn't even in the middle!" After inching the arc ever greater, he thought he felt his frozen feet brush across the submerged chain. He had to wait for another full arcing swing to be sure. At the end of the next one, he forced the hook into the water channel by bending at the waist, and straightening his legs. The submerged hook caught for a split second then pulled free. "At least the next one will have a bit more distance, giving me more time." The added few feet were enough. Using all his weight, he pistoned the hook into the water on the far side of the chain, and it caught. The abrupt stop almost threw Steele from the ball. As it happened, his feet slipped off, and he only managed to keep from falling when his hands slipped down the cable to the top of the ball. He flopped about for a few seconds like a fish on a line, pummeled by the shallow but powerful spillway runoff. Finally, he got a knee over the submerged hook. Once secure, he locked an elbow around the cable. He muscled a loop of chain over the hook assembly, and double-wrapped it around. He just made out the crane through the mist, and frantically waved. Wilkins had discovered a pair of binoculars stuffed in an unlocked cab compartment, and had watched Steele's struggles during the whole event. The second he saw the desperate wave, he inched the crane arm directly above his friend. He hoped the reposition would lessen the amount of any swing when anchor chain was lifted free.

"OK, here we go."

Engaging the winch, he reeled in the cable. Wilkins was afraid to take in too much too quickly, concerned that they might lose the chain. He stopped the ascent long enough to see Steele flip him off with one hand. Three minutes and two hundred vertical feet later, he plopped a bedraggled partner and the captured anchor chain on the roadway.

"Well, look what I've caught."

Steele started to respond sarcastically, then noticed Wilkins' left arm, hanging limp and useless.

"Enough of this rescue bullshit. We've got to get you to a hospital."

"Soon enough, my friend. It's just a little stiff. Let's finish this up. Maybe they'll give us a group rate. By the looks of it, you need admission more than I."

"OK, here's the COA, as Captain Younger would say. Slide that baby over to the center of 3," Steele motioned to the gantry. "We'll take up the slack in the chain and hoist away. With luck, we should pull the near side of the barge underwater."

"Aren't you worried about it sinking all the way past the gate openings?"

"I've got it secured to the dam with those monster hawsers, plus a million acre feet of force should jam it in there. I'm more worried that this gizmo of yours won't have the guts to pull it down in place, once it gets into vertical."

"From an engineering standpoint, I still say we don't have the horsepower to pull it under, and I seriously doubt this procedure is spelled out in any operating manual. If we're *really* lucky and nothing breaks, and we *do* get it under, and if the force is as great as you think, the last twenty feet will definitely be a problem. Maybe we should reconsider running for it."

"One way to find out," laughed Steele. He started up the gantry.

"Where're you going?

"What better place to watch? Besides its out of the rain."

"Well, I hope you realize the strain may topple this spindly thing over the dam. I think the design meant for it to do its lifting closer to the roadway. We could dump it over."

"Hey, man. Over the dam? I've been there, done that a couple times already tonight. Ain't nothin' to it."

They ran the crane south about thirty feet, using the water column on one side, and the center of the barge on the other as reference points. Wilkins extended the crane arm out to its maximum. "If it starts to bend, I'll bring it in."

"Don't break it," Steele chuckled. "They won't let you play with it again."

The cable and attached chain hung loose from the crane arm and curved all the way down to the spillway. With the slack removed it angled directly up and split through the middle of the waterspout. They saw the arm bend as the winch ground in more cable. Wilkins withdrew fifteen feet of it to compensate for the increased tension. They heard a screeching wail as the barge side scraped down along the dam wall.

"It's under," Steele yelled. The shore side of the barge disappeared beneath the reservoir's black water. The opposite side gradually lifted, wooden deck planks spilling off, as the up angle increased.

"Good. Great! You're doing great!" Steele watched the unusual attitude of the construction barge increase, one side angling up and the other slowly submerging.

The superstructure of the crane jerked in vibrating pulses. "We're pushing the envelope on this thing," called Wilkins. "If I reduce the angle on the cable by bringing the arm in further, we won't get any more chain."

"Don't change a thing. Keep winching. She's just about vertical," shouted Steele.

The shrieking was incessant, as the metal hull grated slowly down the concrete of the inner dam wall. After what seemed an eternity, all but ten feet of the barge hull was submerged. The water spouts from gates 2, 3 and 4, dropped off by seventy five percent, their plumes anemic next to those from 1 and 5. Wilkins shut down the winch.

"Each turn is bending the arm instead of retrieving cable. Either we'll lose the arm, or snap the cable," worried Wilkins. He stood, and joined Steele at the reservoir side cab window. "Wow, you sure don't see that every day."

"Nope. But we've got to try and get another few feet. Gates 1 and 5 going at full blast, are still more than the downstream levees can take. Maybe just a few more c.f.s. off the top will make a difference. A few more inches could save lives. Even if the chain or cable snaps, I think the force of the water will plaster that barge in place for awhile."

"You're driving this bus, but I don't like it," Wilkins resumed his position at the control panel.

A loud metallic moan groaned up from the tormented barge just then.

"I think that's the hull caving," guessed Steele. "Any change in the discharge from your side?"

"Nope. A bent hull seems to plug the hole just as well." Wilkins monitored the decreased plumes for any change. "Jeez! Here we go…again."

They felt the vibrating strain on the gantry. Red warning lights flashed all over Wilkins' control panel. Still, he let the winch grind, attempting to gain a few extra few feet of cable. The barge screamed as if in tortured agony and rasped a few more feet down over the submerged openings. They heard two loud snapping reports from directly below. In slow motion, the gantry tilted over toward the dam face, its cab compartment leaning well out over the void. As they started over, Steele looked at Wilkins wide-eyed with a 'what next' look, and began laughing. There wasn't anything else left to do. Maybe it was his exhaustion. Possibly it was a reaction to all the crazed scrambling they had done over the past month. He wasn't sure. He just laughed louder. Wilkins joined in, and they didn't stop until the whole gantry collapsed, its occupants wildly tumbled in the process. The legs crashed across the roadway and parapet, shattering much of its superstructure. The cab teetered to a stop almost seventy feet out in thin air.

"You sure you're up for this?" asked Steele. The big Indian didn't look good. His face was a ghostly white, a vivid contrast to his jet-black hair.

"Like we've a choice?"

"We can sit tight, and wait for help."

"Out here?" Wilkins looked straight down over two hundred feet to the river churning wildly at the base of the dam. "Let's get the fuck outta here!"

The ruined gantry creaked in groaning protest every time they moved. There appeared to be enough reinforcing struts and girders still intact on the gantry to allow a precarious climb to safety. The last thing they needed was to be forced into swinging back to the dam hand-over-hand. Steele was certain Wilkins would never be able to accomplish any such maneuver. Heck, he wasn't sure he could do it himself. With Wilkins setting the pace, they crawled out the floor-way hatch of the cab, onto the bent and twisted leg-struts, and started their dangerous escape.

"Just don't look down," called Steele. "But I'm sort of getting used to the view from this angle," he laughed to himself.

"I'm not looking anywhere. Got my eyes closed tight."

The entire structure of the destroyed crane bounced and shook with each foot they climbed closer to the parapet and safety.

"I wonder if the barge held when we dumped this thing over," Steele tried anything to take Wilkins mind off their dire situation. "I'm sure we broke the chain or the cable."

They both stopped and searched the dam directly below. Just a few isolated waterspouts shot high-pressure spray from the sides of the three middle gates. They obviously were still covered by the barge. "Not exactly water tight," observed Wilkins.

In the distance, they spotted a string of vehicles heading up the hill in their direction, each boasting an impressive array of flashing red and blue lights. A slight graying across the eastern horizon signaled the end of a very long night. Five scary minutes later, the two battered men crawled over the parapet exhausted, but safe.

"Did you notice?" Wilkins muttered.

"Well now what, JW?"

"The rain has stopped."

EPILOGUE

The definition of a 100-year flood or storm is an event that has but a one percent chance of being repeated in any given year. Sacramento water and flood control engineers considered going back to the terminology drawing board after the October 1991 storms. Sheer luck, plus quick thinking and action by two men spared most of the Sacramento metropolitan area and downtown business districts. Had not the prodigious flows from Folsom dam been quickly reduced, hydrologists calculated that over two hundred square miles of the city would have suffered some degree of flooding, with some areas under twenty feet of American River water. By reducing the peak release of over 300,000 c.f.s. from the five destroyed gates down to around 130,000 c.f.s., most of the downstream levee system survived, despite sustained prolonged flows in excess of their rated maximums. Indeed, there were breaks in the flood control system here and there, resulting in significant property damage and loss. However, destruction was minimal, compared to what might have been if that peak flow had been sustained for only one additional hour. Over its three day existence, the rogue storm ran a record 2 million acre feet into Folsom Lake, almost double the previous record. At the State Capitol building, a staggering twelve inches of rain fell in just over seventy-two hours, also a record. Had the levees failed, Army Corps of Engineer experts estimated the ultimate cost would have run into the tens of billions of dollars, not to mention the associated loss of life.

For two days after the storm blew over, inflows to Folsom Lake stabilized at just fewer than 200,000 c.f.s. then began to drop steadily. The reservoir was able to safely sustain the positive difference of inflow over outflow, thanks to the extraordinary volumes of water that escaped during the period that all five gates were out-flowing at capacity, just the time it took Steele and

Wilkins to put a plug in the center three using the construction barge. The engineers estimated that close to 100,000 acre-feet of water blasted through in that period. As a result, the lake level was reduced sufficiently, and gave the engineers enough capacity to work with until inflows dropped off. Taking a page from Steele's ingenuity book, engineers jury-rigged temporary gates using huge sheets of steel, lowered over the side from portable cranes stationed on the roadway, raising and lowering them accordingly by direction of the control engineers. Unfortunately, the construction crane Wilkins commanded in the rescue effort couldn't be salvaged and used in this effort. It collapsed down the dam face, forty-five minutes after he and Steele were whisked to the hospital.

After the event, Sacramento Area Flood Control Agency (SAFCA) officials, only in their second year of existence following the creation of their authority, were called to task by the 400,000 people living and working in some 175,000 homes and businesses in harm's way. Typical of the frustrating process inherent in dealing with many government bureaucracies, five years later, protective measures such as new floodplain designations, new flood zonings, new assessment districts, levee upgrades, dam improvements, plans for additional dams, and much more, were 'still in the discussion stage'.

Steele and Wilkins were snatched from the dam by a phalanx of Sacramento Sheriffs, and hustled off in a four car convoy, sirens blaring and lights flashing, to nearby Kaiser Hospital's emergency room. They were treated for multiple injuries and held 'for observation' for twenty-four hours. None of their various wounds and injuries were serious or life threatening, though the staff cautioned Wilkins that he might not be playing much racquetball for a few weeks. Before their release, Charles Conley informed them by phone from the Caribbean, that Governor Todd wanted to meet, and appropriately thank them with an award ceremony.

"Great," responded Cody on hearing the news. "I'll be there looking like an advertisement for *Johnson and Johnson,* and the big Indian will look like one for *Ace Bandages.*"

In an informal, private ceremony, held at the Governor's mansion rather than in his Capitol office, Jeremiah Wilkins and Cody Steele were honored for 'unselfish acts of heroism'. It was decided by a coalition of State and Federal law enforcement officials representing an alphabet soup of agencies, not to make the affair public for fear it would bring undue press attention to the act of terrorism precipitating the disaster. Everyone at the ceremony except Steele and Wilkins thought it best not to let the public become aware of how truly vulnerable it is to such acts. Dr. Devoney Marsh, DDO Charles Conley, the Deputy Director of the FBI, Governor Todd and his wife, and the Assistant United States Secretary of Defense were in attendance. Following the afternoon observance and during the small reception featuring margaritas, chips and salsa, Cody Steele regaled the dignified group with the story of his rescue by the Atlantic Spotted Dolphin. Everyone smiled and laughed, although no one believed him. The morning after the Governor's reception, Wilkins was flown by private jet back to Hawthorne, Nevada, and Devoney chauffeured Cody back to Sonoma.

The SEAL team and the Marines called in by Conley surprised four of *Wolverine's* men at the King Solomon mine, three miles east of Michigan Bluff. The old gold mine was discovered at the end of a four mile long, one lane, and very tortuous dirt access road, deep within the American River canyon below the town. After a short skirmish, two of the small opposition force were wounded, and all surrendered without further casualties to either side. Pieces and parts of *HAVOC* were recovered, along with volumes of recorded data. After the operation, *HAVOC* was delivered to Lawrence Livermore National Laboratory for analysis. DDO Conley made arrangements with the LLNL staff, allowing Dr. Devoney Marsh to become a member of their super secret team, attempting to create a working reconstruction of the apparatus. According to one of the men captured at the mine, *Wolverine*'s team managed to streamline the device, reducing its size and maximizing the output. They claimed that in so doing they were able to successfully develop and control whatever intensities of output might be desired. On direct questioning, they admitted their leader had been on site, supervising much of the work for the three-day period prior to the storm. They said he and Lew Sharpe conspired to 'blow a few more dams in the States before they were through'. They informed the Marine interrogators that Franz Toscana, the name they associated with the leader, also took detailed notebooks filled with *HAVOC* schematics and many of the ICF modules with him when he departed the site by helicopter. Unfortunately, the men at the mine were in the process of destroying data and machinery when the SEALs and Marines surprised them. It was assumed that much critical information and data were lost. The size of the Michigan Bluff operation was such that it was impossible to keep secret from the small but very aware local population. Federal officials doing 'mop up' were able keep most of the details under wraps from the press through intimidation and obfuscation. However, a one-column article did appear on page 16 of the *Sacramento Bee* the day after the mini-invasion. Concerning the operation, a longtime Michigan Bluff resident, 88 year old Margaret Hanratty, was quoted as saying they hadn't had this much excitement in the old town since her grandmother fell into the outhouse, sixty years ago.

Two weeks later, when the outflows from Folsom decreased enough to safely allow personnel below the dam and into the treacherous river channel, a search was made for the two helicopters believed to have been destroyed by the water columns. Pieces of the KSAC chopper were found directly at the penstock outlets, below the powerhouse less than one-quarter mile from the base of the dam. The bodies of the pilot, a reporter and a cameraman were recovered, together with the main fuselage of the helicopter one mile further downstream. No debris from the CHP JetRanger was discovered until mid-December. The mangled wreckage was found wedged against the bottom of Nimbus Dam, seven miles downstream from Folsom, the stanchion still attached to what remained of its left skid. Despite an exhaustive search for the remains of the pilot, no body was ever recovered. NTSB experts determined that the cockpit was completely destroyed by either a crash from altitude, or the subsequent impact with the dam. Further, they concluded that the pilot's survival in either event was 'highly improbable'.

Nothing of HAVOC was found in the crashed helicopter, or along the course of the American River below Folsom Dam. No ICF modules, no schematics, no logs…nothing. For the next eight years following the event, the planet was to suffer through events of extreme weather unlike anything ever recorded throughout the history of mankind. Unseasonal floods in the Midwestern United States, France, Asia, and South America; off season killer hurricanes in the Caribbean; huge typhoons in horrific numbers throughout the Pacific Rim; pronounced droughts in Africa…year after year. Not to mention global warming. The list goes on and on. Interestingly, China is almost totally spared all extreme weather patterns during this same period. Coincidence?

Had it not been for Ramon Guillermo Vasquez's high maintenance lifestyle, *Partidario* might have survived the loss of over twenty million dollars in pure uncut cocaine when the *Star of India* disappeared forever. Despite frantic attempts to shuffle cartel moneys in order to meet payroll, and forestall demand payments to his supply sources, Vasquez and *Partidario* quickly ran out of money and excuses. His two largest creditors, a well-known Colombian drug cartel and the Russian Mafia, contracted ten oft-used 'mechanics' who caught Vasquez attempting to board a plane out of Rio bound for Los Angeles. They 'escorted' him to the city of Cuiba in central Brazil instead. Cuiba is the gateway to the *Pantanal*, the magnificent everglades of Brazil, an area the size of the continental US. There are few roads and fewer airstrips in the *Pantanal*. The only accesses to this immense, sparsely populated region are thousands of miles of constantly changing waterways. All eleven men boarded a chartered fishing boat, but only ten returned two days later. Deep in the steamy swamps, Ramon Vasquez was stripped naked and left totally defenseless, his wrists handcuffed around a mangrove tree. Anyone who has ever camped near water and tormented by swarming insects may have an inkling of the misery and horror Vasquez must have endured before leaving his earthly existence.

After crashing through the Caribbean, hurricane *Grace* rumbled up the east coast of the US on the down side of her power curve. In the Atlantic, south of Newfoundland and east of New England, the remains of her warm storm elements collided with a massive cold front blowing in from the northwest. The combination resulted in one of the worst storms in recorded history. It boasted winds well in excess of one hundred knots. Mariners and vessels unlucky enough to be caught in open ocean simply disappeared. Wave heights could only be estimated at over one hundred feet, because most measuring equipment within the path of the horrendous weather was overwhelmed or destroyed.

Once the Pacific storm began moving southeast, it picked up speed, eventually blowing itself out over western Utah. After passing over the east slope of the Sierra, hundreds of miles from the Pacific and with its heat source extinguished, the system subsided into just another typical fall event. However, the final chapter of its legacy was the inundation of an eight hundred square mile region of eastern California. It poured over twenty inches of rain on the besieged high country in just forty-eight hours. The epicenter of this biblical deluge was Bridgeport, California.

"Hey white man, how're you doing?"

"Just fine, JW. Thanks for returning my call. How's the Chief business?" asked Steele, clearly pleased to speak with his friend. "I hear your guys were thinking about building Arks during that little storm."

"Yeah. We did get more rain in two days than I've seen in ten years," Wilkins laughed. "How's Devoney?"

"Fine. She's in the galley working on dinner, as a matter of fact. If she wasn't doing something so important, I'd let you ask her yourself."

"Well, give her my very best. Things working out OK for you guys?"

"We'll see. This is a trial run for us both." When they languished in the hospital ten days previous, Steele had told his friend the short version of the relationship history, and details of the conversation out on the step of the Pullman.

"I'll hold a good thought."

"Thanks. How's the great Wilkins' Paiute casino project coming?"

"Canned the whole deal. The tribe won't be needing the income, at least for awhile."

"Oh? Find some money out in the desert?"

"Actually we did, in a manner of speaking."

"How so?"

"Well, I went back out to those bluffs where I discovered you. It was an Indian thing, you know. I needed to be away from people for a while. The landscape was so changed I hardly recognized the place. The volume of rain dumped on that area had to be amazing."

"Why's that?" Steele asked, becoming more and more intrigued.

"Well, those channels and tunnels you explored were flushed and scoured absolutely clean. The force of so much water blasting through such narrow channels literally blew anything and everything in there out all over the high desert."

"So?"

"You wouldn't believe what I found littered all over the place."

"Let's see… skeletons, animals, lots of sand, old car parts…"

"Certainly all that. Also a king's ransom worth of gold, and a bunch of old armor."

"No way!" Steele shouted, prompting Devoney to stick her head out of the galley. "You found the *Lost Conquistador*?"

"If it's not, it ought to be," laughed Wilkins. "It took three pickups and a van to load the whole stash after the archeologists got through taking their pictures, and picking it all over. They tell me it's worth millions just in the gold value alone, not to mention the historical worth of the pieces."

"Hopefully, it all goes to you guys, that is the tribe, right?"

"Looks that way. It might take a few months to establish and finalize the rights, but the attorneys tell us it's a slam-dunk. We won't spend it just yet, though."

"Great!"

"I'm saving you a few choice pieces, knowing how attached you are to the history of this stuff."

"Thanks, Amigo."

"No, thank you. I probably wouldn't have gone back there for a long time if you hadn't sparked my interest the night we met. When are you coming by?"

"Is fishing season still on?"

"Closed here now, but it's open all year round down on the Owens just out of Bishop."

"How's next weekend?"

"See you then, and I'm looking forward to teaching you how."

"In your dreams, JW. Be careful"

"Keep your powder dry."

Over a wonderful bottle of Napa Valley Chardonnay, Cody told Devoney the whole story of the *Lost Conquistador*, and about Wilkins fortunate discovery. Toward the end of his narrative, the phone rang.

"I'm closer, I'll get it," said Devoney. "Hello?"

Cody Steele watched Dr. Devoney Marsh's face cloud in a frown.

"It's Conley. Want to take it?"

-END-

Loose Ends

While *HAVOC* is fictional, with two exceptions, all the locales are not. The settings are all quite real, and I have endeavored to imbue them with the flavor and character so richly unique to each. The only imaginary places are the islands of *Pavao* and *Langosta Cay*. *Pavao*, however, is patterned very closely after an incredibly similar location in Micronesia known now as *Pohnpei*. *Langosta Cay* is purely imaginary. *Rabaul*, the capital of East New Britain, PNG, *was* indeed one of the most beautiful tropical towns on the planet…until 1994. In September of 1994, one week after I was there on assignment, two of the six resident volcanoes mentioned in the story erupted simultaneously. This beautiful and historic destination was virtually blown off the face of the earth, and/or buried in over eighteen feet of ash. I feel quite fortunate to have experienced it the few times I had the opportunity.

The characters of *HAVOC* are all fictional as well. Any similarities with persons living or dead are merely coincidental.

Printed in the United States
16103LVS00003B/76-78